T0354357

HARBINGER

HARBINGER

B.A. Seloaf

iUniverse

HARBINGER

iUniverse books may be ordered through booksellers or by contacting:

iUniverse
1663 Liberty Drive
Bloomington, IN 47403
www.iuniverse.com
1-800-Authors (1-800-288-4677)

ISBN: 978-1-5320-5174-6 (sc)
ISBN: 978-1-5320-5175-3 (e)

Library of Congress Control Number: 2018906728

Print information available on the last page.

iUniverse rev. date: 06/19/2018

~1~

———————— ✳ ————————

Humans are strange.

Seriously, they are. Even those who are considered to be "normal" usually display odd behavior in several areas. The only reason they get away with it is that their kind of weirdness is so common it doesn't stand out as much as, say, someone yelling at the top of their voice every time they see a larch tree. That their own behavior is just as inexplicable doesn't seem to matter.

Another annoying thing about these so-called normal weirdos is that they are often unable to understand behavior or habits that fall outside their own spectrum of weirdness. They might perform completely insane actions on a daily basis, but if someone (usually someone they don't like) does a single thing they wouldn't consider doing themselves, that person is instantly labelled as "weird".

So if you have someone among your acquaintances you find "weird", have a good look at yourself first before making derogatory statements. It makes you look much less like an idiot.

One more thing: if there's something you don't understand – either about another person or some purely theoretical matter – don't proclaim it in front of everyone, and for pity-s sake *don't try to make it sound as if it's someone else's fault that you don't understand the thing in question*. Instead, open your mind and try to see things from the other person's point of view, or do a little bit of research if your lack of understanding is caused by insufficient knowledge. In both cases you'll end up smarter than you initially were, hopefully earning you both greater self-confidence and more respect from your fellow humans.

As humans went, Marsha wasn't all that weird. Sure, she had a few minor oddities like being completely uninterested in sex, accusing elephants of cheating at Yahtzee, having once given birth to half a dozen chickens through her mouth and... all right, all right, she was rather weird, but it was still nothing compared to some of the people she'd encountered in her life, or some of those she would encounter in the near future.

She had once been the chieftain of a small African tribe known as the Khadal. Back then her life had been very simple - her main task had been to make sure the other people in the tribe didn't do anything stupid. Or let me rephrase that: her main task had been to make sure they didn't do anything so stupid they hurt themselves or others. Stupid things of one kind or another was what they did for a living, turning Marsha into more of a babysitter than your standard type of ruler.

All that had changed when one of her friends had gone off to hunt buffalo and didn't come back. After a long and completely unsuccessful search Marsha returned to the jungle north of the Khadal camp to find the friend she'd been looking for, plus another friend who'd got lobbed across the countryside by an erupting volcano, in the middle of a fight against an ancient evil goddess and her not-so-prominent minions. With the help of a motley group of allies they defeated the enemy, which resulted not only in peace but also in the restoration of the ancient Hippo Cult, from which the Khadal unknowingly were descended.

Right now, Marsha was journeying through the vast grasslands far south of her home. The reason for this was that she was searching for something (or someone, depending on how you looked at it). This was a task she'd vowed to undertake, even though it likely meant she'd have to spend several years away from her friends. That didn't matter. She had to do this if the glorious future the Hippo Cult's old prophecies spoke of were to become reality.

The thing – or creature – she was looking for was called the Scion. It was probably the oddest thing Marsha had ever seen – a small, winged hippo which had hatched from an egg that apparently had popped out of an old statue in a cavern below a mountain range far to the south-west of the Khadal camp. During the turmoil that followed its birth the Scion had flown away, leaving Marsha and her friends no clue as to its whereabouts.

Marsha wasn't sure how the odd little creature would bring about the future of hope and joy the prophecies spoke of. She didn't even know what she would do when she found it, if she ever did. All she knew was that this was what she was meant to do. Nothing else mattered.

Well, there was one other thing that mattered just a little bit. Marsha was hungry. She hadn't found anything to eat all day, and her supply of water was running low as well. The food she'd brought with her when she left her tribe had lasted until the day before yesterday; since then she'd lived on what the land provided.

"I should go hunting," she said to herself, then realized she hadn't brought any weapons with her, not even a simple knife. That made her frown. Why hadn't she brought a knife, or better yet a spear? Sure, she was rather fond of fruit and vegetables, but she felt she needed something more solid in her stomach, and a spear would also come in handy in many situations. What if a lion attacked her, for example?

"I've already become lazy," she muttered as she trudged on, looking up as a bird flew past, letting out a mocking cry. "Since we restored the Hippo Cult there's always been someone else to take care of such things. What a fool I was, running off like this without planning further ahead than a week or two."

To be honest, she wasn't sure she would've done much better if she'd had a spear. She wasn't a great hunter like Gemma or Amanda. Her talents lay more in the intellectual field (if such a thing could be said about a member of such a primitive society). Knowing this, she tried to use her head to figure out a way to solve the hunger issue.

She came up with nothing.

"Look at me," she said miserably. "I helped defeating an evil goddess of immense power, but I can't find myself a simple meal. Aren't there supposed to be edible things all over this countryside? Or villages where you can buy food?"

The last thing produced another frown. She realized she hadn't brought anything to trade with. Why on earth hadn't she thought about that? She was supposed to be the smart one in her tribe. Yet here she was, out in the middle of nowhere without even a necklace of lion's teeth to offer in exchange for food.

She knew she wasn't unattractive. Perhaps she could find a man, wiggle her hips a little, and ask him if he had some food to spare while looking deep into his eyes. That was how women made men give them things they wanted, wasn't it? If she'd had a figure like Gemma or Amanda she'd probably get enough food to last her a dozen lifetimes, plus a chest of gold and jewels and three hundred camels. She grimaced. Good thing her looks were only average. What would she have done with three hundred camels?

There was a small grove of trees off to her left. Marsha headed that way to see if there was something edible, perhaps some berry bushes or other plants that wouldn't kill her. Hell, she'd even eat roots if she found nothing else.

She'd almost reached the edge of the trees when a shape emerged between two trunks. Marsha saw that it was a young woman, short and slender with dark hair tied into a knot at the back of her head. She was humming to herself as she stepped out into the sunlight.

"Um, hello?" Marsha said.

The woman looked up, and Marsha saw that she was very beautiful, with large dark eyes like twilit pools. It didn't look like she carried any weapons. In fact, her only possession appeared to be a small leather bag slung across one shoulder.

"Oh, hi," she said, giving Marsha a friendly smile. "I wasn't expecting to meet anyone here. Are you looking for something?"

"Only food," Marsha said. "I ran out a while back. Do you know where I can find any?"

The girl eyed her curiously. "Not from around here, are you? Everyone knows all the food is over that way." She pointed with her right hand. "And over there." She pointed in another direction.

"Oh." For some reason the girl's casual display of knowledge annoyed Marsha. She knew she had no way of knowing where to find something to eat in this unfamiliar land, but she couldn't help feeling that she should know more than this girl, whoever she was. Knowing less than her was like having an alarm bell go off in your head, or like watching the fuel gauge on your car go down to zero. Not that Marsha knew what a car was, of course. At least not yet.

"Don't worry," the girl said. "I have food enough for both of us, and I know where to find more. I'm Jennibal, by the way." She held out her hand.

Marsha shook it. "Marsha. I'm a member of the Hippo Cult."

That made Jennibal frown. "The Hippo Cult? You mean you're worshipping some false god?"

"It isn't false," Marsha said, sounding more defensive than she'd intended. "The Hippo God has spoken to some of our members."

"They must be lying. There's only one true god."

Marsha snorted. "And which one would that be?"

"The God of the Iridescent Cantaloupe."

That made Marsha laugh so hard she had to wipe tears from her eyes and snot from her nose.

"Seriously?" she said. "Where did you get that idea from?"

"I made it up myself," the girl said, sounding as if she was explaining the most trivial matter.

Marsha stared at her in disbelief. "You believe in a god you made up yourself?"

"Yes." Jennibal's beautiful face was dead serious. "It's the god I've chosen to believe in. You can say whatever you want. I know I'm right."

Oh, wonderful, Marsha thought. *The first person I encounter turns out to be a religious fanatic. I'd almost have preferred a rapist or cannibal. At least you know where you stand with those.*

"So…" she said, trying not to sound too condescending. The woman had said she had food, after all. "Do you have any proof of this god's existence?"

"A true believer doesn't need proof, only faith," Jennibal said. "But yes, I've heard him speak to me, inside my head."

That figures, Marsha thought. *Why shouldn't someone who hears voices in her head make up strange gods to believe in? She probably had a difficult birth or something.*

She didn't know it, of course, but in later days there'd be billions of people worshipping either a god that invented things like leukemia in children just to test people's faith in him, or one who rewarded murder with promises of numerous underage girls. Both the followers of the psychopath and the pedophile god claimed their deity to be the only real one, and also insisted they were the most divine and flawless beings ever to exist.

Not even Jennibal was *that* mad.

"Um, about that food…" Marsha tried.

"Ah, yes." Jennibal unslung her bag, rummaged through it a few moments, then produced two fruits roughly the same size as Marsha's fist. "Here you go," she said, smiling happily.

"Thanks," Marsha said, eagerly taking a bite from the reddish-brown fruit. It tasted really good.

All hail the God of the Iridescent Cantaloupe, she thought. *Provider of food for travelers in need.*

Jennibal waited for her to finish the fruit before speaking again. "Hey, feel like coming along? I think there's a village down that way." She pointed to the south-west.

"A village?" Marsha wiped her mouth with the sleeve of her tunic. "What kind of people live there?"

"Not sure," Jennibal said. "But I don't think they're hostile. A bit weird, perhaps, but that's only to be expected."

"Coming from someone who believes in Iridescent Cantaloupe gods they made up themselves, that might actually be a good thing," Marsha muttered to herself.

Jennibal actually turned out to be very good company, at least as long as the conversation stayed away from religious topics. She was friendly, had a decent sense of humor, and a generally positive attitude towards life and the world she lived in. Marsha wouldn't call her smart, not after their initial discussion about Jennibal's patron deity, but she had to admit the girl wasn't the complete airhead she'd first assumed her to be.

"Why did you come to these parts, anyway?" Jennibal asked as the sun sank towards the western horizon. "You never said."

"I'm looking for something," Marsha said. "Or someone, perhaps. Depends on how you see it."

"Oh? That does sound a bit unusual. Care to explain?"

Marsha scratched her head. "We call it the Scion. It's a kind of winged hippo."

The girl regarded her curiously. "And you think I'm weird?"

"Never said you were," Marsha hurried to say.

Jennibal rolled her eyes. "I'm not stupid, Marsha. I saw the way you looked at me when I told you about my God. It's ok, I don't take offense. It usually takes a while for heathen people to see the Light."

Something about the way the girl pronounced certain words made Marsha confused. It was as if she could tell that words like God and Light should be spelled with capital letters. What made her confused wasn't the way the girl said those words, but the fact that Marsha didn't know what capital letters were. Both the Hippo Cult and the Cult of the Raven had written scrolls, but Marsha hadn't had time to learn reading them. She wondered if Jennibal knew how to read. She decided to not broach the subject.

"The Scion does exist," she said instead. "Some of my friends were there when it hatched. They saw it fly away."

"You're doing it again," Jennibal said.

Marsha blinked. "Doing what?"

"Considering things you don't know to be facts. Like with that false Hippo God of yours. You believe he's real because your friends told you they'd spoken to him. And now you believe this hippo bird exists because your friends told you they saw it. Even you must see the flaw in that argument."

"My friends would never lie to me..." Marsha began.

"Not intentionally, perhaps," Jennibal interrupted her. "But people see and hear all kinds of things, especially when under a lot of stress. I know people who claim they've seen images of dead relatives appear before them. How ludicrous is that?"

It was probably for the best that Jennibal didn't know that people still make such claims in this (so-called) enlightened time we live in. She might've ended up in a seizure or something.

"You do believe in something you've never seen," Marsha pointed out.

"That's different. The God of the Iridescent Cantaloupe does exist. I know it."

Marsha gave up.

Evening had turned into dusk when they reached the village Jennibal had spoken of. It turned out to be a settlement of considerable size. Marsha counted to just over fifty huts (a feat that would've taken her old friend Gemma almost an hour, provided there were no major distractions). The huts looked sturdy, as did the people seated in small groups outside them.

The chieftain – a lean, middle-aged man called Ostomy – greeted them with a friendly smile. Marsha noted that he had very white teeth. This was the result of one of the villagers having invented a primitive kind of toothpaste that he gave to Ostomy in exchange for getting to shag the chieftain's wife once a month. Both thought it an excellent deal. Ostomy's wife thought it merely passable.

"It's not often we in the Portapoti tribe get visitors from up north," he said when Marsha had told him her name and where she came from. "What brings you to these parts, my dear Marsha?"

"I'm on a search," Marsha said. "You don't happen to have seen a flying hippo anywhere around here?"

A muffled snort of laughter came from Jennibal.

Ostomy, however, seemed to give the question careful consideration.

"A flying hippo, you say?" he finally asked. "I'm afraid not. What about you, Clyster?"

The chieftain's son – a sullen young man who'd taken an instant dislike to the two newcomers – looked up from his bowl of gruel.

"Hippos don't fly," he muttered. "They're too fat."

"This is no ordinary hippo," Marsha said. "It's the Scion, born from a union between the Hippo and the Raven God."

"Two males can't have offspring," Clyster said, giving Marsha a sour glare.

"Marsha believes in very strange things," Jennibal said. "All civilized people know that the only real God is the God of the Iridescent Cantaloupe."

"Never heard of that one," Ostomy said. "In this village we worship the Orb of Life."

Oh no, not another bunch of religious nutcases, Marsha thought, groaning inwardly. *This might become a very long night.*

She sat in silence for a time while Jennibal tried to convert their hosts to her own made-up religion. Ostomy and his wife Enema, who'd, joined them in the middle of the debate, made polite replies while their son grew more and more infuriated and snappish. In the end the chieftain had to order him to return to his hut, which he did after one last venomous glare at Marsha and Jennibal.

"Please excuse our son," Enema said, refilling Marsha's bowl. The grey-brown gruel the Portapotis ate didn't taste much, but it was supposed to be nourishing and Marsha enjoyed the pleasant sensation of fullness in her stomach.

"No need to apologize," Jennibal said. Waving her hand dismissively. "Many people have trouble grasping new ideas. My own people were the same."

That made Marsha raise an eyebrow. "You never said anything about where you come from, Jennibal. Or why you left."

The girl shrugged. "There isn't much to tell. They were a bit dense. Never understood that the only path to fulfilment lies with the God of the Iridescent Cantaloupe."

"So they drove you away?" Marsha asked.

"No, of course not. They only suggested I tell the rest of the world about the Truth of God, instead of limiting myself to their little village. Very sound advice, considering how feeble-minded they were."

Marsha exchanged a look with the chieftain and his wife. She supposed it was a good thing that Jennibal had followed that "advice". People like her had a tendency to disappear without a trace, or meet with unfortunate and usually lethal accidents if they became too persistent in their preachings.

"This Orb of Life you worship," she said as Enema gathered their empty bowls. "Is it a real object? Something you have here in the village?"

"Of course it is," Ostomy said. "Would you like to see it?"

"Sure," Marsha said. "It sounds interesting."

The people of the village were retiring for the night, giving Marsha and Jennibal sleepy looks as they followed the chieftain through the cluster of huts. One young man's gaze lingered on Jennibal's slim form after they'd passed, earning him a slap when his girlfriend or wife (or whoever the woman sharing his hut was) noticed. Jennibal herself walked in silence beside Marsha, apparently lost in her own thoughts.

At last they came to an open space with smooth, hard-packed dirt. In its center was a wooden stand, about as tall as Marsha's chest. Atop it, resting in a webbed metal holder, was a large sphere of opaque glass or crystal. The light from the dying campfires was reflected in its surface, giving it a reddish tinge.

"Nice, isn't it?" Ostomy said.

Marsha nodded. She couldn't tell if there was something divine about the Orb of Life. It did remind her of the egg she and her friends had been chasing halfway across the continent without actually knowing what it was supposed to do. She'd never seen the egg that had eventually hatched the Scion, except in a very strange dream, but Amanda had claimed she'd felt the life inside it the moment she touched it with her hands.

"May I touch it?" she asked Ostomy.

The chieftain shook his head. "I'm afraid not. This object is sacred to us. No one's allowed to touch it, not even I."

"So how did you get it up onto that stand?" Jennibal asked.

That made the chieftain look confused. "What do you mean? It's always been there. Our ancestors found it and built this village so they could live under its protection."

"And if it falls down?"

This time Ostomy looked annoyed. "It's the Orb of Life," he snapped. "It doesn't *fall down.*"

"Just wait until someone gets drunk and stumbles into it," Jennibal muttered.

"Does it have any special powers?" Marsha asked the chieftain.

Jennibal snorted. "It's just a ball of glass. What powers could it have?"

"You'd be surprised, fair Jennibal," Ostomy said, white teeth glowing in the dark as he gave the girl a rueful smile. "The Orb of Life protects our people from famine, diseases, constipation and enemy attacks."

Naturally, Marsha's brain homed in on the one word that was, beyond all doubt, the least important.

"Constipation?"

The chieftain nodded gravely. "Our bowels always run smoothly. Some people have claimed it's because of the gruel we always eat, but most of us know it's because of the Orb's power."

"Perhaps it used to belong to the God of Digestion or something?" Marsha mused, eyeing the holy relic in a completely new light.

"That should explain why they have such weird names," Jennibal said.

Ostomy frowned as he digested (pun intended) her suggestion. "A God Of Digestion, you say? Never heard of such a one. Where would a being like that reside, if he does exist?"

"He'd probably be indisposed most of the time," Jennibal said, rolling her eyes. "Behind a door with a heart on it."

Marsha hid a yawn behind one hand. "Perhaps we could continue this discussion tomorrow?" she suggested. "It's been a long day, and I'm very tired. Is there some place we can spend the night?"

"You're welcome to use our guest hut," Ostomy said. "It's right next to the one where Enema and I live, so if there's anything you need you can just come over."

The guest hut turned out to be very comfortable, with lots of soft blankets on the floor and thick walls that kept both wind and sound out. Whatever material the hut was made of gave off a slightly musky smell that was far from unpleasant. Marsha wondered if it served to conceal any odors the fabled gastric prowess of the Portapotis might produce.

"Mind if I take the bed nearest the opening?" Jennibal asked. "I usually have to go out and pee in the middle of the night."

"Not at all," Marsha said, lowering herself onto the other bed with a happy sigh. "Sleeping here should be safe enough. If Ostomy spoke truth we don't have to worry about being attacked."

Jennibal snorted again. "Don't tell me you bought any of that nonsense."

"I don't know," Marsha said, stifling another yawn. "There really was something about that orb-thing. It might have belonged to some god or other."

"There's only one true God..."

"Yes, yes," Marsha interrupted. "The big cantaloupe guy. You told me all about it. Let's get some sleep now. I'd like to continue my search tomorrow. Are you coming with me, or will you stay here and try to convert these digestion people?"

"I think I'll come with you," Jennibal said. "The people here are probably too dense to see the Truth of the God of the Iridescent Cantaloupe. Let's hope we find a more receptive people along the way."

"Mmm," Marsha said, already half-asleep. "Preferably with better food."

She jerked awake some time later. It was still full dark outside. How long had she slept? And what had awoken her?

Sitting up in her bed, she peered around, straining her eyes to see in the almost complete darkness. Jennibal's bed 'was empty. The girl must've gone out to relieve herself, like she'd said. Was it some noise she'd made that had disturbed Marsha's sleep?

No, there was another sound. Voices, coming from outside. A sudden feeling of alarm crept into Marsha's bones. What were the villagers doing up in the middle of the night? Somehow she doubted it had anything to do with their smooth bowel movements.

Bright torchlight blinded her. She caught sight of at least two men entering the hut, then she had to cover her eyes with her arm. Someone shouted a command, and Marsha felt the sharp tip of a spear against her chest.

"Don't move!" a sharp voice snapped.

Marsha lowered her arm a few inches, blinking against the light. "What's going on?" she asked, her voice coming out as a squeak.

"Silence!" the man snapped, then turned to address someone outside the hut. "You can come in now, chief."

Another man entered the hut. Marsha recognized Ostomy, the village chieftain. His friendly smile was gone, his face now a hard, stern mask. He looked at Marsha, then let his gaze sweep across the rest of the hut's interior.

"Where's your friend?" he demanded.

"Er, I think she went out to pee," Marsha said. "Chieftain…"

"Search the village and its surroundings," Ostomy ordered. "I'll search this hut myself."

One of the men who'd first entered the hut barked a command, and Marsha heard running footsteps vanish into the distance. Ostomy bent down to rummage through Jennibal's blankets.

"Chieftain, what's happening?" Marsha asked, utterly bewildered by this unexpected turn of events.

"I'm afraid we have to place you under arrest," Ostomy said, picking up Jennibal's bag and ripping it open.

"Arrest? Why would you do that?"

The chieftain looked up, his face so hard it might have been cut from stone.

"For stealing the Orb of Life," he said.

~2~

—————— ✳ ——————

*"Only two things are infinite, the universe and human stupidity,
and I'm not sure about the former."*

- Albert Einstein

There are different levels of human stupidity.

First there's the kind you and I experience with regular intervals, like when we look back on something we did and ask ourselves *"Why on earth did I do that? It was really stupid"*. Then there's the slightly more severe kind, where people don't really understand how stupid they are, doing the same mistakes over and over again. Finally, there are those who can't even follow the simplest of instructions, where the information literally goes in through one ear and out through the other. Those are the people who have trouble managing even the simplest of jobs, usually causing more damage than productivity.

And then there's Ogian.

Some of you might not remember Ogian. Don't worry, it doesn't mean you belong to any of the more stupid groups of people I mentioned above. Ogian is simply a very unremarkable person. Most people don't pay much attention to him. Not unless you get involved in a game of Yahtzee with him, of course.

Yahtzee is Ogian's only passion in life. It's in his heart and soul. He'd play Yahtzee with the Devil himself if there was no one else around. When he plays Yahtzee he feels truly alive. During the game he's king. The rest of the time he's just… him.

You might think that such a devoted player would follow the rules to the letter. Ogian doesn't. He cheats like a goddamn pig.

He's also a big one for showmanship when it comes to Yahtzee. He likes to put the dice on his head and nod them onto the table instead of throwing them like normal people do. If you're unlucky he'll put the dice in his mouth, gargle for a few moments, and spit them out on the table. There are numerous other ways he uses when he plays. Listing them all would make this book twice as long.

Did the word *gargle* awaken any old memories? I thought it might. Ogian belonged to the Elephant People, where one of the most important positions was that of the gargling woman, an office currently occupied by an elderly hag named Hannah. The gargling woman was, through her constant gargling of questionable liquids, in contact with the Elephant God. No one knew exactly how the exchange worked, but isn't that always the way with religion?

Jennibal would, naturally, not have believed in the sincerity of the gargling woman's practice.

But back to Ogian now. Like I mentioned before, Ogian wasn't very smart. He was perhaps as far from smart as is humanly possible. Or not quite. There used to be someone else who was – believe it or not – a little more stupid than he. The person in question was also far better looking.

The one I'm talking about was chieftain of the Telu tribe for a time. She later died when a stone giant crashed through a cliff wall, burying our stupid friend under several tons of broken rock.

But you know what they say about the dead.

You don't?

Neither do I. I just thought that phrase sounded nice.

Ogian, yes. He was at the moment about half a mile away from the rest of his people, on his way to take a dump in a patch of jungle he'd spotted off to the north. He was a bit particular with such things, preferring to take care of his needs at a safe distance from any other humans (or elephants).

Today, however, he was in for a very big surprise.

Humming tunelessly to himself, Ogian strolled in among the trees. It took a while before he found a nice, secluded place with no undergrowth. Hiking up his leather kilt, he squatted down and went about his business.

"Hello, there."

Ogian was so startled that he lost his balance and toppled backwards, landing in the small pile of excrement he'd just produced. Panic suddenly filled him, mingled with bewilderment. He knew he'd examined this place carefully, making sure no one else was around, and yet the voice had come from a place right behind him. How was that possible?

Feeling his cheeks flush brightly, he climbed back to his feet, making sure his clothes covered him properly again before turning around.

A woman, young and beautiful, stood a few feet away, eyeing him curiously. She was wearing a colorful dress of an unfamiliar cut and material, the fabric clinging nicely to her curvaceous form. Ogian was admiring the view when he noticed something odd – a slight shimmer surrounding the woman, as if she wasn't really there.

"Who are you?" he asked.

The woman's gaze grew distant for a few moments, as if she tried to recall something from a long time ago.

"Bathora," she finally said. "I am... was... Bathora."

"I'm Ogian," Ogian said. He thought there'd been something odd about the way this Bathora introduced herself, but figured it probably had to do with different dialects, or simply that he wasn't very good at grammar.

"Hello, Ogian," Bathora said, smiling at him. "Nice to meet you."

"Um, nice to meet you too," Ogian said. "I didn't hear you coming. Have you been here long?" He was painfully aware of the smelly stickiness slowly trickling down the back of his thigh, as well as the somewhat flattened pile at his feet. This wasn't the ideal way to meet a beautiful woman. Not ideal in the least.

"Of course you didn't hear me," Bathora said. "I don't have a real body, so naturally I don't make any sound."

"You mean you're a ghost?"

She nodded. "I... I remember dying, and then I was suddenly here again. I have no idea how that happened, or how long I was gone. All I know is that there's something I have to do."

"Oh?" Ogian thought this sounded interesting. "And what's that?"

The woman gazed into the distance again. This time there was a hardness to her expression, making Ogian want to step away from her. If he did, however, he'd stumble straight into a thorny bush, and he thought he'd already made enough of a fool of himself. Besides, didn't snakes often hide underneath thorny bushes?

"Someone hurt a person I loved," Bathora finally said. "A whole group of people was responsible, actually. I have to find a way to get back at them, and I think you can help me."

Ogian blinked. "Me? In what way?"

"One thing at a time," Bathora said. "I know you're the one I've been looking for, though."

"Are you sure?" Ogian wasn't used to having people look for him, least of all women as beautiful as this one. "I mean, I could get our queen, or perhaps the gargling woman. They know a lot more about things than me."

Bathora shook her head. "No, it has to be you. Will you come with me?"

"Come with you? Where to?"

"Well," Bathora said, wrinkling her nose. "First we'll have to find somewhere you can wash yourself. I might not have a real body anymore, but I can still smell things, and right now you make me wish I couldn't."

"Sorry," Ogian said. He was all too aware of the reek himself. Flies had begun buzzing around him, some of them currently crawling up his leg.

Bathora nodded. "After that... well, I guess you'll have to wait and see. Prepare yourself for a long journey, though."

That made Ogian stare in open-mouthed shock at her. "You mean leave the Elephant People? I can't do that! Who's going to take care of my elephant?"

"Pfft, who cares about an elephant?" Bathora said with a snort. "They're just big, dumb animals."

"Nooooooo!!!" Ogian wailed, tears running down his cheeks. "Our elephants are part of us! We can't be separated from them."

"Well, you certainly can't bring it with you. It'll get in the way."

"Then I'm not going either!" Ogian yelled.

Bathora sighed. "Would you please stop yelling? It's giving me a headache. Or it would, if I'd had a real head. Anyway, if you do this, if you come with me, I'll make you the most powerful man on this continent."

"I don't care! I won't leave my elephant!"

"But think about what you'll be able to do with all that power!" Bathora said, irritation making her voice sharp. "You'll be like a king. More than a king, actually. You'll be like the Elephant God himself."

"I don't want any of that!" Ogian sobbed. "All I want to do is be with my elephant. And play Yahtzee, of course."

A smug smile split Bathora's beautiful face. "Oh? Are you good at Yahtzee, then?"

"Not really," Ogian said, lowering his eyes in shame. "I usually lose, even when I cheat."

Bathora's ghost moved closer to him. A brown, shimmering hand reached out to touch his shoulder. There was no actual sensation of touching, of course, only a faint tingling that Ogian mistook for another fly crawling on his skin.

"You know," Bathora said, her voice low and husky. She looked deep into Ogian's eyes as she spoke. "I could give you the power to throw a Yahtzee any time you wanted to."

It's often said that the way to a man's heart goes through his stomach. This wasn't true in Ogian's case. He saw eating mostly as something you had to do, not unpleasant but certainly nothing to get overly excited about. No, for Ogian, as you might have guessed, the way to his heart went through his dice.

"Really?" he said.

"Really," said Bathora.

"Wow."

Before you get too excited, please allow me to clarify a few things. Ogian didn't fall in love with Bathora (or her ghost) at this moment. He was a rather innocent creature, aware of what made a woman a woman and a man a man, but his mind never lingered for long on these matters. In fact, he'd only experienced something akin to love once, and even then he'd been content with merely speaking to the woman in question a couple of times. He'd felt a bit sad when he had to leave her back at the Hippo God's temple, but had soon found other things to occupy his very limited mind.

"So, do we have a deal?" Bathora enquired.

Ogian stuck a hand into his pocket and drew out the five dice he always kept there. "We sure do, madam," he said.

They set out across the savannah, Bathora leading the way north while Ogian thought about the wonderful new life that awaited him. He imagined the look on the faces of his friends – Kharuba, Bunta-koop and Xylophonidas (don't ask) – when he threw one Yahtzee after another. He'd beat them every time they played, and he wouldn't even have to cheat.

He stopped and frowned. Wouldn't it be cheating if he used the power Bathora had promised him to win? Somehow it felt more dishonest than using the more traditional means of deceit. That kind of cheating required some skill, at least. To be fair, Ogian possessed as little skill in that area as in most other ones, which meant he was usually caught, but the arguing that followed was one of his favorite parts of the game. What would it be like if there was nothing to argue about?

I don't care, he thought. *I'm tired of being a loser. No one will dare make fun of me once I have all that power. I'll be someone!*

That this kind of sentiment could be awoken so easily even in a gentle creature like Ogian proves that anyone starting out at the bottom of the social hierarchy feels a need to climb and to assert himself, usually by pushing down others as this is much simpler than accomplishing something worth admiring. The most despicable of all these low-lives are those who resort to physical violence to make themselves feel strong. As a wise man once said: when you run out of brains, only the fists remain.

Night came, but Bathora showed no sign that she intended to stop and make camp. Ogian stumbled along behind her for a while before deciding it was time to speak up.

"Er, excuse me," he said. "Shouldn't we make camp now. It's too dark to see."

Bathora turned her head, giving him a look as if what he'd said sounded like complete nonsense to her. Then she seemed to remember something, her expression changing to an almost apologetic smile.

"Oh, right," she said. "I'd forgotten you people need to sleep and such. You're probably hungry too. What do you people eat? Grass?"

"Ew, no. Only some animals eat grass. Humans eat meat and fruit and other things that taste nice. Don't you ghosts get hungry?"

"No." Bathora shook her head. "We don't eat, or sleep, or pee. We don't do much, really."

"That must be boring," Ogian said. "Why don't you do stuff like living humans do?"

Bathora rolled her eyes at him. "Don't you think that'd be a bit difficult when you can't touch things?"

"I don't know. Would it?"

The ghost threw up her hands. "You must be the most dim-witted person in all the world," she exclaimed. "I've never seen anything like it!"

Ogian smiled at her. "Thank you. It's very nice of you to say so. I quite like you as well."

"I bet you do," Bathora mumbled. "So, about this camp thing. Do you want to make a fire or something?"

"That'd be nice," Ogian said. "Do you know how it's done?"

"You mean you don't?"

He shrugged. "It wasn't my job back when I was with the Elephant People. I only dug the latrine pits. And filled them up when we moved on, of course."

"How sweet," Bathora said, making a disgusted grimace. "I guess I'll have to show you, then. Go fetch some wood."

"Where?"

"Oh, for the love of... Over there, for example. There ought to be deadfalls among those trees. Can't you think of anything yourself?"

Even with Bathora's guidance, it took Ogian almost an hour to gather enough wood to make a fire and find suitable tools to strike a spark. The ghost seemed at the verge of a mental breakdown (if such a thing was possible for a ghost) by the time she got him to sit down and begin working.

"Strike that stone against the other," she instructed him. "No, not like that, you idiot! It should just glance off the surface. There, that's better. Now blow on the kindling wood. No, not so hard.... ahhh, you blew it out. Now you have to start over again. What do you mean you've forgotten how to begin? A three-year-old would've learned it by now .Hold that stone in your left hand with the smooth surface up, and..."

It took a while longer before Ogian got the fire going. Bathora had found some mushrooms among the trees, and she showed him how to roast them on a wooden spit (he managed to burn some, and also burned his hand a few times when he tried to pry them loose). At long last he got enough food into him to sate his hunger.

"Oh, my," he sighed, leaning back on his elbows and stretching out his aching legs before him. The night breeze was cool but not unpleasantly so, and the fire still provided a nice measure of heat. Ogian realized that he didn't really miss his friends among the Elephant People all that much. On the contrary, it was rather exciting to be out here, in the middle of nowhere, with Bathora's ghost as his only companion.

He shot her a glance where she sat across the fire from him. She was staring intently into the flames, her face looking very beautiful as the firelight sent shadows dancing across it. Ogian figured it was a face many men would fall in love with, not to mention the delicious, curvy figure that accompanied it, but for some reason he didn't feel attracted to her in that way. It might have something to do with her being a ghost and not a real person, but somehow he doubted he'd have felt different if it'd been the real Bathora sitting there. There was just something intimidating about her that told his feelings to stay away and mind their own business.

"Want to play some Yahtzee?" he asked, not knowing what else to ask his new employer.

Bathora looked up, then shook her head once. "Can't touch your dice," she said. "And mine will show whatever I want them to, so it wouldn't be much of a game either."

"You can make your dice show whatever you want?" Ogian asked, eyes widening.

"Of course. That's the kind of power I offered you if you helped me, remember?"

"Ah, of course." Ogian hadn't managed to make that connection. When he tried to put two and two together he usually got stuck on the first two. Strangely, he wasn't too bad at mathematics, probably a result of the endless hours he'd spent playing Yahtzee.

"Can you show me?" he asked when they'd sat in silence for a while.

"Show you what?"

"How you do it. You know, with the dice?"

Bathora watched him with a blank expression for a few moments, then her eyes lit up with comprehension.

"Oh, that," she said with a small smile. "Usually when people asked me to show them something it meant some body part or other. This must be the first time someone's asked me to show them dice tricks. What do you want the dice to show?"

"A Yahtzee," Ogian said without hesitation. "Five sixes. I've never managed that in one throw. Kharuba did it last year, and then I tried to cheat but I don't think they bought it."

Bathora snapped her fingers, and five bone-white dice appeared in her hand. She threw them onto the ground in front of her. They fell into a perfect circle, all five dice displaying six black pips.

Ogian gaped. "Amazing," he said, then coughed as a moth flew into his mouth.

"It's nothing special," Bathora said. "Any ghost could do it."

"They could?"

She shrugged. "Not sure, really. I haven't met any other ones. I'm still trying to work out what caused me to return here."

"What did you do?" Ogian asked. Then, as Bathora gave him a questioning look, "When you were alive, I mean. Were you someone important?"

"Fairly important," she said. "I was the chieftain of a tribe, but I didn't really do anything. To be honest, I was a bit of a dumbass. Pretty much like you."

Ogian felt a surge of warm feelings. Did this amazing woman really think the two of them had something in common? No one had ever said that about him before, except when they wanted to insult someone. "You're just like Ogian" was considered as the gravest insult among the Elephant People.

"You don't seem dumb to me," he said, not knowing how else to return her compliment. "I think you're very smart."

She gave a short, mirthless laugh. "I got a little better just before I died. Not sure how that happened. Might be because I was in the presence of a god."

That made Ogian sit up straight. "You've met a god?" he exclaimed. "Only the gargling woman is able to do that among my people, and she never says anything about what it's like. What did this god say to you?"

Bathora frowned into the fire. "He mostly asked me to take off my clothes," she said sourly. "Gods aren't that different from human males. Lecherous sods."

"Is that god one of those you're going to get back at when we get all that power?"

"No." She shook her head. "There's one person in his service I have a bone to pick with, but that isn't on my list of priorities. Perhaps when I'm done with the ones responsible for my lover's death I'll head over there and finish our business. We'll see."

"So your lover wasn't with you when you met that god?" Ogian asked, thinking that the man must've been extremely handsome and intelligent if Bathora had chosen him as her lover. It would've been a very unpleasant surprise for him if he'd actually met the man in question.

"No," Bathora said. "That was one of the really dumb things I did when I was alive. I left my tribe and went searching for something. I'm not even sure what it was. Almost got eaten by cannibals in the process."

"That's awful!" Ogian said, genuinely shocked. "How did you escape them?"

Bathora let out a long breath and gazed up at the starlit night sky. "I was too stupid to understand back then," she finally said. "My tribe used to serve another god. Or a goddess, to be exact. Her power still ran through its chieftains. I used it, and later my lover used it as well. It wasn't enough to save him, though."

"You mean you've served *two* gods?" Ogian exclaimed. "That's amazing! You must've been one of the greatest leaders on this continent."

She tilted her head a little, an unreadable expression in her big, dark eyes. "Ogian, I couldn't even tell a camel and a giraffe apart."

"No one's perfect," he said, waving his hand dismissively. "I'm still amazed I'm sitting here with someone like you."

"Yeah, well, that's probably because you're almost as dense as I was back then. I still wonder what made me become smarter – dying or being turned into a ghost. Perhaps you should try it and see if it works for you as well."

Ogian wasn't sure what she meant, so he asked another question instead.

"Is that where we're going now? To ask one of those gods to give us his or her power?"

That was two questions, but that's not something you mention in stories like this one. Except that I just did.

"No," she said, her voice dropping almost to a whisper. "I'm done with serving gods. This time I'll be the one in charge. I'll be more than a god. I'll be the one they *kneel* before."

"Wow," Ogian said, stunned by the power of her words. "And what will my part be in all this?"

She looked up at him then, her eyes changing color from their usual dark brown to an intense, glowing amber.

"You'll be the one to herald my coming," she said. "You'll be the Harbinger."

~3~

———————— ✳ ————————

"Stone walls do not a prison make, nor iron bars a cage."

- Richard Lovelace, To Althea, from Prison

When Kat woke up, feeling the hard ground beneath her body, her first thought was, "*Damn, did I have too much to drink again?*". Or, to be honest, her very first thought was "*Fuck, how my head hurts*", but that was more of a general sensation than a thought. Anyway, what she thought right after that was that she couldn't remember drinking the night before, but that was the way it was supposed to be, wasn't it?

"She's awake."

The voice, in combination with the unusual place she'd apparently spent the night in, should probably have alerted Kat that something was wrong, but as the voice in question stated nothing she didn't already know, she dismissed it as unimportant.

With a groan, she rose to her hands and knees and looked up (or as far up as her aching head would allow her). There was a row of iron bars in front of her, each one driven deep into the ground. She frowned at them. Then she looked to the side. There were iron bars there as well.

A cage, she thought. *I'm in a lily-livered cage. How did I end up here? I'm...*

For a moment she couldn't remember exactly who she was. Then it all came back. She was a member of the Hullabaloo tribe, in the north-east of Africa. Her job was to uphold law and order. That made her frown again. Didn't that mean she was supposed to put people behind bars, not the other way around?

She suddenly recalled the voice that had spoken a short time earlier. Climbing to her feet, she turned around, facing the way the voice had come from.

A stocky, grim-faced man was watching her with a sour expression on his face. Kat thought she'd seen him before, even if she couldn't remember his name.

"Who the hell are you?" she snapped.

The man didn't reply. Looking back over his shoulder, he gave a curt nod, then winced as he stretched one of the muscles in his neck.

Another man came into view. Kat hadn't noticed him standing there, behind the sour-faced one. This one, however, was someone she knew all too well.

"You..." she hissed.

"Indeed, me," Clogz said, an annoying smirk on his worm-like lips.

Things were slowly beginning to come together in Kat's head. Last year the Hullabaloo tribe had experienced a wave of criminal activities, from thefts to blackmail and assault, and finally the murder of one of the tribe's leaders. Kat had been in charge of rooting out the band of criminals responsible for this, and had revealed Clogz as their leader. To her frustration he'd escaped, fleeing the village before she could arrest him. No one had seen him since. Not until now, at least.

"So you're the reason I'm locked up here," she said. It wasn't a question.

"You might say that," Clogs said. "Or you could say it's because of what you did. Most of my old companions are dead because of you. I'm afraid that can't go unpunished."

Kat looked at the man who'd first spoken. "You were one of them, weren't you?" she said. "Not one of those we executed, of course. One of those we never found."

The sour-faced man didn't reply this time either. After looking at him for a few moments Kat turned back to Clogz.

"What have you done this time?" she asked.

Clogz tilted his head to the side, that annoying smirk of his widening to an even more annoying smile.

"Let's say there's been a change of regime in the tribe," he said. "I'm running things now. The old chieftain is dead, as are his closest associates."

A sudden chill gripped Kat's heart. "What about my men?"

"The rest of your pathetic little police force are imprisoned just like you," Clogz informed her. "I thought we'd make something more of a... spectacle, of you lot."

"So we're to die?"

Clogz snorted. "Of course. We can't have people like you around, now that things have changed so drastically. I've put together my own force to police this tribe from now on. Naturally, they won't fight the same type of crimes you did."

"What type of crimes will they fight, then?"

"Why, crimes against me, of course."

Kat gritted her teeth. Then she remembered that her head was aching something fierce. She touched the back of her head and grimaced as her hand found a tender bump.

"You attacked during the night?" she growled. "You goat-kissing cowards struck while we were sleeping?"

Clogz didn't look the least bit ashamed. There actually are people who take pride in cheating, boasting about it as if it were some great and admirable achievement.

"Aren't you going to ask what will happen to you and your old companions?" he enquired.

Sudden suspicion filled Kat. "What devilry do you have planned this time?"

The criminal-made-chieftain shrugged. "Oh, just a little something I learned during the time I spent travelling after you chased me away. Let's say it involves you fighting a lion with nothing but your bare hands."

"Oh, is that all?" Kat said, feeling relieved. "What did the poor animal do to deserve this?"

"Hah!" Clogz barked a laugh. "Over-confident as always, I see. This lion is known for its fierceness. We're going to starve it another day or two, to make sure it's desperate for fresh meat. Saves us the trouble of burying you as well."

Kat rolled her eyes. "Both lazy and arrogant, I see. That's not a very good combination if you want to accomplish anything."

"Oh, I have some really grand accomplishments planned," Clogz said. "Too bad you won't be around to witness them."

"I'll witness your downfall, you lily-livered fool!" Kat snapped. "Bringing down criminals is what I do, remember?"

Clogz shook his head ruefully while chuckling softly to himself. Then he gestured to the sour-faced man.

"Keep her well fed. We don't want the lion to finish her *too* quickly."

With that he turned his back to Kat and strolled off into the village. Kat glared after him, clutching the iron bars in a tight grip. She wished her fury would give her the strength to rip them apart so she could run after the bloody idiot and smash his goat-brained head in. But that wouldn't happen. She'd supervised the construction of these cages herself. Nothing short of an earthquake would be able to destroy them, and even an earthquake might not be enough.

Gritting her teeth, she moved over to the opposite side of the cage and sat down on the hard ground. She had to think of a way to get out of this mess. It was possible that she'd be able to defeat that bloody lion they had waiting for her, but she didn't trust Clogz's people to let her go if she did. More likely they'd stick her full of arrows and throwing spears, fool cowards as they were. That meant she'd have to escape. But how?

The best opportunity would be when they brought her to the fight with the lion. She'd be out of her cage, as would her old companions. But they'd be surrounded by armed guards, not to mention a few hundred people come to watch the bloody spectacle. Getting away from that would be all but impossible. No, she had to get out of her prison, free her companions, and get out of the village before Clogz learned she'd escaped.

She stood up and grabbed hold of one of the iron bars. It was solid as the earth itself. She wondered if she could dig her way out during the night but quickly dismissed that idea. The ground here was hard and full of rocks. She'd thought that a good thing when she'd had these cages built. Now she cursed it.

See the possibilities, not the obstacles, she told herself. *If I can't break out of this cage I'll have to find another way. Think, woman!*

There was the sound of approaching footsteps again. Kat swung her head around, ready to hurl some scathing insult at Clogz, but it was only the sour-faced guard returning. She hadn't even noticed that he'd been away.

"Breakfast," he mumbled, bending down to place a basket of bread and fruit on the ground outside the bars. Then he backed off, resuming his earlier position a few feet away.

Suddenly, Kat got an idea.

She spent the rest of the day loafing about in her cage. At noon she did some push-ups, more to pass the time than to increase her strength, and in the afternoon she napped, knowing it might be a while before she got another opportunity to sleep. She ate all the food the guard brought her. Food might also be in short supply in the near future.

A loud roar, not in her immediate vicinity but not too far away, woke her from her second nap. Kat looked in the direction it had come from, memorizing the location and judging the distance. There were a few shouts of alarm, then things calmed down again.

Someone probably came too close to the lion's cage, she thought. *I hope the poor beast bit his lily-livered cock off.*

She saw that the sun had sunk almost all the way to the western horizon. Shadows were lengthening all around her. That meant the moment she'd been waiting for would soon be there, if she'd predicted things right.

If not, I'll most likely be dead before long, she thought, rising to her feet and shaking the stiffness from her limbs. Then she waited. And waited.

Just as she started to suspect she'd been wrong, when almost full darkness had settled over the village, an elderly woman arrived with her supper. She handed it over to the sour-faced guard, who gave it a sniff, frowned, and approached Kat's cage. The old woman left without a glance back.

Kat waited until the guard bent down to place the bowl on the ground. Then she leaped forward, fast as a viper. Her hands shot out between the iron bars, grabbed the man's head and smashed it as hard as she could against the hard metal. The man emitted a low sigh, then went limp in her arms.

There'd been one strong element of risk in her plan. Well, more than one, to be sure, but there was one particular variable that could overthrow it at this early stage. She didn't know if the guard had the key to her prison. All she could hope for was that Clogs was arrogant enough to believe she posed no threat to the dour-looking man. He'd been wrong in that, as we've just seen.

Fortunately, she found the key hanging from a chain around the man's neck. She ripped it loose, fiddled with the lock a few moments, and then the cage's door was open and she was free. She took a few steps, then changed her mind and went back, pulled the still unconscious guard into the cage, locked the door and threw the key as far as she could into the darkness.

The guard's only weapon had been a short knife. Kat knew she could defeat most people with her bare hands, but she took the knife anyway. It'd be useful to have at dinner if nothing else.

The prison cages were positioned at the outskirts of her tribe's village, so no one had witnessed her escape. Most people were probably relaxing after dinner; some of the older ones might already have gone to bed. A few younger couples might also be in bed at the moment, albeit not sleeping.

It took her less than a minute to reach the next cage. Moving like a ghost (a much more graceful one than Bathora's), she came up behind the lone guardsman, who looked half-asleep where he stood. A quick slash with her knife and he was out of the game. She had the cage door open before his dead body hit the ground.

"What?" a gruff male voice said from one of the far corners. "Who...?"

"Shh," Kat hissed. "That you, Bog?"

"Kat?" The burly man was on his feet in an instant. "How did you...?"

"Quiet, I said. If you keep babbling like this we'll have Clogz's entire army here before we know it."

"But you're the one doing all the talking," Bog pointed out.

Kat waved her hand. "That's different. Now, do you know where the others are?"

"I thought I heard Spud yelling something earlier," Bog said. "So he should be in the next cage. Don't know about Weewee."

"You go and free Spud, then," Kat said. "I'm faster and quieter, so I'll find Weewee. We'll meet here when we're done. Got it?"

The man nodded, but naturally Kat couldn't see that in the darkness.

"Got it?" she repeated.

"Yes!"

"Shut up! Geez, how many times do I have to tell you that?"

She found the last member of her old police force in a cage halfway around the village. Even so, she was back at the rendezvous point well before Bog. She took the opportunity to relieve herself behind Bog's old cage. A warrior never passed up an opportunity to sleep or eat or take care of her other needs.

When Bog returned with Spud – a short, bald man with thick arms and a somewhat absent expression on his face – she was already growing impatient.

"What took you so long?" she demanded.

"They were changing guards just as I arrived," Bog said. "I had to wait for the first one to leave before I could strike."

Kat frowned. "That couldn't have taken that long."

"They were kissing. I thought they'd be at it all night, but finally the first guy left."

"So it was a woman guarding the cage when you freed Spud?" Kat asked.

"No."

"Oh. Well. I suppose that's normal these days. Anyway..."

Weewee, the man she'd rescued last, spoke up. He was the youngest of them, barely more than a lad but an amazing spear fighter. At least if you compared him to most other people. If you compared him with Kat herself he was rather poor.

"Aren't we going to leave?" he asked.

"Soon," Kat said. "There's just a small surprise I have planned for Clogz and his lackeys before that."

The moon had risen, providing a pale silver light as they moved through the night. Faint sounds from the distant camp fires sometimes reached them – laughter, the clinking of pots and mugs, and the occasional startled cry as someone played a prank on a friend or relative. Kat led her three companions to a grove of tall trees outside the village.

"Stay here," she ordered them. "Climb up into the trees if you hear something that sounds dangerous."

"Like what?" Spud asked.

Kat was already on her way back towards the village. "You'll know," she called back over her shoulder. Then the night swallowed her.

The sour-faced man was still unconscious when she reached the cage where they'd held her prisoner. She figured he'd have one hell of a headache when he woke up. And it'd take them a while to get him out of that cage. Still, he'd prefer that to being left outside once she set her plan in motion.

They'd left no guard by the lion's cage. Kat shook her head as she saw the key hanging from a hook beside the massive door. Sometimes people made things a bit too easy for her.

"Meow," she said, making a face at the large animal.

The lion simply stared back at her.

"I hear they've been feeding you poorly," Kat went on. "Time to remedy that, don't you think?"

The lion snorted, tossed its head and gave her another dumb look.

"Not much of a talker, are you? Well, I guess that's fine. I can be a bit grumpy when I'm hungry, too. Good thing there's a whole village full of nice, juicy people right over there."

She turned and looked at the small specks of light where the fires still burned. For a moment she felt a faint surge of regret. Not all those people were bad. She wished she knew of a way to lead the lion to those she wanted to get back at. If she ran ahead of it with a slab of raw meat... but no, that'd be too risky. She'd have to accept that some innocent people might get hurt. They'd accepted Clogz as their new chieftain, after all, so they weren't *completely* innocent.

"Try not to eat too many of the decent people," she told the lion while she unlocked the door. As it flew open she swung herself onto the cage's roof, where she'd (hopefully) be out of the lion's reach.

Slowly, the large animal plodded through the opening. It stopped outside, sniffed the air, then let out a low grunt and set off towards the village at a trot. Kat remained where she was, watching the lion disappear into the darkness.

A short time later a terrible roar echoed between the huts. Screams of pure terror followed, and Kat saw dark shapes scattering in all directions. She caught a brief glimpse of the large predator as it chased a group of people between two campfires. Soon the entire village was in turmoil, people running this way and that and screaming at the top of their lungs. Someone had picked up a thick, burning branch and was waving it about madly. There was a loud crash as either the lion or some panic-stricken villager blundered into one of the huts.

Sniggering to herself, Kat climbed down from the cage and vanished into the night, leaving the roars and the screams behind. She knew the villagers would eventually either kill the lion or drive it away. She'd better make sure she and the others were well away by then.

Her companions awaited her among the nearest trees, sending anxious glances in the direction of the village. They'd probably heard the screams and crashes and thought Kat was in the middle of it. When she stepped into view right in front of them they relaxed visibly.

"Kat!" Weewee exclaimed. "What's going on over there?"

"Oh, nothing special," Kat said. "I take it they told you what they planned to do with us?"

Bog nodded. "They were going to feed us to a lion, or something."

"More or less," Kat said with a nod. "They'd starved the poor beast for a day or two. I took pity on the thing and served it a nice buffet."

"No you didn't!" Spud said, displaying the unsavory expression dumb people produce when they think they've caught someone telling a lie or making a mistake and don't realize they're just too dense to understand what the other person really meant.

Kat frowned at him. "Huh?"

"No way you could've cooked up a whole buffet in the time you were gone. And besides, lion's don't eat at tables."

"I didn't mean *that* kind of buffet, you lily-livered imbecile!" Kat snapped.

A malicious grin slowly spread across Weewee's lips. "You mean you let it out and set it loose on the villagers? That's *nasty!*"

"Of course it is," Kat said. "I was the one who came up with the idea, after all."

"I hope the lion bites Clogz's head off," Bog said, his eyes dark with hatred. "And then it can have his balls for dessert."

"Wouldn't it be better the other way around?" asked Weewee.

The big, burly man glared at his younger companion. "Why's that?"

"Well, he won't feel much pain after he's lost his head. Better if the lion saves that for last."

"Oh, right." Bog scratched his head. "Anyway, what are we going to do now?"

"We'll get out of here," Kat said. "That lily-livered lion won't keep Clogz and his goons distracted forever. Once they have things under control again they'll start searching for us. We must be well away from here by then."

"That's enough for now, I guess," Weewee said. "But what'll happen to us after that? We have nowhere to live and nothing to eat, not even any real weapons. We're refugees."

"What kind of geese are those?" asked Spud, who'd had a somewhat limited education.

Kat glanced back at the village they'd just left. Screams and shouts still echoed through the night. Letting loose the lion had really turned the place upside down, but she knew it wouldn't be enough. She wanted to get back at Clogz for what he did, *really* get back at him. But there was nothing they could do right now. Like Weewee said, they were only four refugees without any resources. They'd have to start over, build things up from scratch.

"We'll find something," she said. "There must be people who need skilled fighters. We'll offer our services to anyone who's willing to pay enough."

"I like that," Weewee said, grinning like a fool. "We should get ourselves a name, too. Something really mean."

"What about Kat's Pajamas?" Spud suggested.

"What kind of a name is that?" Bog asked. "It sounds really stupid."

Spud shrugged his thick shoulders. "I dunno. It just came to me."

"Kat's Deathsquad," Kat said.

"That's more like it," Weewee said. "The world will tremble when that name is spoken."

"Kat just said it and I felt nothing," Spud pointed out.

"It's a figure of speech..." Weewee began, but Kat interrupted him.

"We must leave now," she said, picking her way between the tall tree trunks where small puddles of moonlight lit up the uneven ground. The others followed, the four of them vanishing like ghosts into the night.

Behind them the lion let out one last, blood-curdling roar.

~4~

There are some places that seem to radiate malice. They're often dark, barren and generally inhospitable. Places like these tend to attract the nastier elements of the human race, and by *nasty* I don't mean the usual sub-human creatures like golfers, carpenters and dog owners, nor do I mean people with a tendency to get drunk and get into a fight (not necessarily in that order). No, I mean *really* mean people.

The Vale of Uzureth was such a place.

It was located far to the north, where not even the Elephant People had ever journeyed. The vale was surrounded by tall, sharp cliffs, treacherous even to the most sure-footed animals. At its bottom, kept almost completely in shadow even during the day, were scattered rocks and deep fissures from which acrid smoke sometimes rose. Nothing grew in the Vale of Uzureth. Things died there.

The climate was hostile as well – colder than in any other part of Africa, with howling winds and frequent thunderstorms. Strangely, it almost never rained. Rain might mean living things sprouting from the dry, cracked ground, and the Vale of Uzureth wouldn't have that. This was a place for dark people, and accordingly a group of dark people had made it their home.

Seated on a small boulder, watching the dark shadows the campfire sent dancing across the nearest cliffs, was the woman who called herself Little Black Bird.

She was munching on a cookie.

There was nothing odd about the cookie.

There wasn't really anything odd about Little Black Bird.

Except that she was evil.

If someone had asked her what made her evil she'd probably have struggled a long time before coming up with a satisfactory answer. She didn't torture children, didn't sacrifice animals (not unless they were already dead). She didn't drink blood or eat raw meat. But she was evil nonetheless. She belonged to a Death Cult.

Her cult wasn't the typical band of misfits drawn to the occult – people who worship a god with three heads and a phallus like an obelisk, walking around in strange clothes and speaking backwards. They didn't mix strange substances together in the hope it'd give them immortality or other mundane powers. No, her cult was far, far worse.

Or at least that was what she kept telling herself.

They'd done what they could to give the already unfriendly vale an evil appearance. Whenever they found a dead animal they cut off its head and put it on a stake. Little Black Bird (or Birdie, as the others called her) had thrown up the first time she did this. To cover up the incident she'd said it was part of the sacrifice. None of them knew which deity they were sacrificing things to, but all were convinced it was a very dark and nasty one.

Another thing they did was sit by themselves down in the caves under the cliffs for long periods of time. Birdie wasn't sure why that would be considered as evil. It just felt like the thing to do sometimes.

Being stout worshippers of the dark, they were only up at night, spending the days sleeping in the aforementioned caves where they didn't have to endure the accursed light.

Well, that's what they did most of the time, at least.

As nothing lived in the Vale of Uzureth, they had to journey into the surrounding countryside to find food and water and anything else they needed. At night it was too dark to see, even with an ample supply of torches (one of the girls had got lost once and barely managed to find her way back), so they'd made an exception for such tasks. The days were too long to spend sleeping anyway.

"Aren't we going to begin tonight's rites soon, chief?"

Birdie looked up. Demon Viq – a pretty girl with long, dark hair had come up to her. Her brown eyes reflected the firelight so it looked as if they had a reddish glow. It might have given the Death Cultist a properly evil look if she hadn't gotten smoke in her nose and started sneezing violently at that very moment.

"Yeah," Birdie said, finishing her cookie. "Gather the others, will you? I'll bring the sacrifice."

While the other girl was away Birdie went over to a small cavity in one of the cliff walls. She'd chosen the place because its outline resembled a skull. At least if you had a very good imagination.

Inside she found the thing she'd put there earlier that night. It was the small body of the gerbil they'd found dead down by the dry river-bed. Birdie picked it up and carried it back to the fire.

A short time later Viq returned with the other two members of their cult. Lethal Leoma (or Leelee, as the girls had taken to calling her) was a pretty, soft-spoken young woman with mousy brown hair and a pleasant smile. The other was Kel Hell – a plump woman with an enormous rear and a very loud voice. Watching the three of them blabber and giggle like they always did, Birdie wondered (not for the first time) if she'd made a mistake when she picked the members of her cult.

When Leoma saw the dead gerbil she emitted a high-pitched sound that was about as far from evil as anything could be.

"Aw, what a cute little thing!" she exclaimed, ran over to where Birdie sat and began scratching the dead rodent behind one ear.

"Leelee, for the love of..." Birdie cut herself off. Love wasn't supposed to be one of the ingredients in a Death Cult, was it? She tried to come up with a way to rephrase herself (without any success) when Leoma plunged even deeper into the quagmire cute, furry things tended to draw people into.

"Can't we get a live one?"

Birdie gave the other girl a hard look. "We're necromancers, Leelee. We don't deal with live things. And we don't adopt pets."

"But it's so cuuuuute!"

"Necromancers can have pets," Demon Viq put in. "Snakes, spiders and the like. They usually give them long names that are hard to pronounce."

"But snakes and spiders are *nasty*!" Leoma protested. "I want one of these. Er, what is it, exactly?"

"A gerbil," Birdie said.

"Can you eat them?" asked Kel Hell, giving the dead animal a hungry look.

"It wouldn't be more than a light snack for you, Kel," Demon Viq said, grinning at the larger woman.

"Get into position now, you lot," Birdie said, her patience starting to run out. "It's time to begin tonight's rite."

Kel Hell made a pained grimace. "Not one of those tedious ceremonies again. Can't we bake a pie instead?"

"We had pie last night," Birdie reminded her.

"Yes, but that was *ages* ago!"

"There are some cookies left." Demon Viq handed her the jar. "You can have them. I have to watch my figure."

"We should find you a guy," Leoma said with a smirk. "Then he could watch it for you."

"What would we do with a guy?" Kel asked, stuffing two cookies into her mouth and swallowing them without chewing. "You can't eat them."

"We could sacrifice him to the dark powers," Viq suggested.

"Great idea!" Leoma exclaimed. "Then I can keep my gerbil. On second thought, I think I'll want two of them. It'll be like a little family."

"I still think we should bake a pie," Kel said, holding the now empty cookie jar upside down and glaring at it as if its emptiness was a personal affront to her.

"We're necromancers, not bakers," Birdie said. "Gather around now. We still have a lot of work to do tonight."

With some additional muttering, the girls settled down, forming a circle around the dead animal. Kel Hell seated herself on a wooden plank resting atop two rocks. It sagged quite a bit under her weight. The other two sat down on the hard ground, legs crossed.

A flash of lightning lit up the entire vale. A clap of thunder followed a moment later, echoing between the cliffs. Birdie nodded with satisfaction. This was a good omen for tonight's rites.

"Focus your mental energy now," she said. "Picture this gerbil moving its paws, then raising its head."

The four of them stared at the animal for a minute or two, then Kel Hell leaned to the side and released a booming fart.

"Sorry," she mumbled. "Had to."

Birdie sighed. "Kel, how are we ever going to manage anything if you keep breaking our concentration? The rest of us were trying real hard. Right, Viq?"

There was no answer. Birdie turned to ask the girl again but saw she'd fallen asleep. She leaned closer and screamed as loudly as she could into Viq's ear.

"VIQ!!"

"Huh?" The girl jerked awake and gave the others a bleary-eyed look. "Oh, right. Get the gerbil to move. No problem."

"Can I have it as a pet when we bring it back to life?" Leoma asked hopefully.

"We're not going to bring it back to life, Leelee," Birdie said. "It'll be an animated corpse that we'll control. That's the whole point of necromancy, to make dead things do what we want."

"Kel seems to think the whole point is eating as much as you can," Demon Viq said with a toothy grin.

"Will you stop picking on me?" Kel Hell snapped, glaring at the other woman with the same intensity she'd used on the empty cookie jar before. "Or it'll be you lying there at our next rite."

"Only if you sat on me," Viq mumbled, fortunately too low for the large woman to hear.

"What are we going to make the gerbil do if we manage to control its body?" Leoma asked. Her hand reached out to pat the dead animal but quickly drew back when Birdie shot her a warning glare.

"The gerbil will only be the beginning," Birdie said. "Once we've mastered the technique we'll try larger animals, and finally humans. Imagine what we could do with an army of corpses at our command."

There was a long moment of silence, then Leoma spoke.

"Um, sorry, but I can't imagine anything. What about you, Viq?"

The dark-haired girl shook her head. "Nope, nothing really comes to mind. Kel?"

"They could bake us a lot of pie…"

"Girls!" Birdie interrupted, hearing a hint of desperation in her own voice. "This is a Death Cult, for… for darkness's sake! We do evil things. People should fear us. How will that happen if all you think of is food and pets and… and…"

"I can do evil things!" Demon Viq said gleefully. "If a guy gropes me I'll shove a red-hot iron rod up his arse. And I'll laugh while I do it."

Leoma's beautiful eyes widened. "Isn't that a bit harsh?"

"It actually sounds like a good idea," Birdie said, feeling a sliver of hope for their cult's future. "But it shouldn't stop at that. We should tear out the guy's intestines and hang them up to dry between two stakes, and keep his blood in a bucket until it goes foul."

"Ew, that's disgusting," Leoma said. "Imagine how the place would smell. And what would we do with all that rotten blood?"

"There's great power in such things," Birdie explained. "We could use it to summon demons from the world of the dead."

"Are there demons there?" Viq asked.

"Of course there are!" Birdie snapped. "Where else would they be?"

Leoma sniggered. "In Kel's stomach, from what we heard earlier."

"What about you, Kel?" Demon Viq asked.

The large woman looked up. "What about me?"

"What would you do if a guy groped you?"

Kel Hell shrugged. "I'd say thanks."

"Let's not deviate from the subject," Birdie said. "It looks like focusing our wills on the corpse wasn't enough. Let's move to the next stage."

"No!" Leoma gasped, her face suddenly pale. "Not the..."

Birdie held up a long, thin bone needle. "Yes, the blood."

"But you know I can't stand needles! I'm going to faint!"

"This is what necromancers do, Leelee," Birdie said firmly. "Give me your finger."

Leoma's gaze was wild with fear as she stared at the needle. "Is this really necessary? Wouldn't the three of you be enough?"

"We're doing this together or not at all." Birdie leaned over so she could reach Leoma's left hand. The other girl jerked it back. Birdie sighed. "Kel, hold her."

The large woman rose from her seat and knelt behind Leoma. The fear-stricken girl yelped as Kel's thick arms clutched her in a vice-like grip. Birdie wet the sharp tip of the needle with her tongue, then pricked Leoma's left index finger with it. A small drop of bright red blood became visible.

"There. You can let her go now," she said to Kel. She pricked her own finger before tossing the needle to Viq. The pretty girl grinned impishly at Leoma as she slowly and deliberately stuck it into her thumb, then painted her lips with the blood. Leoma yammered weakly and closed her eyes, holding her own hand out as far as she could as if the blood on it was some kind of venom.

Birdie gave Viq an appreciative nod. The girl might be an airhead at times and had a tendency to nod off in the middle of important ceremonies, but at least she had a feeling for proper Death Cult behavior. Perhaps she should assign her the task of ridding Leoma of her faint-heartedness. Her own attempts had all failed.

When Kel finally managed to get some blood out of one of her stubby fingers they all placed their hands on the dead gerbil. Birdie felt a faint throb in her finger as the blood pulsed through it and hoped it meant some of her power transferred itself to the tiny creature. She pictured it rising, dead eyes staring up at her, waiting for her to command it. But nothing happened this time either.

After a few minutes she gave up, pulled back her hand and sucked the blood from her index finger. The others followed her example (except Leoma, who produced a small piece of cloth from somewhere and carefully wiped her finger on it).

"I don't know why we keep doing this," Kel muttered. "It never worked before, so why would it now?"

"The art of necromancy is very complex, Kel," Birdie said. "It's not something you learn in a few sessions. It may take years to master it fully."

"But we've been at it for some time," the plump girl said. "Shouldn't we at least have managed something by now?"

Birdie shrugged. "Perhaps it's like a dam. It holds the water back for a long time, but when it finally bursts everything comes rushing forth at once. We'll have to keep working. Sooner or later we'll discover something that will lead us onto the right path. Just be patient."

"What more can we try?" Demon Viq asked. "It's getting late. Or early, depending on how you look at it."

"Let's try to invoke the dark powers," Birdie decided.

Viq gave her a blank look. "Invoke? What's that?"

"It's what you do with dark powers. It's important to know the right words. I should put together a list so you can practice each morning before you go to sleep."

"I have a book of recipes I read before I go to bed," Kel said.

"Any good words in it?" Birdie asked. "Like dissection or obituary?"

Kel scratched her head thoughtfully. "Not that I can remember. It's mostly stuff like bouillon and fondant. Think we can use any of those?"

"I doubt it," Birdie said. "Anyway. Let's try the invocation now. Everyone stand up."

It turned out Viq had nodded off again, so they had to shake her a few times before she woke up. They formed a tight circle around the dead gerbil. Birdie noticed that the fire had almost died down and suppressed a shiver as the cold night breeze soughed between the cliffs.

"We should hold hands," she announced. "That way we'll channel the power between us and form an unbroken circle of magic. That's how you do these things."

"It is?" Demon Viq asked, stifling a yawn before taking Birdie's proffered hand.

"It certainly is," Birdie said, returning Leoma's smile as the girl took her other hand. Leoma seemed more at ease with this part of the ritual. Perhaps there was hope for her yet.

"O great powers of darkness," she intoned. "Hearken to my call!" *Hearken* was a good word, she decided. "Grant us thy power!" *Thy!* She had to use that one more. Or should she have used *thine*? She'd have to work out details like that before their next session. Now, where was she?

"Right," she continued. "Bring... *Bringeth* unto us the dark fires of the Underworld and fill... filleth us..."

"Fillet was one of the words in my cook book!" Kel Hell exclaimed. "I knew there was powerful magic in it! The eruptions I experienced the morning after I..."

"Shut up!" Birdie snapped, then resumed her invocation. "And filleth us with their mighty essence, because we are..."

"For," Viq interjected.

Birdie gave her an incredulous look. "What?"

"You say *for*, not *because*. Because is too mundane."

"For we are your humble servants," Birdie corrected herself, trying to sound as if she'd intended to use that phrasing from the beginning. It was important to maintain an air of competence, even if she made up all her little speeches on the spot. The girls had to turn to her for guidance and stability – that was what a cult leader was for. And now she'd forgotten what she was about to say again.

"I felt something!" Leoma suddenly cried out.

Birdie was so surprised she almost let go of her hand. "What? What did you feel?"

"It was like a tingling sensation running down my back," Leoma said, eyes shining with excitement.

"Sure a bat didn't crap on you?" Viq asked.

"No! It was cold, almost like ice. There! It came again!"

At the same moment Birdie felt something small and hard bounce off her head. Another landed on her hand, where it quickly turned into a drop of cold water.

"It's a hailstorm, you moron!" she growled. "Let's head inside. This session is over."

They hurried down a steep slope, tripping over loose rocks in their haste to find shelter from the downpour. The hailstones grew larger as the storm reached its crescendo. Some felt sharp as nails as they struck the four necromancers. Birdie had snatched a branch from the dying fire and now held it before her like a dowsing rod. It barely provided enough light for them to find their way to the nearest cave.

As they sat there in the darkness, listening to the thunder and patter of hailstones on the hard ground, an overwhelming sensation of dejection came over Birdie. What was she doing wrong? She'd tried so hard – had found the perfect place for her cult, had devoted herself to worshipping the darkness and the evil powers, had chosen a name that might not be the most menacing but that she felt suited her and made her feel comfortable. And yet she'd failed to conjure up even the tiniest of spirits or animate the simplest of corpses. Never had she felt so much as a hint of response as she tried to use the dark powers.

Except for that one time.

She hadn't told any of the others about the strange sensation she'd experienced down in that deep cave. To be honest, she wasn't certain herself whether it had been real or just something she'd imagined. There'd been something – a kind of presence at the edge of her consciousness. She'd reached for it, and it had passed right through her, vanishing as quickly as it'd appeared. The whole incident had frightened her so badly she'd fled from the cave and hadn't visited it since.

I must go back, she thought. *See if I can find proof that something really happened down there. Only then can I tell the others.*

She rose from the cave's hard floor, went over to the wall next to the opening and grabbed one of the torches hanging there. Demon Viq looked up at the sound.

"Where you goin', chief?"

"Just going to pick up a few things from one of the other caves," Birdie said, not meeting the other girl's eyes. "Be right back."

"Can't it wait until the storm has passed?" Viq asked. "It looks pretty nasty out there."

"Well, nasty is my middle name," Birdie said, attempting a joke.

"Really? I thought it was Claire."

Birdie grimaced. "That name belonged to another person. I'm Little black Bird now. The darkness cowers before me, not the other way around. I'll see you in a bit."

The weather really was nasty. Birdie had to walk almost doubled over as the wind whipped her face, hailstones pelting her cheeks and forehead. The Vale of Uzureth might be the ideal place to form a cult of necromancers, but it was pure hell if you wanted to go out for a walk.

Fortunately, it wasn't very far to the cave where she'd felt the strange presence. She hurried in through the low opening, taking a few moments to catch her breath. The cave's insides were tough, with lots of sharp protrusions jutting out from both walls and floor. It wasn't a good place to play blind man's buff. Not a good place at all.

But, she had to admit, it did look like a place where evil spirits might lurk.

She hesitated, glancing uneasily at the dark corners the torchlight didn't quite reach. What if there were evil spirits here, spirits who weren't happy about living creatures having come to disturb them? Could spirits hurt you? Birdie had a feeling a necromancer should now such things, but no one had ever seen fit to tell her.

"I come in peace," she said loudly. Then she mentally slapped herself. What a silly thing to say. She was supposed to be the master of the darkness and everything that lived in it. If a spirit showed up she'd just... what was the word again? *Compel*? Yes! She'd compel it to do as she wished. She had no idea how such compelling was done, but she figured it'd come naturally to her once the situation arose.

But what if it didn't?

Pushing the fear and doubt away, she moved deeper into the cave. She remembered the way fairly well – out on that ledge, then down that slippery rock face where she'd almost fallen flat on her face last time, crawl through that low passage, and there it was.

The innermost part of the cave was a small, stuffy space with dry, stale air. Its rugged ceiling was too low for even a small woman like Birdie to stand upright, and it sloped down towards the far corner. The place reminded Birdie of a tomb, even if the strangely smooth floor was completely empty.

At least it had been the last time she was there.

A tingling sensation ran down Birdie's spine as she detected a couple of small objects on the ground near the opposite corner from the entrance. From her current position she couldn't make out their exact shapes, only dark forms in the gloom.

Heart pounding, she dropped to her hands and knees, crawling the last ten feet to where the ceiling was so low it almost connected with the floor. Holding the torch in front of her, she stared wide-eyed at the things that had somehow appeared there.

There was a pair of dice – no, *five* dice, all showing sixes, and next to them a glass containing some dark liquid. There was writing on the glass. Birdie leaned closer so she could read it.

Guinness.

~5~

————— ✳ —————

S ome of you might be upset because I made a derogatory statement about dog owners in the last chapter. This does, of course, not apply to every person owning a dog. I was referring to the hardcore dog people - those who love their dogs and hate all other animals. These are the kind of people who, in the case of a fire, would first save their dog and then, more as an afterthought, go back and rescue the rest of their family.

I don't think it's ever been determined why these people are so devoted to their smelly, noisy, drooling companions when they display such aversion for other animals. My theory is that, as the majority of these people are white trash or people with white trash backgrounds, the only creatures foolish enough to love them unconditionally are dogs, and hence all other animals remind them of their inadequacies. But, like I said, this is just a theory.

Marsha didn't hate anyone unless she had a very good reason to, nor did she expect people to like her for no other reason than that she provided them with food. What she did expect was to be treated fairly and to not be accused of things she hadn't done. So right now she was very annoyed, almost furious.

"You've been searching the village and its surroundings for two days!" she snapped, fists clenched so hard she could feel the bones grinding against each other. "Isn't it obvious I haven't stolen your stupid Orb of Life?"

"It definitely isn't," said Ostomy, the village chieftain. "You probably hid it very well, hoping we'd give up the search and let you go. Then you'd pick it up as you left, laughing at us for being so stupid."

"That's absurd! Why would I want that stupid glass ball in the first place?"

Ostomy shrugged. "The reason is of no importance to us. All that matters is getting the Orb back. The future of this village may well depend on that."

"The future of its privies, at least," Marsha muttered to herself.

She was becoming dreadfully tired of being kept a prisoner in this bloody hut. The villagers kept armed guards posted outside at all times, allowing her to go outside only twice a day to take care of her bodily needs. She'd tried to think of a way to escape, but unlike Kat of the Hullabaloo tribe she wasn't a great warrior and she had no lion at her disposal. No, if she was going to get out of this mess she'd have to use her head. She'd made no progress at all in that regard, which made her even more furious.

"What about Jennibal?" she asked. "Any sign of her yet?"

The chieftain shook his head. "She seems to have vanished without a trace. We've looked everywhere, most thoroughly in the huts belonging to the unmarried males."

Marsha gave him a puzzled look. "Why would you look for her there?"

"Because of the way she looks, of course."

She looked blankly at the man for another few moments before comprehension struck her.

Ah, she thought. *That romance thing again. I must learn to understand that stuff better, or I might miss other important things.*

Marsha had never understood why such a large part of people's lives revolved around love and sex. Her lack of interest in people of either gender had caused a lot of speculation among the members of her old tribe, speculations that Marsha herself was completely unaware of. What she did with all the time and energy other people spent fraternizing was also unknown. One possible answer would be that she spent all those hours thinking, but thinking wasn't really the kind of activity that belonged in the Khadal culture, as you've probably noticed by now.

Another thing you might have noticed is that Marsha, though a relatively smart woman by Khadal standards, wasn't very good at arguing her points. She tended to get stuck in her opponent's pattern of thought, unable to talk them down even if her arguments were by far the most sensible.

"Perhaps she took the stupid Orb," she tried, hating herself for putting the blame on the other girl but desperate for a way out of this. "She did leave the hut some time during the night and never came back."

"It's a possibility we've considered," Ostomy said. "But we find it unlikely that she's the thief."

Marsha produced another frown. "Oh? And why's that?"

"Jennibal was a firm believer in that religion with the Omnipotent Cantaloupe, or whatever she called it. A relic belonging to another faith would be without value to her."

"Perhaps she saw your worshipping of it as blasphemy and wanted it removed?" Marsha suggested.

"That's not the impression she gave off," Ostomy said. "She appeared completely indifferent to it. You, on the other hand, displayed an unmistakable interest from the moment I first mentioned it."

Marsha threw up her hands. "This is unbelievable! If you must know, I don't care one whit about your Orb of Life. I was just trying to be sociable. There's nothing wrong with my bowel movements, either."

"That's not what the people who escorted you to the privy this morning said."

"What?" Marsha glared at the chieftain. "They make reports about... about what I do in there?"

"Information is everything," Ostomy said with a tired smile. "You'd be surprised if you knew what can be derived from a person's excrement."

"You mean you *study* it?!"

The chieftain's smile widened slightly, and Marsha decided she'd do nothing but pee from now on, no matter how sick or uncomfortable it made her. These people were much more sick and twisted than she'd thought. Not even the Elephant People's gargling woman would go so far as to... she stopped herself before finishing the thought. The whole idea was too disturbing.

"So, are you going to keep me here until you find your precious Orb?" she asked, feeling that a change of subject was long overdue. "That could take weeks, months."

"Yes, that's one thing I came to talk to you about," Ostomy said. "We've encountered a slight problem here."

"Oh? You're out of gruel or something? By the way, that stuff is rather disgusting."

The chieftain shook his head. "No, it has nothing to do with food. The problem is that, according to our tribe's laws, we can't hold someone prisoner for more than three days. After that he or she must be punished."

Marsha stared at the man in disbelief. "Punished? But you don't know it was I who stole the Orb. You have no proof!"

"That doesn't matter. If we find nothing to indicate that the person is innocent we have the right to pass judgment, and in your case we've decided you'll be found guilty."

"That's insane!" Marsha exclaimed, anger and frustration making her voice shrill. "You can't have me whipped, or whatever it is you do with lawbreakers, because you *think* I committed a crime."

"We're not going to have you whipped," Ostomy said calmly.

Marsha blinked. "You're not? But you said..."

The chieftain held up a hand, silencing her. "Theft of the Orb of Life..." he began.

"... is punishable by death," another voice finished.

Marsha looked up, then scowled as she recognized the young man who'd just entered the hut. Clyster, the obnoxious son of Ostomy and Enema, stood inside the entrance with a self-satisfied smirk on his face. She still had no idea why the fellow had taken such a dislike to her. What she did know, or had at least just realized, was that his hatred went far deeper than she'd thought.

"I guess the prospect of having me killed brings you a lot of pleasure, Clyster," she said, feeling very tired all of a sudden.

The young man's expression didn't change, but the eager light in his eyes was answer enough.

"So," Ostomy continued. "I suggest you come up with a way to prove your innocence fast."

"I have no idea how to do that from inside this hut," Marsha muttered. "Not unless my innocence shows in my excrement somehow."

"Nothing but guilt in there, believe me," Clyster said, a low chuckle accompanying his words. Then he turned and left the hut.

Ostomy gave her one last look. "You have until nightfall tomorrow," he said, then he was gone as well.

As Marsha spent the rest of that evening alone in her confined space, the full meaning of what had just happened began to sink in. They were going to have her killed, executed for a crime she hadn't committed. She'd never see her friends again. And, perhaps most important of all, she'd never find the Scion, which meant that the new Hippo Cult would never enter into the future of enlightenment and glory those old prophecies had spoken of.

She realized she had no idea what kind of wonders they'd miss out on. A few images flashed through her mind – bright chambers full of shiny objects, people laughing as they danced around a large fire, and a strange vision of people sitting in some kind of wagon that moved by itself. She shook her head. This wasn't the time to start hallucinating.

Instead, she tried to think of a way to get out of this mess. If she'd been a great fighter like Gemma or Amanda she might have been able to overpower the guards outside the hut and escape, but she was all too aware of her limited physical abilities. Would it help if she prayed to the Hippo God? Gods were supposed to protect their subjects, weren't they? The problem was that she didn't know any prayers and found herself unable to think one up. She decided the Hippo God was probably too busy to hear her anyway and went back to her non-productive sulking.

Later in the evening she received the usual bowl of tasteless gruel. She left it untouched on the small table by the opening. It might be a pathetic display of defiance, but it was all she could manage at the moment. The minutes crawled by. She continued sulking.

Night came and Marsha found herself unable to sleep. Her stomach felt empty, and she had a sudden craving for burritos. Frowning, she wondered where that notion had come from. She'd never heard of burritos before, much less tasted one. Perhaps they were one of the wonders they'd never get to experience now that the Hippo Cult would remain incomplete for the rest of eternity.

Her head jerked up as a muffled thump came from outside the hut. Someone drew a sharp breath as if to shout, then there was another thump and everything went still again. A slender shape ducked through the opening.

"Hey, Marsha. What's up?"

Marsha rose to her feet, eyes wide with surprise. "Jennibal?"

The girl gave her a dazzling smile, then she noticed the bowl of gruel on the table and let out a delighted sound, whereafter she hurried over and began spooning the viscous stuff into her mouth.

"Er, what are you doing?" Marsha demanded.

She had to wait for Jennibal to swallow before receiving an answer.

"Eating, of course. What does it look like?"

"But…" Marsha was utterly confused. "What are you doing *here*?"

"Eating, for the moment. Please don't interrupt me. I'm starved."

Marsha had to wait patiently until Jennibal had emptied the bowl. When she'd finished, she emitted a happy belch and wiped her mouth on her sleeve. Then she gave Marsha another smile.

"So, how have you been?"

"Er…" Marsha wasn't quite sure how to answer that, so she replied with a question of her own.

"How did you get past the guards?"

The girl held up a large, round object she'd held under one arm. Marsha gasped as she recognized it.

"The Orb of Life! So you did steal it!"

"No, no." Jennibal shook her head, making her long hair swirl around her face. "I found it in clyster's hut. Might have cracked it, though. One of the guards had a hard skull."

Marsha could only gape at her. "You used the Orb to knock out the guards?" Then something else the girl had said registered in her brain. "In Clyster's hut? What were you doing there?"

Jennibal's beautiful face took on a haughty expression. "I wasn't sleeping with him, if that's what you thought. There are limits to what I'd do even for you."

"But..." Marsha's brain was still processing all this new information. "Why would the Orb be in his hut? They've been looking for it for days!"

"As dense as always, I see," Jennibal said with a rueful smile. "My guess would be that he set all this up, hoping we'd get the blame for it. He really is a nasty piece of work, that one. Poor Enema."

Marsha nodded slowly. That sounded just like the thing the young man would do. And of course the others had bought it. No one would look for the Orb in the hut belonging to the chieftain's son.

"You didn't tell me how you found it in his hut," she pointed out.

Jennibal shrugged. "I've spent the last two days trying to find a way to free you. My first idea was to find the Orb and return it to its place so they'd know it wasn't you who stole it. However, that might have resulted in me getting the blame for the entire thing, and I couldn't risk that."

"Naturally," Marsha mumbled. "So what did you do instead?"

"I kept wondering what really had happened to the damned Orb. I spent all of last night looking for it, which was rather stupid of me because these constipation people had already looked in all the likely places. So while I waited for darkness to fall again I tried to think of more *unlikely* places to look. That's when it struck me."

Marsha blinked. "Something struck you. Are you hurt?"

"No, silly," Jennibal said with a snort. "What struck me was the idea that one of the places they wouldn't look was in Clyster's hut. It also made sense that he'd taken it, as he seems to hate us for some reason I haven't figured out yet, and also knew what the punishment for stealing the Orb would be. So I snuck into his hut after he went to sleep and there it was." She held up the Orb as evidence.

"That's amazing!" Marsha said. "But what do we do now?"

"We get out of here, of course."

"With the Orb?"

Jennibal rolled her eyes. "Of course not. What would we want with a stupid glass ball? I'll dump it in Clyster's tent on our way out and give the others a small hint."

The "small hint" Jennibal had planned turned out to be a large arrow drawn in the dirt outside Clyster's hut, pointing straight at its entrance and with the word ORB written in block letters beside it. Marsha didn't know if the villagers would realize the chieftain's son had been behind the entire plot from the beginning or simply think she herself had returned the Orb to them before escaping. Honestly, she didn't care.

They spent several hours stumbling through the night, wanting to get as far away from their captors as possible. Marsha stepped on several things that hurt her foot, as well as a few she couldn't identify (which she was very thankful for, seeing as they felt very unpleasant to the touch). Once they even passed underneath a sleeping giraffe without noticing it in the dark. When the giraffe woke the next morning it found it had acquired a severe case of constipation. All it could remember was having a strange dream about cantaloupes and weird dice games.

Dawn was approaching when Marsha and Jennibal finally decided it was time to rest. By then both of them were completely exhausted and collapsed beneath a couple of tall trees. Marsha, who hadn't eaten anything since the previous morning, was very hungry but much too weary to look for anything edible. Jennibal was already snoring loudly beside her when she closed her eyes and waited for sleep to take her.

When she woke it was almost noon. There was a gnawing sensation in her stomach that she soon identified as hunger. Groaning, she sat up and looked around. Jennibal was still sleeping, her long hair covering most of her face. Marsha shook her gently.

"Jennibal! Wake up! We must be on our way."

"Mmmmmm…" the girl murmured, rolling over on her other side and going back to sleep.

Marsha frowned. She'd always slept lightly and didn't know what to do with people who refused to wake up. Were you supposed to pour cold water over them? She didn't recall hearing the sound of water anywhere during their nightly flight. Then she remembered something Pebe had done once, to bug Amanda. It had earned him a hearty smack but had certainly caught her attention.

She pinched the girl's bum, hard.

"OW!" Jennibal jerked upright. "Stop that! You'll invoke the wrath of the God of the Iridescent Cantaloupe!"

Marsha rewarded herself with a satisfied nod. "Ah, you're awake. Good. What about breakfast?"

Her companion rubbed her sore behind. "What? Oh. I guess it's time for that. What would you like?"

"Er, anything. What do you have?"

Jennibal gave her a perplexed look. "Me? I don't have anything. There was nothing left in my bag so I left it in that hut."

"Then why did you ask me what I wanted?"

"To see if it was something I wanted as well, of course."

This time it was Marsha's turn to frown. "But we don't have anything, so why would it matter what I want?"

"Of course it matters. If we want the same thing you can go out and find it. If we want different things you'll have to spend more time searching, and then I might as well go back to sleep."

"So you're not going to help?"

The girl shrugged. "I did get you away from those Orb people, so I figured making breakfast would be a good way for you to repay me."

"I see." Marsha wasn't sure how to argue against a statement like that. After a few moments of silence she nodded again, rose to her feet and went in search of something to eat. Jennibal yawned, thinking what a strange people the members of the Hippo Cult must be, then dozed off for a while.

After breakfast they resumed their journey, heading west and a little south across rolling hills and through small patches of jungle. Marsha spent most of the time lost in her own thoughts (if it was possible to get lost among such simplistic entities) while Jennibal passed the time whistling jolly melodies and humming to herself. Both of them later agreed it had been a rather pleasant day.

Late in the afternoon they became aware of a low, monotonous thudding sound, coming from somewhere ahead of them and a little to the right. It grew into a louder *boom-boom-boom* as they drew closer.

"What do you think that is?" Marsha asked Jennibal.

The girl tapped her finger against the back of her hand in time with the sounds. "I don't know. Sounds like something's got stuck."

"Do you think we should check it out? Someone might need help."

"Yeah, of the psychiatric kind," Jennibal murmured, but after a few moments of consideration she nodded. "All right. Let's head over there."

Surprisingly, all they found was a single man sitting outside a small tent. He was youngish, perhaps a few years Jennibal's senior, and very tall and lean. His head was oddly shaped, with ears that protruded like trumpets on either side. The repetitive booming sounds came from a kind of hide drum which he absent-mindedly beat with one hand.

"Hello," Jennibal said. "What are you doing?"

The man looked up. The sight of Jennibal standing there, hair glistening in the afternoon sunlight, would have made most males forget what they were doing and have them staring open-mouthed for an indeterminate period of time, but this fellow kept up his monotonous rhythm as if nothing out of the ordinary had happened. Marsha wondered if he was gay.

"Making music," was all he said.

Marsha frowned. "Er, you must be mistaken. I've heard music, and this isn't it."

"I don't know what crap you've heard," the man said, giving her a sour glare. "But this is what real music sounds like. This song is the biggest hit in the whole world. It's played at least thirty times a day everywhere."

"Er, define *everywhere*, please?"

"Well, here for example. And where we used to live."

There was a choking sound as Jennibal tried to suppress a wild gust of laughter. Marsha, on the other hand, didn't find the young man's attitude the least bit amusing.

"You mean it's the song, lacking a better word for it, *you* play the most? That doesn't make it the most popular in the world."

"How do you know what's popular and what's not?" the man snapped. "Are you keeping track of the charts?"

Marsha blinked. "The what?"

"The charts. They show which songs are the most popular right now."

"There are no such things," Marsha said. "And if there were, your song wouldn't be on them."

The man bared his teeth in a dog-like snarl. For a moment Marsha thought he'd attack her, but Jennibal stepped forward before he could say or do anything.

"I'm Jennibal," she said, holding out her hand.

The man ceased his beating on the drum long enough to shake it. "I'm Mongoe," he said, his feral grimace softening to a moderately unpleasant sneer.

"Hello, Mongoe," Jennibal said in her usual chirpy tone. "Er, why are you so sour?"

Mongoe's sneer grew somewhat more intense. "I'm not sour. I'm cool."

"And the difference is?"

The man ignored her question, engrossing himself in his monotonous drumming. After a minute or two Marsha cleared her throat.

"How long is this song you're playing?"

"Huh?" Mongoe looked at her as if she'd just said the most stupid thing he'd ever heard. "This isn't the same song. Can't you hear the difference?"

"No, because there is none."

To her surprise, Mongoe stopped beating the drum this time. He even put the annoying little thing aside and focused all his attention on her.

"Why have you come here?" he demanded. "If you have requests for other songs, then let me know and I might play them later. Just be aware that I prioritize songs I like. People with different tastes are worth less to me."

"Er..." Marsha began, wondering if this Mongoe fellow was quite right in the head. He seemed to live in a tiny, insular world of his own making, where he'd made up rules and truths that suited his own strange fancies.

"We were just looking for some company," Jennibal interposed, once again assuming the role as mediator. "And perhaps to share a meal. Are you alone here?"

Mongoe shook his odd-shaped head. "No, my two friends will be back later. They're out hunting for food. I suppose you can stay, as long as you don't eat too much."

The prospect of spending the rest of the day with this rude, selfish man didn't make Marsha the least bit happy. Finding herself a reasonably comfortable spot on the hard ground, she hoped the food would be worth it. It felt like years since she'd had a really solid meal. Perhaps gruel and fruit were good for the bowels, but Marsha was a carnivore born and bred and felt like her body was about to start deteriorating if she didn't get enough meat.

Not wanting to plunge into another discussion about charts and song requests, she decided to tell this fellow of her purpose in coming here.

"I'm looking for something," she said. "It looks like a small hippo with wings. I don't suppose you've seen such a creature around here?"

Mongoe gave her the kind of look some people produce when they don't understand what you're saying, but for some reason think that's your fault instead of their own.

"A winged hippo?" he finally said. "Such a thing doesn't exist."

Oh, not again, Marsha thought. She had no wish to explain herself to another ignorant, narrow-minded cretin, but she knew her mission was too important to give up this soon.

"It does exist," she said, forcing her voice to remain calm. "It was hatched from the egg the Raven Cult people brought to the Hippo God's temple but it flew away when the Bug Goddess attacked, so now I have to find it."

"What are you talking about?" Mongoe asked, one hand fiddling idly with the drum on the ground beside him. "There is nothing called a Raven Cult. Where did you get that idea?"

"Er, from meeting them, of course," Marsha said. "Why would you say they don't exist?"

"I've never heard of them."

Marsha stared at the man in disbelief. "You mean you don't think anything you haven't heard of exists? What about the Elephant People or the Telu tribe or Mount Azagh?"

"They don't exist."

"They do!"

Mongoe gave her a look that positively oozed of contempt. "How could you know about all those things when I never heard of them?"

"Because I've *seen* them, you idiot!"

"I don't believe you."

Marsha wanted to throw something at the fool man. His attitude was so utterly brainless it made her want to scream. What she didn't know was that Mongoe was a notorious liar, and like many such people he kept mistrusting others, believing them as unreliable as himself. His unwillingness to believe in things he hadn't seen for himself isn't overly exaggerated either. There are lots of people who refuse to acknowledge facts even when they're presented to them in a much more concrete way than what Marsha just did.

During this little explanation of mine Marsha managed to calm herself enough to refrain from physical violence (for the moment, at least). Instead, she thought of a new argument, one she felt the imbecile in front of her wouldn't be able to counter.

"What about me and Jennibal?" she asked with a triumphant smirk. "You hadn't heard of us until we showed up here. Does that mean we didn't exist before that?"

"Are you trying to make some kind of point?" Mongoe said sourly. "Because I don't follow."

If Marsha had had a knife or some other weapon she might have plunged it into the man's heart out of sheer frustration. Fortunately, she didn't have any sharp objects, and before she could take any other drastic measures Jennibal spoke up.

"Look, there are your friends. And they've brought food!"

Two young men were coming towards them, chatting animatedly as they went. One carried a dead animal over his shoulder and seemed to be complaining about how much better the hunting was where they used to live. The other one made mocking comments, accompanied by weird noises that made him appear both stupid and childish.

"Look, Mongoe found himself two little whores," the one who'd made the stupid noises said as they entered the small camp. Marsha instantly disliked him. Jennibal, however, seemed too exalted by their catch to notice the insult.

"Wow, nice catch!" she exclaimed. "Is that an antelope?"

"Klipspringer," said the one carrying the carcass. He dropped it on the ground and dusted off his hands. "Not as good as the springbok living farther west, but it was all we could find."

"It'll do fine, Wurst," Mongoe said, in a slightly more friendly tone than the one he'd used with Marsha. "I'll go find wood for the fire."

Marsha had, to her demise, plenty of time to get acquainted with the newcomers while they waited for the meat to roast. The one who'd called her a whore was called Yeast. He was almost as unpleasant as Mongoe, not outright rude in the same way but incredibly arrogant, which was strange because he was both unintelligent and lacking in class. Marsha figured his arrogance had something to do with the strip of hide he had tied around his neck, because each time he fingered it (which was ridiculously often) his expression turned haughty and he looked down his nose at the others.

The one who'd brought the dead klipspringer was called Wurst. He was, if possible, even dumber than Yeast, rather fat and shabby-looking with greasy, shoulder-length hair and dirty clothes. At first Marsha found him quite companionable, even if he focused most of his attention on Jennibal, but after a while he started to annoy her as much as the two others. He had a way of complaining about everything that quickly got tiresome, especially since he seemed to think he knew how to improve the things he found flawed. In all the time they spent together she didn't hear him come up with a single reasonable suggestion, though.

After about an hour (which felt like an eternity) she decided she'd had enough and went for a walk. The sun had just set, the landscape around her growing darker while the western sky was still bright and beautiful. Birds were singing in a cluster of trees off to her left, and she saw a larger bird in the distance, outlined against the deepening blue of the sky.

Something about that lone bird drew Marsha's eye. Its shape was odd, somehow. She squinted to see better. The bird made a low swoop before vanishing behind a stretch of jagged cliffs. For a moment its form was clearly visible. Marsha felt an icy chill fill her body, and she emitted a gasp.

It wasn't a bird. It was a winged hippo.

~6~

---❋---

*"In the main, ghosts are said to be forlorn and generally miserable,
if not downright depressed. The jolly ghost is rare."*

- Dick Cavett

Ogian was taking a dump again.
This time he'd found a slender tree trunk that had cracked at about waist height, allowing him to seat himself on it with his rear end leaning out behind it. It was a very practical and fairly comfortable way to take care of his business. The forest was silent and peaceful around him, and he closed his eyes and enjoyed the feeling of being by himself, with no one to disturb him as he...

"Diddelidoo, look at all that smelly poo!"

Ogian lost his grip on the trunk and swung around backwards, crashing to the ground with the back of his head ending up in the stinking pile of feces there. Behind him Bathora laughed so hard she almost fell over herself.

"Oh my," she gasped. "You should have seen that! I've never seen anything like it! It was so funny."

With an overwhelming sensation of shame and revulsion Ogian climbed back to his feet.

"Would you please stop doing that?" he whined. "It's bad manners to barge in on someone when he's... when he's..."

"Why would I care about manners?" Bathora snorted. "I'll be a goddess soon. More than a goddess. I can do whatever I want."

Ogian gave her visage a closer look. Bathora's ghost was wearing some kind of light-blue leggings that clung very tightly to her hips and thighs, a checkered shirt of red, blue and white, and a wide-brimmed hat on her head. In her arms she held a strange object, round with a long stem sticking out on one side, thin metal strings stretched across it surface.

"What's that?" he asked, pointing at the thing.

"A banjo," Bathora said. "It's a musical instrument with rodents inside it. Here, listen." She strummed the strings, producing a clear note.

"Very nice," he said. "But what are you going to do with it? And why are you dressed like that?"

Bathora spun the banjo around a few times. "I thought we'd go honky-tonkin'," she said. "It's not often the bar comes to these parts, so we shouldn't miss the opportunity."

"The bar? What's that?"

"You'll see," Bathora said with a bright smile. "But first you'll have to wash yourself. They won't let you in if you've got shit all over you."

They found a nice little lake where Ogian could clean himself. Bathora stood on the shore, plucking a few simple chords on her banjo while he washed. When he'd told her he wanted some privacy she'd said there might be alligators in the lake so she'd better keep watch. He'd thanked her, saying it was very kind of her to look out for him in that way and that he'd never have thought of the risks himself. The only reply she'd given him was a smirk.

When Bathora decided he was presentable again, she led him back through the jungle and onto another of those grassy plains they'd spent so much of the past week crossing. This one looked slightly different, with shorter grass and protruding rocks in some places. Ogian had seen similar sceneries during his long travels with the Elephant People.

"Are there mountains nearby?" he asked, leaping over a rock like a frog with the motor skills of a dead rhino.

"There will be, but not for another couple of days," Bathora said. She was walking in front of him, and Ogian couldn't help but notice how her round, plump buttocks moved inside those tight leggings. Once again, he got the feeling he shouldn't look at this woman in such a way, but he couldn't remember why. Could it have something to do with her being a ghost? He decided that was an explanation as good as any for the moment.

"Do you visit this bar-thing often?" he asked.

"Only once before," Bathora said, glancing back at him over her shoulder. "But I doubt anyone who was there will ever forget that night."

"Oh, why's that?"

She shrugged. "I might've caused a bit of a ruckus."

Ogian had no idea what a ruckus was. He thought it might have something to do with that strange instrument Bathora had played while he washed himself. She'd told him there were rodents inside of it. Perhaps they'd gotten out and frightened some of the other visitors.

That wasn't at all what had happened the last time Bathora had visited the bar, of course. She'd entered the establishment wearing her old garment of office, which looked more or less like a sack that'd been dipped in muddy water. A kindly old woman had bestowed one of her daughter's dresses upon her, transforming Bathora from a mild curiosity to the center of everyone's attention. Things had gotten pretty wild and she'd come within a hair's breadth of being thrown out. She still couldn't recall how the night had ended, but from the headache she'd woken up with she figured it'd been epic.

Ogian couldn't believe his eyes when the bar finally appeared in front of them. The only buildings he'd seen so far were tents and huts, the only exception being the Hippo God's temple, which he'd thought quite spectacular but more than a little bit scary. The bar, however, was something he couldn't have imagined in his wildest dreams (which weren't all that wild most of the time).

"Wow," he said. "When you said we were going to a bar I thought it'd be like, you know, a bunch of people gathering around a fire or something. This is just…" He didn't know words like *extraordinary* or *breath-taking*, so he left it at that.

"Hah, who'd dress up for something like that?" Bathora said as they approached the large building. "Now, a few words of advice: stick to Guinness and peanuts and you'll be fine. I can also recommend their blurbers, if you want something more solid in your stomach. Stay away from the whiskey – too much of that and you might end up in bed with the ostrich."

Ogian blinked. "What?"

"Don't stand there with your mouth open like a misshapen birdhouse," Bathora said, making an impatient gesture towards the entrance. "Come inside. It's time to party!"

The inside of the bar was just as astonishing to Ogian as the outside had been. He'd never seen so many people crammed into such a small place. The level of noise made him dizzy, the different styles of clothing made his eyes want to scream, and…

"They're playing dice over there!" he cried out, a wide (and very ludicrous) smile splitting his face. "I must go have a look!"

"Later," Bathora's ghost said, pointing towards a long, semi-circular counter. "Drinks first."

Ogian cast one more longing glance at the dice table, then followed Bathora through the crowd. In a few cases Bathora literally passed *through* people, causing Ogian to bump into them when he tried to follow. He received a few sour looks and an insult he didn't understand but seemed to have something to do with his parentage.

Once they made it to the bar Ogian forgot about the dice game. All the bottles and glasses and unidentified shining objects made him gawk like a three-year-old child (which, by not quite a complete coincidence, was roughly the level of intelligence he possessed).

"Oh my," he exclaimed. "Where do all these things come from? I've never seen anything like it."

Bathora smiled at him. "That phrase seems to pop up every time I come here," she said. "But to answer your question: the whiskey comes from Scotland, Ireland or the US, the beer is from England, Ireland and, um, not sure about the one called Hakituri. That sounds like a painful way to commit suicide. Anyway, what would you like?"

Ogian had absolutely no idea what she was talking about. Too overwhelmed by the flow of information to answer her question, his eyes instead fell on a very odd occurrence taking place to their right. A man held out a piece of paper to the bartender – a snobby-looking ostrich with large black sunglasses – and received a small pile of metallic discs in return.

"What's that?" he asked, pointing.

"That's money," Bathora said. "You use it to pay for your drinks."

Ogian's face fell. "But I don't have any. How are we going to order anything without that money-stuff?"

The ghost gave him another of her radiant smiles, snapped her fingers and held up a couple of the odd-looking pieces of paper, forming them into a fan and covering her mouth with it. Her eyes twinkled when she saw his expression.

"Being a ghost has its advantages," she said in a low, husky voice.

"But..." Ogian stammered. "I thought you couldn't create real things."

"I can't. These are just an illusion. But I don't think anyone will notice. Here, look!"

She waved her hand, and a few moments later the ostrich came over. His face took on a look of intense disapproval when he saw Bathora.

"Oh, it's you again," he said. "Should I call security at once?"

"No need," Bathora said with an innocent smile. "That sexy dress I used to wear got ruined last year. I'm wearing tight jeans today."

The ostrich reached for a small device with buttons on it. It'd been resting on the flat surface in front of him.

Bathora laughed and made a dismissive gesture with her hand. "Don't worry, lad. I promise you there won't be any trouble because of me tonight. I'm in complete control this time."

After a moment of hesitation the ostrich nodded. "All right, then. What do you want?"

"A pint of Guinness for my friend here," she said, nodding towards Ogian. "I'll just wait for someone to get generous."

The ostrich poured Ogian a glass of some dark liquid with thick foam on top. Bathora handed him one of the pieces of paper, which he quickly dumped into a kind of drawer that seemed to open by itself. He stood silent for a few moments, frowning as he rubbed his fingers together as if trying to feel something that wasn't there, then shrugged and picked out a couple of the metal discs, placing them on the counter.

"Hold on to those," Bathora said. "They're *real* money."

Ogian put the money in his pocket, then picked up the glass and took a sip. The bitter taste made him gag and he came within a hair-s breadth of spitting it out again. Coughing, he glared at Bathora.

"That tasted like one of the gargling woman's brews," he gasped. "Why did you order something like that?"

"Ah, you'll get used to it," she said, giving a young man standing farther down the counter a wink. He almost ran down half a dozen people in his haste to come over to Bathora's side. The look on his face reminded Ogian of a hyena with its tongue halfway to the ground.

"Hey babe," he said, his voice slightly slurred. "That's one hell of a badonkadonk you got there." One hand reached out to touch Bathora's voluptuous behind, his expression momentarily puzzled as it passed right through her body, but then he seemed to decide the drink had played a trick with his perception and resumed talking instead. Ogian didn't understand much of what he said, and after a while he stopped listening.

He almost fell off his stool when someone slapped him on the back.

"Hello, mate! What's up?"

Ogian studied the young man who'd walked up to him, not sure whether he should feel alarmed or not. The fellow looked harmless enough – his skin was unnaturally pale, almost as pasty as those Raven Cult people he'd met last year, his hair light brown and standing on end, and he had one of those weird things across his eyes, although his wasn't as dark as the ostrich's. He was smiling at Ogian, looking like he expected a reply of some sort.

"Um, hello," Ogian managed. "Which tribe are you from?"

That was evidently not what the man had expected. His smile turned into a puzzled expression, but then he shrugged and pointed to the stool next to Ogian's.

"Mind if I join you?"

Ogian looked at the stool, then back at the man. Did he somehow think Ogian owned the chair next to him? Should he tell the man he didn't even own the one he was sitting on? The rules of this place were totally alien to him, filling him with insecurity and unease. So he did what most people, regardless of which time and place they lived in, did to deal with those emotions.

He took a healthy swallow of his drink.

To his amazement it didn't taste as bad this time. IN fact, it sent a wave of pleasure through his body. Filled with this new confidence, he smiled at his companion and nodded towards the vacant stool.

"Please do. I'm Ogian. What's your name?"

The man said something that was too long and complex for Ogian to remember, so he simply nodded and raised his glass as he'd seen other people in the bar do.

"Cheers, um, mate," he said, taking another swallow. This time it actually tasted good.

The man with the odd name sipped his own drink, which was smaller than Ogian's and not as dark. Ogian eyed it curiously.

"What are you drinking, mate?"

"Whiskey," the man said. "Single malt Scotch. You should try it."

Ogian recoiled so abruptly he almost turned his half-full glass over. "You shouldn't drink that!" he squeaked. "You'll end up in bed with the ostrich!"

"Really?" The man didn't seem at all shocked at this revelation. On the contrary, he looked almost eager. "Speaking from experience, eh?"

"Um, no. This is my first time here. My friend's been here before and she told me."

"Ah, I see." The man sipped his drink again. "What did the surroundings look like that time?"

Ogian blinked. "What do you mean?"

The man made a grandiose gesture that managed to encompass the whole establishment and everything around it.

"This place never looks the same twice," he said. "Last time I was here it stood on an island in the middle of a vast ocean. Tonight it looks like we're in Africa or something, although I've seen no cars or houses. Don't you find that fascinating?"

"Um, I guess," Ogian said, not sure what the guy was talking about. "And they do have a talking ostrich."

That caused the man to raise an eyebrow. "What's so special about that?"

"I've never seen one that talks before," Ogian said. "Isn't that odd?"

The man shrugged. "It's always talked."

Ogian tried to see the logic in that statement and failed. A part of him — the part that even in his case might be referred to as *common sense* — knew that talking ostriches was an anomaly, but so much had happened lately he didn't know what was normal anymore. Perhaps this odd-looking man came from a place where all birds talked? Once again, he sought comfort in his drink but found to his dismay that the glass was empty.

He looked at Bathora, who was still standing to his right. The man she was talking to tried to put an arm around her shoulders and stumbled into the counter when he found nothing substantial to touch. Bathora quickly appeared a foot away from where she'd been standing, laughing at the man's clumsiness and asking him if he'd had too much to drink. Then she caught Ogian looking at her and raised a questioning eyebrow. Ogian pointed at his empty glass.

"Good boy!" she said, gliding gracefully across the floor so she stood between Ogian and the man who'd been hitting on her. "Take the drink he bought me," she whispered, pointing to a full glass on the counter. "It's not like I can touch it anyway."

"Won't that make him angry?" Ogian asked, hesitating only a moment before eagerly seizing the glass.

Bathora grinned at him, an identical drink appearing in her hand. She turned back to her companion, downed half her drink in one gulp, laughed and issued some kind of challenge.

"Sorry about that," Ogian said, turning back to his own drinking mate. He took a deep swallow of his Guinness and smacked his lips happily. Behind them there was some commotion as a short, fat youngster was dragged away by two large, grim-looking men. The young man was reeling drunk and making a lot of noise as they threw him out.

"So, what's your occupation, mate?" the whiskey-drinking man asked.

Ogian frowned. "Occupation?"

"yeah, you know, your job."

"Ah." At least that was a question Ogian knew how to answer. "I'm with the Elephant People, digging latrine pits. Filling them up, too," he added proudly.

"You mean at a circus?" the man asked. "That must be exciting."

"It's fine," Ogian said, ignoring the part he didn't understand. He found conversation easier after drinking some of this Guinness stuff, almost as if the right words came to him of their own accord.

"I used to watch circus shows on TV when I was a teenager," the man said with a mischievous smile. "Mostly for the girls in skimpy outfits, of course."

"You know Tiwi?" Ogian exclaimed, having misheard one of the words. "She's the queen of my people. Wow, this world really is a small place."

The man gave him an odd look, then shrugged and pointed towards a funny-looking box standing in one corner. Weird sounds came from it.

"How do you like the music?"

Ogian hadn't recognized the thing for what it was until now. "Ah," he said as comprehension hit him. "So that's where they keep the rodents. Last time Bathora was here they were running all over the place. No one there ever forgot that night, least of all the ostrich. Who did you end up in bed with last time you forgot to bring money?"

This time his companion was silent for a long time as he tried to process the stream of random words Ogian had provided. Ogian himself thought everything he'd said had made perfect sense, even if he had trouble remembering exactly what it was he'd been talking about. The drink seemed to have taken effect in earnest now, filling him with giddiness and a care-free sort of elation. He suddenly decided he'd had enough of this odd-looking fellow.

"Bathora, my sexy friend!" he called out. "It's time to check out that dice table now!"

Bathora shot him a dubious look, then rolled her eyes. "You hold your alcohol even worse than I did," she muttered.

Feeling a little unsteady on his legs, Ogian went over to her. "Just one more beer, please? I'm having such a good time."

She shrugged, then waved the ostrich over and bought him another pint of Guinness. Ogian grabbed the glass with both hands, took a few gulps and belched loudly.

"All right," he said, leaning against the counter to steady himself. "Let's gamble!"

He followed Bathora over to the dice table, found an empty spot and slammed his glass down in front of him. The man standing next to him gave him a disapproving look.

"Whatcha playin', mate?" Ogian said, the words not coming out exactly the way he'd planned but somehow sounding right in his own ears.

"Craps, of course," the man said. "We always play craps here."

Ogian frowned. "Not Yahtzee, then?"

The man gave a disdainful snort. "You don't play Yahtzee at a bar. It's the kind of game you play at home with your kids. Are you gonna bet or just stand there looking dumb?"

"I'd like to do both," Ogian said, a bit confused as to why he'd have to choose. "What am I betting on?"

The man opened his mouth, probably to tell him to buzz off or something even more rude, but Bathora hurriedly butted in.

"Place a dollar on the *no pass* line," she said. "It's a pretty safe bet."

"If you say so," Ogian said, digging through the coins in his pocket. He picked one at random and placed it on the table.

"Not one of those!" Bathora hissed. "That's only a quarter. A dollar is the big one."

"Oh, sorry." Ogian found the proper coin, fumbled a little with it, almost dropped it into his glass before finally getting it into the right spot. The other players around the table made their respective bets.

"Come out throw!" the one holding the dice announced. He made the toss, sending the two dice across the table in an elegant arc. They bounced off the far wall and settled, displaying a six and a five.

"Yo-leven!" the man exclaimed, pumping his fist into the air. Bathora cursed.

"What happened?" Ogian asked.

"We lost," Bathora said sourly. "Damn lucky throw by that trashy pile of filth." She sipped the drink she'd brought with her from the bar. It had an unnatural pink color, a slice of lemon on the side and a purple umbrella sticking up from it. Ogian thought it looked rather silly but wasn't quite drunk enough to point it out.

"Are those drinks affecting you like the rest of us?" he enquired.

"Only if I want them to," she said, picking up the slice of lemon between two fingers and licking it slowly. The man standing next to them suddenly lost all interest in the dice game and focused all his attention on Bathora. She gave him a challenging look, her eyebrows drawing close together. After a while he broke eye contact and began fiddling with the coins in front of him.

"It's your turn, mate," the man to Ogian's right said, handing him the dice. Ogian took them with what he considered an elaborate gesture, then brought them to his mouth like he used to do when playing Yahtzee with Kharuba and his other friends.

Bathora's hand appeared right in front of his face, making him shy back despite knowing the ghost couldn't touch him.

"What the hell are you doing?" she hissed, her eyes glowing with outrage.

"P-Putting on a good show," he stammered. "I always did that back home."

"Well, this isn't your stupid Elephant People. Pull a stunt like that and they'll throw you out. If you're lucky, that is."

He frowned at her. "And if I'm unlucky?"

"They'll throw out your corpse."

"Oh. I see." He took a swallow of beer to calm himself, then looked down at the bets on the table. "What should I bet on this time?"

Bathora made a quick survey of the table, then shrugged and pointed. "Pass."

Ogian fished out another coin and placed it in the required spot. Then he rolled the dice, producing a one and a two.

"You crapped out!" the man next to him said with a snort of laughter. "Way to go, mate."

Ogian gave him a puzzled look. "Of course I crapped out. I couldn't do it here in the bar. Do you know how it usually smells...?"

On his other side Bathora cleared her throat. "He means you lost," she explained. "How much money do we have left?"

He held up the handful of smaller coins that remained. Bathora looked far from pleased as she eyed them.

"This won't do," she said, putting down her drink and adjusting her clothing. "You'll have us broke in no time with those lousy gambling skills."

A distant, well suppressed corner of Ogian's mind tried to tell him to point out that it was Bathora who'd told him where to place his bets. Unfortunately, the rest of his primitive mind didn't listen, instead coming up with what he thought was a very bright idea.

"Can't you use some of that fake money?" he suggested. "It worked well when you ordered drinks."

She shook her head. "The other players would notice as soon as it changed hands. I might make it work once or twice, but after that I'd lose track of which of the coins are real and which aren't."

His face took on a dismal look, and he reached for his glass. It took him three attempts to grab hold of it.

"What do we do, then?" he asked, his voice more than a little slurred.

Bathora thought for a moment, then a sly smile spread across her face. It was an expression no one had seen on her while she was alive.

"I might not be able to do anything about the money," she said, her voice dropping to a whisper. "The dice, however, are a completely different matter."

Ogian had no idea what she meant. The only thing he knew – other than that he was well on his way towards becoming really, really drunk – was that he trusted this woman. This *ghost*, to be exact. He wasn't sure why he had such faith in her. She just seemed to know a lot about the world, like where all those strange drinks came from or how to make music out of rodents. He wanted to be like her, to be able to say smart things and to look good in a pair of jeans...

"I'll have to get my hands on a pair of those," he murmured to himself.

Beside him, Bathora raised an eyebrow. "What?"

"Oh, nothing." He pointed at the dice table, where the other players were placing their bets. "What should I do?"

She shrugged. "Put your money wherever you like. It doesn't matter."

Ogian hesitated for one brief moment, then put his coins in the box marked with the number four. The man standing next to him sniggered.

"Getting desperate, I see," he said.

Ogian only gave him a bright smile and took a swallow from his glass. One of the other players rolled the dice. They bumped against the table's back wall and then, as they were about to settle, they became blurry for the briefest instant. None of the players seemed to notice.

"Little Joe!" the one who'd rolled exclaimed. "Damn, the black guy won!"

The man next to Ogian frowned and muttered something about beginner's luck while Ogian collected his winnings. As the next player grabbed the dice Bathora let her illusion vanish. Her timing was so perfect no one noticed the real dice had showed something completely different. Ogian's admiration for her rose to hitherto unknown heights. This woman really knew how to cheat!

Ogian won the next round, and the next. The pile of money in front of him grew into a small mountain, the frustration among the other players growing at the same rate. Some of them were already giving him looks that had more murder than sourness in them. Ogian was, of course, both too drunk, too dumb and too elated to notice.

"Um, I think it's time to quit now," Bathora whispered to him.

"Quit? QUIT?" Ogian gave her an incredulous look. "But we've only just started! I'm *winning*!"

"Exactly. That's when it's time to quit. A gambler should never get too greedy."

Ogian's face twisted into a pained grimace. "But I'm having so much fun!"

"That's good," Bathora said. "But we can't stay here any longer. Remember our real purpose."

It took Ogian a while to remember that they had another purpose than winning at dice, and still longer before he remembered what it was.

"Making you a goddess?" he asked.

She nodded. "Take the money with you. It might come in handy at some point in the future."

He looked at her with pleading eyes. "Only one more time? Please?"

Bathora hesitated, then gave one curt nod. "All right, then. But one time only."

Grinning happily, Ogian downed the last of his drink, belched noisily, and placed his bet. It was his turn to roll. Making a grandiose gesture that forced the man next to him to duck, he tossed the dice onto the table. They hit the far wall, spun, and settled showing two sixes.

"Boxcars!" Ogian bellowed. "Peanuts and rodents, I won again! I've never seen anything like it! Let's celebrate! Free blurbers for everyone!"

Maddened with joy, he leapt into the air, but as he landed he lost his balance and fell across the table, arms flailing clumsily in a vain attempt to catch himself. One hand struck the real dice, sending them tumbling across the table.

The other players stared dumbfounded at the table, now suddenly having four dice on it, then the man next to Ogian pointed an accusatory finger at him.

"Cheater!" he screamed.

Ogian gave the man an affronted look. Or that was what he'd meant to do, at least. There appeared to be two versions of the man, each one blurry and refusing to remain in the same place. He blinked a few times, stuck his chin out and tried to speak in a haughty voice.

"Don't chou dare chall me scheaterr! I'm the Barhinger... Harbincher... I schall... schall..."

He couldn't think of anything threatening to say, so he settled for waving his fist in front of the man's face.

The man shoved him back. "Oh, up yours, nigger. I had my suspicions about you from the beginning. You're getting it now. Oh yes, you are!"

He pulled up his sleeves, baring thick, hairy underarms. Ogian gave him a bewildered look, wondering what it was the man intended to give him. The people in this bar were strange folks indeed. He was pretty sure the man was angry with him, so why did he want to give Ogian a present?

Suddenly a large snake appeared on the dice table. It wagged its head back and forth menacingly, hissing as its forked tongue tasted the air. The man who'd been about to strike Ogian screamed and jumped back. There were similar reactions all around the table. One of the players called for security.

"Come!" Bathora yelled next to him. "We're out of here!"

Ogian had no idea what was going on, but being a born gambler he snatched up some of the coins on the table before following Bathora towards the exit. He bumped into several people on his way and would probably have been knocked to the floor well before reaching the door if Bathora hadn't shouted at the top of her voice that there was a fire and that people should make way.

The dice players Ogian had cheated weren't as easily fooled, though. The moment Bathora and Ogian disappeared into the crowd the illusion of the snake vanished and they realized they'd been tricked again. Shouting for blood, they pushed their way through the mass of drunk people, reaching the door just as Ogian and Bathora stumbled out into the waning daylight outside.

"Hurry!" Bathora yelled. "They're right on our tails!"

"I'm running asch fascht asch I can!" Ogian slurred, staggering after her. The ground appeared to have become more uneven since they entered the bar, making him trip and lurch as he ran. The shouts and curses behind them came closer and closer.

To their right rose a stand of tall bushes. Bathora made an abrupt turn, then pointed at a small gap between two thick shrubs.

"In there!" she hissed. "And be quiet!"

Ogian did as he was told, crouching down beneath the thick branches. His head spun and he desperately needed to urinate. Bathora's ghost seemed to have vanished. For some reason that made Ogian feel forlorn. He was lost in a place he didn't know, surrounded by men who wanted to harm him, perhaps even kill him. The elation he'd felt during the dice game was gone, leaving only the first vestiges of the angst you feel when alcohol is leaving your system.

He caught a glimpse of two men rushing by outside. One of them looked like the man who'd accused him of cheating.

"Where did the bastard go?" the man shouted.

"Must be here somewhere," the other growled. "You search over there. I'll look among those bushes."

They'll find me, Ogian thought. *I'm surrounded, and there's no way out. They'll find me and kill me. I should've left when Bathora told me to. I'll always do as she says from now on.*

But then there was a shout from somewhere outside, followed by the sound of running feet. Ogian leaned forward, peering out into the gloom.

A figure looking exactly like him was running across the open ground, away from his hiding place. The men from the bar followed it, spitting curses and insults as they ran. Ogian realized Bathora had created another illusion, this one meant to draw his enemies away from him.

The chase was short. When the men had come about two hundred yards from the bar they vanished into thin air, as did the phantom image of Ogian. A moment later Bathora's ghost reappeared right outside Ogian's hiding place.

"It's safe to come out now," she said. "They're gone."

Ogian crawled out from beneath the bushes, getting twigs and leaves in his hair. "What happened?" he asked. "Where did they go?"

"It's the nature of this place," Bathora explained. "Once you get a certain distance from the bar you return to your own time and place."

Ogian glanced around, still not completely certain they were safe. "Can't they come back?"

"Eventually," Bathora said. "But by them we'll be well away from here."

They started walking at a moderate pace. It wasn't long before the bar, with its bright lights and noisy crowd, had vanished from sight, leaving only the familiar night sounds of the African wilderness.

Suddenly Ogian's stomach rumbled. "I'm hungry," he announced.

Bathora snorted. "Serves you right for messing up that pesky dice game. You should've ordered a blurber and kept a low profile. Now I'll never be able to show my face there again."

"I'm sorry," Ogian murmured, looking down at his feet as they moved through the dark landscape. His head was beginning to hurt, and there was an unsettling sensation in his stomach. A sudden convulsion went through him and he bent double, vomiting on the ground. It was the most unpleasant experience he'd ever had.

"There, there," Bathora said, patting him on the head (her hand went straight through him, of course). "It wasn't so bad. I caused a lot more trouble the first time I visited. Tonight was a lot of fun. Don't you agree?"

Ogian wiped his mouth, managing a weak smile. "Yes, it was. We were quite the team there at the dice table. Well, most of what we achieved was your doing, of course. You were awesome."

"I know!" She giggled. "I'll be even more amazing when I come into my full power. Then no one will be able to stop me."

"Stop *us*, you mean?"

She waved her hand, the motion barely visible in the darkness. "Sure, sure. Whatever you say."

Despite the state he was in Ogian felt a warm, fuzzy sensation spread through him .Having Bathora as companion would definitely lead him to greatness. No one would ever make fun of him again. No one would call him a cheater.

They'd refer to him as the Harbinger, and all would tremble as they spoke the name.

~7~

─────────── ✳ ───────────

"As the light upon the leaves of trees, as the voice of clear waters, as the stars above the mists of the world, such was her glory and her loveliness; and in her face was a shining light."

- *J.R.R. Tolkien, The Silmarillion*

There were times when Bazer wished he'd been born a woman instead of a man. He wasn't the kind of person who enjoyed dressing up in women's clothing, nor was he attracted to men. He was simply desperate for sex, and was convinced that no woman, no matter how disfigured, would ever have to experience the anguish that had been his constant condition since he first hit puberty. All women got to have as much sex as they wanted, didn't they?

He wasn't the most attractive of males – his forehead jutted out too far, his nose was large and carried an eerie semblance to a potato, the hair on his head was thin and always standing on end. The only place where his hair grew plentiful was on his back, and there it grew in wild, unruly tufts that would make even the shaggiest of goats frown. Bazer had tried several times to cut it off, tearing various muscles in his arms and shoulders in the process, but the small and scattered portions he managed to rid himself of had only made him look even worse.

Another person might have asked for someone to help with the sheering problem, but Bazer found that much too embarrassing, so he continued looking like a sheep that'd got stuck in a lawnmower. A somewhat defective lawnmower.

His main problem wasn't his looks, though. He had a very awkward personality – whenever he tried to speak to a beautiful woman the words got stuck in his mouth, and if he did manage to say something it always came out the wrong way. He kept dreaming up conversations where he'd be witty and cool and the girl he imagined talking to would melt like wax and start kissing him. When he met the girl in question, however, he barely managed a stammered greeting.

Another strange personality trait he had was that he kept making lists of everything. This might not sound all that deviating – lots of people have at some point made a list of their favorite songs or favorite foods or whatever. Bazer's obsession with lists and rating went far beyond that.

Take this, for example: for years he'd been keeping records of how sexy he thought each girl in his tribe (a rather small tribe, fortunately) looked, giving each one a rating between one and ten every day. Weekly and monthly averages followed, so he could appoint a winner for every given period. The lists and tables covered hundreds of pages by now, and running out of paper had become one of the things he dreaded most.

He'd first become sexually interested in women at the age of twelve and now, at nineteen, he was still a virgin. None of the girls in his tribe had ever looked at him with anything other than revulsion or – at best – indifference. Bazer had been in love (or so he thought) with all of them, usually with several at the same time. He'd even been attracted to his friend's old grandmother, who was rather plump but had – according to Bazer – a really magnificent ass. Not even with her had he had any luck.

He'd tried to think of a way to rid himself of his general reputation as a geek and a weirdo, but had come up with nothing so far. In the end he saw no other way than to leave his tribe and see if he could find a new home, with people who appreciated creatures like him. This was, of course, doomed to fail unless something truly extraordinary occurred.

You probably think that's exactly what's going to happen, that poor Bazer will find the love of his life and that they'll live happily ever after.

Well, he will meet the love of his life, but there won't be much happiness involved.

At least not in the beginning.

He'd been on the road (if there'd been such a thing as a road in the African wilderness during this distant time in the past) for two days. The only living things he'd seen in that time had been two Oryx gazelle, a small flock of kudu and numerous birds. Trudging on through the dry, barren landscape he was beginning to fear that the endless supply of nubile, agreeable women he'd expected to await him out there was only a product of his imagination.

Then he reached a vast expanse of swamplands.

These weren't the swamplands Lulu's old tribe of cannibals had inhabited. No, it was located far to the south, where no one had ever heard of the Orb of Life, Yahtzee or honky-tonk bars. It was a very unpleasant area, full of poisonous snakes and stale, putrid water that could give you all kinds of infections. If Bazer had dipped his manhood into it he might never have been able to fantasize about the girls in his usual way again.

He was still at the outer edge of this perilous region, where the ground was wet and soft but not yet hazardous. The stench was slowly growing worse, though, and Bazer was just about to turn and look for another way to go when he heard the cry.

At first he thought it had come from some bird or other, but when he stopped and listened more carefully he realized it was a human being calling for help. Being a kind-hearted young man in spite of his many strange obsessions, he hurried in the direction the cry had come from, his feet splashing through the increasingly soggy ground.

After a minute or two he reached a spot where the (somewhat) solid ground ended. Ahead was a wide expanse of brown, muddy water, with rotting plants drifting across the surface in some places. The stench was so terrible it made Bazer gag.

Some ten or fifteen feet out in the foul water a young woman was struggling to keep her head above the surface. She looked to be about Bazer's own age, even if it was hard to tell with her face and hair covered in mud. As he watched in amazement she sank beneath the surface, only to appear again a moment later, arms flailing wildly, splashing muddy water all around her.

"Help!" she croaked. "I'm drowning!"

Bazer looked around. There were no trees growing anywhere in this foul place, no bushes large enough to provide him with a piece of wood that could reach all the way out to the girl. For a moment he considered running back the way he'd come and search there, but he figured the girl would probably be gone before he made it back, if he found his way back at all.

"Help!" the girl cried again. "You, monkey man! Help me!"

Not knowing what else to do, he took a step out into the muddy water, but his foot immediately sank so deep he almost fell over. Pulling himself out of the thick, caustic water, he scanned the area more closely, trying to find anything he could use to help the girl. Why hadn't he brought a rope when he left his village? Everyone travelling this accursed wilderness should have a rope with him.

That neither Marsha, Jennibal, Ogian or Kat's little group had brought a rope with them when they set out on their respective trips only shows how stupid and improvident we humans are. Even in our so-called modern age people keep entering into projects without being the least bit prepared, regardless of whether it's starting a family, a business enterprise or simply buying something they really can't afford.

But let's return to Bazer now. The situation he presently found himself in was one he'd fantasized about countless times. Most young men dream about rescuing a girl in distress, usually because they've gotten it into their minds that the reward for such a feat includes long hours of passionate sex. However, standing there in the middle of the nasty bog, each moment feeling like an eternity, sex was the last thing on Bazer's mind. This was an extremely unique occurrence, as he rarely thought about anything else. But isn't that the irony of life?

Just as the girl's head vanished beneath the surface again his eyes caught a glimpse of something large and oblong floating in the water off to his right. All warnings he'd ever heard about how most elongated things floating through dark waters ate people vanished from his mind as he stumbled through the shallow puddles, searching for a way to reach the object.

There actually was a thin strip of more solid ground leading out into the water. Bazer moved cautiously along it, tentatively placing one foot before the other until he'd made it far enough to grab hold of the thing he'd seen .Fortunately for him it wasn't an alligator or a python, only a long, thick piece of wood that had ended up there more or less by accident.

"*Help!*"

The girl's cry sounded more desperate now. Pulling the large piece of wood out of the water, Bazer hurried back the way he'd come. In his hurry he almost misstepped and fell into the water, not once or twice but *three* times. That he made it back at all shows how accurate the term "dumb luck" really is.

Once back on the main stretch of land, he quickly pushed the wooden limb out into the foul-smelling water.

"Here!" he called out. "Grab hold of this!"

The girl did as he said, and Bazer began pulling her back towards him. She coughed and sputtered as he helped her out of the water.

"Here, have some water," he said, offering her the leather flask he'd carried in his pack. It was almost full.

The girl grunted something that might have been a *thanks*, then gulped down a few swallows of the lukewarm liquid. After that she poured some over her head, wiping away the mud as best she could. As the water unveiled her visage Bazer found himself staring in wide-eyed, open-mouthed amazement.

She was by far the most beautiful woman he'd ever seen, more beautiful than anything he could have imagined (and he could imagine quite a lot). Her skin was of a lustrous golden-brown hue he'd never seen before, her long hair a deep auburn color that shone in the bright sunlight. But it was her eyes that had him spellbound from the moment he looked into them.

He'd never seen eyes so large, so bright and so *blue*. Their color was so deep it almost bordered on purple. The brilliance of those amazing eyes struck Bazer like a lightning bolt through the heart.

"You're a twelve," he whispered, almost reverently.

The girl wrung some water out of her hair. "Huh?"

"Ten isn't enough for someone like you," he murmured, still more to himself than to his new companion. "I must expand my rating system."

The girl frowned at him, somehow managing to make the grimace absolutely stunning. Then she felt her cheeks, where pus was dripping from a number of open sores she'd received from being submerged in the putrid water.

"Look at me!" she exclaimed. "I'm all pussy!"

Bazer didn't have anything in his mouth to choke on, but he managed to choke anyway. The girl gave him another disapproving look as he coughed and wheezed, tears running from his eyes and snot dripping from his nose.

"What's the matter with you?" she asked. "Are you sick or something?"

The only reply Bazer managed were a few grunts and other strangled sounds. The girl rolled her eyes at him.

"I've heard humans are descended from apes," she said. "But I always thought the species were separated by more than one generation. Do you think you could manage something a little more eloquent, like, say, telling me your name?"

Bazer finally managed to stop coughing. After swallowing a couple of times he got a few words out, although more as a croak than anything else.

"I'm Bazer. Who are you?"

The girl evaluated this new piece of information far longer than what might seem necessary. Bazer didn't mind. He was more than pleased with simply sitting there looking at her. She was wearing a short skirt made of thin leather, her shapely legs stretched out in a nice L-figure. Her top, although still caked with mud, was made of some other thin and soft material and form-fitting enough to make his heart race. And those eyes...

"I might have been wrong about your parentage," she finally said. "Judging by the sound of your voice there must be a frog there somewhere.

A somewhat disfigured frog,I'd say. But we can discuss that later. I'm Kylee. What were you doing here, out in the middle of nowhere?"

Some of you may wonder why being called the son of an ape and a frog didn't upset Bazer, or why he didn't expect the girl to be more grateful after he saved her life. Unlike Ogian, Bazer wasn't too stupid to recognize an insult for what it was. No, he was simply too amazed that a girl like Kylee would consider talking to him. She was so far above any woman he'd ever met that he had trouble believing she was real.

"What if she's only a product of my imagination?" he mumbled to himself. "Things like that can happen when you spend too long by yourself out in the wilderness, right?"

He tried to look more intently at Kylee, searching for a sign that she wasn't there. She did seem to have a shadow, and there was dried mud on the ground where she'd brushed it off. He reached out and touched a flake of it. It felt real enough.

She studied him with the same mix of revulsion and interest someone would show when watching a bug crawl around under a stone.

"You're not very smart, are you?" It was the kind of question that didn't require an answer. "Perhaps I should use simpler words, if we're to have any kind of conversation. Me Kylee, you Bazer, ugh ugh. How's that? Too complex?"

Bazer cleared his throat. "I'm sorry. I was just wondering if you were really here."

"Oh, look, it talks," Kylee exclaimed, feigning astonishment. "Of course I'm here. Where else would I be?"

"I don't know. Where are people when you just imagine them?"

That made her frown again. "You know," she said. "I think I liked it better when you were just making weird noises. Knowing that you're able to form sentences of more than two words but making no sense whatsoever of what you say is very frustrating. Shall we take this from the beginning again? I asked you what you were doing out here?"

"I was looking for a new place to live," Bazer said. "Somewhere people will like me."

Kylee snorted. "You won't find it. I've only known you for a few minutes and I already dislike you more than anyone I've ever met."

"Dislike me?" Bazer felt his heart sink in his chest, like a drunken hippo in a deep lake. "Why? I haven't done anything to offend you."

The girl shrugged, causing Bazer's breathing system to short-circuit again. "There's just something about you that I found instantly repulsive. It's like when you get something really foul-tasting into your mouth and spit it out without knowing what it was. Except that I can't spit you out. You're just there, looking like a hog's arse turned inside out."

It was slowly dawning on Bazer that this girl didn't like him at all. This was a reaction he was well used to, so it didn't come as a complete surprise, but there was something about the blunt way she expressed her revulsion that made him wonder if a girl had ever loathed him this much before. For his part, he was already head over heels in love with her, ready to dive face first into the putrid water and fight a dozen ravenous alligators with his bare hands if she'd give him the tiniest of smiles.

Knowing Kylee, all she'd give him if he did something like that would be an incredulous stare and a dispassionate shake of the head.

"Perhaps it'll get better once you get to know me," he tried.

She barked a laugh. "Yeah, right. I'd say that was the most goat-brained thing I'd ever heard, but I have a feeling most goats would find that insulting so I'll hold my tongue instead."

"So why are you still here, If you're so unhappy with my company?" Bazer asked.

"Well, I was kinda hoping you'd leave..."

"Leave?" He stared at her in shock. "What kind of guy would leave a girl like you?"

"I don't know. The kind, whatever its scientific term might be, that you belong to?" She looked hopeful.

Bazer tried desperately to think of something to say that would improve the girl's opinion of him. Unfortunately, her incredible beauty made thinking all but impossible. He wouldn't be surprised if he'd learned that several of his major organs had simultaneously shut down.

"You never told me your reason for being here," he managed.

"No, I didn't."

"Is it a secret, then?"

She shook her head. "No, I just don't feel like talking to you."

Normally Bazer didn't feel like talking to beautiful girls, either. There were lots of other things he'd rather do with them. But he found, to his surprise, that things were different with Kylee. He wanted to get to know her, to learn what she thought about different things, what she liked and disliked (all he'd found out so far was that she disliked him, so he figured any other information would be an improvement). Of course he wanted to get intimate with her (any sane heterosexual man would) but that came almost as an afterthought.

"Did you come here looking for something?" he asked.

"Yes, I did."

"What?"

"I don't know." Her gaze became distant for a moment, and it sounded like she spoke more to herself than to him. "There was just something. A feeling. I had to come here, to…" She trailed off, her eyes still unfocused.

"Perhaps you're someone important?" Bazer suggested, hoping it'd make the girl feel flattered. "You know, someone with a unique talent that's needed to save the world from evil."

She snorted. "Don't be daft. I don't have any magic powers or extraordinary abilities. The only unusual thing I can do is talk to birds."

That made him blink. "Talk to birds? You mean you cluck and squawk at them and they answer?"

Kylee spent a long time staring at him, her stunningly beautiful face devoid of expression. When the silence stretched Bazer grew uncomfortable.

"What?" he asked.

"I'm trying to decide whether you were making fun of me, or if that actually was a sincere question. And then I tried to figure out which of the two would have the most negative effect on my opinion of you."

Once again Bazer had trouble following the girl's reasoning. She seemed to read things into whatever he said, always ending up disliking him even more than she'd done before. He began wondering if there was anything he could say that she'd find something positive about.

"And what did you decide?" he asked.

"That I'd rather not find out. But to answer your question – no, I don't make silly sounds or peck at the ground with my nose. My communication with birds is purely telepathic."

"Tele-what?"

She rolled her eyes at him again. "We speak through our minds. Do you know nothing? Except how to be a rat's arse, of course. You're very good at that."

"Thanks," he said. "So, what do the birds tell you?"

"They're birds. What do you expect them to do? Give advice about how to cultivate the land better or how to invent new tools to facilitate our primitive lives?"

"That would be nice," Bazer said. "Do you think they'd know how I'd get a beautiful woman to like me?"

Kylee snorted again. "Count yourself lucky if they told you how to get a retarded baboon to like you. That's about as high as I would aim if I were you."

Once again Bazer found himself at the bottom of the conversational pit. Most people would probably have given up by now, realizing they'd never get anywhere with this girl, but every time Bazer looked at her he felt himself fill with a tingling sensation, giving him new strength and motivation. He didn't have to think about what he'd say next. The words simply came to him.

"What kind of birds have you talked to?"

Kylee had been cleaning her fingernails with a small stick. When Bazer asked his question she looked up in surprise. "Huh? What do you mean?"

Happy that she hadn't found another excuse to rebuke him, Bazer pressed on. "I mean, do you talk to large birds like ostriches, or smaller ones like..." He realized he didn't know the names of many birds, so he just made a vague gesture with his hand.

"There are only small birds where I come from," Kylee said. "Small and stupid. They mostly think about food and mating. Pretty much the same as you, from what I've seen so far."

"Then we should find some larger birds for you to talk to," Bazer said thoughtfully. "Perhaps that's what you're looking for – birds that have some information you need."

Kylee stared at him in silence for a long time. Bazer almost shied back from the intensity in her deep blue eyes, expecting her to lash out at him even more violently than before, but instead she buried her head in her hands and began sobbing.

"Kylee?" Tentatively, he reached out a hand and touched her shoulder. "What's the matter?"

She shook her head, her face still hidden from view. "My life is over," she whimpered.

The situation grew more and more awkward for Bazer. He let his hand drop. It brushed against Kylee's thigh on its way back to him, but he barely noticed.

"What do you mean? Did I say something stupid?"

"No." She shook her head again. "That's the problem. I can take stupid remarks from you. That's something I'm used to, even if I've only known you a very short time."

"Then why are you so upset?"

She looked up then. The tears had made the golden skin of her cheeks glow but hadn't made her eyes red-rimmed. It looked like the girl even knew how to cry beautifully. Her eyes were clear, with a slightly haunted look in them as she spoke.

"Can you imagine what it's like to have travelled this land for weeks without knowing why, and then someone with a brain the size of a bug's bladder comes up with a perfectly reasonable answer? I mean, what's the point of getting yourself a proper education and trying to understand the intricate mechanisms of this world when someone who can only be classified as human by elimination of all other options manages to outsmart you?"

Bazer stared open-mouthed at her. "You mean I did something good?"

"Yes, and I hate you for it!"

"Ah, now we're back to normal," he said, feeling oddly relieved. "You had me worried there for a while."

She stood up and brushed off her clothes, making Bazer's mouth as dry as the last flakes of mud that fell from the thin, clinging fabric. Turning around without a word, she began walking away from him.

"Wait!" he called. "Where are you going?"

"I'm going to do as you said and find myself some larger, more intelligent birds to talk to."

Bazer leapt to his feet and stumbled after her. "Let me come with you."

She stopped and looked back at him over her shoulder, her long, auburn hair swirling around her face. "Why?"

"I don't know. I might be of some help. What if you fall into another bog and need rescuing?"

She sniffed, then resumed walking. "Fat chance of that happening again," she muttered.

"I did come up with that idea about the birds," Bazer continued, desperately searching for an argument that would convince this goddess of a woman to want his company. "Perhaps I'll be able to solve more of your problems if you keep me around."

"One lucky shot doesn't make you an oracle," Kylee said, her back still to him. The way her body moved inside that short, tight leather skirt would've made even Bathora jealous. "Good-bye, Bazer," she went on. "Good luck with your search. You'll need it."

He stopped then. There was nothing more he could do or say. She was leaving him. This was, as I've told you before, far from a new experience for him, but for the first time it really *hurt*. The rejections he'd suffered before were like nothing compared to this. It felt like someone had wrenched his heart out of his chest and squeezed it to jelly right in front of him. Tears began streaming down his face, mingling with the sweat that suddenly broke out all over his body.

"I love you!" he cried, voice shrill with emotion.

It was probably unrealistic to think that such a cliché would have any effect on the woman of his dreams, but for some inexplicable reason it had. Kylee stopped and turned around, raising a questioning eyebrow at him.

"Of course you do," she said. "What does that have to do with anything?"

Bazer took a few hesitant steps towards her. "You're the most beautiful woman I've ever seen," he said. "I've never seen anything like it. Astonishing, simply astonishing." He stopped, frowning at nothing in particular. Why had he said that? It made absolutely no sense. And yet...

Kylee was staring at him, her face displaying a similar expression (although it looked a billion times better on her). She reached out a hand and made a strange motion, like she was tossing or rolling something that wasn't there.

"What was that you said?" she asked, her voice sounding strange, as if she was only half awake.

"I-I'm not sure," Bazer stammered. "There was just this picture in my head..."

"Was it of a strange place with a lot of people?" Kylee asked. She was walking towards him now, slowly but without hesitation.

"Yes!" Bazer moved forward until only a few feet separated them. "They were drinking and playing card and dice games, and there was this snobby-looking ostrich..."

"I know!" Kylee was smiling now, outshining the sun itself. "Didn't those sunglasses look silly on it?"

"Silly indeed," Bazer said, managing a much less radiant smile. "What do you think it means? Why would we get the same vision?"

Kylee sighed, but then the smile returned to her lips. "I'm afraid it means we'll have to stick together, at least until we've figured out the purpose of our meeting. I no longer believe it was a random accident."

Bazer couldn't believe what he'd just heard. "You want to travel with me?" he gasped.

"Not exactly, but it's obviously what we're supposed to do. That I'd rather like to travel with someone closer to my own age and level of intelligence doesn't seem to matter."

That made him frown. "How old are you, Kylee?"

"Twenty."

"That's only one year older than me!"

She nodded. "Yeah, and that basically makes you a child. But that's not my main concern. I'm more worried about having to travel with someone whose intelligence equals that of an amoeba."

Despite the insult Bazer found himself grinning like a fool. "Let's find some of those smart birds, then," he said. "Or even a dumb one, as long as it's smarter than an amoeba."

To his surprise, that made her chuckle. "That was actually a bit funny," she said. "Perhaps travelling with you won't be as much of a pain as I first thought."

Surprising him even more, she reached out her hand to him. As he took it and they set out together, Bazer wasn't sure he could feel the ground beneath his feet anymore.

~8~

———————— ❋ ————————

"A thing of beauty is a joy for ever."

- John Keats, Endymion

The darkness lay heavy over the Vale of Uzureth.

On the ground next to their fire lay something equally heavy.

"I never thought I'd hear myself say this," moaned Kel Hell, clutching her ample belly, "but I don't think I could manage another slice of pie if my life depended on it."

"Well," said Demon Viq. "You did eat as if your life depended on it. I thought those pies would last a whole week. There's less than one left now."

"Want me to sit on your stomach and bounce?" asked Leoma. She'd taken up knitting as a means to pass the time while they waited for Kel to finish eating. Birdie had nothing against knitting – there were many occult patterns and symbols to choose from – but whatever it was the girl was working on had entirely too much pink in it. The color was so unbearably cute it hurt Birdie's eyes.

"Only if you want me to vomit all over you," Kel grunted. "And I wouldn't recommend that."

Birdie stopped listening, instead focusing her attention on the most evil object she'd discovered since coming to this beautifully accursed place. The empty Guinness glass stood on the ground before her, emanating malice and foulness. She glowered at it, trying to force its evil power to transfer to her own body.

She'd transferred its contents to her body by way of her mouth down in that dark, stuffy cave where she'd felt the strange presence. At first it had felt very pleasant – she'd lumbered back to her companions and spent the rest of the night singing and dancing, greatly amusing them for the first hour or two and then annoying the hell out of them when they were trying to sleep.

Eventually she'd passed out, and when she woke up she'd realized what an evil force had lain hidden behind that alluring intoxication.

Shaking her head, she tried to rid herself of the memories of splitting headaches, vomiting and the worst case of the runs she'd ever experienced. She'd been convinced she was dying, and had forced her friends to promise they wouldn't try to raise her spirit once she was gone. But the next day she'd felt better, albeit very thirsty and almost as ravenous as Kel.

"Oh, ye draught of demons!" she intoned. "Let thy cursed power pass onto.. into... unto my mortal flesh! Grant me the ability to spew fire like I spewed vomit when thy foulness filled me. Let my blood become Guinness, burning through my veins like fire!"

She rolled the dice she'd discovered along with the glass. There was something nicely occult about dice, she'd decided. So many dark messages could be found in the patterns they displayed. She especially liked when they came up showing a single pip. It was almost as if the eyes of some dark, demonic creature gazed up at her.

This time, however, the dice showed two fours, one three, one five and one six. Birdie frowned down at them.

"Twenty-two," she said. "What kind of number is that?"

"It might be equal to the number of slices of pie Kel ate tonight," Leoma said. On Birdie's other side Demon Viq chuckled.

"No, I think she had more than that," Birdie said, eyeing the dice thoughtfully. Then, struck by a sudden impulse, she picked up the three dice not showing fours and rolled them again. This time there were two more fours and a two. She picked up the two and rolled it. It came up showing four pips.

"Five fours!" she exclaimed. "That's a... a..."

She scratched her head. There was a name there, at the edge of her consciousness. Mentally, she reached out for it, but it was just out of reach.

"A foursome?" Leoma suggested.

Birdie blinked. "What?"

The girl put down her knitting and pointed at the dice. "Isn't it funny that all of them show four pips?"

"Why would that be funny?" Birdie asked, frowning at her friend. Leelee did have some strange notions sometimes, like when she'd spent half an hour standing on her head in order to see if she'd pee through her nose instead of... the usual way. The top of her head had been sore for three days afterwards.

"Because we're four people, of course," Leoma said.

Frowning, Birdie looked down at the dice. The girl actually had a point this time. Were the dice trying to tell her something? Or were they merely stating something that was obvious for all to see? Damn, why couldn't the stupid things be more specific?

Demon Viq interrupted her thoughts. "Someone's coming."

Birdie's head jerked up. "What? Someone's coming *here*? That can't be. This is the nastiest place in the whole world."

"They must be very nasty people then," Viq said. She'd risen to her feet and was peering out into the darkness.

"How many are there?" Leoma asked.

"Four."

Birdie looked down at the dice. Four pips, four people approaching. Had the dice tried to give them a warning? She had no idea if there was a way for them to indicate if she and her friends were in danger. Suddenly her nerves were all on edge. She reached for the glass of Guinness and cursed silently when she remembered it was empty.

"Do they look dangerous?" she asked.

"I don't know," Viq said. "It looks like three men and one woman. The woman appears to be their leader."

"Are they armed?"

Viq looked down at her. "Why don't you stand up and have a look for yourself?"

"Because then they'll see me and that's not good if they turn out to be dangerous. We should all hide behind Kel until we've found out what their intentions are."

"I'm sure they're wonderful people," Leoma said, beaming like a searchlight. "I'll warm up what's left of the pie in case they're hungry."

"No more pie!" Kel Hell moaned, rolling over on her side so her enormous rear pointed straight at Birdie. Quickly, Birdie stood up and moved over to stand beside Viq. Being spotted by the enemy, no matter how lethal, was still preferable to being in the line of fire when Kel farted.

The four newcomers had rounded a low outcrop and were now coming up the small slope towards their campfire. Three of them were male, just like Viq had said. One was big and burly, one short and bald, and the last young and willowy. It was the woman who caught her eye, though. She wasn't large, but looked strong and very fierce, and she moved with the deadly grace of a natural predator. It didn't take Birdie long to realize she was the most dangerous of the lot.

"Hello," Birdie said. "Welcome to the Vale of Uzureth. I'm called Little Black Bird." She held out her hand.

"Pleased to make your acquaintance, Little Black Nerd," the woman said. "We're Kat's Deathsquad. I'm Kat, the leader." She grabbed Birdie's hand and shook it.

"Nice name... *ow!*" The woman – Kat – had a grip like iron. Birdie felt the bones in her hand grind against each other, sweat breaking out on her forehead as she tried to hold back a groan.

Thankfully, Kat released her hand before it turned to mush. "Nice place you have here," she said, gesturing at the jagged cliffs and animal skulls.

"Thanks," Birdie said, massaging her aching hand. "Er, would you like to stay a while? There's some pie left, if..."

She turned to see if Leoma had heated the pie yet, but the girl seemed to have forgotten all about it. She was staring at the youngest of the newcomers, a silly grin on her pretty face. The young man was staring back at her, his face mirroring her expression.

"I'm Leelee," Leoma said, her voice strangely flustered.

"I'm Weewee," the man echoed.

They continued staring at each other.

Birdie gave the two of them a puzzled look, then glanced back at Kat. The fierce-looking woman seemed as perplexed as she was. After a while she turned back to Leoma.

"Leelee, what's going on...?"

Before she could finished the sentence, the young man stepped over and dropped to one knee in front of Leoma, taking her hand and gently kissing the top of it. Leoma giggled but looked like she found the man's odd behavior pleasing.

"My lady," the man said reverently. "You're the most beautiful woman I've ever seen. My heart belongs to you, now and forever, if you will have it."

"I most definitely will," Leoma said, her grin broadening even more. "I knew the instant our eyes first met that we were meant for each other."

"Oh, for fuck's sake..." Kat swore, covering her eyes with one hand.

Birdie knew exactly how the woman must feel. The two youngsters' behavior was as improper for a band of mercenaries as it was for a group of necromancers. It had been bad enough when Leoma wanted to have a pet. This romance thing was simply too outrageous.

She looked at her other two companions, hoping for some support there, but Demon Viq was eyeing the two love birds with an amused expression, and Kel Hell hadn't moved since the last time Birdie looked at her. Feeling desperately that she needed to regain control over the situation, she spoke to Kat again.

"So, what brings you to the Vale of Uzureth?"

"Huh?" Kat removed her hand from her eyes. "Oh, right. We're fighters for hire, looking for a new contract. This place looked wonderfully nasty so we thought we'd check it out. Are you lot the only ones living here?"

Birdie nodded. "Yes, we are. Everything else is dead, which suits us just fine."

That made the other woman raise an eyebrow. She managed to do even that in a fierce way. "Oh? Why's that?"

"We're necromancers," Demon Viq said. "Death is our life. Well, that and pie, of course, but Kel ate most of those…"

Kat scratched her head thoughtfully. "Sounds like we're in the same line of business, more or less."

"Oh?" This time it was Birdie's turn to be surprised. "You like pie, too?"

"I meant the part about death."

"Ah, sorry." Birdie gave herself a mental slap. It was bad enough that Leoma was making an utter fool of herself; she didn't need to follow her example. Looking to her right, she saw the girl and her new beau talking in hushed voices, their heads close together. She grimaced.

"I don't suppose you have need for a couple of good fighters?" Kat asked. "You know, to provide you with corpses for your rituals, or whatever it is you do."

"That'd be nice," Birdie said. "But we don't have anything to pay you with. Except for the pies Viq here mentioned, of course."

"We can start with that," Kat said. "Gathering and preparing food takes too much time away from our real job. You can take care of all that when you come with us."

Birdie pulled back in alarm. "Come with you? You mean leave the Vale?"

"Of course. You said yourself there's nothing else living here. Without anything living we can't fix you up with any nice, juicy corpses. Besides, it doesn't look like those two lily-livered sops are planning to part ways with each other any time soon."

Birdie glanced at Leoma and Weewee again, and her eyes widened. They were kissing now, holding each other so tightly they looked like one misshapen creature with two heads and eight limbs. She realized Kat was right – there'd be no separating those two.

"So, when are we leaving?" she asked, the idea still alien to her.

"Tomorrow morning."

Birdie swallowed. She should have guessed these warriors wanted to travel during the day. That would mean a large adjustment for her and her companions. Most of all it'd be hard to maintain the dark, ominous atmosphere they'd managed to create here in the Vale of Uzureth. She shivered at the thought of trying to get in touch with the dark spirits with bright sunlight blazing down on them.

But this will be a unique opportunity, she thought. *These people seem to know what they're doing. There'll be a lot of death where they've passed through. And it's not like we've accomplished much here anyway.*

"I accept your proposal," she said, holding out her hand, then remembered what happened the last time she and Kat shook hands and tried to snatch it back, but the other woman had already seized it, squeezing it even harder than before.

"It's a pleasure doing business with you, Little Black Nerd," she said, showing her teeth in a rapacious grin. Birdie closed her eyes and whimpered softly.

So, a little before noon the next day Birdie found herself walking through unfamiliar territory in broad daylight. Fluffy white clouds covered most of the sky, but once in a while the sun peeked through, making her curse and shield her eyes from the bright light. She felt oddly naked out in the open like this, without the reassuring cliffs and soothing thunderstorms of the Vale of Uzureth. There wasn't even a proper cave to seek shelter in.

She was slowly getting to know their new companions. They seemed like a decent bunch, as far as she could tell. Bog, the burly one, didn't talk much, and the bald one with the thick arms seemed a bit slow, but they weren't rude or creepy. Kat and Demon Viq had quickly become fast friends, sharing the same morbid sense of humor, and Leoma and Weewee...

The two youngsters were walking hand in hand a little behind the others, constantly grinning at each other and talking about all kinds of silly things. The soppy sod kept comparing Leoma's beauty to flowers and gems and, oddly enough, to the blade of a spear gleaming in the moonlight. Birdie stopped listening after that.

She let out a sigh of relief when the sun finally sank behind the western horizon and it was time to make camp. Kat claimed Birdie and her companions would have to gather wood for a fire as part of their payment, but as Kel was too tired after the day's long march to do more than sit and complain, and

Leoma and Weewee being the way they were, the task fell on Birdie and Viq. Luckily there were a lot of dry, scraggly bushes nearby, providing them with enough firewood with minimal effort. Soon there was a blazing fire lighting up the darkening landscape, and they began distributing the food they'd brought with them from their old home.

"Well done, Little Black Nerd," Kat said with a mouth full of food. "What kind of meat is this? It's delicious!"

"It's Cryptomus," Birdie said, spooning some into her own mouth.

Kat frowned. "Cryptomus? Never heard that name before. What is it?"

"Mole-rat."

The mercenary woman stopped chewing. Her hands trembled slightly as she clutched the bowl, whose contents had been so appetizing a moment ago.

"We gave you the brain," Demon Viq supplied. "It's the best part."

Kat emitted a strangled sound, her face growing visibly paler. With an immense effort of will she swallowed the food in her mouth, then put down the bowl.

"I think I've had enough," she wheezed.

"I hope we'll pass a lake tomorrow," Viq continued. "Then we can find us some nice molluscs."

Kat stared at her, mouth hanging open.

"Molluscs?"

Viq grinned at her. "Yeah. Awesome stuff. You don't even have to cook them."

The other woman's face displayed pure horror. "You eat them *raw*?"

"Only some kinds," Birdie said. She gave Kat a curious look. "Are you feeling alright? You look like you're going to throw up."

"Must've had too much of your delicious food," Kat grumbled. She grabbed her mug of water and washed her mouth thoroughly. "I'll try to eat less from now on," she finished. "Can't risk getting fat in my line of work."

"Can I have your bowl if you're finished with it?" Kel Hell asked, eyeing the still half-full vessel hungrily.

"Of course," Kat said, all too eager to be rid of the unspeakable contents. "Much too good to waste, this stuff."

"Have you been a mercenary band for long?" Birdie asked.

Kat shook her head. "Not really. Actually, this is our first assignment."

"Oh?" Birdie raised a surprised eyebrow. "What did you do before."

"We were policing our old village. You know, hunting down criminals and such."

Birdie nodded. "That sounds pretty exciting. Why did you leave?"

"One of the criminals we'd been after took over the village and made us prisoners. We escaped, and now we're trying to gather resources so we can go back and have our revenge."

"That's horrible!" Birdie exclaimed. "That you had to endure imprisonment and such, I mean, not that you want revenge. The one who took over your village must be a nasty piece of work."

"Clogz is the worst kind of scum," Kat said, her expression darkening as she spoke. "Killing him won't be punishment enough. Scum like that should... should..."

"Should get a red-hot iron rod up his arse," Demon Viq finished.

"Yes!" Kat's face split into a malicious grin. "That'd be perfect! You're a cruel, vicious woman, Viq. No wonder I like you so much."

Viq grinned back at her. For a time the camp was silent, except for the slurping sounds Kel made as she finished Kat's bowl and the different kind of slurpy sounds Leoma and Weewee made when they kissed. The other two mercenaries had nodded off.

"You up for a ritual tonight, Viq?" Birdie finally asked.

The other woman stifled a yawn. "Not really. I barely got any sleep last night, and then we did all that walking. We don't have a corpse to work with, either."

"We have the dice," Birdie pointed out.

"Roll them, then. If you get five sixes we'll do a ritual."

Birdie pulled the dice from one of her pockets. They looked reddish in the light from the fire, as if someone had dipped them in blood. She tossed them onto the ground. Four of them turned up sixes, but the fifth bounced away and ended up behind Viq.

"What does it show?" Birdie asked.

Demon Viq picked it up, frowned at it, and put it down beside the other four.

"A two," she said.

"You sure?" Birdie asked, eyeing the small, cubical thing suspiciously.

"Positive. Now, if you don't mind I think I'll turn in. There'll be another long slog tomorrow, I suppose."

"Sleep sounds like a good idea," Kat agreed. "Good night, folks."

Birdie sat by herself for a while, looking down at the dice. She was pretty sure the last one hadn't been a two. That strange word had popped up in her mind again when she rolled the dice, and it most certainly didn't signify four sixes and a two. If only she could remember it...

"Might as well try to remember the ostrich's phone number," she muttered to herself, then frowned. What an utterly stupid thing to say. She had no idea what a phone number was and had a feeling most ostriches didn't have one anyway.

That night she dreamed about birds. None of them had phone numbers, which might have something to do with none of them being ostriches, but for some odd reason they were all talking like humans, except all they seemed able to talk about was food and sex. She tried to tell them to stop their inane chattering but when she opened her mouth she could only produce twittering sounds. One of the birds – a particularly ugly one – looked at her and said, "You're a seven. Leoma is a nine, Viq an eight, and Kel... Kel... KEL!"

Birdie woke with a start. That final shout had held such desperation she wondered if the poor bird had been in severe pain. Then she realized it had only been a dream and closed her eyes again, hoping to catch some more sleep before it was time to get up.

"KEL!" This time it was Viq's voice, although it sounded very strained, as if the girl had trouble breathing. "Kel, get off me! I'm dying here!"

Birdie sat up and looked around with bleary eyes. It appeared Kel Hell had rolled over in her sleep and was now lying across Viq's upper body, crushing the poor girl against the hard ground. The big woman was snoring loudly, sounding like an entire herd of warthogs having a singing session.

Viq kept hammering at Kel with her fists, but the large woman refused to wake up. In the end the noise woke Leoma, who gave the scene one long, thoughtful look, then walked over and crouched down beside Kel's head.

"Pie's ready," she whispered in the big girl's ear.

Kel sat up instantly. "Pie? Where? Give it to me!"

"Thanks, Leelee," gasped Viq, massaging her tormented ribs.

They continued their journey west for two more days. The landscape grew slightly less barren – hard, dry wasteland giving way to grassy plains with more vegetation. Having soft things tickling your feet felt odd to Birdie. At one time, when the midday sun shone down on them from an almost unclouded sky, she had to suppress a sudden urge to skip and run through the knee-high grass. Gritting her teeth, she tried to think of proper death cult things, but the only thing that came to mind was an image of a glass of ice-cold beer on a shaded patio. She realized she was very thirsty.

Early evening on the third day since leaving the Vale of Uzureth found them by the shore of a rather large lake. In its center was a small island. This wasn't the island where Amanda had found the funny-looking broccolis after the volcano had hurled her across half the continent. No, it was an island where an abundance of awesome-tasting fruits grew, and among the brooks and clear, shallow pools lay precious stones gleaming in the sunlight. It was always sunny on this island, no matter what the weather was like on the mainland.

And, naturally, this amazing island was the cause of an age-old dispute.

Standing there by the shore, shading her eyes against the setting sun, Birdie saw two settlements, one on each side of the lake. The one to the south was nearer, but it looked rather shabby compared to the one to the north, so after a brief discussion with Kat they decided to head that way instead.

As they entered the settlement Birdie stared in amazement at the neat rows of huts that stretched out before her. She'd never seen constructions so large and fine-looking as these before. Each of them must be able to house as much as ten people without having to cram them together like sardines in a tin. Everything looked very clean, and the people she saw al wore fine clothes and expensive-looking jewelry.

"Hey, Kat," she said. "You should find out if these people need your services. It looks like they have no lack of funds."

"What's a lackophant?" asked Spud, the bald-headed mercenary who appeared to have a somewhat limited vocabulary. "Is it like an elephant lacking ears?"

"More like a mercenary lacking a brain," Demon Viq muttered beside Birdie.

Kat herself ignored the remarks. Her eyes were fixed on a hut that was even bigger and more lavish than the rest. After a few moments she pointed at it with her crude spear.

"Let's go there. It must be where the chieftain lives."

Birdie expected the chieftain of such a prosperous tribe to be extremely well protected, but when they reached the enormous hut they found its entrance unguarded. Inside sat an elderly man at a stout wooden desk, examining a paper he'd taken from a thick pile at his side. Once in a while he made a mark on it with a feather pen.

"Um, excuse me," Birdie said. "May we speak to the chieftain?"

The old man looked up. "Of course. May I enquire about your errand?"

"We have a business proposal," Kat said. "High quality services to offer for those who can pay for them."

"One moment," said the old man, standing up and disappearing between two screens. Birdie noted that the inside of the hut was divided into several rooms with narrow passages between them. It almost reminded her of the caves back in the Vale of Uzureth. Put a couple of skulls here and there and the place would almost feel cozy.

After a couple of minutes the old man came back. "Follow me," he said. "The chieftain will see you now."

They followed him along one of the passages, then turned right and continued down another. Birdie kept wondering why someone had bothered with all those screens when it'd save so much time to just walk straight to the place you wanted to go. Perhaps it was a way for the people living there to find privacy?

Eventually they emerged into a large room, where a plump man in his middle years sat behind a large desk of dark wood. He wore a long, loose robe or kaftan, a heavy gold chain inlaid with rubies and emeralds around his neck. His round, puffy face held a mild expression as he regarded his visitors.

"Welcome to North Pharq," he said, his voice soft but distinct. "I'm Aandu. What can I do for you?"

"Hello," said Birdie. "Um, my friend here has a business proposal for you."

"That's right," Kat said as the chieftain turned his gaze on her. "I represent a band of mercenaries called Kat's Deathsquad. Well, I'm leading them, to be precise. We're looking for someone interested in employing our services."

"That's interesting," the fat man said. "And what exactly is it that you do?"

"We kill people."

Birdie expected the soft-looking man to shy back at that blunt statement, but he only steepled his fingers beneath his double chin and regarded Kat with a thoughtful expression.

"And you're good at what you're doing?" he enquired.

"We're the best. Well, I am. The others are well above average but nowhere near my own level of awesomeness. As a team, though, we're well-coordinated and extremely flexible."

"That sounds very impressive," Aandu said. "And it so happens that we're in need of a group of warriors like you. Have you heard of our conflict with the people in South Pharq?"

Birdie and Kat exchanged a puzzled look. "Is that the settlement on the other side of the lake?" Birdie asked.

The chieftain nodded. "They've been plaguing us for generations with theft, vandalism and assault. Many of us are growing weary of them."

"Sounds like a nasty bunch," Kat said. "What do they have against you? You seem like a peaceful tribe."

"We are," Aandu said. "But we're also rich, while the people in South Pharq are poor. They hate us for it, somehow thinking it's our fault that their lives are so miserable."

"How come they're so much worse off than you?" Birdie asked. "It's not like this side of the lake looks any different from theirs."

The chieftain leaned back in his chair. "There's an island in the middle of the lake," he said. "It's full of wonderful things – food, gemstones, herbs and plants with healing powers. Everything a tribe needs to become prosperous."

Birdie thought she was getting the picture. "And you've laid claim to this island?"

"No." Aandu shook his head. "Anyone can go there and take what they want."

"So what's the problem?"

"The problem," the chieftain said, "Is that we're the only ones who know how to build boats."

"Oh." Birdie's forehead creased in thought for a few moments. "But can't you come to an agreement?" she asked. "Like they'll give you something they have in exchange for a few of your boats?"

"I can tell you haven't met the people in South Pharq," Aandu said with a weary smile. "They're not interested in trade. They prefer to steel things rather than purchase or produce them. They're lazy, unintelligent and hostile, especially towards us."

"Perhaps they're just unhappy," Leoma said, speaking for the first time since they'd entered the large hut. "If you give them some of the things you've taken from the island they might like you better."

"We used to do that," the chieftain said. "But they showed no signs of gratitude. All they did was to want more, and when we didn't give them more they came here and stole from us. When we hid our things from them they started destroying our huts and boats."

"Why didn't you fight back?" Kat asked. "With all that wealth you should be able to arm a large force of fighters."

"We do have weapons of exceptional quality," Aandu said. "But there are no warriors among us. Violence is for low-life scum like those in South Pharq. When they're not harassing us they fight among themselves, which makes their society even less functional. We in North Pharq like to build, to create things of beauty and to expand our own knowledge in order to live happier and more meaningful lives."

"That sounds great," said Birdie. "So why won't the people on the other side of the lake come here and let you teach them what you know? Then they could make their own society better."

"I told you," the chieftain said with a sad expression on his puffy face. "They don't understand that you have to work hard if you want to get anywhere. They want the people who've labored for generations to attain this level of prosperity to simply give them the things they want, claiming that everyone should have exactly the same amount of money and goods."

"And is it like that for the people in their own tribe?" Birdie asked.

The chieftain shook his head. "The rule only seems to apply to those who have more than they do. Those among them who're slightly better off wouldn't dream of giving anything to the really poor ones. Their tribe would probably have been destroyed by internal struggles if they hadn't had us to direct their hatred at."

"So they hate you because you're rich, but they want nothing more than to become rich themselves?" Demon Viq asked.

"That pretty much sums it up," said Aandu with a small shake of his head. "Sounds like bloody hypocrisy to me, but who am I to say? Anyway, many of us think we should rid ourselves of these despicable people once and for all. Do you think your group of fighters could accomplish that?"

Kat opened her mouth to answer, but right them her stomach rumbled so loudly it made even Kel Hell give a start. Leoma and Weewee sniggered.

"Could we discuss it after we've had something to eat?" Kat said, a slight flush to her cheeks. "I, um, have been on a diet lately."

"Why, of course," Aandu said. "I'll have Ydnar bring us refreshments. We can continue our discussion tomorrow morning when you're rested."

They were ushered into another of the hut's many rooms, where they found a large, rectangular table surrounded by a number of chairs. Men and women in long, white robes brought them fruit and berries and drinks in tall crystalline glasses. Birdie sniffed hers and was slightly disappointed when it contained some kind of fruit juice rather than beer.

"What is this?" she asked, picking up a large, round fruit with light-grey, reticulated rind. It seemed to weigh several pounds.

"It's a cantaloupe," the chieftain said. "One of the wonderful things found on the island I told you about. Its flesh is sweet and juicy without being too cloying."

"A cantaloupe?" Leoma said. "I thought that was some kind of clothing."

"No, that's pantaloons," Spud said, fruit juice dripping down his chin.

Everyone turned their eyes on the bald-headed mercenary.

"How do you know a word like that?" asked Kat. "Or are we better off not knowing?"

The man who usually showed such poor understanding of words containing more than five letters shrugged.

"I thought everyone knew the difference between pantaloons and a cantaloupe."

Birdie looked down at the strange thing, somehow getting the impression that it should be glowing. The peculiar notion stayed with her throughout the meal, until she began wondering if the sunlight had damaged her brain in some way.

I wonder if that Spud fellow would know a word like iridescent, she thought at one point. She considered asking the man but eventually decided against it. There was no chance a stupid thing like that could be of any importance.

Or could it?

She gazed down at the cantaloupe, now half eaten, again. Perhaps it'd be safest to carry a few of those things with her, in case...

This time she was almost certain she'd gone mad.

~9~

————— ❀ —————

Distinguishing between what you know and what you believe is something many people seem to have trouble with. This doesn't apply only to people with strong religious beliefs – although the problem is very prominent in their case – but to people in all kinds of everyday situations. I've heard countless people deliver fully detailed accounts of things they know absolutely nothing about, and when asked what they base their account on they reply with things like "That's what I believe" or "That's how I picture it" as if that would be an adequate explanation.

The most annoying among these people are the ones who, when presented with reliable facts to disprove their statements, still maintain that their own belief is correct. I've seen people who, when face with a dictionary or an encyclopedia, shake their heads and say "No, I still believe that..." and so on. One might wonder how people like that can earn any kind of respect, but fortunately (for them) there's always someone equally dumb or – believe it or not – even dumber they can associate themselves with.

So why do these people persist in holding on to their beliefs even when established facts are presented to them? Well, part of it might have to do with an inability to tell a reliable source of information from an unreliable one (I'll return to this subject in a later chapter). A dumb person will "believe what they want to believe" or would rather believe an ignorant friend than a knowledgeable stranger. Or some might just be too air-headed to tell the difference between what's real and what their own underperforming brain has conjured up.

Right now, Marsha was in the middle of a heated debate with someone who refused to accept her first-hand observation as fact.

"I'm sorry, Marsha," Jennibal said, her beautiful face slowly but steadily taking on an expression of impatience. "I know you want really badly for this Scion of yours to exist, but what you saw was no winged hippo. It was a bird, or maybe two birds flying close together, making it look like a bulkier shape."

"It was no bird, you dim-witted fool!" Marsha snapped. "I saw it clearly! We must go after it. At once!"

Jennibal made a grimace. "But I'm *this* close to winning that Wurst fellow over to the God of the Iridescent Cantaloupe. I can't waste an opportunity like this."

"He can't even *spell* cantaloupe," Marsha said with a snort. "He only pretends to listen because you're so damn hot. Let's leave those three idiots now before it gets too dark. Tomorrow it might be too late."

The other woman sighed. "All right, then. But if the God of the Iridescent Cantaloupe becomes wroth with me I'll tell him it was your fault."

"Be my guest," Marsha said. "I'll accept any punishment he deems suitable for my transgressions. Now, let's go, before I forget which way the Scion flew."

They headed south as fast as they could manage while the last of the daylight waned and a crescent moon rose over the horizon. Marsha became more and more frustrated as it grew harder to see. When she'd stumbled and fallen twice Jennibal finally managed to convince her that it was pointless to continue.

"We might pass within ten yards from the Scion without seeing it in this dark," she pointed out. "You don't want that to happen, do you?"

Marsha peered into the darkness, a frantic expression in her eyes. "We could go a little farther. It headed south, in that direction." She pointed.

"That's east," Jennibal said.

Suddenly confused, Marsha looked around. "It is?"

"yeah, you turned left after you crashed into that boulder back there. Are you sure you want to go on?"

Marsha scratched her head. "Perhaps not. It's just…"

"I know." Jennibal took her by the hand and led her over to a dark mound that rose some ten feet above them. "Let's make camp here. That mass of rock and dirt will shelter us from the night wind."

Neither of them knew it, but the pile of rubble before them was the last remnant of the ancient palace where the Raven God and the Bug Goddess had resided at the dawn of time. The open space they'd just passed had once been part of the great courtyard where the Goddess's minions had surrounded the Hippo and the Raven after they'd fled from the palace dungeons. Only a few yards away lay the place where the Elephant God had broken through the wall and scattered enough of their enemies to allow his two friends to escape.

If some ancient power still lingered here, it was too faint for the two women to notice. The Scion had felt it, of course, which was why it'd passed through here little more than an hour earlier. Marsha did experience a fleeting urge to gargle something, but dismissed it as an effect of being thirsty.

When they lay there, waiting for sleep to claim them, Jennibal suddenly spoke.

"Marsha?"

"Mmm?"

"If this Scion of yours really exist and we do find it, what are you going to do?"

Marsha yawned. "Why, tell it to come back home with me, of course."

"What if it doesn't want to?"

Surprised, Marsha turned her head, but of course she couldn't see the other girl in the almost complete darkness. "What do you mean?"

"You told me it flew away as soon as it was hatched. Perhaps it's found itself some other place to stay and isn't interested in going anywhere else."

"That's nonsense," Marsha said. "It's the Scion. It belongs with our Cult. The only reason it flew away was because the Bug Goddess attacked it."

"But wouldn't it have come back when things calmed down?"

Marsha realized she hadn't really thought about this before. "It was newly hatched," she said slowly. "No one ever told it what it was or where it belonged."

There was a soft chuckle next to her. "It's a *god*, Marsha," Jennibal said. "Don't you think it would know such things?"

Marsha lay silent for a long time, contemplating the other girl's words. She had no idea how much a god, newly born or not, ought to know and not know. She didn't even know if she'd be able to communicate with the Scion when they found it, if they ever did. All this time she'd taken it for granted that things would turn out well if she could just track the odd little thing down. But what if it wouldn't?

"I thought you didn't believe the Scion existed," she finally said, trying to avoid the question.

But Jennibal had already fallen asleep.

The following day was warm and humid. Sweat dripped down Marsha's face and back as they walked, while Jennibal's skin only glowed beautifully. At one point, when the midday sun beat down on them even more ferociously than before, the girl took off her clothes and walked in her underwear. It was a sight that would've made Bazer tear his notebook apart and swallow the pieces. At least before he met Kylee.

They found no sign of the Scion anywhere. Marsha didn't know if the creature ever moved across the ground like an ordinary hippo or if it just flew from one point to the next like a bird. Still, she kept looking for tracks and other things the Scion might have left behind, hoping she'd recognize them for what they were if she did find them.

In the afternoon they reached a patch of thick, verdant jungle. Jennibal had donned her clothing again and was walking a little ahead of Marsha, whistling a merry but very repetitive tune to herself. When she showed no inclination to stop at the jungle's edge Marsha hurried to catch up with her, grabbing her arm.

"Sure we should go in there?" she asked.

Jennibal gave her a curious look. "Why not? It's this way we're going."

"But there might be dangerous animals in there. Snakes and such."

"I thought you lived in a jungle like this?" Jennibal said, pointing at the mass of trees ahead of them.

Marsha gave the deepening darkness beneath the impenetrable cover of branches and leaves an anxious look. Strange sounds reached her ears, like the twisted echoes of birdsong heard through a long tunnel. She suppressed a shiver.

"The jungle back home is nothing like this one," she said. "It's much more... reliable. And I've only spent about a year of my life there anyway."

"Ah, come on," Jennibal said. "I'm sure we'll be fine. Besides, wouldn't a mystical creature like the Scion be drawn to a place like this?"

Marsha gave the dark, thick jungle another dubious look ."I don't know. Would it?"

"Sure it would. Come on, now."

Marsha let Jennibal lead the way into the gloomy darkness between the trees. She'd hoped it'd be cooler among those eerie shadows, but instead the air felt thick and difficult to breathe. They had to push their way through thick undergrowth, and sticky liana seemed to clutch at their arms and legs. There were insects too, some with thin wings that fluttered before their faces and by their ears and others that crawled across their skin or got stuck in their hair. Marsha had always felt a strong revulsion for bugs, even before she learned of the evil Bug Goddess, and after half an hour in this despicable jungle she wanted to scream.

After more than a mile of slow, arduous progress they came to a part of the jungle where the vegetation wasn't as dense and thin rays of sunlight reached the ground in some places. Marsha drew a deep breath, relieved at getting something that resembled fresh air into her lungs. She brushed herself off, pulling a fat, hairy leech from her short sleeve.

She was just about to ask Jennibal if they'd stop here and rest for a while when a clear voice called out to them.

"Hello! Who are you?"

Both Marsha and Jennibal jumped at the unexpected sound. It took them a few moments to locate the person who'd spoken. She wasn't on the ground, as they expected, but hanging upside down from a thick tree limb ten feet above their heads.

"Um, hello," Marsha said, studying the woman carefully. She looked to be in her mid-twenties, short and curvaceous with long, curly hair and a pleasant smile. As she watched, the woman swung herself down from the tree, somersaulted once and landed gracefully on the ground.

"Pleased to meet you," she said. "I'm Flamingo."

"Er, isn't that some kind of bird?" Jennibal asked.

"Indeed it is," said the girl. "I was named after them. What are you babes called?"

"I'm Marsha," Marsha said. "And this is Jennibal. Sorry if we seemed a bit confused at first. We didn't expect to find anyone here, least of all up in the trees. Why were you hanging upside down like that?"

"It helps me think," Flamingo said. "I'm working on a new invention, and I'm sort of stuck."

Marsha gave the girl a puzzled look. "Invention? What kind of invention?"

"Come, I'll show you." Flamingo gestured for them to follow her, then loped off between the trees, sometimes dancing more than running. Marsha and Jennibal hurried after her.

Not far away they found a glade where it looked like Flamingo had her abode. There was a kind of hut made from vines and branches, newly-washed clothes hanging from a line between two trees, and a number of strange-looking devices – bowls, tubes and unfamiliar tools. Marsha stared at everything in amazement.

"What are all these things?" she asked.

"Just the usual stuff," Flamingo said, touching some of the clothes to see if they were dry before skipping over to a strange object on the ground. It looked like a large pipe mounted on a sturdy cart. Jennibal walked over and peered into its open end.

"What's this?" she said, her voice muffled and tinny as she tried to stick her head into the opening.

"It's my *kannon*," Flamingo said. "And you shouldn't do that unless you're certain it isn't loaded."

Jennibal straightened herself and backed away a few steps. "Loaded? What does it do?"

"I'll show you." Flamingo rummaged through some things behind the device and picked up a large, round boulder which she fed into the open end of the pipe. Then she took a pinch of black powder from a small bag and put it into a hole at the other end of the pipe, which was bulkier and attached to the cart somehow. "Stand back and cover your ears," she said.

Marsha wondered if she was going to scream, or maybe sing. The girl must have a terrible singing voice if she required them to cover their ears. She did as she was told anyway, watching as Flamingo struck a match and held it to a fuse at the back of the strange device.

The fire quickly consumed the fuse. Marsha was just about to remove her hands from her ears and ask if it was all over when there was a loud BOOM that made her stumble backwards. To her amazement the large, heavy boulder shot out of the pipe with unbelievable speed, landing among the trees at least thirty yards away.

"Wow!" she heard Jennibal exclaim. "That was incredible!"

But Flamingo didn't look at all pleased. "It was a poor shot," she said. "The powder might've gone a bit damp. It's too humid in this place for it."

"Is it some kind of magic powder?" Jennibal asked. "Where did you get it?"

Flamingo chuckled softly, wiping her hands on a rag. "Magic? Of course not. I've made it myself. You mix crystals extracted from bat guano with charcoal and some yellow stuff an old woman gave me once."

"An old woman?" Marsha suddenly perked up. "What was she like?"

"Rather strange, if you ask me," Flamingo said. "She was riding on an elephant and had a breath like nothing I've ever known. Said she got the stuff from a mountain that spewed fire."

"The gargling woman!" Marsha exclaimed. "No wonder this *kannon* of yours can do such amazing things. It's like that gun Fae used to kill Winston, now that I think of it."

"The boulder is supposed to go much farther and faster," Flamingo said, almost apologetically. "Give me a few days to improve it and I'll show you."

"I'm afraid we don't have time to stay here," Marsha said. "We're chasing a winged hippo we saw coming this way last night. Have you seen it?"

Flamingo shook her head. "Can't see much of the sky through these trees. It didn't come through here on foot, at least. What is it?"

"We call it the Scion," Marsha said. "It's the offspring of a union between the Hippo and the Raven God..."

"Both of them male," Jennibal interjected.

"It's of great importance to my people that we find it," Marsha continued. "It's supposed to herald a new era of wonders."

She expected Flamingo to be as skeptical as the others she'd met since leaving the Hippo Cult's temple, but to her surprise the girl's face lit up with excitement.

"That sounds fantastic!" she exclaimed. "Can I be part of it?"

"Um, I guess," Marsha said, taken aback by the girl's reaction. She wasn't sure what she'd expected to find when she left home, but new recruits to the cult had definitely not been part of the picture. As the thought sank in it gave her a strong sense of satisfaction. She flashed Jennibal a triumphant smile.

"I can't wait to see all the other amazing inventions there'll be!" Flamingo went on. "Have you received any hints yet?"

"Um, I think there'll be something called TVW, but I have no idea what it is," Marsha said.

"Come!" Flamingo waved them over to one corner of her glade. "I must show you another thing I've been working on. It's not finished yet, but I hope you'll find it interesting."

Marsha and Jennibal followed her over to an even more peculiar device than the *kannon*. It looked like a cart or small wagon with four wheels and no handle. They exchanged a doubtful look as the girl climbed into it, seating herself behind a roundish contraption attached to the front of the vehicle.

"Come, have a seat!" Flamingo patted the vacant spot next to her, and Marsha saw that there indeed was a seat made of padded leather with a matching back rest. She hesitated a moment before climbing in and seating herself.

"It's comfortable," she noted.

"Of course it is," Flamingo said. "Otherwise your behind would get sore after a few hours of travelling."

Sitting there, Marsha had a strange impression that she should wear sunglasses, and perhaps a thin linen dress and a pair of sandals. Definitely something to tie her hair back, or it'd get in her face when they headed out onto the highway. There was also a very disturbing image of Jennibal posing on the front, wearing only a small bikini. She shook her head.

"So it is a kind of cart?" she asked. "But what are all these for?" She pointed at the multitude of levers and buttons on the board in front of them.

"You use those to operate it," Flamingo explained. "You're right that it's made for travelling, but it's not supposed to be pulled by an animal. It'll move by itself."

Marsha stared at the other woman, certain she must have misheard. "Move by itself? That's not possible."

"I'm sure it can be done," Flamingo said. "I'm using another mixture, but I haven't gotten the formula right yet. Here, look at this."

She turned one of the levers, and a low, coughing sound came from somewhere inside the vehicle. The whole thing shook a few moments, then went still. Flamingo sighed.

"I can't get the engine to ignite properly," she muttered. "But when I do you'll learn the true meaning of *hot wheels*."

Marsha felt very confused. The sensible part of her knew that automotive wagons couldn't exist, and yet she had a queer notion that she'd seen such a thing before, like a feather tickling at her memory but not getting all the way through. These vague sensations had become frequent ever since that day when she'd found the sun rose. Frankly, they were getting very annoying.

"What do you call this thing?" she asked Flamingo.

"Why, a motor wagon, of course. What else would you call it?"

"What, indeed," Marsha mumbled, stepping out of the vehicle and stretching out her legs. The motor wagon might be comfortable but she wouldn't want to sit too long in it without a break. There should be places serving refreshments at regular intervals when you travelled in a thing like that...

They said good-bye to Flamingo a short time later, giving her directions to the Hippo Cult's temple. The girl claimed it'd take her less than a day to get there once she got the motor wagon working properly. Marsha didn't believe her but kept her tongue, not wanting to hurt the girl's feelings. She was such a friendly creature, all smiles and enthusiasm. Marsha was certain she'd be a great addition to her cult.

The evening passed without them catching sight of the Scion again. They left the jungle and headed out onto a stretch of more barren steppe. Marsha marveled over the vastness of this land and its many different sceneries. She was also beginning to understand the futility of following a fast, flying creature on foot.

That night they made camp in a shallow rock basin surrounded by low ridges. They didn't talk much, both of them too eager to get some rest. It took Marsha a while to find a reasonably comfortable position on the hard ground, but once she did she fell into a deep, dreamless sleep.

"Marsha! Wake up!"

Groaning, Marsha opened her eyes. Jennibal was shaking her so hard her teeth rattled. There was a flash of pain as something heavy landed on her stomach – once, twice, three times. Marsha groaned again, louder this time. As she became fully awake she realized the other woman was bouncing on her.

"Jennibal, stop it!" she wheezed. "What's going on? Are we under attack?"

The girl climbed off her. "I saw it, Marsha! I saw the winged hippo!"

Marsha rose to her feet, all drowsiness gone. "You did? Where?"

"Right over there!" Jennibal pointed to the top of one of the ridges. "It was really close. We should be able to catch it if we hurry."

They ran up the dry, rock-strewn side of the ridge, both breathing heavily when they reached the top. Marsha wiped sweat from her face as she peered out over the landscape. The morning was overcast and it felt like there might be a thunderstorm coming. She scanned the area below for movement but found nothing, neither to the west nor to the north.

"There!" Jennibal pointed to the south-east, and there it was, emerging from behind the crest of a hill. It flew low, its wings moving so fast they turned blurry. Marsha followed the creature's flight until it vanished behind a cliff formation off to their right.

"Come!" she shouted, racing down the slope like a mad rhino. Her legs moved of their own accord, somehow managing to keep from falling despite the uneven footing. In her wild frenzy she might even have outrun Flamingo's motor wagon.

She crossed a stretch of open land and flew up the next hill, stopping at its crest to gaze wildly around her. There was a low grunt and a muttered curse as Jennibal caught up.

"Never thought you could run that fast," she said, panting heavily.

"I never had a reason to before this," Marsha said. Her gaze swept across the land like an eagle searching for prey. Why did there have to be so many hills and ridges and cliffs everywhere? It was all but impossible to keep a moving object in sight in this bloody terrain. But… *there!*

The Scion rose into view from behind another rise. It continued to gain altitude, flying west towards a massive cliff formation. As Marsha watched, it crested the jagged tops and vanished on the other side.

"What an amazing little scunner!" Jennibal exclaimed behind her.

Marsha turned her head, raising an eyebrow at her friend. "I thought you didn't believe in its existence?"

The other woman shrugged. "The God of the Iridescent Cantaloupe reveals Himself in mysterious ways."

"Indeed." Marsha began trotting down the hill, more careful this time. The two of them continued at a steady jog towards the cliff formation where the Scion had vanished. As they drew closer they realized it was much higher than they'd first thought, more like a small mountain range than cliffs. Standing at its foot, Marsha looked up at the mass of dark, jagged rock.

"How do we get past it?" Jennibal asked.

"I don't know," Marsha said. "Going around it might take days. We'll have to climb it."

She reached out a tentative hand, grabbing hold of a protruding piece of rock. Heaving herself up, she kicked wildly for a few moments before she found a crevice to stick her foot into. The cliff was incredibly steep, almost vertical, and the rough, uneven stone hurt her bare skin.

"There's another handhold off to your right!" Jennibal called from below. "No, not that high! There. Good. Now, move your right foot up. A little more to the right. There... oh, no!"

Marsha let out a scream as her foot slipped and she fell, hands clawing desperately at the stone but only managing to bruise her skin. Luckily, she'd only come a few feet up and didn't hurt herself too badly when she struck the ground.

"That went well," Jennibal said, helping her up. "Wanna try again?"

Marsha looked at the scratches on her hands and knees. "Not really," she muttered. "But what else can we do?"

"Well, we could try those steps over there. They seem to lead all the way up to the top."

Lowering her arms, Marsha followed the other woman's gaze until she spotted a sequence of narrow but even steps hewn into the living rock. She frowned at Jennibal.

"Why didn't you tell me about them before?"

The girl shrugged. "Didn't see them until now."

The steps proved a much easier climb than the sheer cliff face. Even so, it was far from risk-free. The indentations were only deep enough for half of Marsha's feet to fit, and too narrow for more than one foot at a time. At one point Jennibal, who'd taken the lead, slipped and would have fallen to her death if she hadn't landed butt first atop Marsha's head. Bazer (and quite a few other men) would probably be willing to cut off one arm for a chance to experience that.

They reached the top step without further incidents, climbing onto a ledge that didn't provide much better footing than the narrow steps had. With their backs to the rock wall they edged along it until they found a path or passage leading between two of the highest cliffs. They followed it and were soon engulfed in a cold, hard rock embrace.

After a hundred yards or so they emerged on the other side of the passage and found themselves looking out over a small valley, completely surrounded by tall cliffs. The ground far below lay hidden in shadows, too dark to make out more than vague shapes even during the brightest part of the day. Marsha took a step forward and looked around.

"How do we get down?" she asked.

"Not by climbing, obviously," the other woman said, eyeing the steep cliff wall below them. Then she leaned forward and peered down over the edge.

"What are you doing?" Marsha asked. "You can't possibly consider..."

"I think there's a path down there," Jennibal said. "If we could only find a way to get down to it..."

She frowned, her diminutive brain working so hard Marsha could almost see steam coming from her ears. After a short time she pointed to their left.

"We should go that way."

Marsha gave the treacherous cliff a dubious look. "Why?"

"Because the path slopes downward in that direction." Jennibal pointed to their right. "Logically, that should mean it's not as far below us farther that way." She pointed left again. Marsha's head swung back and forth as if trying to follow an impossibly fast tennis game.

"Right, right," she said, trying to shake the dizziness away. "Just stop pointing. Let's see if we can find a way down."

With extreme caution they climbed along the uneven slope to their left, careful not to come too close to the edge. They didn't have to go far before finding a place where they could see the path clearly, no more than ten feet below them. Marsha lowered herself into a sitting position, then slid more than climbed down the steep slope, landing clumsily on the narrow path.

"You alright?" came Jennibal's voice from above.

Grunting, Marsha pushed herself back to her feet. "Yeah. You can come down. I'll catch you if you fall."

A few moments later Jennibal came scooting down the cliff, landing beside Marsha with a soft thud.

"Ow, my bum," she complained, grimacing as she rose to her feet.

"You should get yourself more padding there," Marsha said. "It'd make travelling in Flamingo's motor wagon more comfortable as well."

Jennibal muttered something inaudible. The two of them started limping down the path. It was rather steep, sometimes turning into a sequence of steps, fifty or more, before levelling out again. The world around them grew darker as they descended.

The path ended near the vale's north-eastern corner. A large cliff hid most of the open space from their view. Marsha led the way around it, and as they turned the last corner they found themselves facing four hulking shapes, snorting and growling menacingly.

"Hippos!" she gasped, taking a step back.

"They're not dangerous, are they?" Jennibal said uncertainly. She reached out a trembling hand. "There. Good boy." She jerked the hand back as one of the large hippos let out a blood-curdling roar and tossed its massive head.

"I don't think these are ordinary hippos," Marsha said. "Look how they stand in a perfect line. They're guarding something."

"Can't you do anything?" Jennibal asked, her eyes wide with terror. "You belong to the Hippo Cult. Aren't these, like, your pets or something?"

Marsha looked at the four large animals. They radiated hostility and menace. She could think of many words to describe them, but *pets* was definitely not one of them.

"I'm looking for the Scion," she said, not expecting the hippos to understand but not knowing what else to do. "Is it here?"

There was no reply. Of course there was no reply. Hippos didn't speak. Trying to communicate with them had been as pointless as...

"YOU'RE ONE OF THEM, AREN'T YOU?"

She jerked as the voice spoke inside her head. Before her the hippos moved aside, a gap opening between them. Through it came the Scion, wings fluttering as it hovered five feet above the ground. It was about the size of a dog, which meant it had grown quite a lot since it was hatched. Marsha wondered if she should fall to her knees or something but decided the ground was too hard and would likely bruise her skin.

The winged hippo regarded her with its strange eyes, unlike both those of a human and an animal. There was intelligence there – deep and ancient despite the creature's young age – but also something else. Was it fear? She thought she must have read it wrong. Why would a god be afraid of her?

"YES," the voice said. "YOU BELONG TO THE PEOPLE OF THE TEMPLE. WHY HAVE YOU COME HERE?"

"Um, I came looking for you, Scion," Marsha said. "I vowed to find you, to dedicate my life to it. And now I have."

"AND WHO'S THE OTHER ONE?"

"That's Jennibal," Marsha said. "She doesn't belong to our people, but she's a nice girl and a good friend. I've come to value her much during our travels together."

"Aw, that's so sweet of you," Jennibal said, putting an arm around Marsha and pulling her into a warm hug. "I like you too, you know, even if you're a bit weird sometimes."

The Scion watched the two humans with a befuddled expression. On either side of it the hippo guards did likewise, albeit with a more feral look in their eyes. Marsha patted Jennibal on her shoulder before turning back to the winged hippo.

"I've come to ask you to return with me to the Hippo cult's temple," she said. "We, um, would like to get to know you better. You're our god, after all."

"AM I?" the Scion said, sounding suspicious and more than a little angry. "YOU ALMOST GOT ME KILLED THE LAST TIME I WAS THERE."

"I know," Marsha said. "That was a very turbulent time. But the Bug Goddess is dead now and our people live in peace. You have nothing to fear."

"SO WHY DO YOU NEED ME TO RETURN IF YOU LEAD SUCH HAPPY LIVES ALREADY?"

Marsha clenched her fists in frustration. Talking to the Scion wasn't at all as she'd expected. There was nothing of the divine wisdom and wondrous revelations that should be part of meeting a god. No, this was more like trying to convince a morose teenager to come back after running away from home. She took a deep breath, trying to compose her thoughts.

"It's in the prophecies," she said. "You're supposed to bring about a new time of wonders. That can't happen if you're down here, lurking in this dark valley."

"A TIME OF NEW WONDERS, YOU SAY. DID THE TEXTS SPECIFY EXACTLY WHAT IT IS I'M SUPPOSED TO BRING ABOUT?"

"Well, not really, but…"

The Scion interrupted her, its voice so sharp it hurt her head. "SO YOU'LL JUST USE ME TO GET WHAT YOU WANT, IS THAT IT? MAKE ME A PUPPET WHILE YOU INCREASE YOUR OWN POWER?"

"I never said..." Marsha began, but the Scion cut her off again.

"I KNOW HOW YOU HUMANS WORK. I SAW IT BEFORE I LEFT THE TEMPLE, AND I'VE SEEN IT COUNTLESS TIMES SINCE THEN. ALL YOU WANT IS MORE POWER FOR YOURSELVES, AND USING GODS AND GODDESSES SEEMS TO BE THE MOST POPULAR WAY TO REACH YOUR GOALS. I REFUSE TO BE PART OF THAT. I REFUSE TO BE A TOOL."

With that, the Scion turned and flew away into the gloom, its four guards following behind it. Marsha stared In despair as it vanished from sight.

"That went well," Jennibal said.

"Stop saying that!" Marsha snapped, glaring at the other woman. "Don't you understand what a disaster this meeting was? Now we'll never ascend into that time of glory and wisdom. We'll continue to be barbarians for as long as the world lasts. It's *horrible!*"

She realized she was crying. Angrily, she wiped the tears from her eyes, stamped her feet a few times and punched the air furiously. It was lucky for her that no one except Jennibal saw her, because she looked incredibly silly.

"We can't give up already," Jennibal said.

"What's the point in continuing?" Marsha wailed. "You heard what the Scion said. It doesn't want anything to do with us."

"Nah, it'll come around," the girl said. "It probably feels insecure, being out here in the wilderness with no one of its own kind to talk to. Let's give it some time and then approach it again."

Marsha gave the girl a long look. "Do you think that'll help?" she said uncertainly.

"Of course it will! Plus, I need to find out the connection between this thing and the God of the Iridescent Cantaloupe. Are you coming or not?"

Marsha stood in silence for a moment as the different emotions warred inside her. At last she nodded.

"I'll come," she said. "You're right – we can't give up just because we had one small setback."

Jennibal smiled, making the gloom at the bottom of the vale seem a little brighter.

"Come on, then," she said. "Let's begin with finding a way out of this miserable place."

~10~

———— ✳ ————

"For night's swift dragons cut the clouds full fast,
And yonder shines Aurora's harbinger;
At whose approach, ghosts, wandering here and there,
Troop home to churchyards: damned spirits all,
That in crossways and floods have burial,"

- William Shakespeare, A Midsummer Night's Dream

"One hundred and sixty-one, one hundred and sixty-two..."
Kat was vaguely aware that a large crowd had gathered to watch her do push-ups with the fat woman Kel Hell on her back. She didn't pay them much attention, though. It was so nice to get some real exercise for once. The woman was wonderfully heavy, so Kat didn't think she'd manage more than two hundred and fifty. Well, she might actually manage some more but she didn't want to exhaust herself before the battle.

"One hundred and eighty-six, one hundred and eighty-seven..."
It felt good to be in a real tribe again. Not that she had anything against those necromancer girls – she'd actually grown quite fond of them - but the things they ate made her want to run away screaming. This was a completely new experience for her – she'd faced countless dangers in her life and never felt any fear, but having to eat something that squirmed or crawled or slithered was simply too much even for her. She'd tried to get her hands on some berries when no one watched but it hadn't been nearly enough to sustain her.

"Two hundred and nineteen, two hundred and twenty..."
"How are you doing down there?" asked Kel from her position on Kat's back. "Getting tired yet?"

"Not at all," Kat said, only a little out of breath. "This might be an alternative career for you. You're like a whole exercising facility."

The big woman giggled. "I don't think anyone's been able to lift me since I was eight," she said. "Might not get many clients."

The crowd applauded when Kat finished her push-ups. She rose to her feet and stretched out her muscles. It was early morning on their second day in North Pharq and she had an appointment with the chieftain in half an hour. If things went as planned there'd be some nice action before the day was over.

Ydnar, the old clerk or whatever he was, was as always seated at his desk just inside the entrance to the chieftain's huge hut. Kat wondered if the old man ever slept or ate or did anything other than work. She had no idea why these people needed so many papers to make their society function. The Hullabaloo tribe had rarely used any papers at all.

Could that be why everything went to hell with it? she asked herself, pausing to give the large piles on Ydnar's desk a sharp look. The papers just lay there, clearly not accomplishing anything. Kat shook her head. It had to be something else, then. Perhaps it had to do with that strange island where all the nice food came from. No wonder those scumbags in South Pharq wanted it. Clogz would probably seize control of it if he knew about its existence.

The thought of Clogz made her clench her fists. She pictured herself with a red-hot iron rod in her hands, the evil usurper bent over in front of her. The sight of his naked rear made her flinch, even if the image was only in her mind. Her revulsion quickly turned to satisfaction when she imagined his screams as she drove the glowing metal up his...

"Miss? Are you all right?"

Kat blinked. The old man had taken his eyes from the papers and was regarding her with a concerned expression on his wrinkled face.

"Um, yes," she said. "Why do you ask?"

"You were salivating. I was afraid you were going to have a seizure or something."

Kat waved her hand at him. "I'm fine. Is the chieftain ready to receive me?"

"I think so. He went into the bathroom two hours ago so he should be back by now, unless his bowels are having an unusually bad day."

"He should find himself an Orb then," Kat mumbled to herself, then wondered why the hell she'd said that. Why would an Orb – even one with a capital O – help against constipation? It had just felt like the most reasonable solution.

She found chieftain Aandu in his office, dressed as always in his silly-looking long robe. In front of him lay even more of those blasted papers. Kat wasn't sure what the fat man was doing with them. His expression seemed more relaxed – even bored – compared to the intensity that always burned in Ydnar's eyes. She filed the information away for possible use later.

"Ah, lady Kat," the chieftain said as she entered the large room. He gave her a pleasant smile and Kat found herself blushing slightly. She couldn't remember anyone ever calling her *lady* before. The word had quite a nice ring to it.

"I've come to discuss terms for our employment," she said, forcing herself to sound stern and professional. This opportunity was far too good to waste and she had to stay focused.

"Ah, yes." The fat man reached for another stack of papers and Kat almost shied back. Was he going to use the power of his damned papers to bend her will to his wishes? And if so, would she be able to detect it or would she be swept along like a reed in a raging river?

"What's that?" she asked, her voice low and tense.

Aandu waved the papers casually in front of him. "Just some calculations I asked Ydnar to put together last night while we enjoyed our wonderful dinner. It's important for us that we get as good a deal as possible."

"And those papers will do that?" Now Kat was really suspicious. Should she demand the negotiations be held in a paper-free environment? She doubted this man would accept that, and then she and her Deathsquad would be without a job again.

Think about Clogz and the revenge you want, she told herself. *No price is too high as long as it means he'll be overthrown. Even if the papers will consume my soul, I must do this.*

"I hope so," the chieftain said. "It all depends on what kind of agreement we'll reach. Do you charge per hour or per enemy slain?"

Kat blinked. "Er, what?"

"Do your clients pay you based on how many people you kill, or how long it takes you to bring down the enemy?"

"Um…" Kat fixed her gaze on the papers, bobbing slowly back and forth in front of her, wondering if they had some kind of hypnotic power. "I had more of a fixed amount in mind," she finally managed.

"Great!" Aandu exclaimed, crumbling the stack of papers together and throwing it into a bin beneath his desk. "That makes things much simpler. Will a hundred gold pieces do?"

Kat's mouth dropped open. She didn't think she'd ever *seen* a hundred gold pieces before. With that much money she could buy everything she needed to bring down Clogz. It was a dream come true.

"We'll need better weapons..." she mumbled, stroking the shaft of the crude spear she'd made out of an old branch and a piece of bone she'd found out in the bush.

"That goes without saying, of course," said Aandu. "You and your men will have your pick in our armory. I'd also like to give you this, as a kind of bonus."

He rummaged through a wooden box and brought out an amulet hanging from a silver chain. It was round and flat, with a shiny surface bearing the image of a single teardrop. It felt cold to the touch as he dropped it into Kat's outstretched hand.

"What is this?" she asked, fingering the cold, hard surface.

"It's an old heirloom that's been in my family's care for centuries," the chieftain said. "It protects you from magic and other divine powers. We never had much use for it here."

"Does it protect you against papers?" Kat asked hopefully.

The fat man gave her a puzzled look. "Papers? What do you mean?"

"Oh, never mind." Kat pocketed the amulet. "We have a deal. Er, would you like me to sign somewhere?"

"I'll have Ydnar draw up the contract," Aandu said. "In the meantime you can have a look at our weapons arsenal. I hope you'll find something to your liking."

A short time later Kat found herself staring at the most amazing assemblage of arms she'd ever seen. There were spears of all possible lengths and thicknesses, each one with an exquisitely made iron blade that shimmered in the torchlight. Daggers and longer blades whose like she'd never even dreamed of lined another wall. She'd never bothered with learning archery, a thing she regretted now as her eyes fell on long rows of bows, quivers filled with arrows hanging above them. This was every warrior's dream, if every warrior had been in possession of a mind capable of imagining such a wealth of deadly objects.

"Well?" the chieftain said.

Kat blinked for the first time since entering the underground chamber. "Well what?"

"Do you think you'll find something that meets your requirements?"

"I might do," Kat said, striding over to the seemingly endless row of spears. She had no doubt she'd find something she liked. What she worried about was how to choose from all these wonderful weapons. She would've liked to take all of them with her, but she'd probably need a hundred carts and four hundred camels for that. She picked one at random and tried its balance. It was perfect.

"I think this one will suit me," she said. "I'll tell the others to have a look as well. They're not very picky."

As she moved on to the knives and blades she thought about what she'd be able to do if she'd had a few dozen men armed with these amazing weapons. She'd vanquish Clogz and his rabble in no time at all. No one would be able to stand against her then.

She picked up one of the longer blades and made a few practice swings. The unfamiliar weapon felt odd at first, but then she began realizing how you were supposed to fight with it. It was faster and more flexible than a spear, even if it lacked somewhat in reach. She decided to bring it with her as well.

"Why do you have so many weapons if you have no fighters?" she asked.

The chieftain shrugged. "We enjoy making things, and we always try to improve our skills. The first weapons we made were of much poorer quality than these. It takes a long time to learn this craft."

"I bet it does," Kat mumbled. She snatched an ordinary dagger from the wall. From now on she'd only use the one she'd brought with her from the village to cut meat. This one was what she'd use in a fight.

"I'm done," she announced.

While she waited for her companions to arm themselves she listened to the chieftain's description of the settlement they were about to attack. It didn't sound like much of a challenge, even if they'd be heavily outnumbered. The people in South Pharq might be cruel and vicious, but most of all they were cowardly and poorly organized. Kat quickly abandoned the plan where they'd wait until dark before attacking. From what Aandu told her it was clear they wouldn't need an advantage like that.

"Are we going to spare the women and children?" she asked.

The chieftain grimaced. "Some of their women are as bad as the men," he said. "They're spiteful and completely without empathy. I guess you can spare them if they yield, but be sure to watch them closely. They'd break a vow as easily as giving it."

"Clogz would've loved them," Kat said sourly. "How well are they armed?"

"Not well at all," Aandu said. "I think they've stolen a few of those badly made weapons I told you about, but by now they've probably become rusty and blunt. The people of South Pharq don't know how important good maintenance is."

Kat nodded. "Any leaders or other important people you want taken prisoners?"

"They have no leaders," the chieftain said. "According to their philosophy no man should be put above another. That never kept them from oppressing those weaker than themselves, of course."

At that moment the other members of Kat's Deathsquad emerged from the armory, chatting and laughing as they compared the weapons they'd chosen. Kat said a quick good-bye to the chieftain before moving over to give them a short briefing.

"Aren't these weapons awesome, chief?" Weewee asked, grinning like a fool. "I wish we'd known about this place earlier. That bastard Clogz could never have taken our village if we'd been armed like this."

"Did the chieftain pay us?" asked Bog, who'd put some silly-looking metal hat on his head and a pair of steel-backed gauntlets on his hands. The latter, Kat thought, must be incredibly warm and uncomfortable.

"Yes," she said. "A hundred gold pieces and an amulet."

"Ah, that's nice," Spud said. "What kind of filling?"

Kat gave the bald man a puzzled look. "Filling? What are you talking about?"

"You know. Bacon, cheese, tomatoes, mushrooms. You can put almost anything in them."

"It was an *amulet*, you lily-livered dolt," Kat snapped. "Not an *omelet*. What would I want with a stupid omelet?"

"Well, we could eat it..."

Kat cut him off before he could come up with more brainless suggestions. "Actually, I have no idea what I'm to do with the amulet. It seems rather useless. Perhaps we could sell it if we ever run out of money."

"Run out of money?" Weewee asked. "Didn't you just say they paid us a hundred gold pieces?"

"Yes, but we'll need a lot if we're going to bring down Clogz. We'll have to hire more men, arm them, feed them and, er, perhaps offer them some kind of entertainment once in a while."

"And where are we going to find all those men?" Bog asked.

"We..." Kat fell silent. Where did you find men who knew how to fight and were ready to travel with them halfway across this lily-livered continent? The only ones she'd ever encountered were the ones she was looking at right now. Slowly, she started to realize she hadn't thought through her plan very well.

"We'll think of something," she said after a few moments. "But first we'll have to vanquish those goat-brained fools down in South Pharq. Are you ready to…"

She cut off when she noticed a short, slim figure lurking behind Weewee.

"What's *she* doing here?" she asked, her eyebrows narrowing.

The young man looked behind him, pretending to be surprised at finding a pretty girl there.

"Oh, I forgot to tell you," he said. "Leelee is coming with us."

"She most certainly *isn't*! You can't possibly be stupid enough to bring someone completely untrained into a battle. She'd only be a liability."

"You mean she'll have mood swings?" Spud asked.

"I said liability, not lability," Kat snapped. She turned to give Weewee another piece of her mind but found that the pretty little necromancer girl had stepped up beside him and was glaring at Kat.

"I'm not leaving Weewee," she said, putting her cute little nose in the air. "He needs someone to look after him."

Kat rolled her eyes. "Oh? So you're his mother as well as his lover now? Tell me, kitten, what exactly are you going to do if something should happen to him?"

"My name's Lethal Leoma, not *kitten*," the girl said haughtily. "That alone should tell you something. I'm also utterly ruthless when it comes to protecting those I love."

"That's all well when you sit around the fire and eat snails or whatever it is you lot have for dinner," Kat said. "But this is a battle we're talking about. There'll be actual killing, and lots of it."

"Exactly! That's why we're coming as well."

With an outraged grimace Kat turned away from Leoma and fixed her gaze on the other three necromancers. They stood lined up as if for a race (although Kat doubted the fat one could run more than a few yards before having to stop for pie). It was the leader, the one called Little Black Nerd or something, who'd spoken. She was looking at Kat with a stubborn expression on her face.

"Death is our trade as well, Katster," said Demon Viq, the one Kat liked best. "We can't miss an opportunity like this."

"Isn't it enough if you check the corpses afterwards?" Kat asked. "They'll still be warm for a couple of hours after we've killed them."

The necromancers shook their heads in perfect unison. "That won't do," Viq said. "We have to be there when the actual killing takes place. That's the only way to study the process of the soul leaving the body. Very interesting stuff."

Kat threw up her hands. "All right, then. But try to stay out of the way. We won't have time to rescue you if you'll get into trouble."

"I'm going to rescue Weewee," Leoma said, moving closer to her lover and giving him a puppy-eyed glance. "Then he'll be eternally grateful to me and won't ever look at another girl."

"Yeah, whatever." Kat turned back to her companions. "Ready?"

They left North Pharq, following the lake's eastern shore until they reached the spot where Kat and Little Black Bird had discussed which of the two settlements to approach. From there they continued more slowly, keeping their progress hidden as best they could. Aandu the chieftain had assured Kat the people in South Pharq kept no sentries or other guardsmen, but moving stealthily was second nature to Kat (her first nature was probably killing) so she employed her skills so masterfully she accidentally caused her companions to lose sight of her and instead follow another trail.

A short time later Kat got her first close look at South Pharq. The settlement looked every bit as shabby as Aandu had described it – the huts were simple and looked so fragile that even the mildest autumn storm would blow them apart, garbage and other refuse lay everywhere, and she could even see a man sleeping on the ground between two huts. A faint but very unpleasant stench reached her nostrils where she crouched behind a large boulder.

"Bloody degenerates," she murmured as she watched another man step up to the one sleeping on the ground, bring out his slimy little thing and piss all over him. The man on the ground didn't wake up.

"Almost making Clogz and his cronies look like civilized people," Bog said beside her.

"No need to get carried away," Kat said sharply. "Now, we'll begin with those huts over there to the left. That'll cut off the escape route for most of them. Then we'll work our way down towards the lake. Who's got the torches?"

No one answered.

Kat bared her teeth as the fury slowly filled her. "Don't tell me you forgot the torches. I specifically told you to bring them."

"I gave them to Spud," Bog said, quickly putting a few feet between himself and his commander.

"Spud?" Kat snarled.

"I gave them to that necromancer girl you're such good friends with," the bald man said.

"Viq?" Kat looked around. "Where is she?"

"Over there," Weewee said, pointing to their right. "Looks like she's nodded off."

"Nodded off?" Kat gave the necromancer, who actually seemed to have fallen asleep with her back against another boulder, an incredulous look. "We just got here. How the hell did she manage it?"

"She can fall asleep anywhere," explained Little Black Bird. "Once, when we dissected a bird..."

"Oh, do spare me," Kat cut her off. "Can anyone please wake the lily-livered woman up and see if she still has those torches. Our plan sort of depends on them."

Thankfully it turned out Demon Viq had the torches in her pack. They lit four of them, one for each member of Kat's Deathsquad (even Gemma of the Khadal tribe might have managed that calculation), and left their hiding place. After a dozen paces Kat looked back to see if all her companions were with her.

"Oh, for fuck's sake..." she groaned.

Bog and Spud were close behind her, but Weewee hadn't followed them. He was still standing by the boulders, kissing Leoma as if nothing else in the world existed. The other necromancers were sniggering at the two of them.

"Weewee!" Kat barked. "Get your lily-livered ass over here, or I'll shove my spear up it so hard you'll wish it was a red-hot iron rod."

"Why would he wish that?" Spud asked. "It sounds very painful."

"Only in the beginning," Kat said.

The bald man gave her a puzzled look. "It stops hurting after a while?"

"No, after a while you either pass out or die."

Behind them Weewee and Leoma finally untangled themselves and the lean youth hurried to catch up. They sprinted across the last stretch of open ground, reaching the nearest huts before any of the inhabitants spotted them. Kat was just about to torch one when a young man in dirty clothes stepped around it. He halted, giving Kat a surprised look.

"Howdy!" Kat said, producing her best, toothy grin.

"Um, hello?" the man replied, apparently not expecting to find a woman with a spear in one hand and a lit torch in the other behind his hut. A few moments passed without either saying or doing anything. Then Kat pointed with her spear to a place behind the man.

"Look, a giant mollusk!"

"Huh?" The man turned his head, then doubled over as Kat rammed her spear into his side. An instant later the hut went up in flames.

"Get on with it!" Kat shouted before darting across a small open space to the next hut. By then the first cries of alarm could be heard from deeper inside the settlement. Kat managed to set fire to three more huts before she had to engage in combat with two poorly armed and even more poorly trained villagers. She dispatched the first with a thrust through the gut, then pulled out her blade and chopped the other's head off. It made quite the display as it sailed through the air in a cascade of crimson blood. Kat grinned happily and popped a walnut into her mouth. Not everything those necromancers ate was slimy and invertebrate.

Lots of people were out now, running in all directions or simply running around in circles, screaming at the top of their lungs and waving their arms in the air. Some ran straight into each other and ended up moaning on the ground. Kat caught sight of Bog running his spear through a man who'd thought he could escape through a gap between two burning huts. He gave her the thumbs-up before vanishing from view.

Kat had lost her torch but there were plenty of burning things to use. Picking up a severed pole from one of the collapsed huts, she ran into the settlement from the north-west, setting fire to another few huts before throwing away the pole to focus on the killing. A couple of men went down, one leaving a small girl behind. Kat patted her on the head and gave her a walnut before moving on.

After killing two more men she ran across a small open space and almost crashed into a young woman, perhaps seventeen years old, who was standing calmly outside a hut, no sign of fear in her youthful face. When she saw Kat her expression hardened.

"I know you're one of them," she said, her voice so cold Kat thought it might turn the air between them to ice.

"One of whom?" she asked, wondering if news of her Deathsquad had somehow reached this place.

"One of the rich scum from across the lake," the girl said. "Either that or you're in league with them. It doesn't matter. I hate you either way."

The girl's simple statement made Kat pause. She'd been subjected to hatred before, but always because of something she'd said or done, not simply because she'd chosen to associate herself with a certain group of people. For some reason she found that more disturbing than if someone had accused her of being a horrible person. She gave the girl a closer look.

"The chieftain said there'd be people like you," she murmured. "Females even more twisted and dangerous than the men. I guess I never really believed him, not until now. What would you have done with your life if we hadn't come here today?"

The girls' dark eyes grew distant, as if she was looking past the conflagration (a word Kat was sure Spud didn't know) and into a world her deranged mind had made up during long nights of frustration, envy and self-loathing.

"I'd destroy them," she said, her voice low but almost vibrating with emotion. "I'd burn down their homes, just like you're burning down ours. I'd give my people justice for their endless years of suffering."

Kat shook her head slowly. People like this seemed to suffer from the same lack of imagination wherever you found them, always repeating the same phrases, thinking the words sounded fancy but not really understanding their meaning.

"And that would be a good thing?" she asked the girl.

"Of course. The world would be a better place once all the rich people were gone and everyone was equal."

"Wrong," Kat said, drawing her blade and plunging it through the woman's heart. "It'd only be better for *you*."

She left the woman's corpse on the ground and went to search for her next victim. By then the entire western part of the settlement was burning, those of the inhabitants still alive heading towards the lake. Their strategy had worked just as they'd hoped. From here on it'd be an easy task to finish the rest of their opponents, caught as they were between the fire and the water.

Another young female came hurtling out of the smoke and ran straight into Kat. She almost drove her blade through the slim body before realizing it was Leoma. The girl had soot on her face and her clothing was torn in some places.

"Leoma? What the hell are you doing here? Didn't I tell you to stay outside the village?"

Leoma looked around with a haunted expression in her eyes. "I can't find Weewee! What if something's happened to him!"

"Oh, for fuck's sake," Kat swore. "Weewee can take care of himself. All you'll do is get yourself killed."

"I must find Weewee…"

Kat grabbed the girl by the arm. She struggled for a while, but her strength was much too feeble to get her anywhere. In the end she gave up and stood still, panting heavily.

"Now," Kat said, pulling the girl with her towards a less dangerous part of the settlement. "Let's go find the others. None of you should run around by themselves like this."

Reluctantly, Leoma followed her through a few rows of still untouched huts. Outside the last one they found Kel Hell, sitting on a young man and delivering hammer-like punches to his face. Kat had to smile. At least one of the necromancers knew how to handle herself in a fight.

"What did the fellow do to deserve this?" she asked. "Did he grope you?"

The big woman looked up. "Grope me? Of course not. I'd have considered that a compliment."

"What, then?"

"He called me fat."

"Oh." Kat made a mental note never to call Kel fat. Even her unmatched skills might not be enough if the large woman directed her mindless wrath at her. She shoved Leoma towards the two on the ground. "Stay with Kel," she said, then turned and ran back towards the smoke and the screams.

It didn't take them long to round up the last of the inhabitants. The fire and smoke had driven most of them down to the lake's shore, where they were pushing and elbowing each other as they tried to get as far away from the inferno as possible. Not even now did they seem able to put up an organized defense.

A few men made one last desperate stand, but those who'd brought weapons had only crude clubs and rusty knives, and Kat's group of warriors dispatched them with barely any effort. Getting rid of the women might have proved hard on the conscience if they hadn't been so unpleasant, spitting and hurling insults at Kat and her companions as they went about their work. The silence that followed when they were all dead came as a relief.

They spared only the oldest women and the youngest boys and girls, sending them on their way with a clear warning never to return to these parts again. Once they'd left Kat looked around. Most of the fires had burned down, leaving only piles of ash and scorched pieces of wood. Corpses lay scattered all over the ruined settlement, more than she could be bothered to count.

Leoma and Weewee had finally found each other and stood off to Kat's right, kissing and whispering soft words to each other. The other necromancers were moving among the corpses, making enigmatic gestures and talking in heated tones. It was obvious they were displeased about something. Kat walked over to their leader, who was crouching by the body of a strong-looking young man lying face-down on the ground.

"What's up, Little Black Nerd?"

The woman looked up, frustration radiating from her whole being. "It doesn't work," she snapped. "I feel nothing. Not even a whiff of air or a slight stir of the senses."

"Um, right." Kat scratched her head with the butt of her spear. "What exactly is it you expect to find?"

"You know," the necromancer said, straightening herself and brushing off her clothes. "Spirits and such. Ways to raise the dead. All the things a Death Cult is supposed to do."

Not knowing what to say to that, Kat looked instead at the other two necromancers. Demon Viq was tugging at a dead man, waving his arms back and forth as if expecting him to wake up. Kel Hell stood a few feet away, giving the other woman a curious look while she munched on a cookie.

"Perhaps you're going at it the wrong way?" Kat suggested.

"Oh?" Little Black Bird scowled at her. "And what do you think we should do instead?"

"I don't know." Kat used her foot to flip the nearest corpse over. "Eat their entrails or something."

The necromancer's face grew pale. "That's revolting!"

"And eating molluscs and rat brains isn't?"

Little Black Bird opened her mouth to retort, but before she could speak they heard another voice, as chirpy as that of a songbird.

"Oh, look at all those wonderful corpses. Astonishing, simply astonishing. I've never seen anything like it!"

Kat swung around, spear raised. A beautiful woman was coming towards them from the south, striding through the carnage as if it didn't bother her in the least. She was wearing a strange kind of tight leggings and a chequered shirt, a wide-brimmed hat on her head. Behind her came a young man with coal-black skin and more primitive garments. He looked to be in really bad shape.

"You've had Guinness, right?" said Little Black Bird to the young man. "I know what you're going through. It'll pass, believe me."

"Before or after I die?" the man said, massaging his temples and grimacing as if in severe pain.

"Who are you?" Kat demanded, focusing most of her attention on the woman, whom she deemed the more dangerous one. There was something odd about her, a faint shimmer around her contours, as if she wasn't really there.

"I'm Bathora," the woman said. "Former chieftain of the Telu tribe. My hung over friend here is Ogian of the Elephant People. And who might you be?"

"I'm called Little Black Nerd," the necromancer said.

The woman – Bathora – covered her mouth with one hand. Muffled snorts of laughter could be heard behind it.

"Bird," the necromancer corrected herself. "Little Black Bird. That's my name."

"I'm Kat," Kat said. "Leader of Kat's Deathsquad. The men over there are my companions Bog and Spud, and those two over there are Weewee and Leelee..."

"Weewee and Leelee?" Bathora interrupted her. "That sounds like comic book characters."

Kat frowned in puzzlement. "Er, what?"

"Never mind." Bathora made a dismissive gesture. "Ogian and I were heading north when suddenly a storm of ghosts erupted from this place. We had to check it out, of course. I must say I'm impressed. Are you responsible for all this carnage?"

"You can see ghosts?" Little Black Bird exclaimed before Kat could speak.

Bathora gave her a casual glance. "Of course. I am one, after all."

This was getting too weird for Kat's taste. Women pretending to be necromancers was one thing, but having to deal with one pretending to be a ghost? The woman's strange clothing and the way her form shimmered must be part of the charade. She opened her mouth to give the woman a harsh rebuke, but Little Black Bird forestalled her once again.

"*You!*" she hissed. "It was you I felt in that deep, dark cave!"

Bathora eyed the necromancer closely for a few moments, then a wide grin spread across her beautiful face.

"Oh, my!" she said. "I always did wonder how that happened. So you're a necromancer. Astonishing, simply astonishing! You're exactly what I need. We should all have a blurber and talk about what we're going to do."

Kat edged closer to Little Black Bird, pitching her voice low so no one else would hear. "Are you saying that one really is a ghost?"

The necromancer nodded. "She is, and I was the one who brought her back to this world. That's the only time I ever managed something real."

Still not convinced, Kat eyed the woman claiming to be a ghost. She wasn't sure how she'd expected a ghost to look – probably wreathed in shadow, with glowing eyes and a large, gaping mouth. This woman looked, well, to be honest she looked a bit dumb.

"Would you mind proving that you really are a ghost?" she asked.

Bathora grinned at her. "Sure. Try touching my bum."

"Er, what?" Kat took a step back, more from surprise than anything else.

"You heard me," Bathora said. "Touch my bum and see what happens." She turned around, displaying a very large but also incredibly shapely rear end. Kat gave the thing a hesitant look. This wasn't a situation she'd expected to find herself in when they'd set out from North Pharq. Bracing up, she reached out one finger to poke at one of the woman's plump buttocks.

Her finger passed right through.

"I'll be damned," Kat said. "You really are a lily-livered ghost."

Bathora's grin was smug as she turned back to face Kat and Little Black Bird.

"Sure am," she said. "But only for a little while longer. See, I'm on my way to become a god, the most powerful the world's ever seen. Ogian here will be my Harbinger. Won't you, pumpkin?"

"I will," said the man. "Bathora will grant me amazing powers."

"Really?" Kat said. "Like what?"

"I'll be the greatest Yahtzee player in the whole world."

"Yahtzee!" Little Black Bird exclaimed. "That's the name I've been looking for. That's when all five dice show the same number of pips, right?"

The man's tortured face suddenly lit up. "You know about Yahtzee?" he said with such enthusiasm Kat almost shied back. "I haven't had anyone to play with since I left my people. Except Bathora, of course, but she can make the dice show whatever she wants."

Grinning, the necromancer stuck her hand in one of her pockets and fished out a couple of dice. Ogian let out a squeal of delight, and the two of them sat down opposite each other, Ogian on the ground and Little Black Bird on the corpse she'd been studying before. They began rolling the dice.

Bathora's ghost eyed them with an amused expression for a while before turning back to Kat. "You're a mercenary warrior, right?" she asked.

Kat nodded. "The best there is."

"Good. Excellent." Bathora nodded her head vigorously. "I will need people like you when I have my revenge. How about you and your friends work for me?"

Kat considered the proposal for a long time. There was something about this woman she didn't like, but she couldn't put her finger on exactly what it was. It was as if her easy-going, pleasant façade hid something much darker and more terrible. And yet Kat couldn't deny that this was just the opportunity she'd been hoping for. If this Bathora woman really would become as powerful as she claimed she'd be the perfect person (or ghost, or whatever) to ally oneself with.

"You spoke of revenge," she finally said. "I, too, am looking for a chance to get back at someone who's wronged me. If I agree to work for you, will you aid me in this cause?"

"Of course, of course." Bathora nodded again, the bun she'd tied her hair into bobbing up and down behind her. "We'll both have our revenge. There'll be so much death those necromancers will pee themselves."

"Then we have a deal," Kat said, holding out her hand. Grinning, Bathora took it – or would have if she hadn't been immaterial. Kat felt a faint chill as the ghost's hand passed right through hers.

"Right," Bathora said, glancing around. "Anyone here into country music?"

~11~

---------- ❋ ----------

"Love, genuine passionate love, was his for the first time."

— Jack London, The Call of the Wild

Kylee was eating a banana, making Bazer drool as she sucked and licked at the sweet fruit. He hadn't been able to take his eyes off her these past two days, which at one point had almost cost him his life when he'd been mere inches from stepping off the edge of a tall precipice. After that he'd begun walking behind her instead and hadn't seen much of the surrounding landscape since.

While he waited for Kylee to finish her banana, he took out his notebook, leafed through the pages until he found the one with her name at the top, and jotted down another twelve beneath the others. The way things looked so far it'd be easy to calculate the weekly average.

"What is it you're writing in that book?" Kylee asked, throwing away the banana peel.

"It's your daily score," Bazer explained.

That earned him a puzzled frown, which – like everything else with Kylee – was absolutely stunning.

"My score?" she asked.

"Yes. I give all girls I meet a score each day, between one and ten depending on how sexy I think they are."

"Riiiiight..." Kylee took a deep breath, making Bazer's mouth go dry once again. "Would you allow me to give you some free advice?"

He smiled happily at her. "Of course. What is it?"

"Well, if you're going to do something so utterly creepy, then don't let the girls know about it. It's not something any woman would find flattering."

"But I want to be honest with you!" Bazer said. "You wouldn't want me to lie, would you?"

She heaved a voluptuous sigh, looking at him as if he was a particularly slow child. "No, but there's a difference between lying and leaving out things that people would rather not know."

Bazer didn't know what to say to that. Nothing he did or said seemed to please Kylee. Well, except for that one time, and then he'd just blurted out something that he didn't understand himself. The feeling of companionship they'd shared then had quickly evaporated, returning Kylee to her usual scornful mood.

At least she hasn't left me, Bazer thought. *That's all that matters. As long as we're still together I have a chance to improve things. If only I knew how.*

They'd kept a mostly western course since leaving the swamplands. Kylee seemed to recall that the terrain in that direction was more mountainous and thus (they hoped) would be the home of the larger birds they were looking for. So far they hadn't found any, though.

"Why did you leave your old people?" Bazer asked, hoping he'd learn more about this amazing woman who despised him so thoroughly.

She frowned at him. "Why do you want to know that?"

"Well, I'd just like to know more about you so I can understand you better."

"It wants to understand me better," Kylee said to herself, looking up at the sky as if asking some heavenly power why it had cursed her with this travelling companion. "*It*... wants to understand... *me!*"

"Is that such a bad thing?" Bazer asked.

"Look, monkey man," Kylee said, leaning forward and fixing him with those large, deep blue eyes. "That thing you call a brain is barely sufficient to keep track of where the food goes in and where it comes out again. Understanding anyone, and me in particular, is so far above you I can't even think of a suitable simile."

"W-What do you want me to do, then?" Bazer stammered.

"Just accept that you're too inferior to do anything but eat, sleep and excrete. That's three things you're able to do. Be happy with that."

"I, uh, I can read and write as well," Bazer pointed out.

"Good! Then you can pass your time doing that instead of pestering me with brainless questions. Now, shall we move on? This place bores the hell out of me. Why did you insist we'd stop here?"

"Actually, it was you who..."

"Shut it!" Kylee snapped. "You've already brought down your daily score to zero. Another complaint from you and it'll get a negative number."

"A negative number?" Bazer asked. "What are those?"

Kylee rose to her feet and dusted off her skirt. "Another concept your brain is too limited to grasp. Come on now. We have to find those birds."

They walked for another few hours, Kylee looking for birds and Bazer looking at Kylee. After a couple of miles they came to a narrow stream, floating through a small gorge and barring their way. Kylee hiked up her skirt almost to her hips as she waded across, nearly giving Bazer a heart-attack in the process. After that he spent the rest of the evening wondering if he should increase her score to thirteen that day. In the end he decided not to, somehow getting the feeling that thirteen was an unlucky number, and not being quite ready to extend his rating system to fourteen yet.

That evening they made camp in a small hollow surrounded by green hills with scattered groves of trees and low bushes. It was a very pleasant spot, and Kylee became more amiable as they shared a late supper. She even wished him a good night before going to sleep.

The next morning Bazer awoke to find her gone. He spent almost an hour searching the nearby groves and hills, calling her name over and over. The morning sun made the leaves glisten and songbirds trilled their sweet melodies, but to Bazer the world seemed colorless and bland.

She's left me after all, he thought. *She got tired of me and left. What am I going to do now?*

As far as he could see he had two alternatives. Either he could forget about Kylee and go back to searching for a new place to live, or he could try to find her and beg her to give him one more chance. There was, he realized, also a third option, but that one involved finding a lake and drowning himself, and heartbroken and miserable as he might be he didn't want to die a virgin.

The first alternative was by far the simplest and most sensible. Kylee had been too far out of his league to begin with. It was a miracle that she'd waited this long before abandoning him. Going after her now would only make her loathe him even more (if that was possible). He should simply forget about her and move on.

But he couldn't do that. Of course he couldn't.

He had to find her. The urge was so strong he could barely think of anything else. This almost doomed his search to failure before he'd begun it, seeing as he couldn't focus his mind enough to decide in which direction to go. But eventually he managed to clear his head enough to form a plan of action.

They'd been heading west, so the most logical option was to continue that way. He should keep his eyes out for large birds and discarded banana peel. Kylee liked bananas. She'd teased him about eating monkey food to show solidarity towards him, her much esteemed travelling companion. Despite the sarcasm the comment had made him feel all warm and fuzzy inside.

He set out across the grasslands, hoping to catch a glimpse of auburn hair shining in the sun, or to see those shapely golden-brown legs disappear behind the next hill. But all he saw was empty wilderness. There was something in the air, though – a strange scent that he couldn't identify. For some reason it made his mouth water.

I must be losing my mind, he thought. *Losing Kylee has made me imagine things. I'd better rest for a while and collect myself.*

He sat down on a boulder, putting his head between his knees. It smelled pretty badly down there, but he didn't care. He closed his eyes and dozed off for a while.

He jerked awake as something hard and sharp pressed against the back of his neck. A similar object poked him in the ribs.

"Get up, unbaked one," a gruff voice said behind him. "Move slow, or will get spear through neck."

Bazer rose to his feet as slowly as his untrained leg muscles could manage. Getting up slowly was much harder than doing it normally, he noticed. How odd, seeing as most other things were more tiring when you did them fast.

The oddest of all, however, were the two creatures who'd captured him.

They were both squat, with thin, angular arms and legs, but the weirdest thing was that they seemed to have no heads, or maybe the heads made up their entire bodies. Either way, the arms and legs protruded from a single blob of golden-brown mass, with small black eyes that looked very much like raisins.

"W-What are you?" Bazer stammered.

"We muffins, unbaked one," the creature standing behind him said. "Me Uga, great warrior and hunter. Half-baked fool on other side be Plop. Decent fighter but slow in head."

"Me not slow," the other muffin said angrily. "Can run faster than you."

"Run fast but think slow as slug," Uga said. "Got brain size of raisin. Small raisin."

Bazer felt a sudden pang of sympathy for the one called Plop. This was almost exactly how Kylee had treated him. He wondered if there were female muffins, and if Plop had developed a system to rate their looks. If they used the term "a hot girl" it might mean something completely different for them, like someone being fresh from the oven.

Another thought struck him, this one far more urgent.

"What are you going to do with me?" he asked.

"You come with us to tin," Uga said. "You prisoner. Fine catch."

Bazer had no idea what a tin was, but he figured it was some kind of village or camp. He wasn't sure if he should be afraid or not. The word *prisoner* did sound slightly better than *food*, but he'd heard unpleasant stories of how some tribes treated their prisoners. Creatures as strange as these might have developed advanced methods of torture, like... He pushed the thought away before the images could get too detailed.

He followed the muffin called Plop, while the one named Uga walked behind him, the point of his crude spear never leaving the small of his back. As they walked, the strange smell he'd caught earlier grew more and more palpable, until it filled his nostrils like a sweeter kind of woodsmoke. He rubbed his nose absent-mindedly.

"Where's that smell coming from?" he asked.

"That be the ovens," Uga informed him. "Is baking day today."

The muffin's words made Bazer slightly more at ease. If these creatures baked things it felt unlikely that they planned to eat him. But then a strange image came into his mind – a piece of what looked like soft meat stuck between two slices of bread, with various kinds of vegetables sticking out on either side.

"A blurber..." he muttered, his lips struggling to form the unfamiliar word.

"You talking to me?" Uga asked behind him.

"Um, no, sir," Bazer said. "Just happened to voice my thought aloud."

"Ah," the muffin warrior said. "Plop do that all the time. Strange habit."

Bazer glanced at the younger muffin walking ahead of him. "He does? I haven't heard him say a word since we started walking."

There was a low chuckle behind him. "That because he no think very much. There, we at tin now."

The tin turned indeed out to be a kind of settlement, albeit very different from anything Bazer had seen before. There were no huts or tents; instead he found himself looking at a long embankment with a multitude of holes dug into its side. Dozens of muffins milled about or stood in the low openings with various tools in their hands. The air was heavy with the strange scent from what Uga had called *the ovens*.

"Ah, captain Uga," said one muffin who'd come up to them. The small raisin eyes leered at Bazer. "Found new unbaked one, eh?"

"Aye, Grub," Uga said. "Ovens warm and ready?"

"Warm and ready," the muffin called Grub said. "You come now and he baked before evening."

"Hold on!" Bazer called out. "What do you mean I'll be baked? You can't bake people!"

Grub looked at him as if he'd said you couldn't drink water. "Must be baked," he said. "Doughy no good."

"But I'll die if... *ouch*!" Bazer had taken a step back and been rewarded with a jab from Uga's crude spear. The weapon wasn't as sharp as the ones his old people had used, but with enough force it might still skewer him. Perhaps that would be preferable to being baked alive.

"Silence, unbaked one!" Uga roared. "You come to oven now. Feel better when properly baked."

Bazer screamed and thrashed about, but more muffins arrived and took hold of his arms and legs. Still screaming, they carried him towards a large stone construction. Intense heat radiated from it, causing rivulets of sweat to run down Bazer's cheeks as his captors brought him closer.

"Stop it!" he yelled, fear and panic making his voice shrill. "You can't do this! It'll be murder!"

A muffin hand appeared in front of his face and pressed something down onto his eyes. Bazer blinked furiously until the raisins fell away, one ending up against the side of his nose, the other bouncing down his chin and vanishing. There was a muttered curse, the muffin's hand disappearing for a few moments before returning with new raisins.

"I'm not a bloody muffin!" Bazer screamed. "I don't want raisins for eyes, and I don't want to get baked. Let me go! Help! Help!"

The heat from the oven was so intense it hurt his skin. The muffins brought him even closer, preparing some kind of tray to put him on before shoving him into the blazing furnace. It wouldn't take more than a few moments, then his life would be over. That realization drained the last strength from his limbs. He even stopped screaming.

"Put him in oven!" one of the muffins shouted. Bazer thought it was Grub.

"Wait!" a sweet female voice called out behind them. "Don't do it yet."

Annoyed murmuring arose among the muffins. Then the ones who'd been carrying him let go, and Bazer collapsed onto the hard ground. Looking up, he saw Kylee coming towards them, a vision of perfect human beauty bathed in golden sunlight.

"Hubba hubba," Uga said. "Hubba hubba hubba."

Most of the other muffins simply stared. Bazer knew from experience that that was a natural reaction when you saw Kylee for the first time. He heard someone wolf-whistle and wondered how a muffin could manage that with lips so dry. Kylee only stood there, her smile more radiant than any sunset Bazer had ever seen.

"Welcome, unbaked lady," Uga said, his voice much softer than when he'd addressed Bazer. "One who rolled you did very good job. Will you bake for me? We make many fine muffinlings."

"Thanks for the offer," Kylee said. "But I don't think a relationship like that would work. And I'm definitely not getting into that appliance over there. I'm hot enough as it is."

Some of the muffins murmured their agreement. Uga and Grub exchanged a look, apparently not sure how to deal with the human bombshell in front of them.

"What can muffins do for you, then?" Uga finally asked.

Kylee pointed at Bazer. "I'd like you to return that… creature… to me. It belongs to me. I've been looking for it all morning."

"But must be baked!" Uga protested, poking Bazer with the butt of his spear. "Is all doughy."

"I know," Kylee said. "Especially its brain. But it requires more preparing, things only another human can do. So I'm afraid I'll have to take it with me."

The muffin shrugged, which looked rather ludicrous with a body shape like that. "Me no want disappoint well-rolled lady," he said. "You take doughy creature. We find other to bake."

"Great, thanks," Kylee said. "Come here, Bazer. You've caused these wonderful people enough trouble today."

Legs shaking, Bazer pushed himself upright, not looking at the muffins as he followed Kylee through their camp. Once out of earshot, she turned to face him with a furious expression on her stunningly beautiful face.

"What do you mean by running off like that? You almost got yourself killed!"

Bazer had to swallow twice before getting any words out. "I-I went looking for you," he stammered. "I woke up and you were gone."

"I was finding us some breakfast. Where else would I have gone?"

"I thought you'd left me…"

She made a grimace, but then nodded as if something had become clear to her. "I understand why you'd react like that," she said slowly. "That's probably what most women would do. But I thought we were agreed we'd look for those large birds together?"

"Yes, but…"

She cut him off with a sharp gesture. "This is where you stop explaining yourself. Anything you say now will only make you look more stupid. That shouldn't be possible, but your stupidity seems to have no boundaries at all. You couldn't even outsmart those muffins."

With that, she turned and started walking away. After a moment Bazer hurried after her, putting a hand on her shoulder.

"Kylee…"

She gave him an impatient glare. "What?"

"Thank you for saving my life .I'd like to…"

He hesitated. What could he offer her as reward for rescuing him from the muffins and their oven? A man usually wanted sex, but he was certain Kylee wouldn't appreciate an offer like that, at least not from him. He didn't have anything beautiful to give her, only his worn note book and a few other worthless things, none of them fit to give to a girl like Kylee.

"Yes?" she said when he didn't speak. "What would you like to do?"

"I-I'd like to do something for you, to show my gratitude. Something that'd make you happy."

She rolled her eyes, looking up at the sky like she always did when he'd said something she found particularly absurd.

"It wants to do something for me," she mumbled. "It wants to make me happy."

"I do!" Bazer said. "I just don't know what to do."

"Well, you could cut off your head," Kylee said. "That really would improve my quality of life. But we might need it to complete our task. I've no idea for what, of course. The only thing it's fit for is to be shoved up a badger's arse."

"But…" Bazer said, utterly confused again. "Why save my life if you want me beheaded?"

Kylee had started walking again. "That's another of those things you're too simple to understand," she said without turning around.

Later that day the landscape began changing around them, turning from grass-covered hills to more barren terrain with sharp cliff formations and hard, dry ground. The sun continued to beat down on them with ferocious heat, causing Bazer to sweat profusely where he struggled to keep up with Kylee, who appeared completely unperturbed by the heat. A few times it made Bazer wonder if the woman wouldn't be able to spend some time inside the muffins' oven and come out again unscathed.

They hadn't said more than a dozen words to each other all day, so Bazer was startled when Kylee suddenly called out his name. She'd been walking some thirty or so yards ahead of him and was now standing atop a rocky outcrop protruding from the crest of a low ridge, the side of which Bazer was in the middle of climbing. She gestured for him to come join her, pointing with enthusiasm at something on the other side.

"What is it?" panted Bazer as he reached the top of the slope. "Have you found something?"

"Have I found something?" Kylee said, shaking her head ruefully. "My dear monkey boy, look over there!"

Bazer looked the way she pointed and felt his face split into a wide smile despite his fatigue. Before and below them lay a stretch of open land, and on its other side rose taller cliffs, jagged and rough. Around them circled large, majestic birds.

"Are... are those eagles?" he asked.

"Indeed they are," Kylee said. "The large ones over there are tawny eagles, the medium-sized ones black-chested snake-eagles. This is exactly what I hoped to find, a veritable smorgasbord for people like me."

"Oh?" Bazer gave her a questioning look. "You're going to eat them?"

She punched him gently. "No, silly. I'm going to talk to them. Come on!"

The next two hours didn't become as dramatic as Bazer had expected. There was no thunder, no eruption of fire from the ground, not even a decent whirlwind or tornado. All that happened was that Kylee stood on the ground, gazing up at the sky as the large birds continued circling around the sharp cliff tops. A few times she nodded to herself, as if saying that the information she received made perfect sense, but otherwise she remained still as a statue.

After a while Bazer grew bored and moved away to sit in the shade with his back to the hard rock. He was about to doze off again when he saw Kylee coming towards him, almost dancing across the uneven ground. Standing up, he went to meet her.

"This is amazing!" she exclaimed before he had time to ask her what had happened. "Those birds had so much to tell me. It's all becoming clear to me now."

"Er, what is?" he asked, unsure what to make of the joy shining in her beautiful eyes.

"Everything, you dumbass! What's really going on in the world, and what my part in it will be. There was so much I didn't know before. I'm almost beginning to understand how someone like you must feel."

Bazer struggled to divide this information into digestible pieces. "What is it that's going on, then?" he asked.

"Oh, it'd take forever to tell you all of it," Kylee said. "The core of it is that something really terrible is about to happen up north, and the ones with the power to stop it are scattered all over the place. We must bring them together, convince them they have to fight side by side or all will be lost."

"The eagles knew all that?" Bazer asked, giving the birds above them a dubious look.

"Yes! They're friends of an ancient creature called the Raven God. He was once the king of all the animals in this land, and he was married to a bug."

"A bug?" This was getting weirder and weirder. "I thought ravens ate bugs."

Kylee nodded. "Their marriage didn't work out, so their kinds have been enemies ever since. There's so much more. The Bug Goddess was killed no more than a year ago, but now there's a new threat – one of her old servants, who also worked for the Raven God for a short time. I didn't quite get the hang of that. Anyway, this new evil might become even more terrible than the Bug Goddess ever was. It has to be stopped."

"Oh. And how do we do that?"

"That was a bit confusing as well," Kylee said, scratching her head in thought. "Most of it seemed to revolve around a creature called the Scion. Their description of it was slightly odd. Perhaps it was I who misunderstood something, but from what they said it appears this Scion is some kind of winged hippo."

"A winged hippo?" Bazer said. "That's certainly odd. What's it supposed to do?"

"They didn't know for certain." Kylee squinted up at the sky as if trying to see things more clearly. "What they do know is that the Scion is confused, even frightened, and that we must help it sort things out."

Bazer stared at her, and not because of her incredible beauty this time. "We're going to help a winged hippo sort out its fears and uncertainties?"

"Yes!"

"How?"

Kylee smiled at him then — a real smile, completely without mockery or scorn. It made Bazer's knees wobble. His mouth was suddenly as dry as the land around them.

"There's a place up north," she said, her eyes glowing with excitement. "It was once home to the Cult of the Raven. The Raven God is still there, imprisoned in a large stone statue. The eagles think that if we manage to get the Scion there, the Raven God will convince it of what it must do. Imagine that, Bazer! We'll get to talk to a *god*!"

"Well, I'm talking to a goddess right now..." Bazer said, then cut himself off. Kylee usually rebuked him harshly for comments like that, and he didn't want to ruin the good mood talking to the eagles had put her in. Dreading the damage was already done, he gave her a hesitant look.

But Kylee's face showed no signs of anger or hostility. On the contrary, she was looking at him with an expression he'd never seen on her face before. It reminded him of the way the girls in his old village had looked at the guys they fancied. But certainly that couldn't...

"Oh, Bazer!" Kylee exclaimed, running forward and throwing her arms around him. "That's so sweet of you." She looked up into his face, then planted a long, deep kiss on his lips.

Bazer emitted a strangled sound, then fainted dead away.

~12~

---- ✳ ----

Distinguishing between reliable and unreliable sources of information has become a much debated subject in recent years, with the internet and social media providing an endless supply of news and rumors. Strangely enough, most people seem to define "reliable sources" as "sources that share my own opinion", allowing them to remain in their own little dream world, where their own beliefs are the only ones that exist. It also appears that the people who advocate this so-called source criticism most strongly are also the ones who'd never question the credibility of a source they themselves agree with.

Right now, Marsha had only one source of information, and she was beginning to suspect that it wasn't nearly as reliable as she'd first thought.

"They went that way!" Jennibal said, pointing towards the south.

Marsha raised one hand to shield her eyes from the bright afternoon sun. "Are you sure? Last time the trail changed direction you said it had turned north. Why would they suddenly be going south now?"

The other woman grimaced. "How should I know? I'm just telling you which way the tracks lead. Come on now, they're probably far ahead of us already."

Reluctantly, Marsha followed her companion across the hard, dry ground. There wasn't much else she could do. Jennibal was by far the best tracker of the two (or at least that was what she'd claimed when they began their search), so Marsha had to rely fully on her abilities if she wanted to find the Scion again.

They'd spent some time searching for a way out of the dark valley where the winged hippo had abandoned them, knowing that its larger, flightless guards must have entered the place somehow. In the end they found a narrow passage leading through the cliffs to the west and followed it until they were out in the open again. After that they'd continued their pursuit in whatever direction Jennibal pointed them.

As they walked, Marsha tried to make out the tracks Jennibal claimed the hippos had made. There were lots of marks in the hard ground, but she found it impossible to tell which of them were made by the large animals and which were simply part of the landscape. She saw similar marks in other places, marks that Jennibal promptly ignored. Whatever it was that distinguished the hippos' tracks, it was beyond Marsha to recognize.

After a mile or two Jennibal stopped, looking from side to side while scratching her chin thoughtfully. It was obvious that she'd encountered some kind of problem.

"Anything wrong?" Marsha asked after a while.

"I'm not sure," the other woman said. "It looks like one set of tracks leads off to the east while the others continue south. I don't know what to make of it."

Marsha couldn't see anything indicating that something as large as a hippo had headed in either direction. She scanned the horizon, hoping to catch a glimpse of something moving. There was nothing, except what looked like a large flock of birds far to the south.

"Perhaps the Scion sent one of its guards out to scout?" she suggested.

"Why would it?" Jennibal said. "It could get a much better view of the surrounding country from the air. Probably move much faster, too."

"Off on some other errand, then?"

Jennibal shook her head. "Unlikely. That Scion thing seemed to have a measure of control over the other hippos' minds, but I doubt it'd be able to give them more complicated instructions. Once they were out of reach they'd go back to being ordinary animals."

Nodding to herself, Marsha once again looked to the south. The birds she'd seen before were closer now. There appeared to be hundreds of them, looking more like a cloud than an ordinary flock. She shrugged and turned back to Jennibal.

"What if we've been following the wrong trail the whole time?"

The girl gave her a puzzled look. "What do you mean? It's obvious the hippos went this way."

"Yes, but we don't know if the Scion was with them. What if it decided it didn't need guards anymore and, like you said, left them to be ordinary animals again."

Jennibal pondered this for a while. A gust of wind blew her long, dark hair into her face and she pushed it away with her left hand.

"Then we're pretty much screwed," she murmured.

"Indeed. So what do we do?"

"We continue following the main tracks," Jennibal said after some more thinking. "I still believe the Scion is with them. No ordinary hippos would move in such a straight line."

"They don't move in a straight line," Marsha pointed out. "The trail has changed direction countless times since we left that dark valley."

"Yes, but..." Jennibal cut off and looked up at the sky. The cloud of birds was almost right above them now, obscuring the sun. A cacophony of cries filled the air, along with a steady deluge of bird droppings.

"What in the name of the God of the Iridescent Cantaloupe is this?" the girl asked.

Marsha didn't answer. Her attention was fixed on the two people coming towards them, moving under the immense cloud of birds as if using it as cover. One was an awkward-looking young man, the other the most beautiful woman Marsha had ever seen. Compared to her Jennibal was merely cute. The two of them were walking hand in hand, which made the contrast between them even sharper.

When the two came closer the young man - who definitely had something unsettling about both his appearance and manners – looked at Jennibal.

"You're a ten," he said. "Before I met Kylee you'd have been the most beautiful woman I'd ever seen. Now you'll have to settle for second place." Then he turned to Marsha. "You're a five," he said, offering no further explanation.

"Um, hello?" Marsha said, not having the slightest idea what the strange man was talking about.

"Please excuse my subhuman friend here," said the beautiful woman. "His brain is functioning on a much baser level than that of normal people. He means no offense."

"He just called me a ten," Jennibal said with a wide smile. "How could anyone be offended by that?"

The girl returned Jennibal's smile, and Marsha swore she could see the world around her brighten. She'd never imagined a creature of such unsurpassable loveliness could exist. It almost made her wish she'd been born a man.

"I'm Kylee," the girl said, holding out her hand. Marsha and Jennibal both shook it (although not at the same time), introducing themselves. The strange, somewhat repulsive man was called Bazer, and appeared to be Kylee's boyfriend. Marsha figured they must be the oddest couple the world had ever seen (bear in mind that she never saw Bathora and Winston together), but seeing as people kept telling her she understood nothing about love she didn't think much more about it.

"So, where are you guys headed?" Kylee asked once the introductions were finished.

"We've been following a trail for almost two days now," Marsha said. "It appears to be leading south at the moment."

Kylee turned to look in that direction, her lustrous auburn hair swirling around her face. "We just came that way," she said. "We saw nothing out of the ordinary. What is it you're looking for?"

"It's called the Scion," Marsha said. "It's sort of a winged…"

"Ah, the Scion!" Kylee interrupted her, her large blue eyes suddenly beaming with understanding. "Then you must be the ones the eagles told us to look for."

Marsha's mouth dropped open. Virtually everyone she'd met on her search so far had mocked her when she said she was looking for a winged hippo. This girl didn't only believe her – she already *knew* what the Scion was. She exchanged a look with Jennibal, but her companion only smiled at her and shrugged, so she turned back to Kylee.

"You… you know about the Scion? How…?"

"Like I said, the eagles told me."

"Eagles?" The thoughts spun in Marsha's head, making her dizzy. Above them the birds screeched, and the cascade of droppings intensified. A few loads splashed onto Bazer's head, making him shriek and wipe furiously at the mess with the sleeve of his tunic.

Kylee nodded. "Yes, I can talk to birds. That's how I learned about the Scion and the great evil rising in the north, and how we had to bring all the good people together to fight it. And now we've found you two. Isn't that awesome?"

"I suppose," Marsha said, still struggling with this new information. Something Kylee had said struck her, and she frowned. "An evil in the north, you say? But the Bug Goddess is dead. We have peace now."

"It won't last long," Kylee said. "One of the Bug Goddess's old servants is about to make herself the most powerful creature this continent has ever seen. We must stop her."

"Her?"

The girl scratched her head thoughtfully, then looked up at the cloud of birds above them. "Yes," she said. "They say it definitely is a woman. What score do you think you'd give her, Bazer?"

The young man looked at her with a sullen expression on his face. "You said you'd keep the birds from shitting on me. Look at me now, I'm all beshitten."

Kylee patted him on the shoulder, careful not to touch any of the sticky spots. "Sorry. I got so excited when I learned these two were also looking for the Scion I forgot to remind them. And *beshitten* isn't a real word. Now get yourself cleaned up properly. Make sure to stay decent - you're among some mighty fine ladies now." She winked at Marsha and Jennibal.

"That's some really disturbing news," Marsha said.

"Nah." Kylee waved her hand dismissively. "He wouldn't undress in front of you unless I told him to. You don't have to worry."

"Er, I meant this old servant of the Bug Goddess."

"Oh, that. Yes, it sounded like some nasty business. I'm not sure how this Scion creature fits into it all, but it was clear we needed it if we were to stop the evil power from destroying the world. Isn't that why you were looking for it?"

Marsha shook her head. "All I knew was that we needed it to bring about a new age of happiness and prosperity for my people. I knew nothing of this new threat."

"That's weird," Kylee said. "According to the birds you're crucial in the fight against the evil being, but you don't seem all that resourceful to me. What about you?" she asked, turning to Jennibal.

The other girl grinned at her. "Oh, I'm just along for the fun of it. My real task is to spread knowledge of the God of the Iridescent Cantaloupe."

The frown on Kylee's face deepened. "That's probably the most ridiculous thing I've ever heard. You and Bazer should get along fine. He's also a few sandwiches short of a picnic, if you know what I mean."

Marsha couldn't help but smile. She was really beginning to like this Kylee. The girl had not only accepted the concept of the Scion as if it were the most natural thing in the world – she'd also dissed Jennibal's made-up deity completely. Her knowledge of this new threat to mankind might also prove vital to the survival of Marsha's people. That the girl had doubted Marsha's resourcefulness was something she was more than willing to overlook, at least for the moment.

"I wonder who this former servant of the Bug Goddess could be," she mused. "The Telu tribe are our allies now that both Winston and Gideon are dead and Gemma's married to Joz. I know of no one else who…" She broke off, a low hiss escaping her lips.

"What?" Jennibal said, giving her a worried look.

"They had another chieftain before Winston took over," Marsha said, trying to remember what Fae and Joz had told her before she left. "They said she went away and hasn't been heard of since. Could she be the one the birds spoke of?"

"It's possible," Kylee said. "We humans all look the same to them. It's hard to get a detailed description."

"But they said she was utterly incompetent," Marsha continued. "I don't understand how she could become such a perilous threat."

Kylee shrugged. "I guess we'll find out sooner or later. But before that we'll have to find the Scion and convince it to join our cause."

"Yes," Marsha said. "We caught up with it a few days ago but it wouldn't listen to us and flew away after a while. Jennibal tracked it as far as this place but we aren't sure which direction it went from here. According to Jennibal the trail is a bit confusing."

"That's not surprising," Kylee said. "You've been going the wrong way the entire time. The Scion is currently in a place almost straight north from here. That's where we were headed when we bumped into you two."

Marsha's mouth dropped open. "You... you mean you know where it is?"

"Of course. Well, the eagles do, at least. I'm just following their directions. They're a lot more reliable than the tracking skills of your Cantaloupe friend, it seems."

Jennibal stuck out her tongue at the other girl. Kylee just grinned back at her.

"This is amazing!" Marsha exclaimed. "But how can those birds know so much, both about the Scion and about this new evil up in the north? I mean, they're just... birds."

"There's a difference between birds and birds," Kylee said. "Eagles are highly intelligent, unlike the smaller birds I tried talking to before. It's pretty much the same as with us humans. I mean, you can hardly believe Bazer and I belong to the same species. Still not sure we do," she added, giving the strange young man a thoughtful look.

Marsha looked at Bazer, then up at the cloud of birds above them. They did look rather well-organized, actually. There were so many of them, and yet they didn't fly into each other or crash into cliffs. Their droppings also kept falling at a safe distance from the small group of humans. As a former chieftain of a very primitive tribe she knew that it took some rather advanced minds to manage all that.

"I still don't know how we'll get the Scion to listen to us," she said. "It seemed very upset the last time we encountered it."

"Oh, we've figured that out as well," Kylee said happily.

Marsha blinked. "You have?"

"Yes. All we need to do is convince it to come with us to the old temple that used to belong to the Cult of the Raven. The Raven God is still there, trapped inside a stone statue, and he'll talk some sense into that poor, frightened Scion kid."

"The Raven Cult!" Marsha slapped her forehead. "Of course! Why didn't I think of that? That's where the egg came from. I should've known it would have some part to play in all this."

Jennibal looked from Marsha to Kylee, an incredulous expression on her beautiful face. "Er, excuse me, but would that be the same egg you spoke of back when we first met? I thought we'd established that you only made that up?"

"Ah, the eagles did mention an egg at some point," Kylee said. "So that's where the Scion came from?"

"Yes," Marsha said. "The Raven Cult people brought it to the ruins of the old temple of the Hippo God, and when we placed it on the altar it hatched and the Scion emerged. I wasn't there at the time, but some of my friends saw it all happen."

"Makes sense," Kylee said.

"You think that story *makes sense*?" Jennibal exclaimed, her whole being radiating disbelief.

"You saw the Scion yourself," Marsha pointed out. "You can't say I made it up now."

Jennibal shook her head. "No, but that tale about statues of ravens and hippos is still utterly ludicrous. There are no such gods, only the God of the Iridescent Cantaloupe."

"You'll see in just a couple of days, cantaloupe girl," Kylee said with a smile. "Because we're heading straight for the Raven God's temple. Unless you'd rather continue following those tracks you claim to see on the ground here?"

Marsha shot Jennibal a triumphant smile. The girl glared back at her. Bazer let out a shriek as another bird shat on him.

"Fine, we're all agreed then," Kylee said. "Off we go."

The next few days were the strangest Marsha had ever experienced. She'd travelled with the Elephant People, had seen a volcano toss one of her friends halfway across the continent, had even seen a woman gargle lava, but nothing could compare with the sensation of constantly having a huge cloud of birds above her head. It was like walking in a bubble where no sun or rain or wind existed, only the endless shrieks and sound of droppings hitting the ground.

And then there was the young man Bazer. He seemed to keep some kind of record over how attractive he found the women he'd encountered over the years, with enough calculations and charts to make Gemma run away screaming (probably after having the number ten jotted down next to her name). The man was weird even by Khadal standards, and that said quite a lot.

"I have no idea what Kylee sees in him," Marsha told Jennibal when they'd made camp after the second day of their journey with the birds. "With looks like that she could've had any man on this continent. Every woman too, if she was inclined, and every god. Why pick that... that creature?"

"I think he's sweet," Jennibal said, munching on a cherry-orange.

Marsha gave the other woman an incredulous look. "Sweet? You can't be serious. All he's doing is write in that twisted note book of his. What's sweet about that?"

"Haven't you seen the way he looks at Kylee?" Jennibal said, pointing at their two companions, standing a couple of yards away and talking in hushed voices. "He really adores her. I'm so happy they've found each other."

Marsha glanced at the two, trying to discern what Jennibal had pointed out but seeing only two people who seemed to have absolutely nothing in common. One was the most beautiful woman she'd ever seen, the other one a man who wouldn't even be called beautiful by his own mother. The greatest difference, however, was that Bazer was so awkward in everything he did and said. He reminded Marsha a little of her old friend Pebe who, now that she came to think of it, had married a very beautiful woman who'd at first appeared to despise him.

"She doesn't seem to think too highly of him," she said thoughtfully. "She keeps calling him monkey-brained and vermin and other rude things."

Jennibal chuckled softly. "That's her way of saying she likes him. It also helps her keep him on the ground. A woman should always make sure a man thinks he's inferior to her. That'll keep their relationship well-balanced."

"I'm not sure I could manage that," Marsha said, frowning as Kylee laughed at something Bazer had said. Above them the eagles kept circling, their shrill cries filling the twilit sky. "Wouldn't it be easier to find a man who likes me the way I am, without all this manipulation stuff?"

"Better find yourself a real simpleton then," Jennibal said. "Any other man would lose interest if you don't keep him on his toes. You'd have to find someone even more stupid than Bazer, and I'm not sure someone like that exists."

"I thought you said you liked him?"

"I do. Never said he was smart, though."

Marsha glanced over at their two companions again. They'd stopped talking. Kylee appeared to be deep in thought, her face a mask of concentration while Bazer watched her expectantly. Once in a while Kylee gazed up at the cloud of birds above them. Finally she nodded, said something to Bazer, and the two of them came over to where Marsha and Jennibal were seated.

"Hey, any of you seen the ostrich?" Kylee asked, lowering herself gracefully onto the ground. Bazer sat down next to her, took out his notebook and began leafing through its pages.

"The ostrich?" Marsha gave the beautiful woman a puzzled look. "I've seen many ostriches. Which one are you talking about?"

"You'd know if you'd met this one," Kylee said. "It wears large, dark sunglasses and serves drinks at a bar."

Marsha frowned. "The only time I've seen someone serve drinks was at the wedding party we had back at the Hippo God's temple. No ostriches involved, only the Elephant People's gargling woman. Why do you ask?"

"Oh, just something the birds told me," Kylee said. "Me and Bazer had the same vision a few days ago, but then this business with the eagles got in the way so we forgot all about it, until he said something just now that reminded me of it. I thought the birds might be able to explain so I asked them. It turned out they did know a little, although most of it didn't make much sense."

"What did they tell you?" Jennibal asked.

Kylee scratched her head. "It was rather confusing, like I said. They claimed there was a place that moved, in ways I didn't quite understand, matching the description I gave them. The one we saw in that vision. A woman appears to have visited it not long ago, along with a man who was obsessed with some dice game..."

"That sounds like someone from the Elephant People!" Marsha said, suddenly much more interested in Kylee's story. "Ogian, probably, or maybe Kharuba. But why would that be of any importance?"

"I don't know," Kylee said. "There's just this feeling, you know, that the vision we had is somehow connected with everything else that's going on. That's why I thought you might know something about it."

"I don't understand any of it," Bazer said while Marsha contemplated Kylee's words.

Kylee patted him on the knee. "That's all right, sweetie. You're just beginning to figure out why you put food into your mouth and not your nose. Leave the more advanced issues to us."

"Why would the ostrich wear sunglasses inside?" Jennibal asked.

"Good question, cantaloupe girl," Kylee said. "The only explanation I've come up with so far is that he's an arrogant douchebag and thinks it looks cool for some reason. It doesn't."

"Or perhaps he went there by car and just forgot to take them off afterwards," Marsha mumbled to herself.

Kylee raised a perfectly arched eyebrow. "What did you say?"

"Oh, nothing." Marsha took a tamarind from Jennibal's bag and bit into it. "What else did the birds tell you?" she asked, wiping red juice from her chin.

"Only that those two caused some commotion at the bar," Kylee said. "The other patrons wanted to lynch them, but they managed to get away. The woman seemed able to create some kind of illusions to divert the others' attention. I've never heard of such a thing before."

"Me neither," Marsha said. "But if Ogian was there, playing Yahtzee or any other dice game, I could bet just about anything that he was cheating."

"That would explain why people got so angry with him," Kylee said, nodding slowly.

"What about the woman?" Jennibal asked. "Could she be the same one the eagles spoke of before? The one who intends to take over the world?"

"It's possible," Kylee said. "There was something odd about the way they described her, as if she wasn't really there. Perhaps this Raven God fellow will know something about it when we get to his temple."

They had to walk for three more days, following the directions Kylee received through her link with the eagles, before they caught up with the Scion and its hippo guards. By then they were completely exhausted, since the last two days had taken them through desert country where the air was so hot it burned their lungs and the sand scorched their feet. They were running low on food and water, too.

"If we don't get out of this hellhole soon we'll have to eat some of those blasted birds," Marsha said. "I bet they're really juicy."

"No need to fret, dear Marsha," Kylee said. "We'll reach the desert's edge before dark today."

"Good," Marsha said, brushing sand and dust from the cloth she'd tied around her head. "I wonder why the Scion would choose to come to a place like this."

"Why don't you ask it?" Kylee said, pointing at something ahead of them. "It's right over there."

Slowly, Marsha let her arm drop to her side and looked the way Kylee was pointing. It was true. The Scion sat perched on a large boulder, peering up at the multitude of eagles circling above. Its four hippo guards were arrayed around it, growling and snorting.

"Are... are they talking to it?" Marsha stammered. "The birds, I mean."

"They're trying," Kylee said, her face muscles tightening as she focused. "There's so much information passing back and forth I can barely make out who's saying what. These creatures don't really communicate the way we do."

"Oh?" Marsha also looked up at the cloud of birds. "What makes them so difficult to understand?"

Kylee pointed at Bazer, who was standing behind Jennibal, looking at her butt as she bent down to clean sand from beneath her toenails.

"Imagine if you could hear everything monkey boy there thought," she said. "Then add about a thousand similar voices and let them all pass through your head."

Marsha contemplated this for a few moments. "I don't think I'd want to have even one Bazer in my head," she said.

"Totally agree," Kylee said, grinning. "These birds are much more decent than that perverted piece of rhino excrement, of course, but interpreting their thoughts is still a constant struggle. There are things I can't figure out even if I've become pretty good at it."

Marsha turned her attention back to the Scion. The winged hippo hadn't moved, but its head was now turned in their direction. She tried to read the expression in its small, dark eyes. It proved impossible.

"Do you think it's safe to move closer?" she asked, giving the large hippos an uncertain look.

"I think so," Kylee said. "The eagles are trying to persuade it that we're friendly and that it's important that it listens to us. I don't think its fully convinced yet, but at least it's prepared to give us a chance."

"Good." Hesitantly, Marsha took a few steps closer to the rock where the Scion waited. Its hippo guards watched her closely, ready to charge at the smallest sign of threat to their master. When Marsha was twenty feet away she stopped.

"Um... hello?" she said.

"THE EAGLES TELL ME I SHOULD ALLOW YOU TO TALK TO ME," came the voice in Marsha's head. Even if she'd heard it before it still startled her.

"That'd be very nice of you," she managed.

"TALK, THEN."

Marsha took a deep breath, then began coughing as she got sand into her lungs. Doubling over, she wheezed and spat until she'd gotten it out again.

"I'M SORRY," the Scion said. "I DIDN'T QUITE GET THAT. WHAT ARE YOU TRYING TO SAY?"

"I'm not sure where to begin," Marsha croaked. "I've received so much new information lately. It seems things are much more complicated than I thought the last time we met."

"TO A SIMPLE MIND THE MOST OBVIOUS THING MAY APPEAR COMPLICATED."

The eagles must have conveyed the Scion's words, for Kylee suddenly burst out laughing. Marsha ignored her, concentrating on what she wanted the Scion to know.

"There's a new evil rising in the north," she said. "It intends to take over the world. We must gather all those with the power to oppose it."

"AND DO WHAT?" the Scion asked, the voice in Marsha's head sounding almost morose, like a teenager who'd been asked to clean his room and enquired why on earth he should do something so unnecessary.

"Why, to fight back, of course," Marsha said, her patience with this insipid godling quickly running out. "We must defeat this evil so people can be allowed to continue living in peace and freedom. Don't you see that?"

The Scion was silent for a while. When it spoke again it sounded tired, dejected.

"YOU CAN'T FIGHT SOMETHING THAT POWERFUL. IT'S POINTLESS."

"We have to try!" Marsha shouted. "We defeated the Bug Goddess. If all of us work together like we did then we can overcome this new threat as well."

She glared at the winged hippo, the two of them remaining silent for a long time. When she received no reply Marsha spoke again.

"Well?"

"WELL WHAT?"

"Are you coming with us?"

"IT DEPENDS. WHERE ARE YOU GOING?"

Marsha sighed. This felt more and more like talking to Pebe or some other scatter-brained member of her old tribe. Weren't gods supposed to tell humans what to do and not the other way around? She tried to stay positive – at least the grumpy little thing hadn't refused her outright.

"We're heading for the old temple of the Raven God," she said. "The eagles tell us he's still there, trapped inside a stone statue. We hope he'll be able to..."

"NO."

Marsha blinked. "What?"

"I SAID NO. YOU CAN'T GO THERE."

"Why not? That's where the egg came from. The people who used to live there are my friends."

The winged hippo took to the air, its wings beating so fast they turned into a blur. Its four hippo guards were suddenly on full alert, moving restlessly back and forth on the ground. Marsha heard Bazer let out a yelp behind her and she took an involuntary step back.

"YOU CAN'T GO THERE!" the Scion shrieked, the voice in Marsha's head so loud and sharp it felt as if her head would explode. "YOU DON'T BELONG THERE! STAY AWAY!"

With that it flew away, its hippo guards following at a thundering gallop. Marsha watched the small creature vanish into the distance, all hope vanishing with it.

"That went well."

She swung around and glared at Jennibal, who was standing a few feet away, eating a sugar plum.

"How can you say that?" Marsha wailed. "It's left us again, and probably for good this time. We'll never get it to come with us!"

"We don't have to," came Kylee's voice from her other side.

Marsha turned in that direction, tears making her vision blurry. "What do you mean? The eagles said..."

"They said we needed to get the Scion to come to the Raven God's temple, yes," Kylee said. "I know that."

"But..." Marsha made a vague gesture in the direction the Scion had gone. "It flew away."

Kylee was smiling like the sun itself. "Yep. And the eagles know where it's going. It let that slip before it left."

"Where?" Marsha asked, despair and confusion making her dizzy. "Where is it going?"

"Exactly where we want it to. The Raven God's temple."

~13~

---- ✳ ----

"I am become death, the destroyer of worlds."

- J. Robert Oppenheimer

"Please, Birdie, just one more game. I'm so bored and no one else will play with me."

"That's because you're a cheater! A lousy, stinking, inbred cheater! I'd rather play Yahtzee with the Great Demon Lord of the Abyss than with you!"

Ogian watched in dismay as the necromancer turned her back to him and stalked away. His primitive brain couldn't comprehend why she was so mad with him. Sure, he'd cheated the hell out of every game of Yahtzee they'd played, but that was no cause for such resentment. If she'd been a true master of the game she'd have cheated right back and done it well.

"Sore loser!" he called after her, punctuating his words with a satisfied nod. It was always good to get the final word in, especially now that he was going to be the Harbinger, wielder of all kinds of incredible powers. No one would dare call him cheater then.

He and Little Black Bird had gotten along so well in the beginning. Her eyes had glittered with excitement when he told her the rules of the Game (he decided that was a good way of referring to it, the capital letter G in particular). They'd felt a strong sense of companionship when they discussed the horrible after-effects of drinking Guinness. All in all, it had been a very pleasant few days.

And then she'd become a skilled enough Yahtzee player to detect his cheating.

He could still remember the stinging sensation when she'd slapped him right across the face. She was a rather petite woman, larger than the pretty one called Leoma albeit not by much, but fury had given her strength and the slap had hurt really badly. There'd been a different kind of hurt when the others had laughed at him as he rubbed his sore cheek. Even Bathora had smirked.

"Let's see who will laugh when I become the Harbinger for real," he muttered to himself, producing what he thought was a fierce scowl. Demon Viq, the necromancer who seemed a bit crazy, walked by just then and raised an eyebrow at him.

"Got something in your nose, Yahtzee boy?" she asked.

Ogian put one finger into each nostril and dug about for a while. "No," he said when he'd finished the examination. "Why do you ask?"

"I don't know. It looked like you were about to sneeze."

Ogian didn't know what to say to that. For a moment he contemplated asking the girl if she wanted to play Yahtzee with him, but decided against it. Demon Viq frightened him a little – not as much as the big woman Kel Hell or the mercenary Kat, but still enough to make him want to keep his distance. He settled for a shrug, then walked on.

He realized he'd liked things better when it was just him and Bathora. The ghost had never scared him, despite being a ghost and a woman who'd soon become powerful enough to bring down mountains and level whole villages with a flick of her hand. Bathora was nice and smart and funny, and very good-looking as well. If his heart hadn't already belonged to...

That last thought made him stop in mid-stride. He'd been about to think of someone, to speak a name in his mind, but it had vanished before he could finish the thought. The same thing had happened before, also when he thought of Bathora as a beautiful woman and not only as his new boss. The whole thing made him very confused.

After Birdie had stopped wanting to play Yahtzee with him he'd tried to introduce some of the others to the Game. The two lovers, Leoma and Weewee, seemed very nice but were usually too busy with each other to pay attention to anyone else, so instead he'd tried the other male mercenaries, Bog and Spud. They were a lot slower than Birdie and had required several tries before learning all the rules, but in the end they'd played some really nice games, until they also discovered that Ogian cheated constantly. After that they wouldn't play with him anymore.

The necromancer Kel Hell was much too big and intimidating for him to consider asking her to play, and the mercenary leader Kat was even worse. She wasn't big, but whenever she looked at him it felt like she tried to come up with the best way to dismember him. He didn't want to think about what would happen if she discovered him cheating.

Following Bathora's directions they'd journeyed almost straight north for the last couple of days. The terrain had grown more barren with each mile they put behind them, until all that surrounded them were sharp rocks and dry, cracked ground. They hadn't seen the sun in two days, and the temperature had dropped until Ogian felt goosebumps rise on his skin. There was a strange, unnerving sensation in the air, as if a storm was coming. Ogian didn't like it.

Hearing voices off to his right, he went that way to see what was going on. The big woman, Kel Hell, was seated on Kat's back, the mercenary doing rapid push-ups as if the weight didn't bother her at all. Little Black Bird sat on a rock a few feet away, a somber expression on her face.

"I don't like her," Kel Hell said. "Are you sure joining forces with her wasn't a mistake?"

"She said she needed necromancers," Birdie said. "And she's the only spirit I ever managed to bring back. I don't want to miss this opportunity."

"She's seeking some kind of revenge," Kat put in. The mercenary didn't even seem out of breath. "There ought to be a lot of death involved. Isn't that what you necromancers want?"

"There was a lot of death at that village," Kel pointed out. "And yet none of us managed anything. Why would things be different this time."

"You must have patience, Kel," Birdie said. "Perhaps the time wasn't right back then. What Bathora is after is something truly incredible, if I understand things right. We must be there to witness it."

Kel sighed, her huge body continuing to move up and down as Kat exercised. "Ok, fine," she said. "I just have a bad feeling about this. There's something not right with that woman."

"She's a ghost," Kat said. "That sort of bothers me. I don't like things I can't kill."

"And I don't like things I can't eat," Kel muttered.

Ogian cleared his throat. "Hello," he said. "Mind if I join you."

"If you're still after another Yahtzee game you can forget about it," Birdie said, glaring sourly at him. "I told you I'm not interested."

"Oh, it's not like that," Ogian said, nodding towards Kat and Kel. "I was just wondering if I could try push-ups like those."

"You really think you could manage?" Kel asked, looking more than a little doubtful.

Ogian shrugged. "I need to be strong if I'm to be Bathora's Harbinger. Better start exercising at once."

"I'm done for today," Kat proclaimed, putting down her knees. "The boy can have a go."

Being referred to as "the boy" angered Ogian. If he hadn't been so afraid of Kat he might have walked over and given her a piece of his mind, possibly accompanied by a punch or two. That had to wait until he received all his new powers, though. Refusing to meet any of the women's eyes, he lowered himself onto his hands and knees.

"This will be interesting," came Kel's voice from a place right above him. There was the sound of shuffling feet, then it felt like a mountain collapsed on him. Before he knew it he lay flat on his stomach, the woman's immense weight crushing him to the ground.

"Please..." he gasped. "You're breaking my back."

"Ah, come on," Kel said. "Push me up. You should manage a few, at least. No one can be that weak."

Ogian was too busy trying to remain alive to even think of doing anything else. The agony in his back made tears sting his eyes, and his vision became blurry. The woman seemed to weigh as much as an elephant. Ogian suddenly wondered if this was how poor old Ballambaro had felt when he got squished under his animal's foot.

"Oh, give the poor boy some respite, Kel," Birdie said. "It looks like he's about to pass out."

"All right, then." The titanic weight was removed from Ogian's back and he finally managed to draw breath. It came out as a low moan.

"That's one poor excuse for a Harbinger," Kat muttered. "I wonder why that lily-livered ghost picked him of all people."

"Can't be his good looks," Kel said, sniggering softly.

"No, then she'd have picked the woman with the eagles," Birdie said, her voice sounding strangely distant.

"Eagles?" Kat sounded puzzled. "What are you talking about?"

"Huh? I didn't say anything. I was only thinking."

"Thinking about what?"

There was a long pause, then Birdie spoke again. "How strange. I don't remember."

"Look," Kel said. "The boy is moving again."

Ogian had finally managed to push himself into a sitting position, wiping tears and dust from his cheeks.

"Aw, look at him," Kat said with mock sympathy. "The poor thing has been crying. Not as tough as you thought, eh, Harbinger?"

"Leave me be," Ogian snuffled, turning his face away so the women wouldn't see the new tears trickling down his cheeks.

"Or you'll do what?" asked Kat. "Run off to mommy Bathora and complain about how mean the girls were to you? The thought of what she'd do then makes me tremble with fear. No wait, she's a ghost, so she can't do anything except say *boo*." She laughed, and the other two women joined in a moment later.

"When I become Harbinger I'll cut out your heart and force you to eat it." The words were out of Ogian's mouth before he could stop himself. There was a time of complete silence, then Kat was on him, hurling him backwards so hard his head struck the ground with a nasty thump. Before he could do so much as yelp she was straddling him, the point of her knife pressing against his chest.

"Are you now?" the woman hissed, her eyes burning with a cold, hard light. "What if I cut yours out right here and now? It'd be the easiest thing in the world." She put a little more pressure on the blade and Ogian felt the edge pierce his skin.

"Lay off, Kat," Birdie said. "Bathora wants the fool kid alive for whatever she's up to. Killing him might ruin our own plans."

Kat grunted. "Right, right. I'll leave his heart where it is for the moment, then. But what about his kidneys? You can survive with only one of those, can't you?" She let her blade slide down Ogian's side, making him shiver.

"Not sure he'd survive having it cut out of him, though," Birdie said. "But if you do, can I have it to experiment with?"

"Sure thing," Kat said, then she leaned down until her face were mere inches from Ogian's. "You'd better behave, boy, or you might wake up without your balls one morning. I'm sure the necromancers could put them to use as well."

She got off him and strode off without another word. Ogian remained where he lay, too stunned to move. The other two women ignored him. No one said anything until Bathora's ghost appeared out of nowhere.

"Are you still loafing about here?" she said, both voice and facial expression reeking of irritation. "You must be the laziest bunch of people on this continent. I've never seen anything like it. Get up with you and move those feet. We're almost there."

"Almost where?" Birdie asked. "Where is it we're going?"

"You'll see," the ghost said. "It'll be *epic*."

They kept their northern course as the afternoon wore on. Around them the landscape grew ever more inhospitable. The ground became uneven and treacherous, with sharp rocks cutting into their feet when they weren't wary, and cracks and gorges suddenly opening right before them. Some were wide enough to swallow a person whole and so deep Ogian couldn't see the bottom.

The sky was darkening as well, and not only because evening had come. Black storm clouds loomed over their heads, bolts of lightning lighting up the northern sky at regular intervals. Thunder rolled in the distance, the sound so deep and ominous it made the air itself tremble.

Suddenly Leoma let out a loud, piercing shriek. Weewee hurried over to where she stood off to Ogian's right, face even paler than usual.

"What is it, love?" he asked. "Are you all right?"

"Snake!" the girl gasped. "I almost stepped on it. It scared the life out of me."

"Get a grip, Leelee," Birdie said from Ogian's other side. "You've seen worse things than snakes in the time we've been together."

"It's this place!" Leoma wailed. "I hate it! It's evil!"

"Exactly," Birdie said. "That's why I like it. It reminds me of home."

"Well said, Nerdy." Bathora turned and gave Birdie a radiant smile. The ghost had changed her attire and was now wearing a long, black cloak and black, heeled boots. Her eyes glowed like dark embers in the fading light.

The necromancer muttered something Ogian didn't quite get but seemed to be about being too dense to remember a simple name. Ogian himself was pretty good at remembering names. It had only taken him a day or two to learn what all the new people were called. He'd had a wee bit of trouble telling the two older mercenaries apart, but it became easier when he started thinking of Bog as the "big one", as the words big and Bog sounded alike.

"That was rather smart of me, if I may say so myself," he mumbled as he trudged on behind Bathora.

"Huh?" said Bog, who was walking beside him.

"Oh, nothing really," Ogian said. "I was just thinking about how much more difficult remembering your name would be if you'd been small."

The mercenary gave him a queer look but said nothing. A light rain began to fall, making the ground slippery and even more difficult to traverse. The big necromancer Kel Hell grumbled something about not having eaten in ages. Ogian was also getting hungry, but Bathora pressed on, obviously not intending to call a halt any time soon. Her face held a frenzied expression, as if something she'd desired for a long time lay just around the next corner.

It was almost full dark when they climbed up a narrow path surrounded by tall, sharp cliffs and, reaching the top, found themselves gazing out across a vast, barren plateau. Right in front of them rose a small mountain, dark and ominous against the storm clouds above. Flashes of lightning lit up its jagged edges and steep precipices. The sight was so eldritch, so completely otherworldly, that the company stood there gaping for several minutes, too overwhelmed to speak.

The necromancer, Little Black Bird, was the one who eventually broke the silence.

"Whoa!" she exclaimed. "And I thought the Vale of Uzureth was the nastiest place on this continent. I never was more wrong."

"What kind of place is this?" Kat asked. For the first time since joining Ogian and Bathora the mercenary looked unnerved.

Bathora's face, already shimmering slightly, looked even more ghostly with the light from the distant lightning flashes dancing across it.

"This," she said, "is a place of power. It's where gods are made and unmade. What you're about to witness here is something no human has ever seen before."

"You mean Ogian is going to say something smart?" Demon Viq asked. She was watching the nightmarish scene before them with intense fascination.

Bathora laughed. "No, of course not. There are limits even to what this place can achieve. But I promise you it'll be spectacular. I'll be at the center of it, after all. Come now, let's go."

They crossed the stretch of hard, open ground – Bathora eagerly, most of the others more hesitant. Ogian was one of the most reluctant ones. He'd seen scary things before – had been there when Mount Azagh erupted, had been part of the charge against the terrible, hulking form of the Bug Goddess, but nothing had ever frightened him so much as this place. The power emanating from it was so menacing, so gargantuan he thought it might swallow the whole world. It made him want to turn and run, as fast as he could, until he was back under the sunlit sky.

When they reached the foot of the mountain Bathora turned and faced the rest of the group. Her eyes were like liquid amber, brighter than Ogian had ever seen them. Her form seemed to have grown taller, looming over them like a smaller version of the mountain itself. Her voice rose above the booming thunderclaps as she addressed them.

"I need Ogian and the necromancer Little Black Bird to accompany me into the mountain," she said. "The rest of you will have to remain here. I doubt this will take long."

"What are you going to do?" asked Kat. She had one hand on the hilt of her sword, her body tense as a bowstring, ready to act at the least sign of danger.

"You'll see," Bathora said. "Come with me, Ogian. Ogian! What in the name of the Cannibal God's smelly farts are you doing? Come back here, before I call security!"

Ogian stopped. He hadn't been aware that he'd started walking away from the mountain. It was as if his legs had moved by themselves, not caring what his brain told them to do. His brain, malfunctioning as always, hadn't told them anything, but that was beside the point. He turned around and forced himself to walk back.

"There, that's better," Bathora said with a satisfied nod. "The fat woman's daughter would be proud of you. Follow me now. You too, Nerdy."

She turned and started walking, seemingly straight towards the mountainside. Ogian and Birdie followed, each step slow and careful. Bathora headed for a patch of rock that looked even darker than the rest of the mountain, and a moment later the shadows had swallowed her.

"Where...?" Birdie began.

"It's an opening," Ogian said, pointing at the black outline. "Come, we must follow her."

They more or less stumbled into a dark passage, winding its way into the mountain through numerous twists and turns. At first Ogian and the necromancer had to feel their way along the uneven rock walls, but after a few minutes a faint light appeared, dancing across the walls and ceiling ahead of them. With it came a sharp, crackling sound that neither of them could identify.

Turning the last corner, Ogian and Birdie found themselves staring at a sight that defied all reason, taking their perception of the world and turning it inside out, taking concepts like *possible* and *real* and gargling them until they were no longer recognizable. Compared to what they saw now the vision of the dark mountain, wreathed in lightning and rain, was no more than mildly unsettling.

The tunnel they'd been stumbling through emerged into a vast mountain hall. Or at least that was what they assumed it to be. About twenty yards ahead of them the world as they knew it ended, and instead there was a wall of fluorescent,electrifying light, its multitude of unnaturally bright colors flashing and crackling so madly it made Ogian's insides want to crawl out through his nose and hide themselves. The noise coming from the otherworldly barrier made his ears hurt.

"By all the dark powers!" Birdie gasped beside him. "This is what I've been looking for my entire life. This is the *real* thing!"

"What is it?" Ogian asked, his voice trembling with fear. "I've never seen anything like it."

"I guess you'd call it a rift in reality," came Bathora's voice, somehow loud and clear despite the deafening noise. The ghost was standing at the edge of the world, a dark outline against the scintillating light.

"A rift in..." Ogian's brain was incapable of understanding the words, much less the concept. "What does that mean?"

"It's where the various dimensions meet," Bathora explained. "The different worlds, if you want to use that term. Come closer. I'll need both of you if this is to succeed."

Hesitantly, Ogian took a few steps forward. The air was hot and stuffy, almost hard to breathe. He could feel the power emanating from the wall of coruscating light, making his skin tingle and his hair stand straight up.

"Fae would have loved this place," he mumbled. "Tom-Tom too, before he became a real man again."

"Stop jabbering and come here!" Birdie shouted back at him. The necromancer had crossed the smooth stone floor and was now standing at Bathora's side.

Sending a quick prayer to the Elephant God, Ogian hurried to join them, positioning himself right behind Bathora. The light was even more blinding this close, making Ogian feel as if the inside of his skull was crackling and vibrating. Sweat broke out all over his body, dripping down his forehead and cheeks and making his eyes sting even more.

"Do you know what to do, necromancer?" Bathora asked Birdie. "You must hold the gate open and pull me through when the time comes."

Birdie nodded. "I can feel it. It's like that time down in the cave, only a million times stronger."

"It'll be even more overwhelming before the end," Bathora said, smiling. "Savor it while you can. This is something you'll experience only once."

The necromancer turned and gazed into the light, her face hardening. "I'm ready," she said.

"What am I supposed to do?" Ogian asked, feeling oddly left out.

"Wait for my instructions," Bathora said. "Then do what I say without questioning. Can you do that?"

"I can," Ogian said. "I've always done everything people told me to."

Bathora laughed softly. "Well, after this you'll be the one telling people what to do. Except me, of course. I'll always be your superior. Oh, well, see you guys soon."

With that, she stepped right into the barrier of crackling light, vanishing from view in an instant. Ogian gasped and turned to ask Birdie what was happening, but the necromancer's face was so taut with concentration and effort he dared not disturb her. Heart beating frantically, he turned back to peer into the wall of light.

Suddenly the necromancer gasped and dropped to her knees. "It's done," she gasped, supporting herself with her hands. "She's back."

Ogian was about to ask what she meant, but right then he heard a voice, loud and powerful and yet strangely familiar. It seemed to speak to him from inside his head, so strong it drowned out all his other thoughts (not that there were many of them).

"COME, HARBINGER. REACH OUT AND TAKE MY HAND."

Bracing himself, Ogian stuck his hand into the barrier of light, gasping as jolts of electricity lanced through his arm and into his body. Then a strong hand grabbed his, pulling him into the inferno. The world ceased to exist, leaving him floating in a purgatory of insanely bright flashes of light and crackling bursts of power. He screamed.

"RECEIVE THE POWER!" boomed the voice in his head, and in that moment it felt like the blood in Ogian's veins turned to fire. The heat seared his bones, permeating through his muscles and setting his nervous system ablaze. Ogian screamed. And then he *changed*.

The hand let go, and Ogian experienced a queer falling sensation. Everything spun around him, making him so dizzy he thought he'd throw up, but what really freaked him out was that he couldn't tell in which direction he was falling. There were no such things as up and down anymore, no fixed points to orient himself by. A long, drawn-out wail emerged from his lips as he plunged into oblivion.

He woke up on the smooth stone floor of the mountain hall, the barrier of fluorescent light crackling and fizzing behind him, feeling like the world's biggest washing machine had centrifuged him for a year. An echo of the burning sensation lingered throughout his body, like the memory of a dream still holding on for a few moments after you wake up.

Someone grabbed him under the arms and tried to pull him back to his feet. Ogian moaned and sank back onto the stone floor.

"Get up, you lousy cheater! We must get out of here!"

Ogian realized it was the necromancer, Little Black Bird. She sounded almost as furious as when she discovered he'd been cheating her at Yahtzee.

"Go away!" he whimpered. "I don't want to go anywhere."

Another tug at his arms. "You'll die if you remain here. Think of all the Yahtzee games you'll never get to play then. Up with you now! I'm not as strong as Kat, or I'd carry you across my shoulders."

Groaning, Ogian let the young woman pull him back to his feet and drag him towards the tunnel they'd entered through. At its opening he stopped and turned his head to look back at the wall of coruscating light.

"Bathora!" he panted. "We can't leave her here."

"Never mind about her," Birdie snapped, pulling at his arm so hard he almost fell over. "She'll find her own way out, and we'd better be at a safe distance when she does."

Ogian had no idea what the necromancer was talking about, but being too stunned to protest he allowed her to lead him back through the dark tunnel. They'd almost made it through when Ogian heard a low rumble rising behind them. Faint tremors shook the living rock surrounding them.

"What's that?" he gasped.

"You'll see soon enough," Birdie grumbled. They turned the last corner and were back out in the open. Night had fallen while they were inside the mountain, and the plain outside would've been pitch dark if their companions hadn't lit a small fire some distance away.

Kat was the first who spotted them. She came trotting over just as Ogian's knees gave way again, dropping him onto the hard ground with a muted thump.

"What happened?" the mercenary asked. "Where's the ghost?"

Birdie opened her mouth to answer, but right then the rumbling sound Ogian had heard before rose to a mighty roar. A large portion of the mountainside exploded outward, and through the opening came a huge, dark shape.

"I HAVE RETURNED!" it roared, in a voice that made the thunder overhead sound like a cat purring.

Ogian's eyes widened. It was Bathora, but not the Bathora he'd spent the past few weeks travelling with. She was at least twelve feet tall, dark and menacing, the supple femininity of her figure completely gone. Her body had become a massive, powerful bulk, her face a terrible mask of midnight shadows except for her eyes, glowing red like dark pits filled with hellfire. The whole apparition radiated terrible, destructive power.

Beside Ogian, the necromancer Little Black Bird watched the creature Bathora had become with a mix of fascination and dread. Kat, on the other hand, was tense as a bowstring, her sword drawn and ready to fight.

"I WILL DESTROY ALL THOSE WHO WRONGED ME AND MAKE THE WORLD TREMBLE BENEATH MY FEET!" Bathora roared. "LET THEM TASTE MY BOOBS!"

There was utter silence for a few moments, then Demon Viq sniggered.

The huge, menacing shape appeared confused, then it said, "WRATH, NOT BOOBS. LET THEM TASTE MY WRATH."

"Will there be lots of killing?" Kat asked, the tension on her face slowly giving way to expectation.

"THERE WILL BE KILLING!" Bathora thundered. "THERE WILL BE DEATH! THERE WILL BE VENGEANCE!"

"yay! And cookies every day!" Birdie shouted.

Bathora turned her burning eyes towards the necromancer. "THERE WILL BE NO COOKIES, ONLY BLURBERS!" she intoned. "AND PEANUTS! AND BAD COUNTRY MUSIC PLAYED BY RODENTS!"

Birdie clamped her mouth shut, her face darkening. Off to their right the big necromancer Kel Hell closed her hands into fists, glaring at the dark apparition with fierce hatred in her eyes.

The Bathora-creature's eyes suddenly fell on Ogian where he lay trembling on the ground. She took a few steps toward him, the ground shaking beneath her mighty feet.

"GET UP, HARBINGER!" she commanded. "YOU HAVE THE POWER I PROMISED YOU. STOP COWERING LIKE A CORNERED MONGREL."

Ogian wasn't sure if she did something to him then or if it was merely his body recovering from the shock, but suddenly he did feel the power inside him. He could *do* things, things no human had been able to do before. Hands trembling with excitement, he reached into his pocket and took out the five dice he always carried with him, tossing them onto the ground and willing them to show what he wanted them to.

And they did. They showed five sixes.

"Yahtzee!!" he bellowed at the top of his lungs, jumping up and down and punching the air with his fists. "Yahtzee! I won! I finally won!"

"YOU'LL WIN EVERY TIME YOU PLAY FROM NOW ON," Bathora said, her shadowy face breaking into a terrible grimace that must've been intended as a smile. "NO ONE WILL EVER DEFEAT YOU AGAIN."

Ogian stared up at the menacing shape, eyes filled with gratitude and awe. "Does that mean I'm a god?" he asked.

The dark apparition snorted, gouts of fire erupting from its nostrils. "OF COURSE NOT. GODS WIELD MUCH GREATER POWER AND GET TO SPEAK IN ALL CAPS. YOU'RE ONLY MY HARBINGER, BUT EVEN THAT IS A HUGE STEP UP FROM THE LOWLY CREATURE YOU WERE BEFORE."

"But..." Ogian began, then had to stop and swallow. "But if I'm no god, then what do you need me for?"

"NOT TO PROVIDE INTELLIGENT CONVERSATION, IF THAT'S WHAT YOU THINK. NO, I NEED YOU TO TAKE CARE OF ALL THE PESKY HUMANS THAT WILL COME IN OUR WAY, THOSE TOO PUNY TO DESERVE MY ATTENTION."

"Ah." Ogian was finally beginning to understand. "You want me to talk to them? Convince them to follow you?"

"NO!!" The roar was so deafening it made all of them cover their ears. Someone – Ogian thought it was the girl Leoma – whimpered softly.

"No?" Ogian said, not sure how he dared speak.

"NO!" Bathora repeated. "YOU WILL CRUSH THEM. LIKE THIS!"

Bathora raised one of her massive arms and pointed it at the mountain. With a crash that made the earth quaver and the group of humans stumble, the solid rock of the mountainside broke apart and collapsed into rubble, burying the opening they'd entered through as well as the tunnel beyond. A cloud of dust rose from the devastation, slowly drifting away on the night wind.

"LET'S WREAK DEATH AND DESTRUCTION ON THIS WORLD!" Bathora roared. "AND LET THE MOST CRUSHING BLOW FALL UPON THE ABOMINATION KNOWN AS THE HIPPO CULT!"

~14~

"My son, ask for thyself another Kingdom, for that which I leave is too small for thee."

- Philip II of Macedon

M arsha had never thought of herself as an overly dramatic person. She tried to keep a level head in all situations, important as well as everyday. People making too much fuss over trifling matters always annoyed her, making her want to scream at them to put things in perspective or simply to get a fucking life (although she never used such powerful language except in her own head).

She'd often heard people say that they'd do *anything* for this or that person, or that a certain person (usually, but not always, the same one as in the previous case) meant more to them than their own life. What Marsha herself had observed, however, was that people tended to care about others only as long as it didn't cause them too much inconvenience. For example, someone who enjoyed hunting could happily bring food to a sick person and feel incredibly good about themselves afterwards, but if the person in question was asked to do something he or she found terribly unpleasant they'd be much more reluctant to offer their assistance. Thus, the conclusion she'd reached was that this unconditional love and caring only went so far.

Looking at the group gathered around her, she wondered how far they'd go in order to protect her and her people. Would any of them turn out to be a great warrior who threw him- or herself into battle with no regard for their own safety? She doubted it. Did any of them possess some unique power that would prove useful in the fight against this new evil? Not unless you counted Kylee's ability to talk to birds, and Marsha failed to see how that could help much against such an all-powerful being. As for wisdom...

"I've been thinking," Bazer announced.

Kylee snorted. "Yeah, and I'm the Raven God's unknown daughter."

"You are?" Jennibal asked, eyes widening slightly. "You never said before."

Marsha shook her head. No, wisdom wasn't a trait this group could contribute with. Perhaps their only purpose was to bring her – and the Scion – to the Raven God's old temple. At least they seemed capable enough to manage that.

"No, seriously," Bazer said. "We don't have much in the way of brute force to throw against the evil in the north, right?"

Kylee gazed up at the sky in that trademark way of hers. "It makes such brilliant observations," she said dryly. "What would we do without its keen perception?"

"Let him finish, Kylee," Marsha said. "It sounds like he really wants to tell us something."

"All right, all right," the beautiful woman said. "At least it'll keep his deranged mind away from our luscious female curves for a while."

Marsha frowned. "I've never heard him speak about me in that way."

"I was talking about myself and Jennibal."

"Oh." That made more sense, Marsha thought. She was perfectly fine with being ignored by the young man. Being plain-looking sure had its advantages sometimes.

"What I meant," Bazer said, "was that if the Scion can control the minds of his hippo guards, then perhaps he could do the same with other hippos. Imagine having hundreds of those huge, powerful animals under your command? It'd be much better than an army of human warriors."

There was silence for a few moments, then Kylee let out a long, agonized moan.

"What's the matter, Kylee?" Marsha asked. "That actually sounded like a good idea."

"I know," the beautiful woman whimpered. "I can't stand it when he does that. It shakes the very foundations of my belief system."

"We of the God of the Iridescent Cantaloupe never waver in our faith," Jennibal proclaimed. "If He sends hippos to do his bidding, then far be it from us to question his wisdom."

Kylee raised her head and gave Jennibal a bewildered look. "Uh, what?"

"We must learn to see the God's hand in everything that happens around us," Jennibal explained. "Sometimes He speaks through the lowliest creatures imaginable just so we'll learn how insignificant we really are."

"Yeah, but even he should draw the line at Bazer," Kylee said. "At a safe distance from him, preferably."

"I think we should present his idea to the Scion when we reach the Raven God's temple," Marsha said. "Anything that might help us in the fight against the evil up north should be welcomed."

They'd all woken up in the middle of last night at the sound of hundreds of eagles screaming in unison – a cry of such agony and trepidation that they jumped to their feet and reached for the weapons none of them had. The minutes it took Kylee to discover what had caused this sudden alarm had felt like a lifetime to Marsha and the others. When she finally relayed the news it did little to ease their fears.

"It appears the evil creature has reached her goal and seized the power she quested for," she said. "She is now virtually unstoppable, a goddess of such power and malice she could destroy the whole world. Things aren't looking too great for us right now."

They hadn't slept much more that night. The eagles remained restless above them, the bombardment of droppings from above more intense than ever. Marsha kept casting anxious glances to the north, as if expecting a huge, glowing shape to appear against the night sky at any moment. Beside her Jennibal was praying to the God of the Iridescent Cantaloupe, mumbling the same words over and over until Marsha knew them by heart. When dawn finally broke it came as a relief. Dark goddesses never seemed as menacing when the sun's warm rays touched your face.

"The eagles say they'll aid us in any way they can," Kylee said after spending some time in deep concentration. "They claim that was how things used to be in the olden days – birds working together with hippos and other land-based animals."

"What can a bunch of birds do against the most powerful creature in the whole world?" Jennibal asked. "Drown it in guano?"

Kylee shrugged. "Bazer?"

"Huh?" The young man had taken out his notebook and appeared to be summarizing the latest scores he'd put down in it. Now he looked up and gave Kylee a questioning look.

"Any ideas about how the eagles can help us against this new evil goddess?" the beautiful woman asked.

Bazer looked up at the mass of feathers and beaks above them, then shrugged. "Let them figure that out. They're very smart birds."

"Thank goodness!" Kylee exclaimed, an expression of blissful relief on her face. "I don't know if I could've taken another brilliant remark. This is more like it."

"I hope he's right, though," said Marsha. "We really don't have much in the way of fighting power."

"What about that Melon God of yours, Jennibal?" asked Kylee. "Can't you call for him to aid us?"

"I spent most of last night praying," Jennibal said tersely. "I'm sure He heard me. He always listens to his subjects, even the least significant ones."

Kylee rolled her eyes. "Yes, but what will he *do*?"

"He hasn't said. Perhaps he's thinking it over."

"Ah, so we're dealing with the slow-minded god of the almighty honeydew?" Kylee said with a mocking smile. "Let's hope it doesn't take him too long to figure something out."

Marsha cleared her throat. "I think we should break camp now. I'd like us to reach the Raven God's temple before nightfall."

Fortunately there were no protests, so the small group gathered their belongings and resumed their journey north. They'd left the desert behind and entered into a somewhat cooler region, with hard-packed dirt beneath their feet and rocky outcrops protruding in several places. In the distance Marsha could see a taller range of mountains.

"I wonder if that's where the Raven Cult's old caverns are?" she said to herself.

"I thought you'd met some of those people?" said Jennibal, who was walking next to her. "Didn't they say where their old abodes lay?"

Marsha shook her head. "Not exactly. Only that it was far west of where I come from and that they lay beneath some mountains."

"What were they like, these Raven people?"

"In the beginning they were really odd," Marsha said, remembering the first time she'd encountered the pale-skinned people with their thick robes. "They seemed to think the sun was the cause of all evil. The *evil eye* was their name for it."

Jennibal glanced up at the midday sun. "That sounds odd, yes. Why would they think that?"

"I'm not sure," Marsha said. "It was a big misunderstanding of some sort. An old scroll with words missing or something like that."

"But they found out they'd been wrong?"

Marsha nodded. "Yes, and then they threw away the thick cloaks they'd used to protect themselves from the sun. They were so pale it hurt the eyes."

"I can guess," Jennibal said thoughtfully, then she giggled. "Bazer would've had a hard time rating their women's beauty with them all covered up like that."

"Well, one of them claimed to have the power to see through people's clothes…"

"What?" Marsha jumped at the sharp sound of Bazer's voice right behind her. "How was he able to do that? Tell me!"

"I don't know for sure," Marsha said. "Perhaps the Raven God granted him the power as a reward for some service he'd performed?"

"I must have a talk with this Raven God once we reach those caverns," Bazer mumbled. "This could revolutionize my rating system."

Late in the afternoon they reached the southernmost edge of the mountain range. The massive rock walls rose steeply above them, their sharp peaks pointing at the sky. Marsha, who'd never seen the Vale of Uzureth or the lonely mountain harboring the great rift in reality, found them rather menacing and inhospitable. Birdie would have given them one brief look and sniffed disdainfully.

They didn't have to worry about not finding the entrance to the Raven Cult's old caverns. The eagles had flown ahead and were now hovering above it, spattering the mountainside with guano. Many perched on protruding crags and narrow ledges, glancing expectantly down at the humans.

"Is this really a temple?" Jennibal asked, watching the small,crude opening with disapproval. "I thought temples were a lot fancier."

"It's not that different from the Hippo God's temple," Marsha said. "I guess the important thing is its power, not its appearance."

"We should go in," Kylee said. "The eagles say the Scion is already here."

Marsha nodded, stepping through the entrance and into a passage much like the one leading into the place her people had made their new home. They moved through a long tunnel, using their hands to feel their way through the darkness, and soon found themselves in a cavernous hall lit by a multitude of candles.

"This is a little more like it," Jennibal said, then her eyes fell on a large hole in the rock wall, across the hall and to their left. Broken rock and other rubble lay piled in front of it. There was a similar-looking hole in the wall across from it. "Or maybe not," she added.

Marsha didn't hear her words. Her full attention was on the large statue standing against the wall to their right – a statue much like the one in the Hippo God's temple, except that this one depicted a creature that appeared to be a cross between human and bird. It had the legs and torso of a human, but the head and wings of a raven. Hovering in front of it, perhaps eight feet above the floor, was the Scion.

The winged hippo turned its head toward Marsha, an unreadable expression in its small, black eyes.

"OH, SO YOU'VE COME," said the now familiar voice inside Marsha's head.

"Yes, I have." For once, Marsha didn't feel captivated by the Scion's presence. Instead she kept her gaze fixed on the statue of the Raven God. It was here, in this very place, that the wondrous egg had first appeared, where it'd dropped into the hands of the young man Drunk. It was also here, she reminded herself, that the Bug Goddess, the ancient enemy of her people, had spent several months, masquerading as a stunningly beautiful woman. That thought made her skin crawl.

"STEP FORWARD," came another voice, deeper than the Scion's and far more imperative, the booming sound filling Marsha's head. This was, she realized, how a real god sounded.

She began walking towards the stone statue, but before she'd taken more than two steps the commanding voice boomed in her head again.

"NO, NOT YOU. THE HOT ONES."

Stopping abruptly, Marsha gazed in bewilderment at the stone statue, then turned left to where Kylee and Jennibal stood.

"I think he means you," she said.

Kylee, standing with her arms crossed, made a grimace but did as the Raven God had said. As she stepped into the candlelight Marsha was sure she saw a red glint in the statue's ruby eyes, as if the god liked what he saw.

"HOLY FU…" The Raven God cut himself off, and Marsha could swear she heard him clear his throat. "YOU MUST BE THE HOTTEST BABE WHO EVER EXISTED," he continued. "AND WITH THE TALENT TO SPEAK TO MY PEOPLE AS WELL. TELL ME, MY LOVELY, HAVE YOU EVER PERFORMED A STRIPTEASE?"

The scowl Kylee directed at the statue was so fierce Marsha thought the stone might crumble and fall apart right then and there.

"No," she said, her voice cold enough to make the North Pole itself shiver. "And I don't plan to do it for the first feather-brained fowl who tries to sweet-talk me."

"FOWL!" The Raven God's outraged scream made Marsha jump. "I'M THE BLOODY RAVEN GOD! HOW DARE YOU REFER TO ME AS FOWL? I SHOULD INCINERATE YOU ON THE SPOT!"

Kylee seemed completely unperturbed by the outburst. "Would you prefer *duck*?" she asked calmly. "You certainly sound like one."

This time there was no mistaking the glow in the statue's eyes. It was obvious that gods didn't enjoy being mocked. From the corner of her eye Marsha saw Bazer giving the strange statue a sympathetic look.

When the Raven God spoke again the voice was lower and more strained, as if he struggled to keep it under control.

"WHAT ABOUT YOU?" he said, and Marsha felt the words directed at Jennibal.

The dark-haired girl looked less confident than Kylee, but her voice was steady as she answered.

"I belong to the God of the Iridescent Cantaloupe. Only at His command will I remove any items of clothing."

"ER, THE GOD OF THE WHAT?" If a god could sound puzzled, the Raven God did.

"The God of the Iridescent Cantaloupe. The only real God. You must know of Him, if you're the one you claim to be."

The Raven God let out a snort, the sound reverberating inside Marsha's head. "I'VE MET ALL THE GODS EVER TO EXIST ON THIS CONTINENT. THERE WAS NEVER A GOD OF WATER MELONS OR WHATEVER IT WAS YOU SAID."

Jennibal clamped her mouth shut, promptly ignoring both the Raven God's words and the jeering smile Kylee shot back over her shoulder. A religious fanatic could probably ignore a kick from a mule if it contradicted their beliefs.

Standing there like a lonely tree caught between two whirlwinds, Marsha tried to collect her thoughts. She had come here for a reason, and it hadn't been to discuss stripteases or made-up gods. Her eyes found the Scion, who looked as forlorn as she felt.

"The reason we came here..." she began, but a voice from the opposite side of the hall interrupted her.

"What's the commotion about, my lord? Did our guest let loose his uncouth guards inside our... oh, there are more of them now. And humans, I see. How yummy!"

A young woman had appeared from an opening leading deeper into the mountain. She was a little taller than Marsha and much prettier, with long, dark hair and long, tanned legs, dressed in a brown robe that seemed made from some kind of hide, a number of small white bones sewn onto it.

Bazer had his notebook out faster than the eye could follow. "Nine," he mumbled, jotting down the score on a fresh page. "Um, what's your name, fair lady?"

"Lulu," the woman said. "I'm working for the Raven God, doing... stuff. And who might you people be?"

"I'm Marsha," Marsha said. "Of the Hippo Cult. The others are Bazer, Kylee and Jennibal." She pointed to her companions in turn.

"Jennibal?" Lulu said, giving the girl a toothy grin. "I like that name. Rhymes with the name of my old tribe. How about you join me for supper? I know just where to put you."

"NO, LULU," came the Raven God's stern voice. "THESE ARE NOT FOR EATING. KEEP YOUR APPETITE UNDER CONTROL."

The woman – Lulu – made a pained grimace. "But I haven't had any real food in *ages*!" she complained, a strange yearning in her eyes as she looked at the other humans. "I can't go on like this anymore!"

"YOU CAN'T EAT THEM."

"Not even a small bite? Please? You'll get my special performance tonight if you let me."

"NO."

Lulu gave Marsha's group one last wistful look, then sighed and lowered her head. "Okay, then. As you wish. But why are they here?"

It was the Scion who answered. "MY... MY FATHER IS TRYING TO CONVINCE ME TO JOIN THEIR CAUSE."

"Oh?" Lulu eyed the group with new interest (not the kind of interest accompanied with potatoes and gravy this time). "And what cause is that?"

"There's a new evil up in the north," Marsha said. She wasn't sure what to make of this Lulu. The woman kept saying strange things, things that made absolutely no sense but managed to unnerve Marsha anyway. Images of black cook pots and aromatic spices filled her thoughts. She shook her head to clear it.

"And you need this cute little critter to defeat it?" Lulu asked, smiling at the Scion. "It can't be very scary, this evil of yours."

"IT IS SCARY," the Raven God said, still sounding a bit grumpy. "SCARIER THAN ANYTHING YOU COULD EVER IMAGINE. IT HAS SEIZED THE POWER OF SEVERAL WORLDS. IT MUST BE STOPPED."

Lulu frowned. "I thought your old enemy was defeated."

"SHE WAS. THIS WOMAN HERE, MARSHA, ALONG WITH A COUPLE OF OTHER PEOPLE, BROUGHT THE BUG GODDESS DOWN. BUT AN EVEN GREATER THREAT HAS ARISEN NOW, ONE NOT EVEN I HAD EXPECTED."

"The eagles said it was one of the Bug Goddess's old servants," Marsha said. "We tried to figure out who, but the only one we could think of was that Telu chieftain who disappeared a while back. I don't remember her name."

"BATHORA," the Raven God said, the name sounding dark and ominous as he spoke it. "YES, THIS NEW THREAT IS NONE OTHER THAN BATHORA, FORMER CHIEFTAIN OF THE TELU TRIBE, WHICH USED TO SERVE THE BUG GODDESS."

"What?!" Lulu's cry was so loud and sharp it made Marsha jump. "Have you become delirious? Bathora is dead. She died right over there when the stone giant crashed through the wall." She pointed to the large hole in the wall and the rubble on the floor in front of it.

"SHE DIED, YES," said the Raven God. "BUT SOMEONE BROUGHT HER BACK. SHE ROAMED THIS WORLD AS A GHOST FOR A SHORT TIME, UNTIL SHE FOUND A WAY TO REGAIN HER PHYSICAL FORM. SHE'S BECOME A GODDESS NOW – A DARK, VICIOUS CREATURE WITH NOTHING BUT MURDER ON HER MIND."

For the first time Marsha saw fear on Lulu's face. "You mean she's coming here? To kill me?"

"SHE MIGHT, EVENTUALLY. BUT HER PRIMARY GOAL IS TO GET BACK AT THOSE WHO KILLED HER OLD PEOPLE, ESPECIALLY THE ONES RESPONSIBLE FOR THE DEATH OF HER LOVER, A MAN NAMED WINSTON."

"Winston?" Marsha's voice sounded strange in her own ears as she spoke the name. "But that means…"

"YES," the Raven God said. "IT MEANS SHE'LL COME FOR THE HIPPO CULT. FOR YOU AND YOUR FRIENDS, LADY MARSHA."

Marsha was halfway back to the tunnel leading out into the outside world before she realized she'd moved.

"I must warn them," she said, fear making her voice shrill. "Gemma, Amanda… they don't know they're in danger."

"HOLD!" The Raven God's voice was so strong and commanding Marsha obeyed it without thinking. "THERE'S NOTHING YOU CAN DO ON YOUR OWN. COME BACK HERE AND WE'LL TALK."

"But…" Marsha's head swung back and forth, her wide-eyed stare shifting between the exit and the stone statue.

"THERE IS STILL TIME," the Raven God said. "NOT MUCH, BUT HOPEFULLY ENOUGH FOR US TO DEVELOP SOME KIND OF STRATEGY. EVERYTHING DEPENDS ON MY SON'S DECISION, THOUGH."

Marsha's eyes fell on the Scion. The winged hippo was still hovering in mid-air, its head turned away from her and the other humans.

"Please," she whispered. "Come with us. Help us save my people."

The Scion was silent for a long time. When it finally spoke it sounded tired, as if it had known decades of hardship instead of barely more than a year of what Marsha considered to be fairly comfortable life.

"WHY DOES EVERYTHING HAVE TO REVOLVE AROUND ME? CAN'T YOU JUST DEAL WITH THIS EVIL BEING ON YOUR OWN?"

"MY SON," the Raven God said gravely. "YOU WERE MEANT FOR GREAT THINGS. WE WAITED FOR THOUSANDS OF YEARS, ME AND YOUR OTHER FATHER. YOU WILL WIN BACK OUR FORMER GLORY."

"BUT I DON'T WANT IT! ALL I WANT IS TO BE LEFT ALONE!"

"Oh, how wonderful," Kylee muttered. "Wise, all-powerful gods yelling at each other like small children. Next they'll accuse each other of stealing the other's toys."

"SHUT UP!" the Scion and Raven God snapped in perfect unison.

"The God of the Iridescent Cantaloupe would never refuse to help His people when they were in need," Jennibal said, directing a disapproving look at the Scion.

"YOUR MADE-UP GOD CAN SHOVE A WATER MELON UP HIS FAT, MADE-UP ARSE," growled the Scion, giving the young woman an angry glare.

"A red-hot iron rod would be more painful," Kylee murmured, her large, deep eyes vacant for a moment. Then she blinked and glanced around, looking slightly confused.

"THE HUMANS CAN'T FACE THE CREATUER BATHORA HAS BECOME ON THEIR OWN," the Raven God said. "NOT ONLY DOES SHE POSSESS TERRIBLE POWERS – SHE ALSO HAS ALLIES AMONG ORDINARY HUMANS, FIERCE FIGHTERS THIRSTY FOR BLOOD."

"BUT WHAT CAN I DO AGAINST SUCH TERRIBLE ENEMIES?" the Scion asked. "I DON'T HAVE THE POWER YOU AND THE HIPPO GOD WIELDED BACK IN THE OLD WAR."

"YOU'RE THE PRODUCT OF A UNION BETWEEN MYSELF AND THE HIPPO GOD," the Raven God said. "BOTH BIRDS AND HIPPOS WILL FOLLOW YOUR COMMANDS. YOU'LL HAVE AN ARMY AT YOUR BACK."

"That's what I said!" Bazer exclaimed.

Marsha could feel the Raven God's attention shift to the ugly little man. The light in the statue's ruby eyes didn't change, but the sensation of skepticism in the air was unmistakable.

"YEAH, RIGHT," the Raven God said. "CLAIMING TO BE SOME GREAT PRODIGY, ARE YOU? I DOUBT YOUR BRAIN IS ADVANCED ENOUGH TO COMPREHEND WHY YOU GET SOAKED WHEN YOU PISS INTO THE WIND. SHUT UP NOW AND LEAVE THE THINKING TO THOSE WHO KNOW HOW ITS DONE."

"Actually," Marsha put in. "He did come up with the idea of putting together an army of hippos on our way here."

"DID HE NOW?" If the Raven God's statue could move it would have rubbed its chin right now. "I DO SENSE A STRANGE KIND OF POTENTIAL IN YOU, NOW THAT I LOOK MORE CLOSELY. IT'S VERY SMALL AND UTTERLY TWISTED, BUT IT'S DEFINITELY THERE. WHAT'S IN THAT NOTE BOOK YOU'RE SO DEVOTED TO?"

Bringing out the book once more, Bazer walked over to the statue and began talking in a low but excited voice, flipping through the pages now and then to show the Raven God one of his weird diagrams or tables. A few times Marsha became aware that the Raven God asked questions, but the words seemed to be directed at Bazer alone. Shaking her head at the weirdness of men – human or divine – she turned back to the Scion.

"We need you," she said. "Me and my people did everything we could to protect you while you were in that egg. Will you help us now, when we face death and destruction?"

Once again the Scion was silent, a searching look in its black eyes as it regarded Marsha. The other three humans were silent, knowing that what came next would decide the fate of hundreds, maybe thousands of people.

"I MIGHT HAVE BEEN WRONG ABOUT YOU," the Scion finally said. "YOU DON'T DO THIS TO GAIN POWER FOR YOURSELF. ONLY OUR ENEMIES THIRST FOR POWER. MY FATHER WAS RIGHT."

Sudden hope kindled in Marsha's heart. "So you'll fight for us?" she asked.

"I WILL. BUT ONLY THIS ONCE. AFTER THIS IS DONE I'LL DO WHATEVER I WANT AGAIN."

"That's all right," Marsha said, smiling as a warm sensation spread through her body. "We won't ask any more of you."

"I'll come too," said Lulu. She stood with her feet firmly planted, hands on her hips and a determined expression on her face.

Marsha gave the woman a skeptical look. "You? Why would you want that? This isn't your fight."

"It most definitely is! I have some unfinished business with this Bathora person. I won't be able to rest while I know she's out there somewhere. Dark goddess or not, she's still a fat-arsed bitch and I'm going to claw her eyes out."

"What do you think?" Marsha asked, eyeing her two companions (Bazer was still speaking to the Raven God, giving him details on what made a woman a nine rather than an eight).

Kylee shrugged. "I see no reason why we shouldn't allow her to come. Like you said, we'll need all the allies we can get."

"I said that?" Marsha searched through her memories, but so much had happened the past few weeks she had trouble telling everything apart.

"Well, someone did," Kylee said. "Doesn't really matter if it was you or not."

"All right. Jennibal?"

The other woman produced a very cute smile. "As long as she doesn't eat us."

Marsha frowned. "Why would she eat us?"

"You haven't figured it out?"

"Figured what out?"

Jennibal was about to speak again, but the Raven God's booming voice interrupted her.

"WHAT'S GOING ON HERE?"

"I'm going with these nice people," Lulu said, giving the statue a defiant look.

"THE HELL YOU ARE! YOU ENTERED MY SERVICE FREELY. YOU CAN'T LEAVE UNTIL I TELL YOU TO."

"I can and I will!" Lulu snapped. "I've served you long enough. This place is boring, and the food sucks. You'll have to find someone else to provide entertainment."

"BUT I JUST LEARNED THIS WONDERFUL WAY OF RATING WOMEN..."

"I won't spend the rest of my life being rated by a lecherous old god who doesn't even know how to clap his hands properly!"

"THAT'S BECAUSE RAVENS HAVE WINGS, NOT HANDS..."

"I don't care!" Lulu's face was bright red from anger, and her fists were clenched so tightly they were going white. "I'm leaving, and if you're not okay with that you can take it up with my *real* god."

A sudden light appeared in Jennibal's eyes. "Would that be the God of the Iridescent Cantaloupe?"

Lulu scowled at her. "What? Of course not. I hate fruit and vegetables. I'll never eat any of that again."

"What will you eat, then?" Kylee asked.

Lulu turned her sharp gaze at the statue of the Raven God. "Right now I might consider some poultry..."

"OH, FINE," the Raven God said with a dejected sigh. "OFF WITH YOU, THEN. I'LL JUST SPEND THE NEXT FEW MILLENIA IN BLISSFUL SOLITUDE, WITH NOTHING TO LOOK AT BUT THESE LOVELY STONE WALLS."

"Sulkypants!" Lulu shot back at him. Kylee sniggered.

A short time later Marsha found herself back beneath the open sky. The sun was setting, painting the western horizon in shades of scarlet and gold. The Scion's four hippo guards had just joined them, the large animals snorting and growling as they watched the humans.

"Which way will take us to your people, Marsha?" Jennibal asked.

"East and a little south," Marsha said. "But I don't think we're heading that way now."

"Oh? Why not?"

Marsha nodded toward the Scion, who was perched on a low cliff. "We must gather that army of hippos first. The land between here and my home is mostly too dry for them. We should find a wet region."

"North, then," Lulu said. "I used to live in the swamplands. There were plenty of hippos around there."

"North it is, then," Marsha said, punctuating the statement with a firm nod. For the first time in weeks she felt like she was on the right path. Before long they'd be facing the most powerful and evil creature who ever existed, but at least they had the Scion with them, and soon they'd have an army of big, strong animals at their command. Things could have been worse.

She just hoped they'd reach her friends in time.

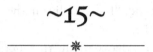

~15~

—————— ❋ ——————

"Little minds are tamed and subdued by misfortune; but great minds rise above them."

- Washington Irving

Kat had never worshipped any gods or goddesses .This wasn't because she didn't believe they existed – she was actually very open-minded about most things in life, religion included. No, the reason for her lack of reverence was that she found it impossible to worship a being who hadn't been able to defeat her in combat, and as no divine creatures had ever walked up to her and challenged her to a fight she remained firmly undevoted.

So, naturally, finding herself in the service of a goddess made her a bit queasy.

She guessed she should have expected this when she joined forces with Bathora. Her big mistake, she realized now, was that she'd never taken the lily-livered ghost seriously. Back then, Bathora had seemed like a complete airhead with an ego as large as her ass, her plans for taking over the world (or whatever her ultimate goal was) sounding more than a little ridiculous. It turned out Kat had misjudged the woman completely. She hated it when she misjudged people.

When Bathora had said they were journeying north to find a place where she'd come into her power, Kat had thought they'd find some magic object or other that would allow the ghost to fire small bolts of lightning at people, enough to kill a few and frighten the rest but not much more. She'd thought she'd be the one to do most of the killing – a deal she was completely fine with – while Bathora produced menacing one-liners and acted like a fool in general. She'd been wrong there as well. She hated it when she was wrong.

But most of all she hated not knowing if she could defeat the creature her employer had turned into. The displays of power Bathora had supplied so far had been quite fearsome, but had also been too few for Kat to perform a real evaluation of the woman's abilities.

"Not even sure she counts as a woman anymore," she muttered to herself where she sat in the high grass, honing her blade with the whetstone she'd got from the armory at North Pharq.

"Huh?" The necromancer, Little Black Bird, looked up from the bowl of multi-legged animals she was eating. One of them didn't seem completely dead.

"Oh, nothing," Kat said. "Just wondering exactly what our employer has turned into."

Birdie shot an uneasy glance across the meadow, to where Bathora's dark, hulking shape stood. Ever since the new Bathora had emerged from that evil-looking mountain up north the humans had kept their distance, avoiding the creature's attention as best they could.

"I know," she said. "I liked her better as a ghost, and I didn't like her much back then. Sometimes I wish we'd never signed up for this."

"We need her," Kat said. "Without her I won't be able to bring down the usurper Clogz, and you said yourself that the only times you've managed any actual necromancy was when Bathora was involved. Without her you'd be back to poking at gerbils."

The necromancer frowned down at her bowl of (as she saw it) food. "Yeah, but at least there'd be cookies."

"What about him?" Kat asked, pointing at where Ogian sat by himself, halfway between Bathora and the rest of them. None of the humans wanted to go near him either.

Birdie shifted her gaze from her food to the former member of the Elephant People. Her frown remained unchanged.

"What about him?" she asked.

"Do you think he's, you know, lost his humanity as well? Is he like *her* now? What exactly can he do, other than cheat more convincingly at Yahtzee?"

The necromancer was silent for a long while. Kat almost wondered if she'd fallen asleep, like Demon Viq tended to do whenever she wasn't doing anything. She'd almost dozed off herself when Birdie spoke.

"I don't know," she said. "Something did happen to him inside that mountain. He gained some powers, but I don't know if it was enough to change him into something other than human. I wouldn't trust him, though. You know what they say about cheaters?"

Kat shook her head. "No. What do they say?"

"How would I know? I was asking you."

Letting her thumb slide along the sharp edge of her blade, Kat gave Ogian another look. The man didn't look all that threatening. Most of all he looked confused. She guessed it must be quite the readjustment for someone who'd been so utterly worthless his entire life to suddenly become something more. Kat herself had always been awesome, so she'd never needed to adjust.

"Watch out, here she comes," Birdie said.

Kat felt the faint tremble in the ground even before she turned to see Bathora's hulking form come towards them. She clutched the hilt of her sword more tightly, her muscles tensing. Even in broad daylight the monstrous shape seemed to radiate darkness and destruction.

"IT'S TIME TO GO," said the booming voice. "GET THE OTHERS TOGETHER."

"Where are we going?" Kat asked, rising to her feet.

"WELL, LET'S SAY IT'S TIME FOR A LITTLE WARM-UP. A QUIET DRINK BEFORE THE REAL PARTY BEGINS. SOME INNOCENT FOREPLAY. YOU GET THE IDEA."

Kat wasn't sure she did, but she wasn't about to admit that. Instead she nodded. "I'll get the others."

They kept the same course they'd done the past two days – east and a little south – as the sun climbed towards its noon peak. Most of them kept quiet, casting uneasy glances at the dark apparition Bathora had become. No amount of time spent around her seemed to diminish their fear. Ogian walked at Bathora's side, looking straight ahead with no expression on his face.

"This hippo Cult you mean to destroy," Kat said as they passed a flock of grazing zebras. "What did they do? I mean, they must be guilty of some terrible crime."

For a moment she thought Bathora would lash out at her, incinerating her or turning her to dust, but the anger and hatred in her shadowy face was directed elsewhere. When she spoke her voice was a low rumble, like thunder rolling between the mountains.

"THEY DESTROYED MY PEOPLE, ALL SAVE THOSE WHO DISAVOWED THEIR OLD LOYALTIES AND TURNED TRAITOR. BUT THEIR MOST DIRE CRIME WAS TO MURDER SOMEONE I CARED A LOT ABOUT. THAT'S WHAT THEY'LL PAY FOR."

"Ah, that sure sucks," Kat said. "It's almost as bad as what Clogz and his lackeys did with my old tribe. I'm so happy you'll give us the chance to get back at them."

Bathora seemed to think for a while. "VICIOUS LOT, CLOGZ AND HIS FOLLOWING, EH?"

"Yup, nastiest bunch I ever knew." Kat ground her teeth together at the memory of being locked inside the cage, of Clogz's self-satisfied smirk when he told her the way he planned to rid himself of her. She hated him so much. The only thing that kept her from screaming her fury was the knowledge that he, and all his cronies, would soon be dead.

"WHAT ABOUT THE REST OF YOUR TRIBE?" Bathora asked. "WILL THEY RISE UP AGAINST CLOGZ'S GROUP ONCE THE FIGHTING BEGINS?"

Kat frowned. "I don't think so. Clogz has gathered all the ruthless ones to him. The rest are too weak to resist. They wouldn't stand a chance."

"INTERESTING." Again, the rumbling voice took on a thoughtful tone. "THEY DO SOUND A BIT SIMILAR TO MY OLD TRIBE. SURE THEY AREN'T RELATED?"

"I thought you said the Hippo Cult were the nasty ones," Kat said.

"OF COURSE, OF COURSE. DID I SAY SOMETHING ELSE? I MEANT THEY REMINDED ME OF THE HIPPO CULT. JUST AS NASTY. MUST BE DESTROYED."

"Good." The moment that word left Kat's lips she felt it didn't belong there, not this close to the demonic creature walking next to her. Shaking her head, she let the sentiment go. Who cared if she'd allied herself with an evil goddess as long as she'd get back at the usurper and his lackeys? Didn't people say the means justifies the method? She frowned again. No, that wasn't what they said, whoever *they* were. But it was something along those lines.

She was still lost in her own thoughts when Bathora's booming voice made all of them jump.

"WELL, HERE WE ARE."

Kat looked around. A few hundred yards ahead of them lay a small village – perhaps twenty huts in a tight cluster. She could see people moving between them, looking like small ants at this distance.

"Looks like a nice place," Leoma said. "Wil we be stopping for lunch here?"

"Lunch!" Kel Hell exclaimed. "The word's like music in my ears. I didn't realize how hungry I was before you said it."

"LUNCH WILL HAVE TO WAIT," Bathora said. "THERE'S SOMETHING ELSE YOU HAVE TO DO HERE FIRST."

"Oh?" Kat said. "Are we going to enlist these people?"

"NO. YOU'RE GOING TO KILL THEM."

The whole company fell silent. For a long time there was no sound, save for the faint rustle of wind through the grass. When someone finally spoke it was Spud, known for his limited vocabulary, who found the word everyone was thinking.

"Why?"

"WHY?" When Bathora spoke that same word it sounded more like a death sentence. "BECAUSE I SAY SO, OF COURSE. YOU NEED NO OTHER REASON THAN THAT."

"But they haven't done us anything!" Birdie exclaimed.

"NEITHER HAD THOSE PEOPLE IN THE VILLAGE BY THE LAKE. I DIDN'T SEE ANY SIGNS OF REMORSE IN YOU AFTER YOU SLAUGHTERED THEM."

"That was different," Kat said, chewing her lower lip. "Those two villages were at war with each other, more or less. One side hired us to fight for them, and we did."

"They were also a nasty bunch," Kel Hell added. "One of them called me a fat cow. That was the last thing he ever said."

The dark, hulking shape took a step toward Kat, who forced herself to stand her ground and not flinch back.

"AND NOW I'VE HIRED YOU," Bathora boomed. "YOU DO AS I SAY, OR I WON'T HELP YOU GET BACK AT THOSE WHO TOOK OVER YOUR OLD TRIBE."

Kat gritted her teeth. This woman – or whatever it was she'd become – had the nerve to *blackmail* her! It didn't matter how powerful she was – no one blackmailed the leader of Kat's Deathsquad. At least not if they wanted to be around to see the next sunrise.

But she knew Bathora had outmaneuvered her. Kat needed the lily-livered bitch if she was to have her revenge. Getting back at Clogz was more important than the lives of a handful of weaklings. She'd kill the people in that stupid village, even if it left a sour taste in her mouth.

"Fine," she mumbled. "We'll do it."

"NO!" The cry came from Leoma. The girl's face was red with anger, tears brimming in her blue eyes. "This is evil! Weewee, you mustn't do this!"

With a growl that made the air itself tremble, Bathora reached out one massive arm. A bolt of white-hot fire shot out, straight towards Leoma. At the last moment Weewee managed to pull her out of the way, the two of them stumbling to the side, eyes wide with fear.

"I DON'T KNOW WHY I STILL KEEP YOU ABOUT," Bathora roared. "YOU'VE SERVED YOUR PURPOSE. I HAVE NO FURTHER USE OF YOU, PATHETIC EXCUSES FOR NECROMANCERS."

"They stay," Kat said firmly. "Harm any of them and you'll regret it."

Bathora's eyes were like blazing fires when she fixed them on Kat. "ARE YOU THREATENING ME, LITTLE MERCENARY?"

"I don't make threats," Kat said, meeting the terrible gaze. "Only promises."

Bathora contemplated this for a while, then nodded. "ALL RIGHT, THEN. PROMISES ARE FINE. IF YOU'D THREATENED ME I'D HAVE SQUISHED YOU INTO A BLURBER, WITH YOUR BLOOD AS KETCHUP. I'M NOT SURE WHAT I'D USE AS TOMATOES – PERHAPS I COULD SLICE UP YOUR KIDNEYS OR SOMETHING. ANYWAY, WHERE WAS I?"

"Er, you sent us to kill the people in the village," Kat said.

"WHAT VILLAGE?"

Kat reached out her arm and pointed tentatively at the small settlement to the south-east. "That one."

The dark apparition looked at the village as if seeing it for the first time. "AH, RIGHT. THIS GODHOOD THING GETS CONFUSING AT TIMES. THERE ARE SO MANY THINGS I KNOW I SOMETIMES CAN'T TELL MY OWN THOUGHTS APART FROM WHAT'S GOING ON IN OTHER PLACES. ANYWAY, GO KILL THOSE PEOPLE SO WE CAN MOVE ON."

"What do you want me to do?" Ogian asked. "I don't have a sword, and I wouldn't know how to use it if I had one."

"YOU DON'T NEED A SWORD, YOU IDIOT!" Bathora snapped. "USE YOUR POWER. PUT SOME HUTS ON FIRE. MAKE THE GROUND ERUPT BENEATH THEIR FEET. BE *SCARY!*"

Ogian gave the village a hesitant look. "I could make grimaces at them..."

"GO!" Bathora roared, and this time even Kat obeyed without thinking. She ran towards the village, the other members of her Deathsquad following close behind. When they reached the first huts she stopped and gave the place a closer look. Everything seemed utterly peaceful. The few people who'd noticed the arrival of the newcomers stood placidly, watching them with kind, unafraid eyes.

"Where is your chieftain?" Kat demanded. "I want to talk to him."

A smiling, round-faced man came walking towards them. He looked to be in his late forties, with thin lines creasing his face and an almost bald head. His clothes were simple but looked well-made.

"I'm the chieftain of this village," he said, offering Kat's company a slight bow. "What can I do for you."

"We're going to kill you," Kat said. "I want you to make resistance."

The only reaction she received was a raised eyebrow. "Why?" the chieftain asked.

"Because it'd make me feel better, you lily-livered fool! Go get your weapons now!"

Still smiling, the chieftain tilted his head to one side, as if studying the behavior of an interesting animal.

"We don't have any weapons," he said.

"What?" Kat gave the man an incredulous look. "How do you defend yourselves, then?"

"We don't. We prefer to meet hatred and violence with love."

Kat stared at the man as if he'd just said he breathed tar instead of air. "With love? How the hell does that work?"

"We believe that the reason people become violent and hateful is because they haven't received enough love. So all we have to do to turn them away from that dark path and back into the light is give them the love they need."

"I'm surprised you're still alive," Kat muttered to herself, then addressed the chieftain once more. "So you mean you won't resist if we attack you?"

The chieftain shook his head. "We'll open our hearts and receive you with love. We don't believe in negative or destructive thoughts."

Kat sighed. "Fine, then. You do that. Don't say I didn't warn you, though."

When all the villagers were dead Kat spent some time looking at the smoldering remains of the huts. That goat-brained Ogian fellow had slowly but steadily warmed to the task of Harbinger, screaming "Yahtzee!" at the top of his lungs as he pointed his hands at each hut in turn, causing them to burst into flame. None of the villagers had raised a hand against them, making their task easy from a practical point of view but much harder emotionally. The other members of her Deathsquad appeared sullen as well, walking by themselves or standing in silence, looking down at the ground.

"WONDERFUL, WONDERFUL," came the voice Kat had begun to dislike very much. Bathora's monstrous shape lumbered towards her, her fiery red maw open in a terrible grin.

"How did I do, mistress?" Ogian asked, looking like a child expecting praise for managing to tie his shoe laces.

"WELL ENOUGH, DEAR. FULL HOUSE, TO SPEAK YAHTZEE LANGUAGE. THE FAT WOMAN SENDS HER COMPLIMENTS." She emitted a repulsive, bubbling chuckle.

"What do we do now?" Kat asked.

Bathora shrugged her massive shoulders. "THE NECROMANCERS SAID THEY DIDN'T WANT TO EXAMINE THE CORPSES, SO I GUESS WE MOVE ON. OUR NEXT TARGET WILL BE THE HULLABALOO TRIBE."

For a few moments Kat stared blankly at the dark abomination, then she recalled that the Hullabaloo tribe was the name of her old people. She'd spent so long thinking of herself and her companions as *Kat's Deathsquad* that she'd almost forgotten who she'd been before. Whenever she'd thought of her own home she'd only pictured the hated Clogz and what she wanted to do to him when she returned.

"Oh, great," she said. "We'll have to find Demon Viq an iron rod, then."

It took them a couple more days to reach their destination. They passed east of the Vale of Uzureth, continued south and east for another two days, and finally approached Kat's old village from the north. Standing on a low hill, Kat remembered the last time she'd gazed upon her own home. It felt so long ago, as if the memories belonged to another person from another time. She shook the thoughts away, focusing entirely on her long-awaited revenge.

"Are you and Ogian going to strike first?" she asked Bathora. "To wreak some of that death and destruction you spoke of?"

Bathora's massive shape loomed over her, reminding her of a black watch tower where she stood atop the hill. The dark goddess's face lay hidden in shadow, making it impossible for Kat to make out any expression.

"NOT YET," she said, her voice a low, deep rumble. "LET'S GIVE THEM A CHANCE TO EXPLAIN THEMSELVES FIRST. YOU KNOW, CONFESSING THEIR CRIMES AND SUCH BEFORE WE SEND THEM TO THE ETERNAL REST."

Kat frowned up at the inhuman face. "You want to *talk* to them? That won't work. Believe me, I've tried."

"WE'LL SEE," Bathora mused. "OH, YES. WE'LL SEE."

Kat felt her mood darken as Bathora gave Ogian instructions. He was to proceed along with the humans while Bathora herself followed at some distance. Kat had no idea what the lily-livered monstrosity had in mind, but she suspected she wouldn't like it. Why give Clogz and his followers a chance to prepare themselves when the most logical thing would be to strike, hard and brutal, while their enemies were still unaware of them?

Once within shouting distance of the village's northern edge they stopped. Some of the villagers had noticed their approach and were eyeing them uneasily. Ogian stepped forth and shouted in a loud voice.

"I am Ogian, Harbinger of the Goddess Bathora. We mean you no harm. Let the one named Clogz come to us, so we may discuss our intentions with him."

The villagers scurried away, vanishing between the long rows of huts. Kat saw a few familiar faces among them, although the expressions they held were different from what she was used to – wary, skittish, as if afraid to make one wrong move. Apparently the atmosphere in the village had changed along with its government.

A short time later she saw a group of men come towards them. At their head was Clogz, and with him a strong force of warriors, probably the strongest and most ruthless ones he'd been able to find. Kat's fingers tightened around the hilt of her sword when she saw the man who'd had the nerve to lock her up in a cage. And then she saw something that made her almost as furious.

Behind the warriors came a group of ordinary, unarmed villagers, dragging the carcass of the lion Kat had released before escaping the village. The dead animal showed signs of rot in many places, and flies buzzed around it. Judging by the grimaces on the men's faces it must have given off quite the stench, too.

"So you've returned," Clogz said, offering Kat a very unbecoming sneer.

"I have," Kat said coldly. "And I see you don't have enough sense to bury the dead. I can't say I'm surprised."

Clogz waved a hand in the direction of the lion carcass. "I just wanted to show you how we dealt with your little pet. It didn't cause the damage you intended. Nor will you and your little band of outlaws."

Beside her, Bog muttered a curse. Spud and Weewee merely looked at Clogz, their faces dark with anger. Ogian shuffled his feet, then spoke slowly and carefully, as if afraid he wouldn't get the phrasing right.

"A new time is coming," he began. "A new power is rising. I am its Harbinger."

"That's very impressive," said Clogz, his tone implying that he wasn't at all impressed. "So what do you want from us?"

"Well, most of all I'd like to play Yahtzee..." Ogian said, then cleared his throat. "But that'll have to wait until later. We've come to discuss your part in this new order."

"And what order would that be? What is this new power you're speaking of?"

"UM, THAT'D BE ME."

Kat almost jumped out of her skin when she heard Bathora's voice right behind her. The foul creature must've used some uncanny power to sneak up on them unnoticed. By the look of astonishment on Clogz's face she figured he'd been as startled as she.

"I..." Clogz began, for once unable to find a snide comment. "I can't say I've seen anything like that before."

Bathora produced that gut-wrenching chuckle again. "PEOPLE USED TO SAY THAT WHEN I WAS ALIVE TOO, BUT THEN THEY WERE USUALLY REFERRING TO MY BUM. SOMETIMES I MISS THOSE GOOD OLD DAYS, EVEN IF I WAS DUMBER THAN A BAG OF HAMMERS BACK THEN. OH WELL, THAT'S ALL IN THE PAST NOW."

The new chieftain of the Hullabaloo tribe digested this for a few moments before deciding to dismiss it all as irrelevant. "Who are you?" he asked instead.

"BATHORA, AT YOUR SERVICE, MUCH ESTEEMED USURPER. OR I EXPECT YOU'RE THE ONE WHO'LL BE AT MY SERVICE, IF YOU POSSESS THE LEAST BIT OF SELF-PRESERVATION INSTINCT. I HEAR YOU'RE A VERY RUTHLESS MAN."

"I, um, I guess so," Clogz managed.

"GOOD. I HAVE A BUSINESS PROPOSAL FOR YOU. WOULD YOU LIKE TO HEAR IT?"

"I do."

"FINE. EXCELLENT. THIS IS HOW IT GOES. I'M ABOUT TO CONQUER THE WORLD, AND I'LL NEED PEOPLE TO FIGHT FOR ME. THE ONES I HAVE DIDN'T TURN OUT AS WELL AS I HOPED. WOULD YOU AND YOUR TRIBE LIKE TO JOIN FORCES WITH ME?"

"What?" Kat exclaimed, turning her gaze – and with it the full force of her wrath – from Clogz to Bathora. "You treacherous, goat-kissing, slug-brained, wart-infested…"

"SILENCE!" Bathora thundered, then addressed Clogz again. "THERE'LL BE RICHES AND POWER FAR BEYOND ANYTHING YOU CAN IMAGINE, AS LONG AS YOU'RE PREPARED TO DO WHATEVER I TELL YOU. DO WE HAVE A DEAL?"

Kat felt frustration rise within her as a wide smile spread across Clogz's face. She hated that expression, hated the man, hated Bathora, but most of all she hated that she'd been deceived and had been played for a lily-livered fool. And she was beginning to suspect she and her friends were In terrible danger.

"We do," Clogz said. "I'll be happy to serve you. What will your first command be?"

Kat didn't have to look at Bathora's bestial face to know it displayed a self-satisfied smirk. The tone in the booming voice was enough.

"KILL THESE HUMANS."

Kat had her sword out before Bathora had finished the sentence. The other members of her Deathsquad followed an instant later. Weewee placed himself protectively in front of Leoma, his own weapon flashing in the sunlight.

"Get the necromancers away from here!" Kat shouted. "We can't keep them safe and fight Clogz's men at the same time. There are simply too many of them."

"I'm staying with Weewee!" Leoma insisted. "I'm not going anywhere without him!"

Kat wanted to punch the stubborn wench, but right them the fastest and boldest of Clogz's spear fighters fell upon them and she had to focus all her attention on holding them off. Her sword slashed and cut at arms and chests while she used the spear in her left hand to parry the thrusts aimed at her. For a moment her opponents drew back, unused to this new way of fighting, but then they regrouped and came at her from both left and right and Kat had to retreat a few steps.

Beside her Bog and Spud fought back to back, fending off half a dozen of Clogz's men. Two lay dead at their feet but more kept coming – it looked like Clogz had had more men ready just out of sight and now threw them into the fray to increase his advantage in numbers even more. Kat cut down one of her opponents, and for the briefest instant the ground lay open between her and Clogz, standing by himself some fifteen yards away. She dashed towards him but only made it a few steps before someone whacked her across the shoulders and she stumbled to the side. By the time she regained her balance she was completely surrounded by grim-looking warriors.

"Dung-brained swine!" she growled, preparing to fight till her last breath. She might never get her revenge, but at least she could take some of these lily-livered traitors with her into the grave.

She was just about to hurl herself at the nearest opponent when a blood-curdling roar came from somewhere behind Clogz's warriors. Shouts of alarm followed, a few turning to shrieks of sheer terror. The warriors surrounding Kat hesitated, heads turning to see what had caused the commotion. Kat followed their gazes, and what she saw made even her staunch heart race faster.

The dead lion, left on the ground when the fighting began, was now standing on its four legs, its massive head thrust forward, sharp fangs bared. Its rage was clearly directed at Clogz's men, the ones who'd been responsible for its death.

"It's alive!" someone hollered.

No, Kat thought. *Not alive.* She'd seen the animal's eyes as it turned its head in her direction. They were dead eyes, with no light or emotion in them. The lion's movements were also off – stiff and jerky, as if reluctant to obey the commands they were given.

She looked behind her, and there was the necromancer Little Black Bird, standing with her arms held high, a look of fierce determination on her face. For an instant their eyes met, and the young woman gave Kat an almost imperceptible nod. The tiny gesture was all Kat needed.

"Come!" she shouted at her companions. "We must get out of here while they're distracted."

Two men were blocking her path, both staring open-mouthed at the ghastly form of the zombie lion as it sprang clumsily at another terrified warrior. Kat ran her sword through the gut of the one to her left. He didn't even appear to notice it. Kat was past him and away from the rest of Clogz's fighters before he'd hit the ground.

"Stay close to me!" she shouted, forgetting that none of the others - least of all Kel Hell – was able to match her speed. She sprinted across the flat, grass-covered ground, thinking that if they only got far enough away they'd find freedom and...

A huge shape appeared right in front of her. Kat skidded to a halt, almost tearing her ACL in the process. Bathora's dark form loomed over her, looking as furious as a thousand storm clouds on a really bad day. She pointed a finger like a black spear at Kat.

"YOU'RE OUT OF THE TRIBE!" she roared. "SUCH INSOLENT BEHAVIOR CAN'T BE ACCEPTED! I'VE NEVER SEEN ANYTHING LIKE IT! I'VE THROWN PEOPLE LIKE YOU OUT BEFORE, NEVER THINK I HAVEN'T. SOME WEREN'T EVEN IN THE TRIBE TO BEGIN WITH. GET OUT, OR I'LL CALL SECURITY!"

Kat knew she should be afraid, but all she could feel right then was blazing hatred for the creature who'd betrayed her, who'd left her to die at the hands of her most reviled enemies. She stood her ground, raising her sword in a gesture of defiance.

"I'll kill you, you rat-faced, lily-livered cow!" she spat. "Goddess or no, I'll strike you down! You've known me as Kat until now, but from this moment on you can refer to me as Death."

"OH MY," Bathora said, a hint of amusement in her booming voice. "AREN'T YOU A FEISTY LITTLE THING? FINE, THEN. IF YOU WON'T RUN, THEN YOU WILL DIE."

She held out both of her massive arms, and a torrent of destructive power shot out from them, straight towards Kat. Too late, Kat realized what a mistake it'd been to challenge a creature of such immense power to a fight. Now she'd die, as certainly as if one of Clogz's warriors had impaled her on his spear, and there'd be no one left to stand against the enemy.

But the crackling burst of power never hit her, or perhaps it hit her without causing any harm. All Kat felt was an electric tingle and a stab of intense cold against the skin of her chest. The thick lance of power rebounded, shooting back towards Bathora. The goddess only managed a startled yelp before the full force of the blast struck her, flinging her back at least twenty feet. The ground shook with the impact of her landing.

Kat stood panting, unable to make sense of what had just happened. The cold sensation on her chest lingered, and after a few moments she reached inside her tunic and pulled out the amulet she'd got from Aandu, the chieftain of North Pharq. She'd completely forgotten about it. Now she recalled the words Aandu had spoken, words she'd dismissed as superstitious gibberish back then.

It protects you from magic and other divine powers. We never had much use for it here.

"No, but I found a use for it," Kat mumbled to herself. "Protection against divine powers, eh? I bet the fat-arsed bitch never saw that one coming."

The sound of running feet made her swing around, the amulet still clutched tightly in one hand, but it was only her companions finally catching up to her. All looked unhurt, except for a few scratches here and there. Little Black Bird looked pale and exhausted, leaning on Demon Viq for support.

"Nice job with the lion," Kat said, grinning at the necromancer.

Birdie looked back over her shoulder. There was still chaos among Clogz's men, even if the lion had stopped moving. It'd be a while before their leader got them back together.

"That's what they get for trying to outlaw cookies," the necromancer said, touching her forehead with one hand and grimacing as if in pain. Demon Viq put an arm around the other woman's shoulders to steady her.

"It was Bathora who wanted to outlaw cookies," Spud said.

"We know, Spud," Kat said. "No need for a clarification."

The bald man gave her a puzzled frown. "Who's Claire?"

"I'll tell you later," Kat said. "Right now we need to get as far away from here as we can."

Kel Hell pointed at Bathora's motionless body, lying on its back like a monstrous insect. Thin wisps of smoke rose from the dark, massive form.

"What are we going to do with her?"

Kat shrugged. "We must leave her here. She's too heavy to carry with us."

The large necromancer gave her an incredulous look. "I wasn't talking about taking her with us. I meant, are we going to finish her off while she's out?"

"That would be the coward's way," Kat said. "If I'm going to kill her I want to offer her a fair fight."

"But..."

"Watch out!" Weewee called out. "Here comes Ogian."

The former latrine digger of the Elephant people came scampering across the field, huffing and puffing. Apparently fitness wasn't among the powers Bathora had granted him. Despite his harmless appearance Kat felt her muscles tense. She had seen what this man could do, and she was the only one with a magic amulet to protect her.

"What do you want, Ogian?" she demanded when he was a couple of yards away.

"I came to check on Mistress Bathora," Ogian said, panting heavily. "What have you done to her?"

"She's only having a nap," Demon Viq said. "All the excitement today wearied her out."

Ogian gave Bathora's motionless form a quick glance, then nodded. "Ah, ok. No need to worry then, right?"

"Right," Kat said. "But I think you should remain here and keep an eye on her. You know, in case something dangerous shows up."

A look of worry came over Ogian's face. "Something dangerous? You mean like that lion? Do you think it'll come after us?"

"You never know," Kat said. "But I'm sure you could handle it if that happened."

"I guess," Ogian said. "Everything was so confusing back then. Why was everyone fighting?"

"You'll have to ask Bathora that when she wakes up," Kat said. "We must be off now."

"Off?" Ogian gave her a querulous look. "Where are you going?"

"Um..." Kat couldn't think of any explanation the imbecile might find feasible. Fortunately, Demon Viq came to her aid again.

"We're going to fetch dinner," she said. "Aren't you hungry?"

Ogian spent some time searching for the correct answer to this question. In the end he merely shrugged.

"Well, we are," Kel Hell said. "We'll be back soon. And who knows, we might even join you for a game of Yahtzee."

The stupid man's face lit up like a beacon. "Really?"

"Really. Just remain here and try to stay out of trouble."

Kat cleared her throat. She'd noticed that Bathora was beginning to stir where she lay. It wouldn't be long before the foul creature was back on her feet, probably even more furious than before.

"Let's get moving," she said, setting out at a brisk walk. "There isn't a decent blurber place within a dozen miles of here."

"For which we are so very grateful," Birdie mumbled, giving Bathora's huge form one last scowl before following Kat.

~16~

———— ✳ ————

I have often wondered if there's anyone above the age of twelve who likes snow.

Lots of people claim they do, yes, but I'm far from certain they actually *like* the snow.

Hm, perhaps I put the wrong word in italics. Does it become more clear what I mean if I say I'm far from certain they actually like *the snow*?

All right, I'll try to clarify. The most common reason people have for liking snow is that "it brightens things up". Some closer investigation shows that they only find this pleasant when they're in a car or inside their house. No one's ever said they enjoy trudging around in the snow, getting wet and cold and bringing a shitload of water and salt into their living quarters. So is it really accurate for these people to claim they like snow?

Traffic is another example of something that doesn't harmonize well with snow. I have a friend who once uttered that "I hope there'll be a lot of snow this winter". Everyone else present looked at him as if he were an utter fool until it struck me that he was the only one who worked within walking distance from his home. It would've been a bit worrying if someone had seriously considered it a good thing to be forced to spend three times as much time getting to work and back each day for an entire season.

People also argue that snow is good because children have a lot of fun playing in it. That's true enough, but do these people ever give a thought to all the elderly men and women who break their arms and legs each time the streets are filled with snow and ice? Probably not.

Marsha had never seen snow, so she wasn't able to establish whether she liked it or not. Judging by her personality, she would most likely have found it impractical and cumbersome. Also, being used to a much higher level of temperature, she'd assuredly find winter in the northern parts of the world highly unpleasant.

Something she knew she didn't like, though, was mud.

As a person used to sitting on the ground she'd received some very unpleasant surprises upon entering the swamplands. Mud was wet and cold, and seeped into places Marsha didn't want things seeping into. It had taken her two whole days to get out of her old habit of sitting down on the ground whenever she wanted some rest, and by then it felt like she had mud *everywhere*.

Walking through the soggy terrain was also both tiring and treacherous. Even with Lulu as a guide there'd been several occasions when a member of their company had been close to drowning. Marsha still shivered when she remembered the time she'd sank all the way to her neck in the foul-smelling muck.

Lulu, yes. It had come as a shock to Marsha when she eventually learned the woman was a cannibal. It appeared everyone else had known for quite some time by then – even Bazer, who generally was a bit slow on the uptake. Marsha guessed the concept of cannibalism was so alien to her she had trouble picking up the signs. No one had ended up in Lulu's belly so far, though, and it turned out she'd once been a good friend of Marqamil of the Raven Cult, a man much respected among Marsha's people.

Bazer had spent some time sulking after the Raven God refused to grant him the power to see through people's clothing. Kylee had tried to comfort him, explaining that there wouldn't be much point in rating women's beauty if you could see through their clothes every time you looked at them. They'd all receive the same score over and over again, she said. Bazer had remained in a foul mood until the beautiful woman exposed a little more of her luscious body than she usually did. After that the ugly little man had looked like he wouldn't need food or water for at least a week.

A loud roar made her jerk upright and almost fall off the rock she was sitting on. It had only been one of the hippos, of course. Even after this many days Marsha hadn't been able to get accustomed to the ear-splitting sounds the formidable animals let out at regular intervals. The farts they released as often were almost as loud.

They'd gathered two dozen of the huge animals since coming to the swamplands. The Scion claimed he could control many more of them than that, but a strange sense of urgency had begun creeping up on Marsha, reminding her of how she'd felt last year when she was returning home with the Elephant people. She knew they couldn't stay here much longer, that her people needed her.

The hippo who'd roared lumbered over to where Bazer sat and glared intently at him. After a while the young man started to cringe and gave Kylee, who was sitting on a boulder a few feet away, a pleading look.

"Why is it looking at me like that?" he asked.

Kylee shrugged, causing her blouse to stretch tightly across her ample bosom. "It's probably trying to figure out which species you belong to. It took me a while to figure that out, and I'm infinitely much smarter than a hippo. Don't expect it to move away any time soon."

The hippo grunted, gave Bazer a quick sniff and headed back to the nearest mud puddle, where it joined a few of its hippopotamine comrades. The splashing sounds, which had become a natural part of the background noise, grew louder for a few moments before returning to its normal level.

"Looks like those beasts aren't as slow as you thought, love," Bazer said.

Kylee snorted. "Must've been your body odor that drove it away. Those large nostrils must be a curse when in your company."

"Want to continue the game?" Jennibal asked. She was sitting on a low tree stump, her shapely legs stretched out in front of her. "It's not like we have anything else to do while we wait for the Scion to return."

"Sure," Kylee said. "It was your turn."

"Right." Jennibal thought for a few moments. "Each of you describe the other with a word beginning with the letter G."

"Gorgeous," Bazer said immediately.

"Grotesque," Kylee replied an instant later.

Jennibal laughed and clapped her hands. "Well done! You go, Bazer."

"Okay," said the young man. "Name something that turns you on and begins with the letter B."

"Nice try," Kylee said.

"Belly buttons," said Jennibal.

There was an awkward silence. Kylee suddenly became very engrossed in the milkweed plant growing by her feet. Above them an eagle screeched.

"What?" Jennibal asked, glancing from one to the other with a bewildered expression.

"That's not the kind of information you want Bazer to possess," Kylee muttered.

"Oh? Why not?"

"Because, you know, he's *Bazer*."

"Ah." Sudden comprehension showed on Jennibal's face, followed by a very cute blush. "Well, not all belly buttons qualify, of course. His, for example, is a massive turnoff."

Bazer, who'd grabbed the garment covering his upper body and begun pulling it up, froze and shot Jennibal a resentful look.

"You've never seen my belly button," he pointed out.

"No, and I'd prefer for it to stay that way. The images in my head are more than enough."

The three of them continued their bickering for a while longer, but Marsha stopped listening. An uneasy feeling had come over her, one she couldn't really come to terms with. It felt almost like a predator was stalking her which, of course, was totally absurd.

Something sniffed her right behind her ear, making her jump to her feet with a startled yelp. Her feet slid on the slippery mud, her arms flailing wildly before she managed to regain her balance.

"Oh, sorry," came Lulu's voice behind her. "Didn't mean to frighten you."

Marsha glared at the cannibal woman. "You shouldn't sneak up on people like that, then. And most of all not *sniff* them."

"Sorry," Lulu said again, looking as if she meant it. "Old habits die hard, I suppose, and I haven't had anything to eat all day. I guess my instincts took over for a little while."

"Better get something to eat before they take over completely," Marsha said.

Lulu smiled at her. "Great idea. Care to join me?"

"Er, no, thanks," Marsha said, hurriedly taking a few steps away from the cannibal woman. "I need to relieve myself. Back in a few minutes."

Her need to urinate had only been moderately pressing, but she found it a bit frightening when Lulu got into what the others called her big-black-kettle mood (whatever the hell that was supposed to mean), and felt she had to get away for a while. It wasn't that she expected the cannibal woman to start gnawing at her, more like a desire to escape unwanted attention. Going away to relieve herself had been the only excuse she'd been able to think of.

Marsha's feet splashed as she made her way towards a dense grove of swamp trees. Walking in mud was actually very pleasant, she decided. It kept your feet cool and had a soothing effect on your soles. The tickling sensation as she rubbed her wet, muddy toes together was almost enough to make her giggle.

Mist began swirling around her feet as she reached a patch of dry ground and continued in among the trees. She glanced around to make sure that pervert Bazer hadn't followed her, then squatted down to take care of her business. The mist felt cool and damp against her skin, almost unnaturally so.

When she stood up she noticed that she was completely surrounded by milky whiteness. She frowned, trying to remember which way she'd come from. All she'd normally have to do was follow the loud noises the hippos made, but she found to her dismay she couldn't hear anything at all. The thick fog seemed to drown out all the natural sounds, except...

Marsha tilted her head to one side and listened. There was a strange sound coming from somewhere ahead of her – an eerie keening unlike anything she'd ever heard before. Was it one of her friends singing? It didn't sound like any of them, but it was the only sound she could make out, so she started walking towards it.

Walking through the impenetrable mist felt like wading through muddy water. She had to step carefully, unable to see where she put her feet. Fortunately, the ground appeared both dry and even, with short grass and moss cushioning her steps. The keening grew louder, pulling her towards it with invisible fingers.

Without warning, Marsha stepped out of the mist and found herself back beneath the open, overcast sky. Empty wasteland lay before her as far as the eye could see. Behind her rose a thick wall of grey-white mist, perfectly straight as if hewn from stone. It made Marsha think of old tales she'd heard long ago, of barriers between two worlds, like between the world of the living and the dead.

Is that it? She asked herself. *Have I accidentally entered the world of the dead? And if that's the case, how do I get back?*

The strange, mournful sound still filled the air. Marsha looked around, trying to locate its source. Her gaze fell on a large boulder about ten yards away. Atop it crouched a small shape, its clothing blending into the surrounding landscape so perfectly she hadn't noticed it the first time she looked in that direction. She took a few hesitant steps toward it, and the creature slowly turned to face her, the keening stopping as its familiar eyes found hers.

"Pebe?" Marsha was so startled by the unexpected encounter she stopped in mid-stride and simply gawked.

"Hello, Marsha," Pebe said. "It's good to see you again."

"But..." She brushed a hand across her eyes, wondering if this was a mirage of some sort, but Pebe's form remained as solid as before. "What are you doing here? Where's Tiwi and the other Elephant People?"

Pebe looked thoughtful for a few moments. His voice sounded odd when he finally replied, as if he was describing things he saw with his inner eye.

"She had other things to do. I came alone, looking for you. They said you needed my help."

"They did?" Marsha's joy at seeing her old friend was slowly turning to confusion. This wasn't Pebe's usual way of speaking. Had he changed so much in the year he'd spent with the Elephant People?

Pebe nodded, slowly rising to his feet. "Yes. I have something you require if you're going to succeed in this. Will you come and get it?" He gave her an expectant look.

Something in his eyes made Marsha take a step back. "I...," she began. "I don't think..."

"No worries," Pebe said. "I'll come for you instead. Just remain where you are."

He walked slowly towards her, and as he moved his form changed, until it was no longer human but lizard-like, with scales and claws where there'd been skin and fingers before. The elongated jaw opened wide, so very wide, exposing rows of sharp teeth.

Marsha couldn't move. Either it was dread holding her in place, or this creature used some power to compel her. Incoherent thoughts raced through her mind – the bitter irony of getting away from a hungry cannibal woman only to be eaten by this horrifying creature, sadness at never getting to see her friends again, worry that the rescue operation would fail now that she wouldn't be there to oversee it.

The creature's jaws seemed to fill the entire world. It was close enough for her to smell its rotten breath. Soon the jaws would snap shut and there'd be no more Marsha...

A blast of something searingly hot shot past Marsha's left ear. The creature who'd been about to devour her burst into flame, screeching in agony as the fire consumed its flesh. Marsha stumbled back, the intense heat burning her skin. The sickening smell of burning meat and hair filled her nostrils.

Something slammed into her from behind, throwing her face down into the mud. She tried to get up, but whoever had attacked her pushed her head down into the cold wetness. Muddy water filled Marsha's mouth and nose, choking her. She tried to scream, but there was no air left in her lungs. She was drowning.

And then her head was above the surface again. She sputtered and coughed, spitting out what felt like gallons of thick, muddy water. Gasping, she finally managed to get some air back into her aching lungs.

"There you go, Marsha. Take a few deep breaths. You'll be fine."

Marsha realized the one who'd tried to drown her was sitting on her back. Strangely, that was also where the voice that had spoken came from, and it was the voice of someone she knew.

"Jennibal?" she gasped. "What are you doing?"

The pressure on her back vanished and she heard soft splashes as the girl moved around to squat in front of her.

"I'm sorry, Marsha. Your hair was on fire. That's why I doused you like that. Are you doing okay?"

Marsha allowed her friend to help her back to her feet, then wiped mud and some kind of slimy plant from her face. "Yeah," she said. "I'm all right. What happened?"

Jennibal glanced down at the smoldering remains of the creature that had assumed Pebe's form. "That thing almost had you, If the Scion hadn't returned when it did we might not have made it here in time."

"The Scion?" Marsha looked around until she found the winged hippo, hovering about two meters above the ground off to her left. "It was you who killed it?"

The strange creature gave the smallest of nods, its small, black eyes fixed on Marsha.

"So you can breathe fire now?"

"IT APPEARS SO, YES."

Marsha scratched the back of her head. "You never said anything about that."

"I DIDN'T KNOW IT UNTIL NOW. IT SORT OF JUST HAPPENED."

"An ability like that might prove useful in the fighting to come."

The Scion's mouth twisted into a disapproving sneer. "I'D RATHER NOT DO IT AGAIN. IT TAKES A LOT OUT OF ME, AND THE AFTERTASTE IS REALLY DREADFUL."

Marsha nodded slowly. "I see. Thank you for saving my life, though. I really appreciate it."

"PLEASURE'S ALL MINE. BUT PLEASE TRY TO BE MORE CAREFUL THE NEXT TIME YOU NEED TO PEE."

"I'll try." Marsha became aware that there were three large hippos behind the Scion. Neither one looked familiar. "New recruits?" she asked.

"YES. THERE ARE A FEW MORE BACK AT THE CAMP. I THINK THESE WILL BE THE LAST ONES, THOUGH."

"Yes." Marsha nodded her agreement. "I had this feeling earlier today. Like something telling me we were in a hurry."

"I KNOW," said the Scion. "I FELT IT TOO. WE SHOULD MOVE ON AT ONCE."

Marsha had to ride back to their camp on the back of one of the hippos. It was a very uncomfortable experience, but her legs had felt too shaky after her incident with the shape-shifting creature for her to trust them to carry her back across the treacherous ground. Once back among the rest of her companions she sank down on the muddy ground, for once not caring about the unpleasant seeping.

"A scorched lizard, you say?" Lulu's forehead creased in thought. "That doesn't sound too bad. Kinda exotic. Are you sure we can't stay while I head over for a quick bite?"

"I'm afraid not," Marsha said. "We'll be off as soon as the Scion gets the hippos together."

"Ah, that's a shame. Let's hope we find something nice and juicy on the road, then."

Not wanting to think about what the cannibal woman thought of as *nice and juicy*, Marsha turned to look to her left, where Kylee and Bazer were preparing themselves for the next stage of the journey. At the moment the beautiful woman appeared to pick lice from her lover's hair, giving him sharp reprimands about personal hygiene as she worked.

"They're so cute together," Jennibal said, smiling as she watched Kylee pinch the ugly little man's ear so hard he cried out.

"Were you, um, romantically involved with someone in your old village?" Marsha asked.

Jennibal gave her a look as if she'd been asked if she ate rocks for breakfast. "Of course not. My heart belongs to the God of the Iridescent Cantaloupe and none other. It's still sweet to watch other people in love, though."

"I see," Marsha said, not seeing at all what the girl meant. "Well, here comes the Scion. Time to leave this place."

They spent the rest of that day marching through the wilderness, their course due east and a little south. After a couple of hours they reached a broad river, its muddy brown water flowing slowly towards the south like a huge amount of spilt gruel.

"We'll have to build a raft of some sort," Marsha said. "Some of us can't swim."

Lulu had suddenly gone pale as a sheet (a light brown sheet, to be sure, but there doesn't seem to be an alternative expression for people with more pigmented skin so I'll stick with the usual one).

"I-I'm not sure I can manage that," she stammered.

Kylee emitted one of her patented snorts. "What's the matter, cannibal chick? Afraid of deep water?"

"No," Lulu said. "It's just that the last time I went down this river on a raft I almost got eaten by some nasty mud creature. It happened right after that Bathora woman destroyed my old village. Not one of my best days, that one."

"Well, we have to get across somehow," Marsha said. "I'm sure there won't be any mud monsters attacking us this time."

Actually, the very same mudman which had attacked Lulu on that fateful day was at the present lurking near the river's opposite shore. Fortunately for the humans, one of the hippos stepped on it after swimming across, squishing it into a loose mass of goo unable to cause any harm for several hours. By the time it had repaired its body the company had safely paddled across and were gathered on the eastern side.

"Let's make camp here," Marsha decided, watching the dark forms of the eagles silhouetted against the setting sun. "No point stumbling through the dark."

The Scion made a quick survey of the land from above, proclaiming the place free from danger upon his return. The hippos swam and wrestled in the turbid water while the humans prepared a late supper. Marsha didn't eat much, unable as she was to get the stench of the burning lizard-creature out of her nostrils. It was deep into the night before she managed any sleep, and dark dreams kept disturbing her rest. When dawn came she felt like she'd had no sleep at all.

That day took them across the vast plains of the savannah, with small patches of jungle in a few places. At one point they passed a large pile of dung that Marsha took as a sign that either the Elephant People or her friend Emkei had passed through here not long ago. Jennibal gave the fly-covered pile a frown, muttering something about the Orb of Life not being needed in this neighborhood.

The following day was much the same, except that they passed no dung heaps. In the evening they came to a large lake with a single island in its center. None of them knew it, but this was the island inhabited by the peaceful broccolis, where Amanda had landed after the volcano had tossed her across half the continent. The broccolis were still waiting for the visit she'd promised them.

They'd just made camp by the lake's southern shore when the Scion came whizzing across the water at high speed.

"THERE ARE PEOPLE COMING THIS WAY!" The voice in Marsha's head sounded excited, almost breathless.

"People?" Marsha stood up and glanced around. "Where?"

"FROM THE NORTH-EAST. THEY'LL BE VISIBLE TO YOU SOON."

The eagles, who'd been perching in the nearby trees or soaring majestically above the lake, had suddenly become restless. Wings flapped and screeches filled the air. Marsha glanced up with a puzzled frown, then turned back to the winged hippo.

"Do they look dangerous?" she asked.

The Scion shook its head. "THE EAGLES SAY THEY'LL BECOME OUR ALLIES, THAT THEY'LL HAVE AN IMPORTANT PART TO PLAY IN THE BATTLE TO COME."

"Yes," Kylee said thoughtfully, a look of intense concentration on her beautiful face. "They mentioned this the first time I talked to them. The pieces are falling together."

"But who are they?" Marsha said, still not fully convinced the newcomers would be friendly.

"WE'LL SEE," the Scion said. "IT WON'T BE LONG NOW."

Sure enough, a few minutes later Marsha saw a group of people come into view, rounding the lake's south-eastern corner and continuing towards them. Some of them looked like soldiers; the rest seemed to be ordinary young women. One of them was large, albeit not nearly as big as Emkei. When they reached Marsha and her companions one of the soldiers – a fierce-looking young woman – stepped forth and nodded in greeting.

"Hello," she said. "I'm Kat, leader of Kat's Deathsquad. And who might you be? A travelling menagerie of some sort?"

"Er, no," Marsha said. "I'm Marsha of the Hippo Cult. The others, well, it's a bit complicated."

Bazer had moved up beside her, scribbling furiously in his notebook while giving the female newcomers searching looks. Kat eyed him curiously.

"Hey, what's wrong with your face?" she asked.

Kylee stifled a burst of laughter behind one hand. "It's always been like that," she explained.

"Really?" Kat raised an eyebrow. "I'm surprised no one's shot him by accident yet, thinking him a... a..."

"A mix of a half-digested frog and a monkey whose face got stuck in a meat grinder?" Kylee supplied.

"Yes! Exactly!" Kat nodded her approval of the description, then she caught sight of the Scion for the first time. "And what the hell is that thing?"

"Um, that's the Scion," Marsha said. "It's a divine creature who can breathe fire."

For some inconceivable reason that made Kat smile. "Is that so?" she mused. "I advise you never to try that stuff on me. You might get a very unpleasant surprise."

Marsha eyed the woman more closely. She wasn't tall but looked strongly built, armed with an unfamiliar weapon that looked like a very large knife as well as with a short, fine-looking spear with a sharp metal point. It was obvious that she knew how to handle herself in a fight, but Marsha had no idea why she'd claim to be resilient to fire. Perhaps she was only good at boasting, like her friend Pebe or Tiwi of the Elephant People.

An awkward silence had fallen over the two groups of humans. Marsha exchanged a look with Kylee before turning back to Kat.

"Anyway," she said. "It appears we have a common enemy. Have you heard of a woman named Bathora?"

Kat's eyes narrowed at the mentioning of the name. "Heard of her?" she spat. "I *served* the lily-livered trollop for a time. We all did. Biggest mistake I ever made."

As Kat's eyes narrowed, Marsha's widened. "You mean you've met her? Since she came back from the dead?"

"Uh huh." Kat nodded. "She was a ghost at first. That wasn't too bad. But then she and Ogian went into that mountain, and when she came back out she'd become something else. A kind of dark goddess. That's when I really started hating her."

"Ogian?!" This time Marsha's mouth dropped open. "Kinda dumb fellow? Cheats at Yahtzee?"

"That's the one," Kat said. "He was the first to ally himself with the Bathora woman. She calls him her Harbinger. He got some powers too, back in that foul mountain. Still as dumb as before, though."

Marsha stood there, looking like an utter fool while she struggled to digest this new information. Ogian was Bathora's chief servant? Kind, gentle, utterly brainless Ogian, a man she'd travelled with for weeks and whom she'd believed unable to hurt a fly. Well, unless it beat him at Yahtzee, of course.

Something else Kat had said caught her attention. "You said you used to serve her. What made you leave?"

"The fat-arsed cow betrayed us," Kat said, poking holes in the ground with the butt of her spear. "She promised us we'd get back at the ones who took over our old village, but once we got there she allied herself with the usurpers instead. We barely made it out of there alive."

"So you're all from the same place?" Marsha asked, eyeing Kat's motley company. They didn't really look much alike.

Kat shook her head. "Only me, Bog, Spud and Weewee came from the Hullabaloo tribe." She pointed at each of the three men in turn. The one named Weewee was kissing one of the young women – a pretty little thing she imagined Bazer would give at least a nine on his twisted scale.

"And who are the others?" she asked.

"They're necromancers," Kat said. "We've been travelling together for some time now. This is Little Black Bird, their leader. The others are Demon Viq, Kel Hell and Loony Leoma."

"Lethal Leoma," the girl corrected her, taking a short break from her kissing session.

"Right, Lethal Leoma. We've been travelling at high speed since escaping from Bathora. Before we met you... what's the matter, Birdie?"

The necromancer called Little Black Bird was staring up at the cloud of eagles above them. "I dreamed about this," she murmured. "Before we came to North Pharq. We have to help these people, Kat. It's important."

"If you say so," Kat said, winking at Marsha as if to apologize for the other woman's odd behavior. "But let's get to know them a little better first. What tribe did you say you belonged to?"

"The Khadal tribe," Marsha said. "It's become part of the Hippo Cult now. That's where I'm from, at least. The others, well, they're from all over the place."

"The Hippo Cult!" the one called Demon Viq exclaimed. She was a pale, dark-haired woman with a mad glint in her eyes. "That's the one Bathora said she'd destroy. This really is too much of a coincidence to be, well, a coincidence."

"Who's this Quincy you accuse of being dense?" said the short, bald man Kat had called Spud. He didn't appear to be very smart.

"Never mind that, Spudman," said Demon Viq, patting him gently on the shoulder. "Go fix us something to eat while we take care of the important stuff."

"Okay," Spud said. He bent down and started rummaging through his pack. Marsha suddenly realized she was rather hungry. It had to be a product of all this excitement.

"We are on our way back to help my people," she said, turning back to Kat. "Will you join our forces?"

Kat gave Marsha's company a dubious look. "You do realize Bathora has over a hundred warriors at her command, right?" she said. "Plus her own and Ogian's powers. I'm sorry, but you lot don't look like you'd be much use in a fight. What did you plan to contribute with?"

"The Scion can control the minds of those hippos," Marsha said, pointing towards the lake where the large animals were splashing about and rolling around, emitting roars of delight. "They'll be a powerful force. And then we have the eagles, and the Scion himself, of course."

"I see." Kat scratched her chin thoughtfully. "We might actually have a chance then. A small one, but a chance nonetheless. At least things look better than they did an hour ago."

"And here comes the food!" came Spud's gruff voice from behind Kat.

"Great!" Kat said, grinning at Marsha as Spud handed her a large, green fruit. "Just stay away from anything the necromancers eat," she cautioned. "They eat things most people wouldn't even touch."

"I'll remember that," Marsha said, starting to peel her fruit. It both looked and smelled very pleasant.

"Thanks," Jennibal said as she received a large, light-grey fruit. "What is this?"

"It's a cantaloupe," Spud said.

Jennibal's eyes widened, and Marsha watched in amazement as the girl dropped to her knees, bowing her head low while holding the fruit as if it were the Orb of Life or something.

"You're the God of the Iridescent Cantaloupe!" she exclaimed, her voice trembling with reverence. "I am your humble servant. Lead, and I will follow."

The bald man gave her a blank look. "Huh?"

"Long story," Kylee said, grinning at the stunned expression on Spud's face. "But I have a feeling you might get laid at some point in the near future."

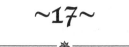

~17~

———— ✳ ————

"Deep into that darkness peering, long I stood there, wondering, fearing, doubting, dreaming dreams no mortal ever dared to dream before."

- Edgar Allan Poe

Ogian was having a nightmare. It wasn't the kind of nightmare he normally experienced, which usually involved him being in a large crowd and suddenly realizing he was naked. Nor was it the kind of nightmare where someone's chasing you and you can only move your limbs in slow-motion. No, this nightmare had eagles in it. Lots of eagles.

He was walking through an unfamiliar landscape, searching for something he couldn't remember but knew he had to find. The world around him was eerily silent, at least until he heard the flapping of wings above. Before he could look up an eagle landed atop his head, causing him to yelp with surprise. He tried to shake it off, but all that earned him was a splash of bird droppings on the back of his head. The eagle screeched into his ear, the sound so loud and sharp it was physically painful.

Another eagle appeared, this one flying straight into his face, sharp beak tearing at his skin. Ogian screamed, waving his arms furiously to get rid of the obnoxious bird, but suddenly there were many more of them, so many he could see nothing but feathers and beaks and talons. When he opened his mouth to scream again he found his mouth full of slick feathers. He spat them out, but immediately found his mouth full again.

I never should have drunk that potion, he thought, then wondered why such a strange thought had entered his mind.

"THE POWER!" came another voice, one he recognized but couldn't place. "USE YOUR POWER!"

What power? his thoughts screamed in his head. *I just dig latrine pits. I don't have any power.*

"YOU'RE THE HARBINGER, YOU FOOL! TOAST THOSE BLOODY FOWL!"

Ogian remembered then. He'd gone into that mountain, and when he came out again he'd become something else, something more than he'd been before. There was power inside him, power he could use to destroy things. A person with such powers didn't need to fear a flock of stupid birds.

He lashed out with his power, completely at random. Loud explosions echoed around him, sending clouds of feathers in all directions. The eagles screeched. Then they were gone.

When his vision cleared Ogian found that he was no longer in that unfamiliar place. Instead he stood in a dark room, or perhaps it was a large cavern. In the distance was a bright, unnatural light. Against it he could see the outline of three men.

"Kharuba?" Ogian asked, squinting against the brightness. "Bunta-koop, Xylophonidas? What are you doing here?"

"We're disappointed in you, Ogian," Kharuba said.

"In me? Why's that?"

"You've cheated at Yahtzee."

Ogian frowned. "I've always done that. You've never complained before. Why now?"

"You used to do honest cheating," Bunta-koop said. "Not anymore. What you're doing now isn't fair play. We can't accept it."

"I don't need your acceptance!" Ogian snapped, feeling the anger rise within him. "I'm the Harbinger now. I can do whatever I want!"

"No one will play with you," said Xylophonidas. "Never again."

Ogian opened his mouth to retort, but his friends were suddenly gone. Where they'd stood loomed two massive shapes. Both had human bodies, if larger than any human Ogian had ever seen, but their heads belonged to animals. The one to the right had the head of a hippo, the other one that of an elephant. Ogian couldn't make out their features, but he could feel a strong sense of disapproval radiating from them.

"Who... who are you?" he stammered.

"You know who we are," said the elephant-headed creature.

And Ogian did. He'd seen the statue of the Hippo God several times while he and the other members of the Elephant People stayed by the temple in the jungle. No one save the gargling woman had ever seen the Elephant

God, but even someone with Ogian's limited intelligence could identify the other creature. Suddenly sweat broke out all over his body, his knees becoming unsteady.

"What do you want from me?" he demanded.

"You've become one of my people's enemies," the Hippo God said. "I'm displeased."

"And why would I care?" Ogian snapped. "You're no god of mine. I don't have to listen to you."

"Would you say the same about me?" asked the Elephant God, its voice deep and calm, with a hint of sadness in it. "Am I no longer your god?"

"I..." Ogian hesitated. Was he still a member of the Elephant People? Bathora had never made it clear if he belonged to her now, or if he was some kind of freelancer. "I'm the Harbinger," he finally said. "That's all that matters."

The Elephant God sighed. "I'd hoped it hadn't gone this far," It said. "What you're doing now, son, it's wrong. You've become an instrument of the most evil power the world's ever seen. Nothing but grief and suffering will come from this."

"That's not true!" Ogian shouted. "I *am* something now! Before this I was nothing but a laughing stock. Now I'm *important!*"

"You're deluding yourself," said the Hippo God. "No one thinks you're important, not even the one you serve. She's only using you to get what she wants."

"I don't care!" The anger had made Ogian's voice shrill. "I'm the best Yahtzee player who ever lived! *No one can beat me!*"

"I could."

Ogian blinked. The two massive shapes were gone, in their place a diminutive female shape. Her voice was vaguely familiar, like an echo from times long past.

"Who are you?" Ogian managed. "Where did you come from?"

"Don't you remember me?" the woman asked. "We've met before."

Ogian strained his poorly functioning brain so hard his head began to hurt. It was as if there was something there, only just outside his reach, memories and feelings he wanted to touch, to bring back into his conscience. But every time he reached for them they were gone, dissolved into nothingness.

"No," he said. "I don't remember you."

The woman was silent for a while. When she spoke again there was such sadness in her voice it almost made Ogian weep.

"I thought I meant more than that to you," she said. "But it appears I was wrong."

"Tell me your name," Ogian said. "Maybe I'll remember then."

The woman shook her head. "There's no use. The person who cared about me is gone. The creature you've become will hurt my people, hurt the ones I love most. I will leave you now."

"No!" Ogian didn't know why, but he wanted desperately for this woman, whoever she was, to stay with him a while longer. Only she could answer the questions he had, only she could tell him what he should do.

But she was gone.

And a moment later Ogian was awake again.

At first he couldn't remember where he was. This was nothing unusual – as someone who'd spent his entire life travelling it happened more often than not, but during his time with the Elephant People he'd always known whom he'd see when he opened his eyes in the morning. These past few weeks had involved so many new acquaintances, causing different faces to pass through his mind, but as the last vestiges of the dream left him he recalled that he was with Bathora and the Hullabaloo tribe, on his way to destroy their enemies.

He got up from his sleeping blankets and ducked out of his tent. Only he, Bathora and the chieftain Clogz were allowed to sleep in tents – the rest of the warriors spent their nights beneath the open sky. As he stood there, still in a foul mood after the strange dream, he wondered once again at their numbers. The camp was huge, larger than any settlement he'd seen before coming to the Hullabaloo tribe a couple of days ago.

As always in the morning, he needed to relieve himself, and perhaps take a dump as well. He started walking through the camp, passing Paer the tomato guard and the others in charge of their supplies. Ogian didn't like Paer – the man was a pig just like his father, a nasty old man to whom Bathora had assigned the task of making blurbers. The only time Ogian had tried one of the man's abominable creations he'd spent the rest of the evening puking his guts out. That hadn't improved his opinion of the man in the least.

Some of the warriors shied back when he walked past them. That made him feel a little better. He might not be a twelve-foot goddess like Bathora, but he was the Harbinger and they should show him proper respect. Even so, there was an unpleasant sensation nagging at the edge of his mind, telling him that he'd cheated his way to this position and should feel nothing but shame. The voice was faint but persistent, refusing to go away no matter how hard he tried.

One good thing their visit to that strange mountain had brought with it was that Bathora could no longer sneak up on him the way she'd done as a ghost. Also, if he focused hard, Ogian could tell if one of the humans was approaching. This meant he could take a dump without fear of being discovered, giving him a wonderful sense of freedom and control over his own life.

When he'd finished his business he returned to camp. The warriors were already preparing for the day's march, loading their possessions onto the simple carts they used for transport. Paer inspected the huge pile of tomatoes he was in charge of, occasionally picking one out and giving it a closer look. The man really was a jerk.

Bathora had been a bit grumpy ever since the incident outside the Hullabaloo tribe's old village. Ogian didn't really understand what had happened there — it appeared Kat and the others they'd travelled with had suddenly decided to turn on them. Kat had even attacked Bathora and somehow managed to knock her unconscious. Bathora had been very vague during her explanation of how that had happened, as well as with the reason behind Kat's betrayal.

Another thing he didn't understand was that all the members of the Hullabaloo tribe seemed to hate Kat and her companions with a passion. The reason for their hatred was unclear, but Ogian thought it originated from some old conflict he knew nothing about. He wondered if Bathora had known about this enmity when she decided to recruit Clogz and his people. Someone as smart as her should have known there'd be trouble. But these things were probably too complicated for someone like him to understand.

That day's march passed as in a daze for Ogian. Thoughts didn't race through his mind — a more accurate description would be that they crawled like a sloth on very strong sedatives — but for someone like Ogian that was enough to keep him fully occupied for hours on end. The sensation that there was something important he ought to remember was stronger than ever, like an itch on the back of his head that wouldn't go away. And then there was the image of his old friends looking at him with disapproval in their dark eyes. What had he ever done to deserve that?

"That's one hell of a gloomy look, Harbinger."

Ogian jerked back to awareness. Clogz, the Hullabaloo chieftain, had walked up beside him and was now regarding him curiously. Ogian managed a weak smile.

"Just thinking," he said. "Um, where are we?"

"A few hours south-west of where we were this morning," Clogz said. "Has Bathora told you where we're heading?"

Ogian shook his head. "She doesn't talk much these days. It was nicer back when she was a ghost. We had a lot of nice talks then."

"I can guess." The chieftain's gaze grew sharper. "Tell me, how did she become the way she is now? I've never seen anything like it before."

"That's what she keeps saying," Ogian murmured.

Clogz raised an eyebrow. "What?"

"Never mind." Ogian put one hand into his pocket to make sure the dice were still there. Their touch always gave him comfort. "We went into this mountain," he said. "There was a barrier of flashing lights. Bathora went into it, and then she pulled me through as well."

"That's fascinating. What was it like in there?"

Ogian shrugged. "I don't remember, really. The light was blinding, and my whole body tingled. I don't know how long it lasted."

"And when you came back out you had some kind of power?" Clogz asked.

"Yes. I can throw a Yahtzee any time I want now. And I can make things explode."

The look in the chieftain's eyes reminded Ogian of a hungry animal. His voice sounded strange when he spoke, as if he'd been without water for days.

"When this is over, do you think you could show me that place?" he asked.

Ogian smiled at him. "Sure. It was very far north, but I think I could find it again. We could ask Bathora..."

"No!" The man's outcry was so sharp it made Ogian jump. "Don't tell her. It'd be better if it was only the two of us. Like you said, she hasn't been very friendly of late."

"That's true," Ogian said. "I wonder if it has anything to do with the blurbers."

Clogz gave him a puzzled frown. "The what?"

"Oh, nothing. I'm sure that nasty old man will get them right eventually."

That evening they made camp at the base of a small mountain range. Ogian was on his way to fetch his dinner when he spotted Bathora standing outside the camp, looking like a huge, black boulder in the fading light. She was staring at the mountains as if their dark slopes held images only she could see. Ogian hesitated a moment, then cautiously walked up to her.

"What are you looking at, Mistress?" he asked.

"WE'RE GETTING CLOSE NOW," Bathora said without turning her gaze away from the mountains.

Ogian looked in the same direction as the dark goddess but saw nothing out of the ordinary. "Closer to what? There are only those mountains over there."

"YOU'LL SEE," Bathora said, her voice the soft rumble of a herd of buffalo trotting across the savannah. "TOMORROW YOU'LL SEE."

She said nothing else, so after a while Ogian left her there and went in search for something decent to eat. He stayed well away from the foul stuff Paer and his father were making, instead heading for a group of men who appeared to be preparing a nice-smelling stew.

One of them, a man named Utoto or something, looked up when Ogian approached. "Oh, look, it's the Whoremonger. Going to join us, are you?"

"Yes," Ogian said, wondering if the man had trouble pronouncing difficult words. "Your food smells good. Want to play some Yahtzee while we wait for it to finish boiling?"

"No Yahtzee tonight," said Ahlan, a sour-faced man with a fading scar on his forehead. "It ruins my appetite."

The third man, a quiet fellow named Loord, put aside the spear he'd been sharpening. "I quite like Yahtzee," he said. "We can play a game or two before we eat."

Ogian's face brightened. "That's great! Is it okay if I begin?"

The other man nodded. He had a round face with even rounder eyes and short, stubby hair with a bit of red in it. Ogian had never heard him speak more than a few words before, but found that he was good company if a bit stuck in his own world. He threw the dice, smiling slyly as he made them show a moderately good result.

"Oh, my," he said. "This doesn't look good. I'll keep the two fours and hope for better luck next."

He rolled the dice twice more, making a third four appear along with a five and a six. "Three of a kind!" he announced. "That's twenty-five points for me."

"Twenty-three," said Loord.

Ogian pretended to count the pips again, then nodded. "Ah, you're right. My bad. Now it's your turn."

His opponent threw the dice, coming up with two sixes, two fives and a one. To Ogian's amazement he picked up all dice save the one.

"Sure that's a good move?" he asked helpfully. "You were close to a full house there."

Loord shook his head. "I always do the categories from top to bottom. First the ones, then the twos and so on."

"That doesn't make sense," Ogian said. "You can't possibly win when you play like that."

"No, but it has to be done in straight lines. Things get too messy if you don't follow a pattern."

Ogian watched with a mix of fascination and disbelief as the strange man rolled the dice twice more without getting any more ones. He realized he might not even have to cheat to win against someone like Loord. For some reason that made him feel very bad, like the whole point of the game had been lost.

"Small straight," he said after his second throw in the next round. He'd planned to go for the large straight but felt too sorry for his opponent to go through with it. "Thirty points. Is that okay with you?"

"Of course," Loord said, looking puzzled. "That's what you get for a small straight."

"Just making sure," Ogian said, jotting down the score. "I don't want to appear too greedy."

They continued playing, Ogian getting further and further ahead of his opponent. In the last round it looked like Loord would actually manage a Yahtzee, getting four twos in his first throw. Unfortunately, his next two throws yielded a four and a six and he finished with a miserable eighty-seven points to Ogian's three hundred and forty-nine. Oddly enough, the man seemed rather pleased with his performance.

"I did get the small straight," he said as Utoto handed him a bowl of stew. "I think this was the first time that happened."

"Congratulations," Ogian said, then narrowed his eyes as he watched Loord gobble down his food without even bothering to chew. "Why the hurry?" he asked.

Loord gulped down the contents of his mug before answering. "I must finish my food before the sun sets," he said. "It was a close call tonight."

"Ummm, why's that?" Ogian asked. "Are you afraid the food will go bad if you take too long? It really doesn't."

"No, it's not that," Loord said, putting down his bowl and rising to his feet. "I'm off to bed. I always go to bed just after the sun has set."

"Why that early?" Ogian asked, eating his own food without any hurry.

"Because I must be up two hours before dawn," Loord said. "I always rise two hours before dawn."

Ogian rubbed the side of his nose, smearing it with thick sauce without noticing. "That's very early. Do you have some special task that requires you to get up then?"

"No, I just want to be ahead of the rest of you. Anyway, good night, all of you. See you tomorrow."

Sucking at his spoon, Ogian watched thoughtfully as Loord strode off through the camp. When he was sure the man was out of earshot he turned to the others.

"Is he always that weird?" he asked.

"Yeah," said Ahlan. "No wonder the two of you get along so well."

"Thanks," Ogian said. "He wasn't much of a Yahtzee player, though."

The strange dream didn't come to him that night. Instead he dreamed about standing in a jungle glade somewhere, facing a young female hippo. He had no idea how he knew the hippo was female, nor why he felt such affection for it. Then Bathora came lumbering between the trees and sat on the hippo's back, crushing it to the ground.

"FINISH IT, HARBINGER," Bathora commanded, giving the helpless animal a hard smack on the head. "FINISH IT OFF FOR ME."

Ogian took a step closer, then hesitated. The hippo turned its head towards him, giving him such a pleading look it broke his heart. He knew he couldn't kill the poor beast. Something deep inside him wanted to help it, to strike down Bathora the same way that brave woman Kat had, but he knew she'd kill him if he raised a hand against her. So he simply stood there, until finally the dream faded and he woke up.

The following morning, as he was eating his breakfast, Ogian felt faint tremors in the ground beneath him. At the same time the people around him fell silent. Looking up, he saw Bathora's massive shape coming towards him. The dark goddess rarely showed herself in the middle of the camp like this, keeping mostly to herself or being completely out of sight. Her presence unnerved the humans, and even Ogian felt a little uneasy.

But Bathora appeared in an unusually good mood as she crouched down next to him. Even squatting she was taller than any human, looming over Ogian where he sat. She placed a heavy hand on his shoulder, almost toppling him over.

"TODAY IS A GREAT DAY FOR YOU, HARBINGER," she boomed.

"It is?" Ogian said. "Is there a Yahtzee tournament or something?"

"WHAT?" Bathora's expression darkened a little. "OF COURSE NOT. THIS IS FAR MORE IMPORTANT. TODAY YOU'LL PROVE YOUR WORTH TO ME – REALLY PROVE IT, FOR THE FIRST TIME."

Ogian looked up at the shadowy face and the glowing red eyes. "How will I do that, Mistress?" he asked.

"ON THE OTHER SIDE OF THOSE MOUNTAINS LIES THE HOME OF MY OLD TRIBE," Bathora said, pointing to the peaks south-west of their camp. "THEY'VE TURNED AGAINST ME, JOINED FORCES WITH MY GREATEST ENEMIES. I'VE NEVER SEEN ANYTHING LIKE IT. WE'RE GOING TO DESTROY THEM."

"Destroy them?" Ogian rubbed his chin as he gazed the way Bathora had pointed. "You mean, like, kill them?"

"OF COURSE I MEAN KILL THEM. WHAT OTHER WAY CAN YOU DESTROY A TRIBE?"

"I don't know. Wouldn't it be enough to blow up their huts or something?"

Bathora bared her long, sharp fangs in a terrible snarl. "THAT WON'T BE PUNISHMENT ENOUGH FOR WHAT THEY DID. WE'RE GOING TO WIPE THEM FROM THE FACE OF THE EARTH, AND YOU'LL BE THE ONE TO DO IT?"

"Me?" Ogian shied back, a sharp stone pricking his bum as it scraped across the ground. He was suddenly feeling *very* uneasy.

"YES, YOU," Bathora said firmly. "YOU'RE MY HARBINGER. IT'S TIME YOU START ACTING THE PART."

"But…" He made a weak gesture to indicate the mass of humans around them. "Can't the warriors do the killing?"

"THEY'LL DO SOME OF IT, YES. BUT I NEED YOU TO PUT ON A MORE SENSATIONAL SHOW. A REAL POWER DISPLAY – SOMETHING NOBODY'S SEEN FOR A THOUSAND YEARS. PEOPLE MUST LEARN WHAT HAPPENS WHEN THEY DEFY ME."

Ogian looked away. "I don't want to do it," he said, his voice barely more than a whisper.

The large, red eyes flashed with anger. "WHAT DO YOU MEAN YOU DON'T WANT TO DO IT? YOU NEVER FALTERED WHEN WE DESTROYED THAT VILLAGE UP NORTH."

"I only blew up huts then," Ogian said. "Killing people is different. It's… it's wrong, son. Nothing but grief and suffering will come from this."

"WHAT ARE YOU TALKING ABOUT?" Bathora asked, more puzzled than angry now. "OF COURSE THERE WILL BE GRIEF AND SUFFERING. THAT'S THE WHOLE POINT OF IT!"

"I'm not going to kill those people!" Ogian wailed. "And I'm not going to let you crush that poor beast. It's cheating, and you know it! We can make the dice show whatever we like, and we don't have to do the categories in any particular order!"

Bathora eyed him curiously for a while. "YOU REALLY ARE A WEIRD ONE," she finally said. "BUT THAT DOESN'T CHANGE ANYTHING. YOU'LL LEAD THE ASSAULT ON THE TELU, AND YOU'LL TEAR THEM APART LIKE THE FILTHY LITTLE WORMS THEY ARE."

"I won't…"

"DID I MENTION THEY'RE YAHTZEE HATERS?" Bathora said with a sly smile.

Ogian clamped his mouth shut, eyes narrowing as he faced Bathora. "Yahtzee haters?"

She nodded. "THEY OUTLAWED YAHTZEE AFTER I LEFT. ANYONE CAUGHT PLAYING IT WILL BE EXECUTED."

"The *bastards!*" All the fear, all the unwillingness was gone from Ogian's mind. Red-hot fury filled him like the thick, bubbling lava of Mount Azagh. He rose to his feet, straightening himself.

"GOOD, GOOD," Bathora said, nodding her monstrous head. "I KNEW YOU'D SEE REASON. SHALL WE GET READY, THEN? WANT A BLURBER BEFORE WE BREAK CAMP?"

"I'm ready," Ogian said, voice hard as steel. "I'll have neither food nor rest until these Yahtzee haters are destroyed."

"THAT'S MY BOY," Bathora said, putting a huge arm around his shoulders. "WINSTON WOULD'VE BEEN PROUD OF YOU."

A couple of hours later Ogian found himself gazing at a pretty large array of huts and tents. People were milling about, carrying out all kinds of everyday tasks. He saw none of it, though. To him, they were like rats, vermin crawling across the filthy ground. They needed to be destroyed. Every single one of them.

"My men are awaiting your command, sir," Clogz said beside him.

"I'm not sure there'll be anything left for them to kill once I'm done," Ogian said. Then he gathered his power and focused all his hatred on the settlement before him.

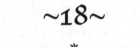

~18~

————— ✳ —————

"There is no friendship, no love, like that of the parent for the child."

- Henry Ward Beecher

Gemma sat on a rock outside the Hippo God's temple, looking down at the baby boy cradled in her arms. After almost three months she still had trouble grasping that the strange little creature had come out of her body. Lying there with his thumb in his mouth he looked so cute, so content, so... so utterly ridiculous!

"Just like your father," she murmured, stroking the short, black fuzz on the infant's scalp.

Her life had changed dramatically since little Niq came into the world. Gone were the long, wonderful hunting trips and the exploring adventures she, Marsha and Amanda used to undertake with regular intervals. Instead she spent her days making silly noises to a creature who didn't understand even the simplest of words, and when she didn't do that she wiped up poo. Lots of poo.

And, she realized to her amazement, she loved this new life. She loved it so much it almost frightened her.

She was still sitting like that, wondering at the changes mother hood could bring to a person, when Little Niq woke up, yawned majestically, looked up at her and raised his small hand towards her face.

"Bah bah bah bah!"

"Bah bah yourself," Gemma said. "I see your vocabulary hasn't improved since this morning. That's all right – nor has mine."

She lifted the cloth-wrapped bundle so she could kiss the brown little forehead. Niq reached out, his small hand poking at her nose, eventually found a nostril and began exploring it. Gemma had to focus hard to avoid sneezing.

"What treasures grand may fall into your hand, when your fingers seek inside a nose so sleek?"

Gemma looked up and smiled. "Hello, Amanda. What's up?"

The voluptuous woman smiled back at her, then squatted down and began making even sillier noises than the ones Gemma usually produced, poking at little Niq's cheeks and chin. The baby made a delighted sound and drooled a little for good measure. Gemma wiped it away with a corner of the cloth she'd wrapped him in.

"Aren't you Amanda's little nugget?" Amanda cooed, laughing as Niq released a very loud fart. "Sounding just like your daddy there."

"Everyone keeps saying how much he looks like Joz," Gemma complained. "Is there nothing at all of me in him?"

"I'm sure there are similarities that will become more apparent as he grows up," Amanda said. "He'll probably end up with a brilliant intellect, an athletic build, a perfectly shaped butt..."

"... and a gift for mathematics?" Gemma muttered. "Yeah, there are lots of useful traits he could inherit from me."

"Quit moping," Amanda said, giving her friend a toothy grin. "Not many kids can boast about having a mother who helped save the world. You're holding the son of a legend right there, Gemster."

"I suppose." Gemma looked down at Niq, who'd gone back to sleep. "If only Marsha could bring the Scion back so we'll see some of those wonders Tom-Tom keeps talking about."

Amanda puzzled over this for a moment. "Well, the fish we had for dinner yesterday was pretty wondrous," she finally said.

"You mean we got through all that trouble to get better fish?" Gemma said incredulously.

"No, of course not," Amanda hurried to say. "I just figured the changes would come more slowly, like a tiny little bit at a time. Doesn't that make sense?"

Gemma sighed. "Sure. I just wonder how Marsha is doing. She's been gone a long time now."

"I'm sure she's fine," Amanda said. "She'll come back one day and then we'll throw a huge party. Is Joz still with the Telu, by the way?"

Gemma nodded. "He said he'd have to stay a couple of days to help an old friend rebuild his hut, but I suspect his real reason was that he wanted one night of undisturbed sleep, with no baby waking up twice an hour screaming his lungs out."

"That's men for you," Amanda said with a wink.

"I'll teach my son to be a more responsible person," Gemma said, giving the sleeping baby a meaningful look.

"Good luck," Amanda said. "It's never worked so far."

Both women turned their heads at the sound of raised voices from the temple's entrance. A moment later Tom-Tom, the new High Priest of the Hippo Cult, pushed his way past a group of young men lounging about in the shade. The tall, handsome man looked like he'd just seen the dead come to life (which had actually happened to him little more than a year ago).

"Get everyone together!" he gasped. "An attack is coming!"

The two women were on their feet in an instant, Gemma still holding the sleeping baby in her arms.

"An attack?" she said. "That's not possible. There are no hostile tribes anywhere nearby."

"Even if there were we'd handle them easily," Amanda said. "We have many strong warriors here."

Tom-Tom shook his head vigorously. "This is much more serious than that. The Hippo God himself warned me. He wouldn't do that unless we were in real danger."

Gemma and Amanda exchanged a look. Neither of them was completely certain about the part the Hippo God would play in the glorious future the old writings predicted for their people, nor did they trust the High Priest's ability to communicate with the deity very far. But something had clearly upset the man, and they wouldn't dismiss his warning without giving the matter a thorough examination.

"Did he say what manner of threat we're dealing with?" Gemma asked. "The Bug Goddess is dead, and so are all her minions. I don't know of any other enemies."

"It's some kind of new evil," Tom-Tom said, the urgency in his voice matched by the restless shuffling of his feet. "The Hippo God didn't have time for a more detailed explanation. He just said to gather everyone and prepare for battle."

"All right, then," Amanda said. "From which direction is this attack expected to come?"

"From the north," the High Priest said. "The dark forces attacked the Telu camp a couple of days ago and now they're coming here."

"What?" Gemma exclaimed, suddenly feeling all cold inside. "But Joz is there with them! What happened? Did the Hippo God say?"

Tom-Tom gave her a look full of compassion and sadness. "The whole camp was destroyed along with everyone in it. I'm truly sorry, Gemma."

"NO!" Gemma began trotting towards the temple's entrance. "I must go there! He might still be alive. He *must* still be alive! Where's my spear?" The motion combined with her loud shouting woke little Niq up and he began wailing furiously. Gemma looked down at him as if wondering how the thing had ended up in her arms.

"Calm down, Gemma," Amanda said. "The Telu camp is several days' journey from here. Even if you ran like a cheetah there'd be nothing you could do for Joz and the others."

"But..." Gemma looked around with a panicked expression on her face. "I must..."

"You must defend this place," Amanda said. "Your people need you."

"But what about Joz...?"

Amanda put a gentle hand on her shoulder. "What about little Niq? Would you just run off and leave him here? What would happen to him when the attack came?"

Gemma closed her eyes, holding back the scream she wanted so badly to release. Amanda was right, of course. Her place was here, with Niq and Emkei and the others. Joz's fate was beyond her power now.

"All right," she said. "But I'll need someone to look after Niq while we prepare our defenses."

"Ginger is over there," Amanda said, pointing at the robust, elderly lady who'd been the Khadal tribe's medicine woman. "I'm sure she'll take good care of him."

Gemma had just deposited the baby into the loving hands of the medicine woman when there was a shout from one of the trees to the east of the temple.

"Warriors coming!"

"Not already!" Gemma moaned. "I'd hoped we had at least a couple of hours to prepare."

"Those can't be the attacking force," Amanda said, peering into the shadows between the trees. "They look badly battered, and the one leading them looks very much like..."

"Joz!" Gemma shouted. With a few long leaps she was across the clearing and in her husband's arms. Joz looked like he'd been through hell a couple of times, and then through a car wash and a large garbage disposal unit. Gemma took no notice of his torn clothes and the dried blood on his face and body, though. Joz was here. He was alive. That was all that mattered.

"Gemma!" he gasped. "We have no time for this. They'll be here soon."

"I know," Gemma said. "We've already begun preparations. Those bastards will get a very unpleasant surprise when they get here.."

Joz shook his head. "No, you don't understand. We can't fight this enemy. It's useless."

She gave him a puzzled look. "What do you mean? Of course we can fight them."

"You didn't see them, Gemma." There was such despair in Joz's eyes it almost made her step back. "The things they did..."

"Tell me," she whispered. "Who are they?"

"It's Bathora," Joz said. "I don't know how it's possible, but I swear it was her. Well, not the Bathora who used to lead the Telu. This was something... else. But I swear it was her."

Gemma stared at her husband in disbelief. "Your old chieftain? But you said she was harmless. Stupid, but harmless."

"The creature she's become is everything but harmless," Joz said. "And she has a huge force of warriors with her. And then there's the Harbinger."

Gemma blinked. "The what?"

"The Harbinger. He was the one who led the attack on the Telu camp. Sent waves of power tearing through the panicked people. Made the earth erupt beneath our feet and made tents and huts burst into flame. He strode through the destruction like a demon from hell, and yet I could have sworn I'd seen him before."

"What do you mean?" Gemma asked. "If you'd seen a creature like that before I'm sure you would've told me about it."

Joz shook his head. "It can't be possible," he murmured. "But he looked just like one of those Elephant People. The one who kept cheating at Yahtzee."

Gemma racked her brain until she came up with a name. "Ogian? Is that the one?"

"I think so," Joz said. "I only saw him a few times, so I could be mistaken. But it looked just like him."

Gemma tried to recall everything she knew about Ogian. He'd been the most placid creature imaginable – kind, docile, rather dumb. The monster Joz had just described didn't fit the image she had of the man at all. But if that Bathora woman had turned into a murderous creature of evil, then who was she to say something similar couldn't have happened to Ogian? She turned back to Joz.

"Come," she said. "We can talk more while we prepare the defenses. There might still be enough time."

"But…"

"I don't care if it's hopeless! We must try! Or there won't be a future for little Niq and all the other children. There won't be a future for *us*. Are you coming or not?"

Joz stared at her, eyes wide amidst the dirt and blood on his face. Slowly the hopeless ness gave way to determination and resolve.

"All right," he said. "Let's do it."

About an hour later Gemma found herself a hundred yards north of the temple, hewing away with an axe at a thick tree trunk. All around her people were working, doing everything they could to form barriers and prepare other means of defense. Amanda, being by far the strongest woman Gemma had ever encountered, carried large boulders that she put together into a wall behind which the defenders could take shelter.

"That barrier should hold them back a while," said Emkei, who was standing in the middle of everything without actually contributing.

Gemma wiped sweat from her brow. "I hope so, but we have neither the time nor the men to erect one around the whole temple area, and if what Joz says is true they might be able to blast their way through it. We have to do something, though."

"Yes." The seer's puffy face wore the gravest expression Gemma had ever seen on it. "Those creatures won't settle for defeating our people. They intend to wipe us from the face of the earth."

"We won't go down without a fight," Gemma said. "The Hippo Cult has faced terrible odds before."

"Yes, but…" Emkei fell silent when the sound of a loud explosion reached their ears. "That must be them," she said, unable to hide the fear in her voice.

"It sounded close," Gemma said. "Are all who can't fight gathered inside the temple?"

"They are," came a chirpy female voice from right behind them. Startled, Gemma spun around, axe raised, but it was only Fae. The short woman looked her usual odd self, with bones sticking out from her hair in all directions. She was holding a spear casually in one hand.

"What are you doing here, Fae?" Gemma demanded. "You're no fighter. Get back inside the temple."

"No way!" Fae said. "I won't stay behind while the rest of you face danger out here. Too bad my gun doesn't work anymore – I'd have preferred it to this more primitive weapon." She waved her spear a little.

"Do you have any skill at all with that?" Gemma asked, eyeing her friend critically.

Fae shrugged. "I'm the most agile member of the cult. I should be able to cope. And Tom-Tom will be there with me."

"Tom-Tom can't fight either," Gemma said with a frown. "He'll just be in the way."

"He claims the Hippo God has granted him some of its power," Fae said. "Just like in the old days, he said."

There was another explosion, this one so powerful it shook the ground.

"Ready yourselves, then," Gemma said, throwing the axe aside and picking up her spear. "It'll begin any minute now."

They arrayed their fighters as best they could along the hastily erected barriers. Gemma was all too aware of how few they were – their line of defense was stretched painfully thin both to her left and right. If the jungle hadn't been so dense there'd be even larger gaps with no defenders.

Beside her Joz was leaning heavily on his spear. He'd washed the blood and dirt off his face, but that only made the weakness and fatigue more visible. Gemma gave him a worried look.

"Sure you're up for this, love?" she asked.

Her husband emitted a low grunt. "There isn't much of a choice, is there? It's either fight and die or remain behind and die. The choice is simple."

"Yeah." Gemma weighed the spear in her hand. There'd been a time, not too long ago, when the feeling of its hard, smooth wood was all she craved. Now it reminded her of how much she wanted to hold little Niq, to see his silly-looking face one more time before the end.

"There they are!" came a call from her right. Gemma pushed the thoughts of her child away, focusing her attention on what lay ahead of her.

On the other side of the barrier was a small stretch of open ground where the defenders had cut down the trees. Shapes were now emerging from the shadows between the trees at its far edge – fierce-looking warriors armed with long-shafted spears and small, round shields. They were hollering like madmen as they advanced.

"So many," said Fae, who was standing on Gemma's other side.

It was true. Gemma didn't even try to count their enemies. They seemed to fill the open area, and more kept coming from the north. Rocks came flying across the barrier, forcing Gemma and her comrades to duck. Something soft struck a boulder right in front of her, splashing red juice across her left cheek.

"What the hell was that?" she grumbled, wiping the stickiness away with her arm.

"Not sure," Joz said. "But it looked very much like a tomato."

There was no time to wonder about this any further, for the foremost attackers had reached the barrier and were trying to climb across it. Some got struck down as the defenders positioned in the nearby trees hurled rocks and short spears at them, but that barely halted their progress. Gemma ran her spear through one who'd suddenly appeared right in front of her. She caught a glimpse of Amanda hurling a whole tree trunk at a group of attackers before another enemy leaped across the top of the barrier and engaged her.

"Hold them back!" she shouted, waving her spear to block a savage thrust from her foe. "Don't let them across!"

"Trying!" Fae called out from Gemma's left. The small woman darted back and forth like a dancer suffering from vestibular neuronitis, stabbing wildly with her spear whenever an enemy came within reach. It didn't look like she'd managed to kill anyone yet – her random, rapid movements seemed to cause more confusion than harm among the attackers. Gemma supposed that was better than nothing, but...

The barrier in front of her erupted in a cloud of broken rock and wood. Gemma tumbled backwards, crashing through a low stand of undergrowth before coming to a dazed halt some fifteen feet behind where she'd stood a moment earlier. Black spots danced across her field of vision. She blinked a few times until she could see clearly again.

A dark shape stood in the breech the explosion had created. The tree trunks to either side had caught fire, making it look like the figure was wreathed in flames. It raised its arms toward the sky, roaring in a voice not quite like thunder but fairly loud anyway.

"I am the Harbinger! I have come to destroy you all!"

"It really is him," Joz gasped, pushing himself to his feet and staggering backwards. "It's Ogian!"

"He's changed quite a bit since the last time I saw him," Gemma said. She was back on her feet as well, spear raised in front of her. The weapon suddenly felt like a child's toy in her hands, so utterly useless against the power of the creature standing there among the flames.

"I would have liked to take a dump before the battle!" roared the Harbinger. "But there were no good opportunities. This makes me extra mad!"

He swung his arms around, sending crackling sparks of energy flying in all directions. Then he pointed his hands at the ground before his feet, and a wave of explosions shook it, causing earth and stone to burst into the air. The explosions came straight towards Gemma, blasting everything in their way to pieces.

"Stop!"

Gemma had raised one arm to shield her face from the blinding explosions. As she lowered it she saw that the devastation had stopped a few feet in front of her, an unnaturally straight line dividing the unbroken ground from the Harbinger's ruination. A tall man was standing between her and the Harbinger, arms outstretched in a gesture of defiance.

"Tom-Tom," Gemma whispered. "But how…?"

"In the name of the Hippo God, I command you to step back," Tom-Tom declared. His voice sounded different from anything Gemma had heard from him before – not particularly loud but full of power and conviction. For a moment the dark shape of the Harbinger seemed to shy back, the destructive force emanating from it shrinking. Then he straightened himself, and new tremors shook the earth.

"You dare stand in my way, cultist?" he roared. "As you wish, then. You have power, but not even a Full House can stand against a Yahtzee. Prepare to die now!"

A lance of blue energy shot out from the Harbinger, incinerating the air itself. Tom-Tom made a sweeping gesture with his left hand, and a shield of pure white appeared in front of him, deflecting the Harbinger's attack. Another bolt, this one glowing like liquid fire, tore through the air. Tom-Tom staggered backwards and to the side, his shield barely surviving the impact. The Harbinger advanced, a triumphant look on his face.

Gemma didn't see how the battle between the two men continued. Enemy warriors had begun pouring through the breach in the barricade, far too many for the scattered defenders to hold back. Gemma saw two middle-aged men, people she'd known since she was a little girl, cut down when they tried to fend off almost a dozen enemies. Their bodies vanished from sight as more hostile warriors kept coming.

"Rally to me!" she shouted. "The barrier has fallen! Retreat!"

She waited for the others to obey her order, but for some inconceivable reason they all ignored her. Annoyed by their lack of discipline, she repeated the words again with the same lack of response. The third time she used so much force the words seemed to fill her whole head as she thought them…

Wait. Gemma's anger turned to confusion in the span of a heartbeat. Had she only spoken the order inside her head? No wonder no one had obeyed her. Making sure her mouth was open this time, she shouted the command as loudly as she could.

As I've mentioned at some point before, Gemma could produce extremely loud shouts. She could also make her voice so high-pitched no human ear was able to perceive the sound. Fortunately, the shout she emitted now was pitched at a normal level. It was also so loud it made both her companions and their enemies cease their current activities and cover their ears.

"Dammit!" Gemma growled as, once again, no one did what she'd told them to. "Why isn't anyone listening to me? And why is everyone standing with their hands over their ears?"

Thinking that leading by example might prove a better strategy, she ran back a dozen or so paces, slipping in behind a large tree to conceal herself. As she did, her butt bumped into something. Or, as she noticed when she spun around with her spear raised, *someone*.

"Oops, sorry," she said with an embarrassed smile.

"My pleasure," Joz said, grinning back at her.

She punched him softly on the arm. "Oh, shush, you."

"Watch out!" he cautioned. "Here they come!"

Fighters on both sides had recovered from the shock of Gemma's incredibly loud shout and were now producing their own measure of noise as they battled each other with renewed fury. As the attackers pressed on, Gemma's people retreated by pure necessity rather than as a result of her order. Gemma pressed her back to the tree (which thought it a very pleasant experience) and waited for the right moment to appear.

When the first attackers came into view she leapt out from her hiding place, stabbing wildly with her spear. Two enemies fell before they even became aware of her presence. Another went down an instant later, while off to her right a fourth fell to Joz's spear.

"Fall back!" Gemma shouted, darting away before their enemies could reorganize themselves. This time more people obeyed her command, running towards her from left and right until a small group had formed around her .

They continued fighting in this manner for a few minutes, making quick lunges at the enemy before seeking shelter among the trees again. It worked well enough until they reached the more open ground that surrounded the temple itself. Then there were no more places to hide.

"What now, Gemster?" Joz asked, wiping sweat and blood from his face. His spear was in as poor condition as he, full of notches and cracks.

"I guess we remain here until it's over," Gemma said. She managed a tired smile when she saw Amanda burst out from between the trees to her right, a small group of defenders following her. Then she spun around in alarm as a blood-curdling wail split the air, but it was only Fae, shooting through the air with her arms wrapped around a thick liana. The small woman smashed feet first into a group of attackers, throwing them head over heels to the ground before the liana rebounded and sent her flying backwards with a more panic-stricken scream.

"Stand your ground!" Gemma shouted. "Don't let these barbarians reach the temple unless it's over our dead bodies!"

The attackers came towards them. There seemed to be even more of them than before. Gemma saw Amanda smash one enemy's head to bloody pulp with a single blow, then she was engaged in combat herself, waving her spear with all the might she had left. She wouldn't give up, not as long as she could stand and hold a spear. These were good fighters, but she could take them. She'd take them all if she had to.

Through the haze of battle frenzy she became aware that the ground was shaking. She watched in horror as a huge, dark shape came crashing through the trees, throwing whole trunks aside as if they were mere branches. The attackers drew back a little, as if uncertain what to make of this new apparition.

"I AM BATHORA!" the creature roared in a voice like thunder. "I HAVE COME TO DESTROY YOU ALL! THIS IS PAYMENT FOR WINSTON, AND FOR GIDEON, AND FOR ALL THE OTHERS WHO DIED BECAUSE OF YOUR ABOMINABLE CULT! WHO DARES TO STAND AGAINST ME?"

There were a few moments of silence as the booming sound of her voice echoed off the temple's stone wall. Then a calm voice spoke.

"I do."

All eyes turned to see who'd spoken. Emkei stepped into the open space that had formed between Bathora's monstrous form and the cowering defenders. The seer's puffy face showed no sign of fear, only calm acceptance and unyielding confidence.

"Emkei, no...!" Gemma exclaimed, but the large woman was already several paces ahead of her, moving without hesitation until she stood right in front of Bathora. Emkei was by far the biggest woman Gemma had ever seen, but Bathora made her look like a small child where she towered over her like a dark mountain wreathed in malicious power. The glowing red eyes looked down at the Khadal woman with a mix of curiosity and amusement.

"MY, AREN'T YOU A FAT ONE?" she rumbled. "YOU MAKE THE WOMAN AT THE BAR LOOK LIKE A STICK. I'VE NEVER SEEN ANYTHING LIKE IT. OH WELL, I COULD DO WITH SOME EXERCISE."

She reached down her massive arms and wrapped them around Emkei's ample body, obviously intending to lift the Khadal woman off her feet. There came a couple of low, rumbling grunts as Bathora struggled with the heavy load. Finally she managed to hoist Emkei into the air and tossed her aside. Gemma could have sworn the ground shook almost as much when the seer landed as when the dark goddess had approached through the jungle.

"THAT WAS THAT," said Bathora, rubbing her massive arms as if massaging away an ache. "NOW, WHERE'S MY HARBINGER?"

Just as Bathora finished speaking there was a loud explosion from somewhere behind the trees to her left. A dark-robed figure came flying through the air, landing in a motionless heap on the ground. Thin wisps of smoke rose from the limp form.

"Tom-Tom!" Fae shrieked, dashing over to kneel beside her fallen husband. Soft, whimpering sounds could be heard in the sudden silence.

Bathora gave the strange-looking woman a closer look. "YOU!" she hissed. "I BANISHED YOU FROM MY TRIBE! YOU CALLED ME A FAT-ARSED COW! SOMEONE CALL SECURITY! HARBINGER, WHERE ARE YOU?"

"Right here, Mistress." Ogian strolled casually out from between the trees, tossing a couple of dice from one hand to the other. Bathora gave him an outraged scowl.

"WHERE HAVE YOU BEEN?" she demanded. "I HAD TO COME HERE MYSELF TO MAKE SURE EVERYTHING WENT ACCORDING TO PLAN."

"Sorry, Mistress," Ogian said, making the dice disappear inside his dark robes. "The Hippo Cult man provided an unanticipated measure of resistance. He's been incapacitated now, as you can see." He motioned to Tom-Tom's unmoving form on the ground.

"VERY WELL," Bathora said. "LET'S FINISH THIS BUSINESS BEFORE THE BLURBERS GROW COLD. YOU, THE HIPPO CULT, HAVE BEEN FOUND GUILTY OF MURDERING MY FORMER LOVER WINSTON AND SEVERAL OTHER MEMBERS OF MY OLD TRIBE. THE PUNISHMENT FOR SUCH A GRIEVOUS OFFENCE IS DEATH. ANY QUESTIONS?"

No one said anything. All the remaining Hippo Cult fighters stood motionless, arms hanging limply down their sides. The display of inhuman power Bathora and her Harbinger had provided had taken the last of the fight out of them. Now they were only too aware of how hopeless any further resistance would be. Not even Gemma could find it in her to issue one last desperate attack.

"FINE, THEN," Bathora said with a curt nod of her monstrous head. "THIS IS WHERE YOUR PATHETIC LITTLE CULT ENDS. READY, HARBINGER?"

Ogian took a step forward and Gemma wondered at how completely different this dark, menacing creature was from the dim-witted but kindly man she'd met not much more than a year ago. He carried himself differently, walked differently, even talked differently.

"Ready, Mistress," he said.

"KILL THEM ALL!" Bathora boomed. Both she and Ogian raised their arms, destructive power beyond human comprehension crackling around them. Gemma knew this was where it'd all end – herself, Joz, little Niq, all the others she loved.

But another darkness swept in over the open space, this one emerging out of the western sky. At first Gemma thought it some unnaturally fast stormcloud, but as it descended on Bathora and Ogian she realized it was a mass of large birds, hundreds or thousands of them. Before either Bathora or her Harbinger had time to react they were enveloped in a cloud of screeching eagles, beaks and talons ripping at their dark forms. At the same time came a rumbling sound like subterranean thunder, the ground trembling as a number of huge beasts came crashing into the open space, trampling all enemies unfortunate enough to get In their way.

"Hippos!" Amanda hooted beside Gemma. "An army of hippos!"

But Gemma paid her friend no attention. Her eyes had fallen on a group of warriors who'd entered the scene right behind the hippos. Their leader was a young woman, not particularly large but very fierce-looking, the other three battle-hardened men. And behind them came a small woman, looking extremely frightened where she stood at the edge of the trees.

Marsha had returned.

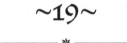

~19~

*"He made me see what Life is, and what Death signifies, and why
Love is stronger than both."*

- Oscar Wilde, The Canterville Ghost

Watching the chaotic scene before her, Kat realized they'd arrived in the nick of time. Bathora's warriors had conquered almost the whole battlefield, pushing back the ones she assumed to be Marsha's people all the way to the wall of the rather ugly temple. Some of them were still putting up a desperate fight, among them the hot woman with the thong displaying her buttocks so gloriously that Kat guessed must be Gemma and the voluptuous one that could be none other than Amanda. Despite their bravery it was clear they wouldn't have lasted much longer without help.

But the arrival of the hippos changed everything. The massive beasts crashed into the warriors from the Hullabaloo tribe, trampling them under their heavy feet or using their powerful jaws to crush bones and muscle into pulp. Their charge was the most epic thing Kat had ever witnessed, turning the tide of battle in mere seconds. Screams of pain and terror filled the air where there'd been shouts of rage a moment earlier.

"Attack!" Kat commanded, pointing with her weapon at the huge mass of enemies. "It's time those lily-livered goat lovers pay for their crimes!"

She led the way into the battle, following the path of trampled ground the hippos had left behind them. The other members of her Deathsquad followed, the points of the spears from the armory in North Pharq glistening in the afternoon sunlight.

The four of them wouldn't have made much of an impact a few moments ago, but the eagles and hippos had spread such chaos among the enemies that Kat and her companions didn't encounter much resistance. They stabbed and hewed and cut their way through the panic-stricken warriors, leaving their own trail of corpses behind them. Kat wielded her long blade in one hand, her short spear in the other. The new style of fighting felt so natural to her she wondered how she could ever have fought any other way.

She'd just left another enemy dead at her feet when she caught sight of the hated face she'd hoped to find. Raising her blade as in salute, she called out her challenge.

"Clogz! You lily-livered bastard! Come and fight me!"

For a moment she thought she saw a flicker of hesitation in the man's face, but then his features hardened and he came towards her, pushing aside those of his men who blocked his path. He stopped a few feet away, regarding Kat as if she was something the cat (pun intended) had dragged in.

"So you're still alive," he said, his voice so cold Kat couldn't tell if he was disappointed or not. "Was this thing with the birds and the hippos your doing?"

"Not really," Kat said. "I just tagged along to see the show. And for the pleasure of killing you, of course."

Clogz snorted. "You've fled from me twice already. Why not make it a third time?"

"I'm done fleeing," Kat said, scowling at the man who'd usurped the leadership of her old tribe. "I only did it last time because I was betrayed. It won't happen again."

"Very well, then." Clogz raised his long spear. "It's your funeral."

He leaped at her with such speed she wondered if Bathora had somehow granted him some of her power as well. She was forced to use both her weapons to parry his first series of attacks, snarling like an enraged beast as she fought. Their weapons rang together over and over until Kat almost felt a little out of breath. She figured that was more because she'd had a really large breakfast, though.

Clogz might have outmaneuvered most other spear fighters, Kat's companions included, but he had no experience fighting someone like her. Once she'd fended off his initial onslaught she began an offensive of her own, using her two weapons in patterns that put her opponent off balance, forcing him to step back as blows and cuts kept coming from unfamiliar directions. The hard mask his face had displayed also began to falter, uncertainty and fear showing through. Kat, on the other hand, felt a triumphant grin form on her own visage.

Using the shaft of her spear she batted aside Clogz's weapon, stepping inside his reach before he could respond. Her blade shot out, fast as a viper, slicing him twice across the belly. Emitting a strangled sound, Clogz doubled over, dropping his spear and clutching his wounded midsection. Kat smashed the shaft of her spear into his face, sending him flying a few feet back and ending up flat on the uneven ground (however the hell that's done).

Kat stepped over to where he lay and looked down at the half-stunned man. "You should never have put me in a cage," she mumbled. "Big mistake."

She raised her blade for the killing blow, but then a sharp voice called out from somewhere behind her.

"Wait! Don't kill him yet!"

Scowling, Kat swung around, about to snap at the newcomer that this really wasn't the time to get soft-hearted and merciful, but when she saw who'd spoken she knew mercy was the least likely thing to occur.

Demon Vic came trotting towards her, a mad grin on her face and evil light shining from her eyes. In her hands was a long iron rod, its tip glowing red-hot like a sunset painted in blood. The necromancer waved the thing at Clogz, still lying dazed on the ground.

"Get him up. And turn him over. Quickly, before this thing cools down."

Grinning back at the other woman, Kat grabbed Clogz by his collar and yanked him up to a kneeling position.

"This is going to hurt," she hissed into his ear as she flopped him over so he stood on his hands and knees, back turned towards her and Viq.

"Pants down, please," the necromancer commanded.

Kat used her sword to cut loose the string holding the Hullabaloo chieftain's breeches up. The sight of his bare arse was as far from pleasant as the man himself had been.

"Taking aim!" Demon Viq shouted, holding the iron rod out in front of her. "Three, two, one, NOW!"

Kat actually had to look away when the other woman drove her instrument of torture home. Clogz's screams echoed through the jungle, so full of agony Kat cringed involuntarily.

When the usurper finally passed out and the terrible screams ended Kat let out a long breath she hadn't realized she'd been holding. While Demon Viq retrieved her iron rod and moved back towards the temple, stifling a yawn as she went, Kat drove her blade through Clogz's limp body, piercing his heart to ensure he was dead.

Lifting her gaze, she tried to get an overview of the situation. The hippos were still raging through their enemies' ranks, stomping and crushing as they went. The ground was littered with mauled and mangled corpses, piles of hippo droppings interspersed between them. Those who remained alive were desperately trying to get away, but the eagles kept swooping down on them, causing panic and confusion and many ran straight into each other and fell to the ground in tangles of arms and legs.

Two extremely tight clusters of birds hid the forms of Bathora and Ogian almost completely. Kat saw one of Bathora's thick arms flail about in a vain attempt to get rid of the clawing and hacking nuisances. The few she managed to smash were immediately replaced by others.

"Follow me!" Kat shouted to her companions. "At them now, before they manage to break free!"

She'd only taken a few steps when a massive explosion made her stagger back. Blackened feathers filled the air along with the sickening smell of burnt flesh. When the smoke blew away Kat saw Bathora's monstrous form looming over the carnage, her shadowy face looking more murderous than ever. Her glowing red eyes found the mass of birds still enveloping Ogian.

"USE YOUR POWER, HARBINGER," she boomed. "LET'S HAVE CRISPY CHICKEN WINGS FOR DINNER TONIGHT."

But Ogian didn't respond. Soft, whimpering sounds came from somewhere inside the cloud of flapping wings and clawing talons. With a growl that would have made any lion bow its head reverently, Bathora reached out her arm, sending a torrent of power to incinerate the eagles around Ogian. The former Elephant People man looked utterly horror-struck when he finally became visible again.

"It was like in my dream!" he gasped. "Except I couldn't do anything. I couldn't reach my power."

"NO MORE WHINING!" Bathora roared. "GET YOURSELF TOGETHER AND HELP ME GET RID OF THESE ABOMINABLE ANIMALS. THEY'VE CAUSED ENOUGH DAMAGE ALREADY."

She held out her arm, clenching her hand into a dark fist, and one of the hippos exploded in a shower of blood and gore. A moment later another one met the same fate, and then a third.

"No!" Kat screamed, darting forward with both weapons raised, but then a compact shape shot past her, its wings beating so fast they became blurry. The Scion opened its mouth and a thick stream of fire shot out towards the dark goddess.

Kat opened her mouth to cheer, but the cry of elation died on her lips when she saw a cloud of dark power form around Bathora, sucking in the clear afternoon light and plunging the world around the dark goddess into gloom and despair. The darkness also swallowed the Scion's fire, leaving Bathora without as much as a singed hair strand.

"YOU!" she bellowed, directing all her fury at the winged hippo. "YOU SHOULD NEVER HAVE BEEN ALLOWED TO EXIST! DIE, SPAWN OF EVIL!"

With that, she let forth a blast of power so immense Kat thought the sky itself might crumble and collapse over their heads. Not even the Scion, offspring of two ancient gods, could ward off an attack like that. With a shriek that echoed through Kat's mind it was thrown to the side, tumbling head over heels through the air until it crashed into the crown of a tree at the edge of the clearing. Branches and leaves erupted into flame, black smoke spreading across that whole part of the jungle.

"THERE," Bathora said, dusting off her hands. "ONE PROBLEM LESS TO DEAL WITH. WHO'S NEXT?"

"Try me!" Kat shouted, stepping into the open space in front of the dark goddess and giving her a good scowl.

Bathora looked down at her, the expression on her inhuman face darkening as recognition came.

"SO YOU'RE HERE TOO, LITTLE WORM? I GUESS I SHOULDN'T BE SURPRISED. VERMIN ARE ALWAYS DRAWN TO OTHER VERMIN."

"The only vermin here are you and your ilk, you traitorous bitch," Kat snarled. "You should watch out for those necromancers. They eat all manners of slimy creatures."

"I SHOULD STRIKE YOU DOWN," Bathora mused. "BUT I HAVEN'T FORGOTTEN WHAT HAPPENED LAST TIME. HOW DID YOU GET MY POWER TO REBOUND BACK AT ME LIKE THAT? IT WAS ALMOST AS IF..."

She trailed off, and Kat could feel a faint tingling sensation spread across her skin, as if an invisible finger was probing at her. Suddenly the amulet grew ice cold against her chest.

"AH," Bathora said, nodding to herself. "A PROTECTIVE TALISMAN OF SOME SORT. THAT CERTAINLY EXPLAINS THINGS. WELL, THERE ARE WAYS TO GET AROUND SMALL OBSTACLES LIKE THAT."

"Do it now, Kat!" Weewee shouted from somewhere behind her. "Kill her while you still can!"

Kat rushed forward, moving faster than she ever had before in her life, but an unseen force tugged at the chain around her neck – a kind of suction, thin like a needle but incredibly strong. With a sharp sound the chain cracked and the amulet ripped away from her body, falling to the ground.

"HAHAHA!" Bathora's triumphant laugh echoed through the jungle. "I WAS UNABLE TO USE MY POWER TO HURT YOU WHILE YOU WORE THAT THING, BUT NOTHING KEPT ME FROM TEARING IT AWAY FROM YOU AS LONG AS THE POWER DIDN'T TOUCH IT OR YOU DIRECTLY. NOW YOU'RE DEFENCELESS AGAIN, LITTLE MAGGOT!"

Suddenly Kat was flying backwards through the air, landing twenty feet behind where she'd stood before. The impact drove the air from her lungs, and she lay gasping for a few moments, unable to move a limb.

"I SHOULD FIND SOME SPECIAL WAY TO KILL YOU." Bathora's voice came to her as through a thick mist. "PERHAPS BREAK THE BONES IN YOUR BODY ONE BY ONE UNTIL IT GIVES OUT. OR I COULD..."

"No!"

The voice that spoke was thin and shrill, but somehow it managed to pierce through Bathora's mighty rumble. Pushing herself to a sitting position, Kat saw Marsha's petite form place itself between her and the dark goddess, like an ant defying a full-grown elephant. Bathora gave the Hippo Cult woman an amused look.

"LADY MARSHA, I PRESUME. I'M HONOURED TO FINALLY MEET YOU. NOW, WAS THERE SOMETHING YOU WANTED TO SAY TO ME?"

"Yes!" Marsha said, her voice sharp as a blade as it rang through the clearing. "Leave Kat alone. This has nothing to do with her. It's me you want."

"IS IT NOW?" Bathora seemed to contemplate this for a few moments. "PERHAPS IT IS. AFTER ALL, YOU AND YOUR PEOPLE WERE THE ONES RESPONSIBLE FOR WINSTON'S DEATH."

Marsha gave a curt nod. "Indeed. Except you shouldn't put the blame on any of the others. They acted only on my command. I take full responsibility for what happened to your former lover. Kill me and let the others go."

"Marsha, no!" cried the one Kat thought to be Gemma. "Don't do this!"

"It's how it has to be," Marsha said, not taking her eyes off Bathora's huge form. Behind her, the other members of their company hesitantly came into view – Jennibal, the four necromancers, Kylee and Bazer, and finally the cannibal woman Lulu. They stood together, these people from all over the continent, joined together seemingly by coincidence. Kat climbed back to her feet and positioned herself beside them.

Bathora remained silent a while longer, then an idea seemed to pop into her head. A terrible smile split her shadowy face, displaying long rows of sharp fangs.

"LET'S PERFORM A SMALL TEST," she said, her voice softer but just as malicious. "HARBINGER, COME HERE!"

The man who'd been standing off to her left slowly stepped up beside her. His clothing was disheveled after his escapade with the eagles. Kat saw stains of guano on his shoulder and right arm. She had to smile. It looked like Bazer wasn't the only one the birds enjoyed crapping on.

"Yes, Mistress," the Harbinger said.

"KILL THIS WOMAN," Bathora commanded. "IF YOU DO, I'LL SPARE THE REST OF HER PEOPLE. IF YOU DON'T THEY'LL ALL DIE."

The Harbinger turned his face to Marsha. For a moment he stared blankly at her, then his eyes widened. His hand trembled when he raised it to his mouth.

"It's... you..." he whispered.

"Hello, Ogian," Marsha said.

"I...I..." Ogian swallowed hard.

"You must do it," Marsha said. "Kill me, and all the others will be safe. I beg you to do it."

The man's face twisted into a grimace of such agony Kat almost felt sorry for him. "I can't," he whispered.

"You must! She'll kill me anyway, along with all the others. I'm the only one who needs to die, but you have to do it."

Ogian shook his head. "I can't. I remember now. You were in my dream. I didn't recognize you, but now I know it was you. You said the person who cared about you was gone. I almost was. But I'm back now."

"What is he talking about?" Kylee asked. "He seems even more incoherent than Bazer."

"Shush," Jennibal said. "Can't you see they're sharing a tender moment. It's supposed to be like this."

Beside her, the necromancer Leoma nodded, taking Weewee's hand as she watched the drama with a hint of moisture in her eyes.

Marsha, on the other hand, looked utterly bewildered. "Dream? I don't understand."

"I knew there was something important I had forgotten," Ogian said, eyes still fixed on Marsha. "That happens sometimes when there's too much to think of. But now I remember what it was. I love you, Marsha. That's why I can't kill you. Not even if the future of the whole world depended on it. I'm sorry."

"Aw," said Jennibal, wiping a tear from the corner of her eye.

"Aw," echoed Leoma, burying her face in Weewee's chest.

"Men," muttered Kylee, rolling her eyes.

"VERY WELL," Bathora rumbled. "YOU DISAPPOINT ME, HARBINGER. TURNS OUT YOU'RE NO MORE THAN A SOPPY SOD AFTER ALL. I HAVE NO USE FOR LOSERS LIKE YOU."

She reached out an arm, and a blast of power struck Ogian in the chest. For a moment he remained upright, hands clutching the gaping hole in his body, then he fell face down onto the ground. Thin wisps of smoke rose from the corpse.

"No!" Marsha screamed, covering her face with her hands. More screams came from other parts of the clearing. Then everything grew still. Even the remaining hippos and eagles were silent.

"That went..." Jennibal began, but Marsha cut her off.

"Don't say it went well!" she wailed. "Ogian is dead! He might have made some poor decisions and even committed murder, but he wasn't evil at heart. His death is a great tragedy!"

Jennibal gave the other woman a look full of compassion. "I know," she said. "I was going to say it went rather poorly. I'm sorry, Marsha. I know what it's like to lose someone dear to you."

"You do?" Marsha said, wiping at the tears running down her cheeks without much success.

"Well, not really, but it's the kind of thing you're supposed to say." Jennibal smiled as Spud came limping and put an arm around her. The mercenary had received a few cuts but none looked serious.

"SORRY TO INTERRUPT YOUR DISCUSSION," Bathora rumbled. "BUT SEEING AS THE HARBINGER FAILED TO CARRY OUT THE TASK I GAVE HIM, IT LOOKS LIKE I'LL HAVE TO KILL ALL OF YOU MYSELF. CAN SOMEONE PLEASE TUNE DOWN THE MUSIC FOR A WHILE? LAST ORDER FOR TONIGHT."

Kat knew she had to act fast or they'd all be dead in a matter of moments. Problem was, she couldn't think of anything that would stop Bathora. Her weapons lay on the ground ahead of her, too far away to reach, and they wouldn't do her much good anyway. Bathora would strike her down before she'd taken two steps towards them.

"The lily-livered cow has won," she muttered to herself. "Even if she cheated her way through the whole game."

Power crackled between Bathora's outstretched hands. It looked like the dark goddess was preparing something particularly nasty as the battle's grand finale. The ground beneath Kat's feet began trembling, and there was a roaring noise…

Kat blinked, then turned around. The roaring sound came from the south and kept getting louder. One by one, her companions also turned to see what might cause such a sound. It was unlike anything Kat had ever heard, almost like something from a different world.

Something came towards them at incredible speed. At first Kat could only see two bright lights moving between the tree trunks, but as the sound grew to an almost deafening level she realized it was some kind of wagon with four wheels, seemingly running on its own accord. It came to a halt right behind the stunned spectators, rattling and letting out puffs of smoke through a pipe at its rear. The strange wagon held a single occupant – a young woman with long, curly hair. She took off the odd-looking black accessory that had covered her eyes and beamed at everyone.

"Hello," she said. "Sorry I'm late."

"Flamingo?" Marsha exclaimed, her voice full of disbelief. "How did you…? I mean, I wasn't expecting you."

The newcomer turned off the wagon's engine and stepped out, still smiling radiantly. "I told you I'd come as soon as I could. Didn't get the wagon to work properly until yesterday, though." She gave the strange vehicle an affectionate pat.

"That's great," Marsha said. "But I'm afraid you chose a bad time to arrive. That creature over there is just about to have us all eradicated."

Flamingo glanced over to where Bathora stood, still working on whatever devilry she planned to unleash on them.

"Looks like a nasty one indeed," she said. "Good thing I brought my *kannon* with me."

She went over to the back of the wagon, and Kat noticed that a kind of trailer was attached to it. On the trailer stood a strange, tube-like contraption. Next to it lay a couple of large iron balls.

"I don't think that thing will do much good against a creature of such power..." Marsha began.

"Oh, you just wait and see," Flamingo said. She stepped onto the trailer and laboriously began pushing the *kannon* off it. The thing must be incredibly heavy, because she could barely move it even though it ran on two wheels.

"Let me give you a hand with that," Kat said, hurrying over and giving the thing a good push. It rattled down off the cart, making deep tracks on the soft ground.

Flamingo gave her a grateful smile. "Thanks. Think you could turn it around and aim it at that evil-looking creature over there? It looks like she's almost done with her sorcery."

With a grunt of effort, Kat managed to push the *kannon* around the wagon until its open end pointed straight at Bathora. While she worked Flamingo fetched one of the iron balls, rolling it across the ground until it lay next to the long iron tube.

"Can it really shoot those?" Marsha asked, eyeing the large lump of iron dubiously. "They look awfully heavy."

"They *are* heavy," Flamingo said, wiping sweat from her brow. "But much more accurate and causing more damage than a boulder." She turned back to Kat. "My strong friend, would you mind loading it into the *kannon*? It's too heavy for me to lift."

"Sure thing," Kat said, reaching down and picking up the iron ball as if it weighed almost nothing. While she stuffed it into the tube's opening Flamingo produced a bag of black powder and a piece of string. She fiddled at the other side of the tube for a few seconds, then looked up.

"All set," she said. "Take a few steps back, and cover your ears."

Marsha and Jennibal, the only two who knew what to expect, quickly put some distance between themselves and the strange contraption. Kat watched with interest as Flamingo struck a match and lit the fuse at the back of the *kannon*. Off to her right, Bathora finished her spell-weaving and reached out her arms to launch her attack at the remaining Hippo Cult people.

BOOM!

The sound of the explosion caught Kat by surprise. She'd seen Bathora and Ogian blow things to pieces before, but the blast from the *kannon* exceeded everything she'd experienced before. Through a cloud of smoke she saw the iron ball shoot through the air at unbelievable speed, striking Bathora in the stomach. The dark goddess staggered back, emitting a startled "Oof!". The blast of destructive magic intended to destroy the cowering humans shot straight up into the sky instead, its only victim a small bird that Kylee wouldn't have shed a single tear over.

Flamingo let out a curse that made even Kat flinch. "Tough bitch to kill, that one," she muttered, watching Bathora pick up the iron ball and study it carefully.

"THIS DOESN'T BELONG HERE," she growled, tossing the heavy object aside.

"Neither do you," Kat mumbled, then turned back to Flamingo. "What now?"

"Let me try one more thing," the young woman said. "It's a prototype I was working on right before I came here. I don't know if it works."

"Give it a shot," Kat said. "It's the only thing we have, and I doubt that lily-livered buffooness will let us live much longer."

Flamingo hurried back to the trailer and picked up another iron ball. This one was smaller than the first and apparently light enough for her to carry without too much strain. She loaded it into the tube, then inserted more black powder and lit the fuse.

"You might consider crouching down behind the car," she said, covering her ears as she followed her own advice.

There was another loud BOOM. The iron ball shot out from the *kannon*'s opening so fast the eye could barely follow. It flew true, striking Bathora in the chest. Kat felt a pang of disappointment, knowing this smaller ball would cause even less harm than the first one, but her misgivings proved unfounded. As the iron ball struck its target it exploded with a force so great Kat thought it had blown all of them to kingdom come. A blinding light filled the entire world, then everything turned black. Her ears rang and she realized she was lying on her back, soft and slightly damp ground beneath her. She groaned and struggled back into a sitting position, rubbing at her aching eyes.

At first she saw nothing. Then, as her vision returned, she saw nothing but smoke. After another couple of moments she became aware of a shallow crater where Bathora's huge form had stood, scattered flames eating at the grass around its edges, smoke rising from the ashes.

"It worked!" Flamingo shouted jubilantly. She rose from her cover and began performing a celebratory dance. Off to her left Demon Viq, who'd slept through all the drama, stirred and produced a majestic yawn. Bazer picked up the note book he'd dropped and, gazing across the devastation at Gemma and Amanda, jotted down two very high numbers on a fresh page.

None of them knew this, but at the exact moment of Bathora's death Clyster of the Portapoti tribe died of volvulus. Also, on the far island of Madagascar, the first stone giant in a thousand years was born – the daughter of Tai-X and his wife Phe-B, a lovely little girl of fifteen hundred pounds they decided to name Hel-N. If someone had told Mongoe of all this he wouldn't have believed it.

"Is… is she dead?" Leoma stammered, uncertainly eyeing the spot where they'd last seen Bathora.

"Let's go have a look," Kat said. She went over to pick up her weapons before slowly approaching the crater. At its center lay a young woman, head resting on one arm as if asleep. Her body showed no signs of injury – not unless you counted a few soot stains on the white, sack-like garment she wore – making it easy for Kat to identify her. It looked like Bathora had returned to her human form in death, her appearance similar to what she'd used when Kat knew her as a ghost.

"She's so beautiful," came Flamingo's voice at Kat's side. "What a shame she had to turn evil."

"Yeah," Kat said, feeling Bathora's neck for a pulse. There was none. "Bloody shame."

"What are we going to do with her?" Flamingo asked. "I doubt Marsha's people will want to have her buried here, so close to their own abodes. She wasn't very nice to them, was she?"

"No," Kat said. "She wasn't very nice at all."

"What, then?"

Kat was trying to come up with an answer to that question when another voice spoke behind them.

"Let me take care of her."

She turned to see Lulu, the cannibal woman, stand there with a gleeful expression on her pretty face. If Lulu had been a dog, she'd definitely have had two tails. Kat frowned at her.

"What are you… oh, I see."

"I've wanted to do this for such a long time," Lulu cooed. "There was nothing but mush left the last time she died, and by the time I got all the boulders away it had all gone bad. This time it'll be perfect."

"You're going to eat her?" Flamingo asked, her face contorted with revulsion.

"Of course!" Lulu said. "Not her bum, though. There must be enough cholesterol there to give an entire tribe heart attacks. The rest looks tender and sweet, though."

"Lulu is a cannibal," Kat explained. "And don't be alarmed," she continued as Flamingo shied back. "I've travelled with her for days and she didn't even nibble at me."

"I had a feeling I'd be the one ending up in the cook pot if I'd tried that," Lulu said, stepping into the crater and kneeling by Bathora's corpse. She lifted one of the limp arms and gave it a sniff, obviously liking the aroma because she emitted a pleased sound and began licking her lips.

"Bon appetite," Kat said, turning around at the sound of approaching footsteps. The voluptuous Hippo Cult woman who'd been a leader among the defenders came towards her, smiling brightly.

"Hi, I'm Amanda," she said, holding out her hand.

"I'm Kat." Kat took the woman's hand and gave it a good squeeze.

Amanda's smile widened as she squeezed back.

Kat frowned and squeezed harder.

The other woman's grip grew harder still.

Kat squeezed as hard as she could, sweat slowly trickling down into her face.

Amanda laughed and squeezed so hard Kat could feel the bones in her hand grate against each other. Kat gasped, the pain in her hand so intense she felt tears form in her eyes. She was about to let out a pitiful moan when the other woman finally let go.

"Nice to meet you," she said, giving Kat a respectful nod before striding off to introduce herself to the other newcomers. Kat followed her with her gaze, rubbing at her aching hand, for the first time in her life unable to think of anything to say.

The sound of convulsive sobbing caught her attention. A few paces away Marsha had knelt by Ogian's corpse, burying her face in the man's curly hair. Between fits of sobbing and whimpering she spoke soft words into the dead man's ear.

"Oh, Ogian. Why did you have to die when we'd just found the way back to each other? I should never have left you to go search for the Scion. Now you're lost to me forever. If only I could speak to you one last time."

"Er, I might be able to arrange that," said another voice, breaking the silence that had followed Marsha's last words.

The necromancer, Little Black Bird, stood not far away, looking down at the dead man and the mourning woman with a thoughtful expression on her face. Marsha's tear-streaked visage turned towards her.

"You can?" she said, the faintest hint of hope in her weak voice. "How? He's dead."

Birdie nodded. "I can't give new life to his body, but I could try bringing him back as a ghost, the way I did with Bathora. If you give me your consent, of course."

"Please!" Marsha beckoned for the other woman to come closer. "Please try. I'll give you everything I have."

The necromancer smiled as she walked over and knelt beside Marsha. "That won't be necessary," she said, placing a hand on Ogian's head. "It's what I always wanted to do."

A small crowd gathered around to watch in silent expectation as the necromancer worked – Kylee and Bazer, Leoma and Weewee, Jennibal and Spud, Flamingo, Bog, Kel Hell and Demon Viq, Gemma, Amanda and the other Hippo Cult people. All of them stood there together, everything that had happened that day suddenly forgotten, only caring about what was to come next.

Out from between the smoking and smoldering trees to the west the Scion came limping. One of its wings hung broken and useless down its side, and its whole body was covered with soot. It stopped at the edge of the clearing, watching the humans in silence.

A collective gasp arose when a spectral shape suddenly took form, rising from Ogian's motionless body. Slowly, one part at a time, it grew more substantial, until a vaguely translucent manifestation of the former Elephant People man stood above his corpse, looking more than a little confused.

"Ogian!" Marsha exclaimed, leaping up and trying to throw her arms around him. Naturally, they passed right through the shimmering form.

"Lady Marsha?" the ghost said. "Where are we? What am I doing here? And who are all these people?"

Marsha took a step back, tears still streaming down her cheeks, but this time they were tears of joy. She smiled at the bewildered ghost, undisguised thankfulness in her dark brown eyes.

"Don't be alarmed," she said. "I'll explain it all to you."

~20~

———— ✳ ————

"Though lovers be lost love shall not; and death shall have no
dominion."

- Dylan Thomas

So, once again, Marsha had to endure three weddings in one day.
She had no idea why people had to get so soppy every time they
happened to save the world from a deadly threat. Couldn't everyone just
be happy with that and go on with their lives? No, they had to pledge their
eternal love for each other and kiss in public a number of times before leaving
the stage to the next pair of star-crossed lovers. It had almost come as a relief
when it was time for Ogian's funeral. Sure, there'd been a lot of grief, but she
preferred that to all the romantic nonsense. That the ghost of the person they
were burying stood next to her during the ceremony also helped.

Her face took on a sudden frown. Weren't there supposed to be four
weddings and one funeral? She had no idea where that notion came from,
only that it felt right somehow. She shrugged. Too late to do anything about
that now.

Marsha had never been one to cry at funerals. She could never understand
people who wept whole rivers, and the moment the ceremony was over they
were all happy and laughing again, as if nothing had happened. To her grief
was something lingering, a feeling you had to live with for a long time, not
just while you put a body in the ground. Many people thought her insensitive
because of her lack of tears. Marsha wondered if it wasn't the other way
around.

She almost jumped out of her skin when Flamingo's car came roaring
between the trees, passing only a few feet to her right. The curly-haired
woman waved at her and beeped a few times before vanishing into the jungle.
The strange vehicle had become a major hit among the tribe's children (and a
fair number of adults as well). They never got tired of screaming as Flamingo

pretended to drive straight into a tree or cliff, only to veer to the side at the last possible moment.

"Damn, I want one of those for myself."

Marsha turned and gave Fae a curious look. "You do?" she asked.

The small woman nodded, making the bones in her hair bob back and forth. "Yeah. Imagine racing through the dark on a warm summer night, the wind blowing back your hair, hoping you won't crash into a sleeping elephant…"

"Um, sounds kind of dangerous," Marsha said.

"That's the point!" Fae grinned happily at her. "Life's supposed to be exciting and dangerous and *wild*. You must admit things would be a bit dull here if not for Flamingo. Did you know she might be able to reconstruct that gun I shot Winston with?"

Marsha shook her head. "No, I didn't. When did she say that?"

"I've been spending a lot of time with her and Kat, studying that wonderful *kannon* of hers. Kat is so excited about it. Says it'll revolutionize warfare forever. Not sure who she's going to fight now that both Bathora and that Clogz fellow are dead."

"She'll find someone," Marsha said. "People like her always do."

"She'll have to find new companions, though," Fae said, smiling to herself. "I mean, now that both Spud and Weewee are married they'll have other things to do than fight."

"Or at least move on to a different kind of fighting," Marsha said, thinking about all the arguments she'd heard among the married couples of the tribe.

"Yeah," Fae said, obviously following Marsha's line of thought. "But that's part of the experience. A husband's chief purpose is to annoy his wife. That and… well, you know."

Marsha cleared her throat. "Speaking of husbands, how's Tom-Tom doing?"

"Better. That Ogian fellow gave him a nasty blow, but he has the blessing of the Hippo God and expects a full recovery."

"That's good," Marsha said. "According to Gemma he saved many people back there."

Fae nodded. "He did. It was just like in the ancient days, when they were fighting the Bug Goddess for the first time. Or so he tells me, at least."

The two women parted ways. Marsha began walking back through the mass of revelers. There was someone she had to see. Well, more than one someone, actually, but she preferred to deal with matters one at a time.

She passed a small group of people cheering Kat on as she was doing push-ups with Emkei on her back. The mercenary woman claimed the immensely fat seer was the only one who could provide her with exercise hard enough for her to reach her new goal – to become as strong as Amanda. Marsha, who'd seen Amanda beat elephants to death with her bare hands as well as toss boulders into volcanoes, wondered if Kat would ever reach that level of strength. She had to admit the woman seemed determined enough, so who knew?

Off to the right she spotted the necromancer, Little Black Bird, seated on a fallen log next to Demon Viq, who had – as usual – fallen asleep despite all the noise and commotion around her. Birdie waved at Marsha, who strode over and seated herself next to her on the log. It wasn't very comfortable.

"How are you doing, Birdie?" she asked. "I never thanked you properly for what you did with Ogian. You gave us a second chance to be together. Thank you."

Birdie waved the comment off. "It's no big deal. I'm just happy I finally learned how to do these things."

"What are you going to do now?" Marsha said. "Will you return to that place, the Vale of...?"

"Uzureth," the necromancer provided. "I don't know. There really isn't anything for me to do there anymore. I guess I'll have to look for work elsewhere."

"You're welcome to stay," Marsha said. "Everything will be provided for you."

The other woman gave her a tired smile. "Thanks, but there wouldn't be much for me to do. I think I'll hit the road, look for people who want to employ my services, even if they're a bit odd."

"I see. Will the others come with you?"

The necromancer let out a short laugh. "I doubt it," she said. "Leelee will stay with her husband, and the other two saw our Death Cult mostly as a fun game." She shot a sideways glance at Viq, who snored softly where she sat.

They sat in silence a short time, until Marsha grew restless and stood up. "Have you seen the Scion?" she asked.

Birdie shook her head. "Barely seen it since the battle. I hope it wasn't badly injured."

"It looked fine the last time I saw it," Marsha said. "But there are a few things I want to speak to it about. Please let me know if you see it."

"Will do," Birdie said, turning back to her own thoughts as Marsha moved on.

People were singing and dancing all around the Hippo God's temple. There was such an abundance of food and drink that it made Marsha wonder if the prophesized time of wonder and glory was simply a reference to what was produced in the kitchen. The former necromancer Kel Hell had quickly established herself as the head baker, providing everyone with a never-ending supply of pies and cookies. The delicious aroma her work spread through the caverns had made Amanda suggest that she change her name to Swell Smell.

"Lady Marsha!"

Marsha groaned inwardly as two of the newly-wed couples came skipping towards her. It wasn't that she didn't like them – all had become incredibly dear to her. She just preferred to keep the soppiness at a safe distance, preferably out of sight.

Leoma was the one who'd called her name. She was holding Weewee by the hand, pulling him along as she hurried towards Marsha. Right behind them came Jennibal and Spud, the former looking more radiant than ever and the latter, well, looking like he usually did.

"How did you like the ceremony?" asked Leoma. "Wasn't it wonderful? I don't know when I cried the most, when we were up there ourselves or when we watched the others."

"Yes, it was very nice," Marsha said. "Have you...?"

"I was afraid the holy man wouldn't get the part with the God of the Iridescent Cantaloupe right," Jennibal interrupted her. "You infidels have so much trouble grasping the truth, even when it sits right in front of you."

"Perhaps you should have used a larger cantaloupe," Marsha said. "It was a bit difficult to see when you were standing at the back."

"Maybe so," the beautiful girl said. "But everyone could see Spud. Isn't it incredible that he's lived so long without being aware he was the one true God?"

"He didn't even know of cantaloupes until a couple of weeks ago," Weewee said with a crooked smile.

"Are the two of you going to stay here with us?" Marsha asked Leoma.

"We'd love to," Leoma said, eyes sparkling with joy. "Gemma has found us a really beautiful chamber, all warm and dry, and we're going to have lots of pets. Lots of children too, in time." She giggled and leaned her head against Weewee's shoulder.

"We're staying too," Jennibal said. "Just look at all these lovely people, all waiting to be converted to the true faith. Now that we've discovered who Spud really is there'll be no way for them to ignore our preachings. Right, love?"

"Yeah," Spud said. "Pretzels should never be ignored. Every sermon should involve at least one kind of pastry."

"He hasn't got the hang of this ecclesiastical stuff yet," Jennibal said apologetically. "I guess things like that take time, just like with your Scion. Good thing he has me to show him the way. Right, love?"

"Yeah, babe," Spud said, patting her on the rump. "You're almost as defined as me."

"That's *divine*, love."

"So is this," he said, squeezing her behind a little harder.

"Um, I should be on my way," Marsha hurried to say. "Got some things to take care of. See you guys later, okay?"

She scurried off without waiting for an answer. In her hurry to get away from the newlyweds she managed to get herself turned around and was several dozen yards into the jungle to the south-east before noticing. Muttering to herself, she made a wide circuit to avoid further contact with the revelers, only to bump into the third newly-wed couple, standing by themselves near the eastern edge of the open space in front of the temple.

Kylee and Bazer didn't appear as love-struck as the other two couples. Well, at least Kylee didn't. Most of all she looked bored, standing there in all her glory while Bazer seemed to have trouble keeping his tongue from hanging out halfway down his chest.

"For the thousandth time, ape boy," Kylee said with a sigh. "We're not going to have sex now."

"But we've just been married!" the ugly little man protested. "That's what people like us are supposed to do!"

"On our wedding *night*, yes," Kylee said. "It's only afternoon. Keep your slimy little worm in check a while longer."

"But there's no reason to wait. It'll be an experience you'll never forget."

Kylee rolled her eyes. "That's what I'm afraid of."

"Um, hello," Marsha said, stepping out from between two thick tree trunks.

"Oh, finally someone sensible to talk to," Kylee said, giving Marsha a smile that could have made the sun go home and sulk for a millennium. "I don't suppose you're interested in adopting a semi-human male? It's almost housetrained and doesn't have too many fleas."

"No, thanks," Marsha said. "Do you regret your marriage vow already?"

"Of course not," Kylee said. "I'll take him back tonight. Just wanted a few hours respite from his endless nagging about how much he wants me and how much glorious sex we're going to have."

"I've prepared a whole new section in my note book," Bazer said proudly. "I'm expecting our weekly average to be…"

"It has prepared a new section in its note book," Kylee said, looking like she wanted to sink into the ground and never return. "Isn't that wonderful?"

"I can make another section where you rate my performance each time," Bazer said with a sly grin. "If you want…"

"No," Kylee said sharply. "I don't, and nor do you. I'll let you know if I'm not satisfied with your… performance. In fact, you should assume your performance is insufficient unless I specifically tell you otherwise. That way I'll have to do much less talking."

Marsha left them there, bantering back and forth like they'd always done. She wasn't sure how well those two would fit into their society. It was easier to picture them with the Elephant People, right next to Tiwi and Pebe. She figured the Hippo Cult men would welcome Kylee with open arms, at least. The woman stood out even among such beauties as Gemma and Amanda. She wondered if that would cause any serious trouble.

As she approached the temple, she caught sight of her two oldest friends lounging on a grassy mound near its entrance, much like the way they'd done the last time there'd been a wedding spree. The only difference was that Gemma was cradling her son, making silly little noises at him. Marsha went over to join them.

"Marsha!" Amanda called out when she saw her friend. "I've made up a new rhyme: *A god of a melon is nothing to dwell on, but a hippo with wings is what happiness brings.*"

"Very nice," Marsha said. "I doubt Jennibal will like it much, though."

"Naw, she seems like a nice girl," Amanda said. "I don't think she'll be offended."

"She thinks that bald fellow she married will be the one to bring about the new time of wonder," Gemma said, winking at Marsha.

"Let her think that," Marsha said. "As long as it comes I don't care who takes the credit for it."

"I haven't noticed much of a difference yet," Gemma said. "There are all these new people, but life here is pretty much the same as it was before."

"It won't happen in a year or two," Marsha said. "Things like that take time. We have to be patient."

"That Flamingo chick brought some amazing stuff with her," Amanda pointed out. "She might come up with more if she decides to stay. Has she said anything about her plans, Marsha?"

Marsha shrugged. "It sounded like she wanted to stay. She's been too busy driving people around in that car of hers to talk much about the future."

"That's good," Amanda said. "She's a lot of fun, even if she's a bit nuts. Life here could get really interesting with her around."

"Indeed." Marsha was about to speak again when little Niq woke up and began wailing like an air raid warning alarm. Gemma rocked him back and forth, making hushing sounds that had no apparent effect.

"I think he's hungry," she finally established. "I'll head inside to feed him."

A sudden thought struck Marsha and her forehead creased in worry. "Has any of you seen the Scion?" she asked. "I've been looking all over. You don't suppose Lulu has...?"

"I doubt it," Amanda said. "She's been so full after eating that Bathora woman she's done nothing but lie on her bed and moan, clutching her stomach and releasing thunderous farts."

"Oh," Marsha said. "That's good, I suppose."

"Are you sure it's a good idea having someone like that around?" Amanda asked. "Who knows what she'll do once she's digested her last meal and gets hungry again?"

"Joz seems to like her," Gemma said. "They both hated Bathora so they probably feel some kind of kinship. He claims she's perfectly harmless."

"Where is Joz, by the way?" Amanda said. "I haven't seen him all afternoon."

"I'm sure he..." Gemma broke off, suddenly looking uncertain. "I'll see if I can find him before I feed little Niq. See you later."

"And I'll continue searching for the Scion," Marsha said, turning to leave.

"Oh, I almost forgot," Amanda said. "I saw it inside the cavern earlier this afternoon. It flew into the great hall."

"Ah, thanks," Marsha said. She hurried back to the temple's entrance and through the long tunnel. There were torches placed at regular intervals, making shadow versions of Marsha dance along the walls. Flamingo claimed she could make lamps that would burn much longer and steadier, but the first one she manufactured had exploded when she tried to light it. Her eyebrows had still not grown back out.

She found the Scion perched on the altar in front of the large statue of the Hippo God. The fire that always burned in the brazier below illuminated the small shape in shades of red, yellow and orange. The winged hippo held its head low as if listening. Marsha left the shadows at the tunnel's end and approached cautiously. She was perhaps five paces away when the Scion's voice sounded in her head.

"HE SAYS THIS IS WHERE I WAS BORN. I DON'T REMEMBER ANYTHING BEFORE I FLED FROM THE BUG GODDESS. ISN'T THAT STRANGE?"

"Not really," Marsha said. "Most humans don't remember anything before they're four or five years old. It's the way things are."

"THEY BROUGHT ME HERE IN AN EGG," the Scion went on. "HOW UNDIGNIFIED."

"It was a very beautiful egg," Marsha said. "I only saw it in a dream, but the memory of it is as clear as if I laid eyes on it a moment ago. I don't think there's ever been an egg like that before."

"IF YOU SAY SO." The winged hippo was silent for a while. When it spoke again it sounded frustrated. "I DON'T KNOW HOW TO DO IT, YOU KNOW."

Marsha blinked. "Do what?"

"BRING ABOUT THIS NEW TIME OF WONDERS YOU ALL TALK ABOUT. I COULDN'T EVEN SAVE YOU FROM THAT DARK GODDESS. SHE TOSSED ME INTO THE TREES LIKE A BAG OF GARBAGE."

"I wouldn't worry so much if I were you," Marsha said. "You're here now and we're all safe. Let's deal with each new day as it unfolds."

"THAT'S WHAT HE SAID," the Scion murmured.

"The Hippo God?" Marsha lifted her gaze to the large stone statue. In the light of the fire its eyes seemed to glow a deep, dark red. "I've never been able to hear his voice."

"HE DOESN'T SPEAK MUCH. NOT LIKE MY OTHER PARENT."

"Well, I guess that's because he's a bird..." Marsha began.

"HEY, I'M HALF-BIRD TOO!" The Scion interrupted her. "WATCH HOW YOU SPEAK TO YOUR PATRON DEITY."

"Um, sorry," Marsha said, feeling some heat rising in her cheeks.

"WHY DID YOU COME HERE?" the Scion asked.

"I..." Marsha broke off. Why had she wanted to see the Scion? She'd been detained so many times on her way she'd forgotten why she'd been searching for it in the first place. "I guess I wanted to ask you what we're to do," she finally said.

This time the voice in her head sounded puzzled. "WHAT DO YOU MEAN?"

"You know." She made a vague gesture with her right hand. "As your subjects and such."

"I HAVE ABSOLUTELY NO IDEA."

"Oh. Well. Okay." She scratched her head. "I suppose we'll continue as before, then."

"YOU DO THAT."

As she left the winged hippo, whom she'd travelled across half the continent to find, facing countless dangers along the way, she couldn't help but wonder if they really needed the morose little thing. It hadn't provided much help, except with that nasty creature in the swamplands. Most of the things they'd been forced to do by themselves – her and Jennibal and Flamingo and Kat and all the others. And now it looked like they'd continue with that.

"Perhaps that's how prophecies are fulfilled," she said to herself as she emerged back into daylight. "They tell you what's going to happen and it's up to yourself to make certain it does. Pretty smart, really."

The party was still going on outside, but Marsha felt even less inclined than before to take part in it. Instead she walked around to the back of the temple, where the battle against Bathora had been fought. She knew that was where she'd find him.

Ogian's ghost stood in the middle of the clearing, gazing down at the grave that bore his name on it. The look on his face was sullen, contemplative, so completely unlike the naïve, fatuous, asinine features she'd come to know while she travelled with the Elephant People. Whatever death had done to him, she decided it was a definite improvement.

"You know," he said as she stepped up beside him. "I can't help but wonder if there are two people buried there – both Ogian and the Harbinger – and if I really am related to either."

"You're Ogian," Marsha said. "You were always Ogian. The Ogian you are now is a product of everything that happened to you in life, both the good and the bad. You just look at it from a different perspective now."

The ghost emitted a low grunt. "So you mean there's still some of that vicious, murderous monster inside me? Why do you want me around, then?"

"We all make bad decisions," Marsha said. "Sometimes they have more dire consequences than we expect. You paid for your mistakes with your life. No need to punish yourself further."

Ogian thought for a long moment (something that never happened while he was alive). "You may be right," he finally said. "So what am I supposed to do now?"

"Live with me," she said, then grimaced. "Well, not technically, but you get what I mean. I don't want one of those stupid wedding ceremonies, only to spend the rest of my life with you by my side."

"Are you sure?" Ogian said, regarding her with doubt on his face. "It wouldn't be like the real thing. I can't give you any physical love, for example, not even a touch."

She waved her hand dismissively. "I was never interested in those things anyway. And there are lots of other things two people can do than have sex."

"Like what?"

She reached into her pocket and fished out a couple of dice.

"Yahtzee?" she asked.

A wide grin slowly spread across Ogian's face. "You know I can make the dice show anything I want, right?"

She shrugged. "I don't care. Losing suits me just fine, as long as I do it in your company."

They sat down there, right beside Ogian's grave, and Marsha threw her dice, studied the result with a disapproving frown, picked up all five dice and threw them again, and then repeated the procedure a third time.

"I positively suck at this," she said. "What am I supposed to do with such a result?"

"I'd put it under Chance," Ogian said helpfully.

Marsha sniffed and jotted down the number on a piece of paper. Ogian made five slightly transparent dice appear in his hand, grinned as he put them in his mouth, let them rattle a while in there before spitting them out again.

"Yahtzee!" he exclaimed, punching the air with his fist.

Marsha glared at him. "Couldn't you have saved that for later?" she asked. "You know, to make the game a *little* exciting, at least."

"I'm sorry," Ogian said, face dropping. "I guess I got carried away. I promise I'll do better from now on."

"Good," Marsha said, giving him a warm smile. "I'm sure you will."

Printed in the United States
By Bookmasters